THE BEGINNING OF SORROWS

ENMESHED BY EVIL . . .
HOW LONG BEFORE AMERICA IS NO MORE?

GILBERT MORRIS, LYNN MORRIS, ALAN MORRIS

THOMAS NELSON PUBLISHERS®
Nashville

Published in Nashville, Tennessee, by Thomas Nelson, Inc.

Published in association with Alive Communications 1465 Kelly Johnson Blvd., Suite #320, Colorado Springs, CO 80920

Scripture quotations are from the KING JAMES VERSION of the Holy Bible. Printed in the United States of America

ISBN 0-7852-7000-0

Printed in the United States of America
2 3 4 5 6 7 8 9   05 04 03 02 01 00

To Douglas E. Freeman, our favorite Screaming Eagle.
Thanks again, Uncle Buddy, for taking that hit
for us on the road to St. Lo.

And no marvel; for Satan himself is transformed into an angel of light.

—2 Corinthians 11:14

PROLOGUE

———◆———

I T WAS FRIGHTENING, but uncommonly beautiful.

The eerie bluish green lights began as narrow as a laser pointer's beam, then grew longer, thicker, then bent and twisted and danced. The ribbons grew, separated, whirled in circles, spirals, filament clouds of hallucinatory loveliness in the impenetrable darkness of the cave's small, hot chamber.

One of the dancing circles brushed against Dr. Niklas Kesteven's forearm. To his consternation, he was so tense—and so enthralled—that he almost screamed.

The ring of light disintegrated at his touch, and he felt nothing, not even the brush of air.

But, the touch of the unearthly seemed to energize him. Whirling, he fell to his knees and scrambled out the narrow opening into the cavern's wide subterranean passageway. Five men huddled against the far wall, their eyes wide with fright under the miner's lights mounted on their helmets.

"Cover that opening with one of the solar blankets," Kesteven ordered them brusquely. "Seal it as best you can." He turned and ran up the passageway toward the cave entrance. His going was awkward; he lurched and shambled, for he was a big man and he didn't fit well in parts of the underground hallway.

The five men left behind looked weakly rebellious. The smallest of them, a young Russian man named Vaclev Mikhailovich Mirinov, was their guide. The other four men were sturdy Georgian "pack mules"—bearers. They watched Mirinov warily.

He blinked rapidly, staring at the maw of the secret chamber. "Better do as he says, I guess. He's paying the bills." After seeing that the men had a silver solar blanket and were gingerly tacking it around the opening with pitons, Mirinov went to see about Dr. Kesteven.

The big half-Russian, half-melting-pot-American was standing just outside the cave entrance, shouting into his SATphone. "I don't know what it is, Alia! Which is why I'm telling you that *we* need to grab the samples, and fast!"

His face changed, and then his voice changed. "Love of my life, listen to me. It could be an electrochemical phenomena, or it could be animate . . . like *Lampyridae.* Fireflies. Only smaller. I just don't know yet. But no matter which it is, I've got a—a sense about it, a blood and guts instinct that we need it, Alia. It's important. It's really important. You've got to trust me."

He waited, and Mirinov got the impression that the other end of the connection was silent too.

Finally Kesteven's tense expression relaxed. "Where are we?" he asked Mirinov.

Mirinov shrugged. "This mountain has no name."

"No, I mean who does this mountain belong to? Is this Georgia? Azerbaijan? Dagestan?"

"I don't know, Dr. Kesteven. Nobody knows."

To Mirinov's surprise, Niklas Kesteven grinned. It was like a shaggy grizzly bear showing his teeth. "Nobody knows? That's good, Vaclev Mikhailovich. That's good. Hold on, Alia."

His SATphone, which was merely an earpiece with a wire wisp of an amplifier that he could position in front of his mouth, was connected to a portable Cyclops. Mirinov was fascinated as he watched Kesteven rapidly push keys on the keypad. Everyone—at least everyone in America, and the wealthier citizens of Russia—

had a Cyclops in their home, of course. But Mirinov had never seen a unit this small.

The six-inch-square screen showed a grid, then numerical notations. "Alia. I'm at 47.355° longitude, 41.280° latitude. Send an atmospheric sample kit, an electrical engineer's toolbox, and a full microbioassay kit. When can you get here?"

He listened. "Then black-ops it. Probably best. Of course I set the RS voice scrambler for the call, Alia, I'm not an idiot. So when?"

He paused, then nodded. "I'll be waiting."

Untangling himself from his SATphone wires, he laid the Cyclops on top of a nearby flat rock. With furious haste, his great meaty fingers flew over the keys. Once he placed his thumb over a square red icon in the lower left corner of the screen, and the Cyclops said in a colorless female voice, "SID tools authorized." Kesteven touched a few more keys, and the blue grid appeared again, this time with a flashing yellow dot in the center of the screen. He turned to Mirinov.

"Don't move this, don't even touch it. In about fourteen hours, a black dot will appear on this screen, heading toward the yellow dot," he told the younger man. "Come get me as soon as you see the black dot."

Mirinov stared uncertainly at the Cyclops thinking, *I'm supposed to stand here and look at that thing for fourteen hours?*

Niklas grabbed his backpack and headed back into the cave, but turned at the entrance, just before he stepped into the murky blackness. "Vaclev Mikhailovich," he said patiently, "I'll send the mules back up. You can take turns watching."

Mirinov nodded with some embarrassment.

"And Vaclev? If you should see any black dots, any at all, before four o'clock tomorrow, all of you get into the cave. Do you understand me? All of you get into the cave, and bring all the equipment with you. Except the Cyclops, don't touch that. And no fires tonight."

"Yes, Dr. Kesteven."

Kesteven stepped over the line of light into the darkness.

At eight minutes before two o'clock the next day, local time, a tilt-wing V-22D Vindicator buzzed over the mountain and reeled down a bulky package to Dr. Kesteven. He disappeared back into the cave.

The bulky, spiky chopper waited, slowly circling, sometimes hovering as if impatient.

When Dr. Kesteven returned, the chopper dropped lines and reeled him and his precious package in. Dr. Kesteven never gave a backward look—or thought—to his five companions. The helicopter's high, throbbing whine faded into the distance.

Vaclev Mirinov turned to his bearers. "Let's go. Now. Hurry."

One of them exclaimed, "Now? But we had no sleep last night!"

Vaclev Mikhailovich Mirinov shook his head stubbornly. "Did you see the insignia on that helicopter? Oh, of course . . . it was in English. It was the Sixth Directorate. Commissars. American, I guess. But it doesn't matter, does it?"

"No," the man agreed hastily. "We must leave now."

Within half an hour, they were scrambling down the nameless mountain. They never spoke of Dr. Niklas Kesteven, or the odd events of that long day and night, to anyone.

Sixteen hours later, another Vindicator appeared on the mountain. An eleven-man squad, dressed in black with no insignia at all, line-dropped down. They took many samples in the chamber—air, soil, geologic. Then they sealed the cave with native rocks. Within twenty-four hours all entrances to the cave were disguised so expertly that no one, except the commissar squad and perhaps Dr. Kesteven, could ever recognize it.

But no one, not even the men who knew exactly where it was, would ever see the cave again.

PART I

EARLY SPRING

Professing themselves to be wise, they became fools, and changed the glory of the uncorruptible God into an image made like to corruptible man, and to birds, and to fourfooted beasts, and creeping things.

—ROMANS 1:22–23

O Rose, thou art sick.
The invisible worm
That flies in the night
In the howling storm

Has found out thy bed
Of crimson joy,
And his dark secret love
Does thy life destroy.

—WILLIAM BLAKE, "THE SICK ROSE"

ONE

THE ROUGH YELLOW ROCKS flecked with mica moved—but Zoan knew that this could not be. *Rocks do not move,* he thought and fixed his eye on the spot where the lambent beams of the rising crimson sun touched the earth in front of him. Zoan himself sat as still as a candle in a crypt watching the thin line of pale light move imperceptibly over the solid rock on which he sat.

The rock moved again but this time Zoan smiled. *A lizard.* He relaxed and met the gaze of a foot-long lizard who had flattened his lithe body against the coarse rock. The golden eye of the lizard regarded him with a sentient alertness. For nearly ten minutes neither man nor lizard moved one centimeter. It was as if the two were carved out of the rough impasto of sandstone on which they rested. As if drawn by a magnetic force, the red wafer of a sun rose from behind the broken lines of the hills that stood as rugged sentinels blocking off the valley.

All was still and all was silent except for the sigh of the breeze. Zoan reached out his hand.

Extending his forefinger, he bent forward until his hand was two inches from the lizard's face. The malevolent eye of the lizard flickered as whatever primitive process that passed for thought stirred him. His tongue flickered out, touched the finger of the man. Once—twice—three times. He did a series of rapid push-ups, flipped his body in a sudden contortion, then scurried away to disappear into a small crevice under an uplifted slab of basalt.

Coming to his feet in one smooth motion, Zoan stood for a moment considering his encounter with the lizard. *It would be nice to be a lizard—to be able to change colors anytime I wanted.* He was pleased to think of changing his coppery tan to meld in against the brilliant reds of the sandstone cliffs or the dark brown color of the earth itself. It was a way he had of always putting himself inside the being of any bird or beast or reptile that passed his way. For one brief moment, he became a lizard, felt his scales scraping against the rocky surface of the canyon floor, heard the slow slogging of his lizard heart. He felt the hunger for living food and felt his claws tighten as the sharp concept of a crunchy grasshopper formed in his lizard brain.

This sudden metamorphosis—the putting aside of his human flesh and putting on the body of the lizard—had not been a thought but merely an impression that came and left like the desert breeze. It was an unconscious exercise that had been with him for as long as he could remember. Such moments were the most pleasurable element in Zoan's barren existence.

Zoan had always been conscious of time, space, and the physical senses on the surface in a way that he could not explain, nor could anyone understand. For him, time was not a long line that one plodded along in a linear fashion. Rather, it was a meandering river that he could step into or out of, always changing, never the same. Yesterday was like ten years ago. Dr. Kesteven had told him once, "A smart man said, 'Time is but the stream I go a-fishing in.' You're like that man. You move back and forth through time in your head, Zoan, just as most people move back and forth through space."

Without haste, Zoan moved slowly across the green grass that was just beginning to show the signs of the year's age. His looks were not notable; indeed, he was nondescript. He was no more than of average height or weight, had brown hair of no particular beauty, and the only thing about his face that ever called attention were his eyes. The pupils were much larger than normal, which gave him a deep, dark-eyed look. They also tended to dilate excessively in low light. Zoan could see in the dark much better than humans who were born in an ordinary fashion.

As he crossed the fields, Zoan's mind was bisected by the two worlds that were his. He knew only these two worlds; together, they had been his whole life.

The first world lay under the arching blue heavens. It was composed of green grass and sandstone cliffs with pinon trees and scrub brush, and the ranch, which was laid out neatly with a white framed house, a red barn behind it, four more sizable outbuildings behind that, a corral where the horses were kept, and a large green pasture where the four dairy cows now stood grazing, their heads down. This picture-book world was set in the larger one of yellow sand and dark green foothills leading to the lifting hills that ringed all with their serrated peaks.

This was the best world for Zoan, for he was a part of it in a way that he was not of his other world, which lay beneath the ranch. As he walked about now, his eyes moved from point to point, sweeping the landscape, taking in the vultures that circled lazily miles away in the high azure sky.

The massive, circular laboratory lay concealed deep beneath the canopy of sky and yellow sun and green grass. The two worlds were sharply delineated by the surface of the earth itself. Even as Zoan reached over to pat the large dog that came up to nuzzle his legs, he was aware of the powerful engines throbbing beneath his feet. The massive dynamos were the heartbeat of his second home. This world could not be seen by human eye, not even by those who flew over it from time to time.

Zoan's two worlds were as separate as the medieval heaven and earth or perhaps earth and hell. The one buried deep in the bowels of solid stone was illuminated by cold, fluorescent lighting and powered by mighty atomic-fueled dynamos. It was a cold, clinical world and Zoan was never sorry to ride the elevators up through the colors of the different levels and emerge under the canopy of space and smell the odors of life. Each time he left the laboratory and emerged into the world of warm sunlight, it was like a new birth. The very moment he left the house that concealed the elevators, he was invaded by the sense of *life*. Always he could feel, somewhere deep down inside his very being, the life, the force, the very breath of animals and of men that moved in this world.

Suddenly, Zoan stopped dead-still, for something had come to him. It could not be called a thought but was more a combination of nerves and memory—a galvanic force of sorts. He had often felt this visitation, and always it came to him much like the small electric shock he had felt sometimes during his testing when he was young. The feeling was not painful, but all of his outer rational faculties were abruptly halted as the sensation flowed over him. Even had Zoan been capable of such philosophical reasoning, he could not have isolated the organ that received this impression. It was not the brain or the heart; it was much clearer than any thought or impression that came through these organs.

Once Dr. Kesteven had told him that butterflies knew how to fly to the coast, and then launch out blindly over the pathless ocean. Dr. Kesteven had said, "No scientist has ever been able to explain how they know there's something out there. All the eye can see is water. But they leave; if there's no island there they all die. But there *is* an island, and they fly there, and they stay there in winter. I've been there when they've covered the rocks, looking like a multicolored garment of red and yellow and blue and green, alive and fluttering. But how do they know that something is there? We don't know. I don't think we'll ever know."

Zoan had pondered the force that instructed the butterflies to go to a place they had never known, and had come to believe that whatever power led them was like the inexplicable feelings and instincts that came to him sometimes. He understood nothing of how or why these impressions came, any more than did those colorful butterflies. But time and again he had been *invaded* by something, and he always obeyed blindly.

And now he knew without question that something was wrong. Quickly he broke into a trot, and like a hound on a scent he moved from one point to another. He traversed the scant green grass of the pasture, at other times leaping easily over the yellowish rocks with the few inches of soil that composed the mantle of the earth. He sniffed the air and his eyes probed constantly as he loped across the field. *Something is wrong!* He knew this, but he had no concept of what might be setting off such strong signals inside his head and along his nerves.

Finally he saw the black-and-white yearling that he had taken such pride in. The calf was standing on the border of a field close to a group of evergreens that formed the base of a mountain that shouldered its way out of the earth, rising like a burly giant. Zoan broke into a dead run, flowing over the rocks like a shadow. His eyes were dilated, the pupils enormous, as he swept in front of the yearling, who stared at Zoan wild-eyed and snorted with sudden alarm.

At the exact instant that Zoan flanked the calf, he turned and saw the lithe form of the jaguar. The North American jaguar, which was thought to have been extinct in the last century, was now very much alive, and roamed the West at will. She was at once graceful and frightening, this feline, in the way of big cats. Her face was round, the ears clipped, with emerald green eyes that dominated the face. The tawny coat with rosettes of deep rich brown rippled with tightened tendons. She was made for killing; those sharp incisors were for tearing, the powerful claws to hold helpless prey securely, flawless muscles of that special powerful beast's quality so superior to humans. She was crouched, a quiver shimmering along her flanks.

Zoan faced the magnificent cat, motionless as stone. The savage light of blood-lust fired in the green eyes. Suddenly, without warning, she launched herself. The movement was too quick to follow, just a tawny flash of light. Zoan, unafraid and stern, threw up his hand and cried out with a loud voice, a sound from the depths of his soul. Mid-leap, the jaguar dropped. Growling gutterally, she advanced, her paws silent on the green grass. She stopped right at Zoan's feet, looked up at him with those hypnotic green eyes . . . and then, like a kitten, started rubbing her face against Zoan's leg. She was big enough and strong enough that she almost unsettled him.

He leaned down to rub her head, right between the ears, just as he knew she would like. "No, you can't have calf for breakfast. But never mind, I'll find you something else you'll like." Zoan gave one glance at the yearling. "You go back to your mother, you foolish calf." Sharply he clapped his hands. Wild-eyed, the yearling wheeled and raced across the field, his hoofs making a miniature thunder that faded quickly. "Come along, Cat," he murmured, giving the jaguar a final pat on the sleek flank. He ambled toward the barn, and the jaguar followed him as meekly as a pet dog.

A simple, clean peace washed over Zoan. *The Wrong is over and the Bad Thing didn't happen.* He felt good about this and began to sing. He had a pleasant, surprisingly deep baritone voice and the song he sang was an ancient one. He had no idea how old it was, and he didn't know what the words meant. It just seemed he had always known it.

Ring around the rosy,
Pocket full of posies,
Ashes, ashes, we all fall down.

"How did he do that, Niklas?"

Alia Silverthorne watched Zoan and the jaguar. She was standing beside Dr. Niklas Kesteven, a big, shambling man with thick, curly brown hair worn very long. Indeed he was built so strongly with his barrel chest that he seemed to overshadow her. He had watchful eyes, dark brown shaded by thick lashes, and a mustache and beard of the same shade. His teeth were big and white and there was a small space between the front two that he had never felt it worthwhile to repair.

He turned to study the woman who stood beside him. "You're curious about things, aren't you, Alia?" He examined her in an analytical fashion—much as he would have examined an insect under a microscope. As a scientist it was his habit to put everything in a box, but he had not been able to do this completely with this woman. She was twenty-five years old, twenty years his junior. Methodically he picked out from the gray depths of his brain the facts concerning Commissar Alia Silverthorne. Such statistics came easily to Kesteven, for he had that sort of memory.

He knew, for example, that Alia had failed to make it through Navy SEAL training. The fact that no woman ever had did not comfort her, and the fact that the navy had given her the opportunity didn't minimize her antagonism toward all things military one bit. *As the Bard said, Hell hath no fury as a woman scorned . . .*, he reflected, and Alia Silverthorne could simmer with fury, though she never had with him. However, he had long known, and seen, that her failure was a bitterness that lurked under the surface of her confident and smooth demeanor.

After Alia's tour of duty with the U.S. Navy, she had applied to the Sixth Directorate, the enforcement arm of the Man and Biosphere Project. Though they preferred to be called "the MAB Project compliance monitors," they were in fact enforcers, and well-trained and elite ones at that. Alia was well-suited for this job, for she was, though rather short, extremely strong and agile. She had a tremendously short reaction time, for she had mastered every form of the martial arts in existence, and was deadly in hand-to-hand combat. Her daily training schedule—self-imposed—was still excruciating. Niklas supposed she was still punishing herself for not being good enough to be a SEAL.

"Yes, I am curious," Alia was answering his idle question. "I always have been. I've just got to know how that boy stopped that jaguar from having the calf for breakfast."

Niklas slipped his arm around the woman. He had the sense of tight strength in her firm body, and he clearly felt her reaction to him. He had always been good with women, able to read them, able to bring them to do whatever he wished them to do. This one, however, was a little different; perhaps that was why he kept her close. Even now he felt her instinctive response—she turned slightly, moving so that she pressed more closely against him—yet at the same time he sensed that part of her was holding back. Still, when she looked up at him, there seemed to be no aloofness in her gaze. Her eyes were golden brown, with an areola of hazel around the pupils, lending her a strangely intent look. Alia had straight, no-nonsense brows and her heavy brown hair was cut in the rather masculine manner that was so fashionable among female commissars: short, spiked crew on top, with a small queue bound behind her head with a plain silver ring.

She was impatient with his casual assessment of her, particularly the way he was making foul faces at her hair. Niklas hated her hair. "Go on, Niklas, tell me about your pet, Zoan. You never have. I've heard some of the lab rabble call him 'Frankenstein.' Why is that?"

Kesteven withdrew his arm from around her waist and leaned against the side of the Humvee V. The two had come out at dawn to watch the sunrise, and had watched, unnoticed by Zoan, as he had encountered the jaguar. Kesteven had been a professor for many years and there was still some of that in him. Although his lecturing days were over, he did enjoy explaining things to Alia. "Zoan's the only successful product of two programs in the SS Biome lab—Experimental Embryology and the Structured Embryonic Development Studies."

"Oh, that's EE and SEDS. I remember the static about them."

"Exactly. They were formulated to bring a human embryo to full-term in an artificial environment."

"Yes . . . but they sort of faded off the screen . . ."

"Little wonder." Kesteven's voice grew chilly and his eyes suddenly flared with something close to anger. "The EE/SEDS team were fools. For twenty years, at the beginning of the century when the demand for artificially carried children was great, they tried. The embryos were fertilized artificially, then implanted into mechanical incubators."

"Twenty years? With no success at all?"

"Not for fifteen years. All the embryos died, most of them in the first trimester. Then they had a breakthrough from '15 to '28, about a 50 percent success rate in bringing the embryos to the second trimester. Two percent of them came to the third trimester. But only one embryo was ever carried to full-term in the incubators."

Alia studied Niklas Kesteven's eyes. She was a strong woman in ways other than physical, and she wasn't intimidated by him, not exactly; but her relationship with Niklas was not at all what she wanted. He treated her with condescension sometimes. Although she was not brilliant, she was keenly intelligent. Her only formal education had been in military tactics and strategy. With no scientific background at all, Alia felt ill at ease around him, as he often showed such disdain for anyone who was not a scientist, and a brilliant one at that. However, Niklas usually was affectionate with her, and kind most of the time. Alia knew about all of his other women, but she comforted herself with the fact that he always came back to her. She did not know it, but Niklas Kesteven was her greatest weakness. Now she frowned and asked tentatively, "So— you're saying that Zoan is a creation of that program?"

"Yes. Actually he's *my* success. It was I who thought of adding allantois to the amniotic fluid in the incubators. It wasn't part of the protocols, but the EE/SEDS team trusted my judgment."

He watched her, his eyelids dropping to conceal his eyes. It gave him a mildly supercilious expression, and Alia gave in to his ego and asked him, "All right, Niklas, what is allantois?"

"It's an element of reptile and bird eggs, not normally found in human embryonic development. It stores and purifies the nitrogenous wastes of the embryo. Zoan was the first implant to have allantois added and he was brought to full-term. Oddly enough, he was the only one who ever survived; soon after his birth the program was canceled. He was the first, and the last . . ."

A frown creased his face. "Zoan wasn't a strong baby. He suffered from 'failure to thrive,' a condition that had all but disappeared from medical technology. Put simply, it meant that he was sickly. It was a fairly common syndrome in the previous century, in the babies of alcoholics and drug abusers. But it was unheard of by the time Zoan was born. Anyway, he had respiratory infections, colic, inexplicable fevers. He had jaundice before he was a month old. I didn't think the little yellow worm was going to make it." He laughed harshly. "That was when the EE/SEDS team ran fast and took cover."

"What did they do? Throw him in the sterile waste receptacle?" Alia grunted.

"Not quite that bad, but I think Zoan would have died if it hadn't been for me. He was being kept in a sterile lab with no color, no toys, no visual or audio stimulation. I told them to act like they had some trace of human brain cells and paint the room, play some music, hang a mobile or two. I told them to talk to him."

"Did they?"

He shrugged, his sharp eyes narrowing as he watched the barn door where Zoan and the jaguar had disappeared. The sun's rays, slanting over the gold and vermillion desert, were growing warm, and Niklas's cheeks above the heavy beard were flushed. "Doubt it. They wouldn't have had any idea what to say to a baby, unless they quoted him the periodic table or explained the DNA helix to him . . . still, it might have made a difference if they even did that . . ."

"What do you mean?" Alia asked curiously.

"Zoan survived, yes, but he still hasn't thrived. Not mentally. As soon as he grew older, the assessments showed that he was different, and that's why there was never a lot of publicity about this 'success' of EE and SEDS."

Alia nodded. "They didn't want to publicize him."

"Yes, even when he was very young, the lack of energy, physical and mental, was obvious. Zoan was almost nonresponsive to any intellectual stimulus. He just seemed mentally unable to process information or to recall it. His physiological testing was exhaustive. He's perfectly normal, including all brain wave patterns. He does have one interesting anomaly—an extremely high visual acuity. But that's the only abnormal thing about him. That we can objectively measure, anyway."

"But—aside from charming jaguars—how functional is he in reality? He doesn't seem very intelligent at all."

"Well, that's the wrong word to use with Zoan. He's functional, all right, it's just on a level that I haven't quite figured out yet. And the cooks and maids and other peons call him Frankenstein because he has almost no social skills."

"Because he's a lab creation."

"Yes, although that's not scientifically accurate."

"Well, you can't really say he's human."

Niklas gave her a hard-eyed stare. Alia, like most people, had not seen many people who were different, or odd, in any way. Most embryos who were determined to be handicapped were aborted promptly. Those that weren't were institutionalized immediately. Society these days was not so tolerant of any individualists, for any reason. "I'd not be so quick to say that," Niklas said in a bored tone. "Zoan's just different. Unique, you might say."

"You still haven't explained how he stopped the jaguar from attacking the calf."

"I can't tell you that, but I have observed that he has a strange affinity with animals. He almost seems to join himself with them. I've studied it, off and on, for years. He's very good at taking care of animals, better than the vets."

"But what does he actually do with himself?"

"He does janitorial work, things like that. And he does take care of the farm animals. He even helps the vets sometimes with the biome samples we bring here. Last month someone brought in a wounded coyote; I forget what was wrong with it. Anyway, the vet told me that Zoan knew better than she did how to take care of him."

Alia eyed him with a hint of disbelief. "You're fond of him."

"He's fond of me." Kesteven straightened, rubbed his beard restlessly. "Zoan's always at ease with me. Never asks questions or demands attention. He's always been that way."

Alia noticed that Kesteven did not exactly respond to her observation directly. It came to her suddenly that he was not a man particularly fond of anyone—really even of her. This pained her but, as always, she took great pains not to let Niklas know. In an odd way, she felt that this way Niklas had lost and she had won.

———————

Every day was the same to Zoan. When he was in the laboratory world of bombproof glass and titanium and reinforced white concrete, he felt somehow enslaved and subdued. But even when he was up under the blue sky and happy, one day was still much like another. This day had passed as had the others; he had milked the cow, fed the chickens, gathered the eggs. He had visited the biome animals that came and went, some to be studied, some to be tagged, some to be attended if they were sick or injured. On this day they had four rabbits, eighteen semi-wild mustangs, two prairie dogs, and a tarantula. He had spoken to all of them, and had told the attending veterinarian in a numb singsong tone that there was nothing wrong with that one lady prairie dog, except she had a burr stuck in her paw that was fevering her. He'd gotten it out, but the vet had better soak her paw and give her some medicine. Zoan had also mentioned in passing that she was pregnant with six kits. The vet, who was accustomed to Zoan's mystical ways with animals, hadn't asked any questions, and had hurried to medicate the female prairie dog.

Now, as the darkness gathered, he dawdled his way reluctantly toward the house, trying to ignore the dread that always came when he left the surface and descended into the earth.

From the outside the ranch house looked like a perfectly normal house. Even the inside had an ordinary appearance—a kitchen, a great room with an enormous fireplace, five bedrooms, four baths, massive western furniture. The veterinarians who made rounds of different labs, and usually two commissars, stayed in the house. It seemed perfectly normal.

But there was one room that was different, and now Zoan approached the door carefully, as always. It frightened him, in a vague and formless way, to leave the soft world of grass, and dirt, and trees, and to pass through this door. It was just a bedroom. But one wall was different. It had no paintings, no decorations. It was simply a blank wall of an indifferent grade of old paneling. His jaw working, Zoan walked to stand in front of the blank wall and muttered, "Zoan."

A slight humming sounded. The wall slid sideways into a track, and then, with a very slight metallic hum, the twelve-inch-thick elevator door slid upward. Zoan stepped inside. The only elevator or access to the lab level was an anonymous white box. As the great door closed behind him, he braced himself for the descent. It was fast and smooth, but Zoan always felt a teeth-gritting jar that was more in his head than in his body.

Level One of the lab complex was a sort of guard room and communication center, and a full squad of commissars was always there. Two elevators on the north and south sides of the circular structure accessed the five lab levels. Normally anyone and everyone who came and went in and out of the lab were cataloged by the commissars, even if they didn't stop them to do so. But they never gave Zoan a second look; indeed, it seemed as if they never saw him at all. He moved in his slow, deliberate way to the lab elevator and again said quietly, "Zoan." The steel door slid open, and he stepped into the mirrored cubicle, which he hated even more than the numbing white one from the ranch bedroom.

The only signals or indicators on the elevator were the color indicators as the elevator moved downward through the various levels. The flash of colors—bars imbedded in one panel of the mirrors—fascinated him as they always did. He had memorized each level, and repeated them automatically as he passed them and the lights flashed. The highest level was painted green and he whispered, "Zoology." Blue—"Climatology." He watched as the yellow flashed warm gold. "Geology." Blinding white flashes: "Botany." Finally the elevator came to rest, red bars flashing luridly. He sighed, "Microbiology."

The door slid open and Zoan resignedly entered into this other world. He moved slowly down the corridor, which was painted a light, lifeless gray, as were all the rooms he'd ever lived in. A red band of color was implanted in the center of the corridor floor and again along the walls at waist level. All levels were coded with their own signal color, so if one found himself on the wrong floor, the color code would alert him to where he was.

Zoan turned and passed into the kitchen and deposited the eggs and the milk, which he had put in two gallon containers, on the smooth surface of the counter that flanked one wall. Everything was smooth; there was no roughness. Acrylic, shiny steel, and glass offered no grain or break. Everything was the same pale gray, and the lack of color, as always, depressed Zoan. He heard some of the staff in the cafeteria, and slipped out the back door into the hallway. They taunted and teased him, which really didn't bother him; but he felt tired, and wanted to sleep, not talk.

Zoan plodded along to his own room, which was a cubicle that shared a bathroom with the Red Level janitor's supply room. He entered and looked around for one moment, wishing he could sleep outside under the starry sky. The room was windowless, of course. Exactly ten by fifteen, it contained a bunk, an old metal locker, a shelf with a few books, a tiny pull-down desk and uncushioned oak stool.

It was a neutral place with no decoration, except each wall, aside from the one with the inevitable Cyclops screen, was completely filled with photographs of animals, all taken by Zoan himself. Dr. Kesteven had given him a camera two years earlier, and now the walls were covered with pictures of the wildlife of the desert. Hawks and vultures and blue jays caught by the telephoto lens crowded one wall. Another was adorned with enlargements he had made of the jaguar, a puma, an elk, a ten-point buck, and a red wolf. There were whimsical pictures of baby gophers and quick lizards and scuttling spiders, each photo capturing their movements of life.

Zoan painstakingly touched a combination of keys on the Cyclops wall pad, the only control command he had ever bothered to learn. The screen stayed dark, but the gentle strains of Debussy wandered into the small room. Stretching out on the cot and locking his fingers behind his head, for a long time Zoan lay still, listening to the music, lulled. He loved music of almost every kind, and once he heard a song he never forgot the tune or the words. His head was cluttered with music, though he rarely called any one song or score to the forefront.

He lay for four hours, sleeping dreamlessly. When he awoke he was hungry, so he went to the kitchen. The evening meal was over, and he cleaned up the mess that the kitchen workers always left for Zoan to clean up. Everything was quiet, and the lab seemed deserted, though Zoan knew, of course, that there were twenty-six people on the Red Level right now. Sitting down at the worktable, he ate a bowl of cereal and drank two large glasses of the fresh milk that he had brought in. Zoan always ate whatever was available and never complained.

Finally he left the kitchen and began to roam the Red Level. He had spent his life here; there were no surprises, and there was nothing for him to see. Once he had asked Dr. Kesteven to let him sleep outside, but after he received a negative answer, it never occurred to Zoan to ask again. Now he moved silently through the corridors, his mind longingly centered on the world so far above him.

He decided to go see if maybe Dr. Kesteven was working late. Sometimes—not every time, but sometimes—Dr. Kesteven would let him stay in the lab while he worked. A dull sense of loneliness filled Zoan, and he hoped that maybe tonight he would get to stay in Dr. Kesteven's lab. Aside from the animals and music, his only pleasure in life was being with Niklas Kesteven. He stopped at Dr. Kesteven's lab door, said "Zoan," and he was glad to see the door rise on the air hydraulics to let him in.

But the lab was dark, with only the harsh halogen light over Dr. Kesteven's worktable still on. Disappointed, Zoan moved to the table and switched it off. But the door—a regular wooden door—into Dr. Kesteven's private quarters was ajar, and voices came through it. Automatically Zoan stopped to listen, for he had no sense, no instinct, to tell him not to eavesdrop.

It was two voices, and Zoan identified the second voice with bitter disappointment. The woman was with the doctor, and that meant there was no chance that Dr. Kesteven would talk to him, or let him visit. Zoan's hearing was almost as acute as his sight and he remained still in the deserted lab, listening. Maybe the woman would leave soon.

". . . *Thiobacillus chaco*," Dr. Kesteven was saying, "is a chemosynthetic bacterium that utilizes energy from the earth itself—minerals—rather than the sun-based photosynthesis process for food."

"As usual, Niklas, I don't know what you're talking about."

"Alia, I want you to try to understand, as difficult as it may be for you. I wish you had an inkling of any scientific theory." Niklas's voice was rather thick, his arrogance barely concealed, but then he grinned widely and softened. "This organism is going to be very important in my life, Alia, and it would be good if you could share it with me. I believe I can put it so that you will understand it."

Alia, dressed in a flowing one-piece lounging robe, was seated across from Dr. Kesteven, curled up in a black leather armchair. He was sprawled on the sofa opposite her, across a sterile expanse of glass and steel table. Both were drinking amber-colored brandy out of thick cut-glass goblets. Alia knew that when Niklas drank he eventually relaxed and grew more expansive. This was what Alia wanted: for him to soften, and for him to talk to her.

"You've been working on this thing for two years now, Niklas," she said, cocking her head to the side, her eyes sparkling. "Ever since I came and fetched you from the middle of nowhere in the Caucasus Mountains. I took a big risk for you, you know. That was hardly within the United States' jurisdiction, to steal a big scientific discovery. Aside from the fact that I really didn't have the authority to send a Vindicator and crew to personally pick you up."

"When I got back and the Third Directorate understood what I'd found, they approved. You didn't get reprimanded, did you?"

"No."

"In fact, you were promoted soon, weren't you?"

Her eyes narrowed. "You're not going to try to tell me that the reason I got promoted to third commissar of the Shortgrass Steppe Biome was because of you and that silly bug. That's not true and you know it, Niklas. I got promoted because of my dedication and success as a field coordinator."

Kesteven shrugged carelessly. "Two days after you picked me up, an eleven-man squad went in. They took more samples but no one, not even those men, knew exactly what I had found."

"So what was it?"

Kesteven's dark eyes wandered to a point somewhere over Alia's left shoulder and stayed unfocused, dreamy. "You'll have to take it by faith, Alia . . . but then, a lot of science has to be approached, at least in the beginning . . . by a leap of faith." He roused, then took an appreciative sip from the fine old goblet. "It was something like Saint Elmo's fire, I thought at first, which is a purely inanimate electrical reaction. Then, when I could see that it was a sort of meaningful pattern, I thought it was something like fireflies, or some of the marine crustaceans that produce phosphorescence. After a long, hard study, I did find that it was animate, a chemoautotroph. Sulfur crystals were found in its cells, which means that the bacteria feed on sulfur, then oxidize it into energy. But that didn't explain the light phenomenon."

He paused for a while, brooding. Alia waited, barely touching her drink. At length, Niklas said in a voice curiously reserved for him, "*Thiobacillus chaco*, which I think we can assume had been in the refined atmosphere of the sealed cave for an unknowable time, took a static charge from the air we introduced. But instead of frying it—as it would have any other organism without *chaco*'s peculiar qualities—it actually converted the extra electrons into light. Not heat, like other organisms attempt to do with an electrical charge. Into light. It's—unheard of."

"Why is that so important?" Alia asked quietly. She refilled his glass and waited until he drank half of it down.

"Alia, no living thing has ever been cataloged that produces an electrochemical reaction. Until *Thiobacillus chaco*, no one ever considered that it might be possible for a living organism to utilize a positive electrical charge in such a way."

She stared at him, understanding the concept but unsure of the ramifications. For once, he was lost in his own thoughts and didn't notice her confusion.

"I named it *chaco*," he said dreamily. "That's an old Spanish-

Indian word for 'the children of light.' Millions and millions of them join together, end to end, and they form light strings. In quantity they have a way of dealing with the electrical charge. The charge sweeps through the chain of linked bacteria, creating the coronal discharge—the blue-green light effect. They become airborne, through a mechanism I still haven't been able to quantify. Once any one of them touches the earth, the circle separates, neutralized. In effect they break the circuit. The charge dissipates into the earth so it's grounded."

Niklas was half-drunk now, and eyed her blearily. "You don't understand what it means, do you?"

"Not—not really. I mean, I understand the basics of what you're saying, Niklas, but I'm just not certain I understand the implications."

A touch of contempt returned, but he continued intently, "Here, my dear woman, is a living organism that could live through what was, in proportion, a killing electrical charge. It's like a child surviving a direct hit by lightning—and here's the really important thing, the really life-changing, world-changing thing. *Chaco* doesn't just live through it." He shook his head in wonderment and his liquor-dulled eyes grew bright. "It actually controls electricity through biochemical processes." He took another sip, more cautiously now, and went on, "I didn't realize the immense significance at first, and I had to do a lot of research in other fields, like physics and electrochemistry and even electrical engineering. But now, finally, I'm certain."

Outside, in the lab, Zoan was in a somnambulant state. All the words of the two inside came to him clearly and he would be able to repeat the conversation word-for-word in the future. The words themselves meant nothing to him, the concepts as unreachable as if they had been speaking in Greek. But something about the tone of Niklas's voice frightened Zoan. It was exactly the same apprehension that had come to him earlier on the surface, when the jaguar was stalking, though Zoan didn't know yet what the Wrong was, what the Bad Thing was that was about to happen. Now he got the same sense, as he listened to Dr. Kesteven talking loudly and with a slight slurring of his words. Zoan kept thinking, *Something is Wrong. Some Bad Thing here . . .*

Zoan had been frightened of many things, but never of Dr. Niklas Kesteven, and Zoan wasn't even certain now whether his fear was of Dr. Kesteven, or of his incomprehensible words, or of the woman, or just something carried in the air itself. But he did know he was afraid; his tanned skin dimpled with goose bumps. Numbly, Zoan left the lab, skimming back to his own cubicle for comfort and security. The lab door closed soundlessly behind him. Niklas and Alia never knew that their conversation had been overheard.

Niklas was saying expansively, "Only a few inventions have changed the world, Alia. Gunpowder. The discovery of antibiotics. The digital computer, laser technology. But this is more significant than any of those. Consider this." He got up, rather unsteadily, and touched the snakelike black lamp with the low light on a table by Alia's chair. With a quick movement he twisted the neck so the bulb glared full on Alia's face. She stared up at him unblinkingly, the harsh light making her pupils tiny needle points. Niklas, a little deflated, deflected the lamp slightly and went on in a softer tone, "Did you know that we are using the very same technology for this lamp, and that one, and the overheads, that a man named Thomas Edison invented almost two hundred years ago?"

"No," she answered, still defiant, her head thrown back to stare up at him.

"It's true. The very same outmoded, old-fashioned way of producing light. The same outmoded, inefficient manner of transporting electricity. The same old, tired wires and conduits and circuits . . . But shortly, very shortly now, Alia, everything will change. The entire world will change. Because of *Thiobacillus chaco.*" He sat back down, tossed down the last of the drink, and grinned his canine grin at her. "Because of me."

Alia Silverthorne moved over and sat down in his lap, leaning against him. The time for talk was over, she knew. "I love a man who has power," she said in a hoarse voice.

"No one loves a man with power. They fear him," Kesteven said thickly. And then he put his drink down and reached for her.

———◆———

Zoan could not escape the sense of danger—somewhere, hidden, waiting—that had crept over him as he had overheard the conversation between Kesteven and the woman. He tried to blot it out with work, but that didn't succeed. For hours he walked through the desert alone, hoping that the companionship of the wild deer, shy and elusive, or the cougars, or even the vultures that circled overhead, might remove, somehow, the words that he had heard. They kept playing over and over again in his head. He had no idea why they made him afraid; they still meant nothing to him.

For three days he did not speak to a soul, but no one noticed, for that was not uncommon for Zoan. As Dr. Kesteven had said, he had no social skills, and unless he planted himself directly in front of someone and addressed them, they rarely even knew he was there. He was burdened by a heavy weight—and there was not one living soul he could share it with.

Finally, on the fourth night after overhearing Niklas and Alia's conversation, he fell into a deep and profound sleep. He began to hear what he thought was music, but his sleep was so deep he didn't recognize it as such. Once his mind rose almost to the conscious level, and he thought fuzzily, *I've left the Cyclops on*. But then he dropped back down into that colorless, lightless, odorless place where he stayed when he was not roaming one of his two worlds.

He knew what a symphony was, for Dr. Kesteven had taught him that. It was a piece of music in several parts. What followed came to him in the movements of a symphony.

The first movement was like a flute that began on a low-pitched note and rose slowly. There were no words, but as the music continued it became in his mind a message that was felt rather than understood in his conscious, rational faculties: *Leave this place . . .*

The message was clear, and although Zoan was in a comalike sleep, he could not mistake it.

The second movement sounded like a violin. It was a comforting sound, smooth, with the notes rising and falling like liquid over his spirit. Here again there were no words, but clearly as if it were etched in stone, Zoan seemed to see the message. *I will show you what you must do . . .*

There was a long silence, a long waiting. Finally Zoan began struggling through the levels of consciousness. As he moved upward toward understanding, fear began to creep in. But before he came to wakefulness, even as doubts started gnawing at the corners of his mind, the third movement arose, and this time it was like a distant trumpet, blowing a solid, clear, golden note. The melody had a triumphant note. It sounded like something Zoan had heard before but couldn't quite bring to remembrance. He waited, sleeping, knowing that whatever the trumpet was saying would become clear, and it did. It seemed to surround him rather than coming in through his ears or through any of his senses, and the message was unmistakable: *Don't be afraid . . .*

All of this, the music and the message, came to him whole, like a fine piece of embroidery. The dream, the symphony, and the words were delicate and interwoven in an intricate pattern, yet each theme had an identity that could not be confused with the others.

Zoan came out of sleep instantly. He stood up and waited until the music faded, as if it had traveled a distance away from him. Then he was surrounded and cloaked by the silence. "Leave this place," he whispered, "—I will show you what you must do—don't be afraid." He repeated the words many times, and as he did so, the movements of the symphony echoed deeply in his spirit. Somehow he knew the music would always be there, and joy swept through him.

More logical minds might have waited and examined the meaning of the dream or the vision but Zoan was not such a being. He knew somehow that what he had heard had more reality than the concrete and steel that formed the circular laboratory. With deliberation, he pulled on his clothes and packed his knapsack until it bulged. Throwing it over his shoulders, he went to the elevator, swallowed, and said, "Zoan." Once again, he was feeling apprehensive. *I'm leaving my home.* But then the golden notes of the trumpet sounded again somewhere deep down inside him. *Don't be afraid,* and then the violins, *I will show you what to do.* And finally the flute, *Leave this place.*

The lab elevator deposited him at Level One. Not a single commissar looked up or saw Zoan. Two of them were hunched over Cyclops, engrossed in something on the screens. Four others were in an anteroom, and raucous laughter floated out. Zoan went to the last elevator, spoke his passname, and left the Shortgrass Steppe Biome Lab XJ2197.

A decrescent moon hung low in the sky, and the pale light of the stars was waning. They made a constellate glow that held him for a moment, and then his friend the dingo, with one blue eye and one brown, came to him whining. "Hello, Dog." Reaching down, he caressed the rough head, and thought, *What about my friends?*

The "friends" that he thought of were not the workers, nor even Dr. Kesteven, but the animals. He waited, thinking, perhaps, another message or word, or maybe just a bit more of the symphony . . . but nothing came. Finally he walked over to the corral and opened it. The mustangs whinnied, breaking the silence of the predawn. One, the grizzled old lead stallion, came and nuzzled against Zoan's hand. Without a word, Zoan patted the coarse, wiry shoulder. "You want to come, Horse? It's time to leave this place."

Obediently, Horse (which was the only name Zoan had for him) trotted after him, and naturally all the rest of the horses plodded along after him. They had no sooner reached the end of the cultivated yard, stepping out of the gloom of a stand of ironwoods onto the desert sands, when a lithe, shadowy figure appeared.

"You come too, Cat. We're leaving here. This is not our home anymore." He sensed movement above and looked up. Sticking his fingers in his mouth, he whistled and soon he heard the rustle of wings. A magnificent red-tailed hawk descended and lit upon his shoulder. "We're leaving, Bird," he said. "It's time to go now."

He moved quickly and surely then, for he had cut the cord that had bound him all his life. Now he moved surely, his odd, darkened eyes on the high mountains. Suddenly hearing a noise overhead, Zoan stared upward. A black dot appeared; in the shadowy morning, before the sun rose, no one else but Zoan could have seen it at all. It was flying low and very fast. They flew over the lab often, and Dr. Kesteven had told him what these were. It came to his mind without effort, and he said aloud, "F16 Tornado. A German plane."

They were like birds of ill omen, these planes, with their deadly sleek lines and their mysterious runes. Zoan could clearly see the iron cross in black, outlined in red, that adorned the side of the fuselage. He stood still, watching until the whistling roar had passed and faded into silence.

He turned and trotted along until he reached the line of trees that ringed the base of the first mountain. And then man, horse, cat, dog, and bird were silently swallowed up by the evergreens.

TWO

—◆—

I T LOOKS LIKE HOME."

Vashti Nicanor spoke softly, and that surprised her comrade Darkon Ben-ammi. Vashti was not a woman of smooth edges and satiny manner. Though she was a striking woman, with great dark eyes and raven-wing eyebrows accentuating them, her mouth was a little firm for a woman's, her brow so determined, the line of her jaw of such flinty strength. Darkon made no response to her moment of forgetfulness, however. He followed her wistful gaze to the ground dashing past the helicopter's side door only three hundred feet below.

"You're right, Vashti," he agreed. "But only a New Zionist would find this the most beautiful part of this tour." Though they defiantly termed themselves "New Zionists," disdaining the religious overtones of "Jews," they both knew that they missed the only home they, and all Jews, had ever known—Israel. Both of them lived in Beersheba, on the edge of the Negev Desert. Now they flew over a likeness of it: a desert plain of a thousand tints of browns and golds. It was a harsh land, with no cheerfully bright primary colors and no soaring trees or awe-inspiring mountains, only hardy scrub bushes and thirsty ground-clinging succulents. It was lovely to their eyes.

"Now you'll get to see something pretty," a deep voice drawled right behind them. "This scrub's kinda harsh, isn't it?"

Vashti and Darkon exchanged secret "I'm amused" signals, invisible to anyone but the two of them. They'd worked together so long, so hard, and so successfully, that they almost had developed a mental telepathy. "Yes, Lieutenant Darmstedt," Darkon agreed. "It's a dry and thirsty land."

"Yup," was Ric Darmstedt's succinct agreement to the poetic observation. "But we're coming up on Mesa Verde. I think it's real pretty, the colors in the cliffs and all. And how about those old cliff dwellers? Did you know that nobody's figured out yet who those people were, what they did, or why they left?"

"So I heard," Vashti said dryly. "I can't imagine Americans not being able to find the answer to something." Darkon gave her a heavy-lidded glance of warning, and Vashti shrugged. She thought the big, handsome, blond Alaric "Ric" Darmstedt was something of a clown, with his slow drawl and constant jokes. He was of German heritage, too, and that might have had something to do with Vashti's impatience with him, though she never would have admitted it out loud.

"Give us a low-and-close, Lieutenant Fong," Captain Slaughter ordered the pilot.

"H-U-A, Cap'n," Fong returned smartly. It was the "Heard, Understood, and Acknowledged" all-purpose response that had been a catchphrase of the 101st Airborne for more than one hundred years.

Fong banked the helo sharply to the right, and dropped about four hundred feet into a slash of a canyon. Unfortunately, the two Israeli "advisers" had been lounging so nonchalantly at the helo's open pod doors on the left side that both turned turtle and slid all the way to the right side of the helo. Luckily, those bay doors weren't open. Both of them banged noisily against the interior wall.

"Aw, man! Fong, look what you did!" Lieutenant Darmstedt protested. "Here, ma'am, let me help you—"

"I don't need your help," Vashti snapped, struggling to regain her equilibrium and her dignity. "And don't call me ma'am."

"No, ma—sir," Darmstedt said lamely. After all, the woman was a colonel in the Israeli air force. He couldn't just call her, "hey, you."

But the new AH-64D Apache helicopter was just as smooth as it was silent, and it only took a few seconds for Vashti to jump to her feet on the now-level floor. With a pointed glance at Darmstedt, who was helplessly hovering and fidgeting, she grabbed Colonel Ben-ammi's outstretched hand and hauled him up. Ben-ammi had a round, jolly paunch and was gasping a little with surprise. "Now, what is the emergency that we needed to take a combat dive to see?" Vashti huffed.

"Sorry, Colonel, for the spill," Captain Slaughter, who was copiloting, said. But he didn't sound very sorry. "I just thought you might want to see the cliff ruins."

They were eerie. Tucked under great cliff overhangs and fronted by soaring pine and fir, the ancient city of golden stone and cunning masonry work was hidden from all eyes, unless you happened to have an agile and maneuverable helicopter like the Apache.

"No one ever sees them, I guess, except us. And maybe some Green techies working in this biosphere, but I doubt it. Those fat, wallowing Vindicators they use couldn't cut in and out of a canyon like this," Captain Slaughter continued with relish.

This was getting back down to business, Vashti thought with satisfaction. She ignored the poignant sight floating by the hovering helo's pod doors and studied the members of Fire Team Eclipse generally, gauging who to try to worm some information from.

The pilot, Lieutenant Deacon Fong, was of no use, even if he hadn't been busy flying the helo. He was half Chinese, half American, and so was his personality. He could be just as boisterous as any American male Vashti had ever seen, but he clamped up tight and became infuriatingly "inscrutable" when she tried to talk to him of important matters.

Captain Concord Slaughter, tall, rangy, sandy-haired, casually handsome, was almost as bad; he was polite, respectful, and forthcoming on all technical information that he had been ordered to give the Israeli "advisers." But his interaction with Vashti and Darkon was exactly the same as any captain's would be to any higher-ranking officers. Nothing personal, just business.

Sergeant Rio Valdosta, Con Slaughter's right-hand man, might talk a little. But he was more wary when Captain Slaughter was around, and when they were on a practice mission. Even though this mission was kind of ambiguous and lighthearted—they were just taking a practice flight to test some of the helo's new features— Valdosta was still a little tightly wound.

Lieutenant Ric Darmstedt would, of course, talk the ears off a water buffalo, Vashti reflected, and would never say anything worth listening to. His best friend on Fire Team Eclipse, however, was another matter. It seemed that David Mitchell rarely said anything unless he took some time to decide if it was worth saying. His carefulness was nothing like Ric Darmstedt's required attention time, for it seemed to take him forever to finish a sentence in his agonizingly slow Texas drawl. Sergeant David Mitchell just didn't talk much, that's all, but when he did he sounded fairly sensible.

Vashti chose him.

They were using their helmet comm system, though the Apache was silent-running and they probably could have heard each other speaking in a normal conversational tone. Still, airmen have their habits. She focused on him, and David, a nice-looking young man of quiet face and ways and long-lashed light blue eyes, met her gaze with a friendly half-smile. She asked, "I believe you're from Albuquerque, Sergeant Mitchell? So this is your land? How do you feel about this program that has so changed your lives in the past twenty years?"

"You mean the Man and Biosphere Project, Colonel?"

"Yes. That's why so much of your land is deserted now, isn't it? Like these magnificent ruins—" She gestured out the open bay doors, but unfortunately they'd gained altitude, and all that was out there now was the twilight sky. "I mean, those ruins we just saw. No one lives here, no one is allowed to visit here?"

David Mitchell answered in measured tones, "That's correct, Colonel Nicanor. This is part of the Shortgrass Steppe Biome, and these lands are cared for by the Man and Biosphere Second Directorate. The human population has been redistributed to sustainable development areas."

"You sound just like that beautiful blonde lady that is always on Cyclops," Vashti joked. "You say these high-sounding words, but what does it mean? How can a bloodless thing like a directorate take care of the earth? What do they do, issue it standards and rules of order? And what does it mean, 'sustainable development areas'? I am curious, you see, as I hear and see this all over the West since we've arrived."

Sergeant Mitchell nodded soberly. "Yes, here in the western United States, the Man and Biosphere Project is about 85 percent complete, so you are right, ma'am, it's a much bigger part of our lives than in the American South, say, or along the eastern seaboard, where you and Colonel Ben-ammi have been."

The Israelis, who truly were colonels and pilots in the Israeli air force, were also members of Mossad, the Israeli intelligence organization. They had just been "invited" to Fort Carson, Colorado, by some genius in Washington to "advise" the 101st on the new Apache prototype. Actually, Fire Team Eclipse had been briefed that the Israelis were to be treated and addressed as if they were advisers, as a courtesy to the Israeli government. But actually they were to do a lot of advising *to* the two colonels, mainly on the Apache's weapons modifications and improvements, and especially on its two most secret new features, the Bioscan Definition Array and the Crossbow Navigational System.

After his oh-so-gentle reminder that he knew Ben-ammi and Colonel Nicanor had been in Washington for the last month, and therefore certainly understood all about the MAB Project by now,

David Mitchell continued. "To answer your questions, Colonel Nicanor, the five directorates are responsible for overseeing the re-wilding of as much of the land as possible, so that America can be returned to its ecological native innocence," he recited in a bored tone.

Valdosta snorted, and Lieutenant Darmstedt punched his ribs so hard they could hear the thump even through their helmets. Valdosta shut up. Deadpan, David went on, "And the human population is assigned to certain areas, called 'co-op cities,' or just, 'co-ops,' that the directorates feel can best sustain a human population and urban development without damaging the ecosystem surrounding it."

"Ah, I see," Vashti said gravely, noting Valdosta's expression of disgust and Lieutenant Darmstedt's too-obvious attempts to keep him as neutral as Sergeant David Mitchell was. The exchange had taught her much, but not enough. She pressed on, "But you didn't answer my original question, Sergeant Mitchell. How do you—all of you, the American people—feel about this sweeping project, with all the changes it's made in your culture?"

Politely, David Mitchell answered, "Feel? What do you mean, Colonel? It's the law of the land. We all uphold the laws of this country to the utmost of our abilities."

"Of course," Vashti said in a bored tone that she hoped would disarm the sudden wariness that flared in David Mitchell's big, innocent blue eyes. She should have known better, she should have learned better by now in her eight years of intelligence work. Never, *never*, ask a man from whom you're trying to gather intelligence how he *feels* about the information. All it does is make him shy like a startled bird.

Darkon gave her a covert glance both of knowing and understanding. He'd been in Mossad for more than twenty years, and he would never have been so clumsy. But since this was just the beginning of their attempts to understand the undercurrents of the Man and Biosphere Project in America, Vashti's gaffe that gave a sort of warning to Sergeant David Mitchell wasn't really significant. Vashti knew that before long, if Darkon spent much time with Fire Team Eclipse, they'd all be running to him, telling him about everything as if he were their father. Vashti comforted herself with the knowledge that there were many other situations where she could extract information much more easily than her partner could. This all-male soldier-boy network was really much more suited to his particular talents.

Captain Con Slaughter twisted in his right front-facing copilot's seat to face the main cabin of the helicopter, where the other three members of Fire Team Eclipse and Vashti and Darkon were sitting. "Sergeant Valdosta, why don't you and the team demonstrate some of the special features of this great new helo to our advisers? Valdosta, you take the weapons systems; Darmstedt, you take flight control and navigation; and Mitchell, you take communications."

Everyone stood up; Vashti and Darkon started toward the pilots' cabin, expecting as usual to have to lean over into the tiny space to see the displays and controls. Sergeant Rio Valdosta, a short, powerfully built young man with thick paratrooper's legs and wide shoulders, jumped up from the bench seating along the helo's starboard wall. "Look here," he began, then quickly amended, "uh—Colonels—sirs. The Apache AH-64D has four redundant control panels built right into the main cabin. Any and all systems—except the actual piloting of the craft—can be controlled from any one of the four stations back here." He touched a button, and a panel in the helo's wall slid down silently to reveal a Cyclops II flat screen and a pull-down keyboard. Amusingly, a stool—obviously on air hydraulics—popped up out of the floor for the operator to sit comfortably at the computer. Vashti and Nicanor exchanged looks: *Americans.*

The soldiers showed emotion now, all right, Vashti thought. They were as excited as ten-year-old boys with their new toys. And, she had to admit, they did have some wonderful toys. This helo, which was the newest under the American Multi-Task Force guidelines, was designed to fill slots that used to require two or three different aircraft types. It was a troop transport, attack helicopter, ground-cover aircraft, air-to-air combat weapon, and covert insertion-extraction stealth craft. It could do anything except make MRE's—Meals, Ready to Eat—that all soldiers for the last century had learned to hate. And Vashti wondered about that. *Knowing Americans and their heaven-high demands of comfort, there's probably a kitchen and a bar on this can, hidden somewhere in the walls and floor like everything else.*

Valdosta, Darmstedt, and Mitchell gave Vashti and Darkon lectures on their assigned topics, and then Valdosta said into his helmet comm, "Sir? Would you please key in the authorization codes for the BDA and Crossbow?" These two features were still classified Most Secret, and only Captain Con Slaughter had the codes to download them to the accessory databases in the main cabin.

"Keyed in," Slaughter said. They watched the Cyclops screen, and suddenly incomprehensible numbers, letters, symbols, and line graphs flew by at speeds incomprehensible to the human eye.

"These are the Crossbow raw readings," Darmstedt said, and suddenly he actually sounded as though he had some intelligence. Vashti did have to reluctantly admit to herself that Darmstedt was highly intelligent, as he seemed to have more expertise than anyone else on the team with the high-tech complexities. "This feature can gauge any environmental influence on the helo, and then automatically compensate. If it starts raining, it can adjust all the radar-sonar settings. If a power line is up ahead, it can either alert the pilot or make a flight adjustment on its own, or both. When it gets dark, it turns on the lights," he finished, with a lopsided grin.

"Sounds as if you don't need pilots anymore," Darkon said, with a hint of wistfulness.

"Actually, we tried some unmanned aircraft, both fixed-wing and helos," Darmstedt told him, reverting to his professional voice. "But they never could achieve satisfactory success rates, even though the technology plainly exists. There are just too many variables, and even a Cyclops can't figure out all of them."

"What about the weapons systems?" Vashti asked. "Does Crossbow interact with them?"

"No ma—sir," Darmstedt stammered. "It's just an environmental compensation, not a weapons manager."

"Let's try the BDA," David Mitchell said enthusiastically. He was particularly interested in this toy, which was not only a brand-new piece of equipment, but also a brand-new concept.

"You tell 'em about it, Sergeant Mitchell," Darmstedt said generously, though he was more proficient and knowledgeable about the tool. At least he didn't have to try to figure out what to call Vashti Nicanor for a few minutes.

"The Bioscan Definition Array," David said proudly. The screen changed to a digitized topographical map of the ground below. "What it does is find life-forms, scan them with biosensors, and then identify them . . . including their size, weight, gender, temperature, pulse, respiration. The BDA can even give genetically coded information, such as the color of their eyes or hair."

"That's impossible," Vashti scoffed.

"No, Colonel, it really works," David said, his eyes twinkling. "We tried it out yesterday. Hey, Lieutenant Darmstedt, would you give me a hand? I'm not sure I remember . . ."

They worked on the keyboard for a few moments, as Ric Darmstedt gave David quiet instructions. "I got it, sir, here we go. Hey, look—man, there's something huge down there!"

"Yeah, must be Godzilla," Ric Darmstedt said dryly. "Look, David, you gotta use a little bit of sense. Nothing's that big, so it's got to be a lot of little somethings . . . that's it, reset the parameters, tell Baby BAD what you want . . ."

It was a herd of mustangs, running swiftly through the desert night. The outline of each horse was shown on the screen, an odd sort of electric blue line drawing, and it actually recorded their individual movements, even down to the flow of their manes.

"The display is kind of like a visual aid," Darmstedt explained, without adding "for dummies," for which David Mitchell was grateful. "It's not really very accurate, it's just sort of an artist's rendering of the raw data that Baby BAD is receiving. Now, if we want to see what's really up with these horses—" He poked a few keys, and the screen changed to columns of letters and symbols.

Ric Darmstedt was facing Vashti and Darkon, and wasn't really looking at the Cyclops screen. But David Mitchell was, and he leaned forward and whistled. "Sir, look," he said softly.

Ric turned and narrowed his eyes at the columns of data. "I can't believe it . . . where'd he come from?"

"And where's he going?" David murmured.

"What is it?" Vashti demanded. The readout was nonsensical to her; she thought it might truly be a Godzilla, whatever that was.

Darmstedt pointed to a block of information on the screen. "Look at that. It's a Homo sapiens. A man about twenty years old, weighs one-forty-eight, five feet ten inches tall. Brown hair, brown eyes. No weapons. He's riding the lead stallion."

Darkon asked thoughtfully, "I begin to see the wonder of this BDA. The old thermal imaging never would have picked him up, would it?"

"No, sure wouldn't, sir," David answered, staring as if hypnotized at the screen. "Hey, Lieutenant Darmstedt, can you zero in on him and get some more detailed genetic information? There's something funny here . . ."

"Sure," Darmstedt answered. Using the joystick, he made some slight exterior adjustment to the scanners, and pushed some more keys. Soon a readout of the Homo sapiens filled the screen.

"Look," David said. "This man's showing some kind of weird

protease. See the anomaly warning? The BDA says he's actually got some kind of—maybe—yeah, either bird or reptilian protein-base code in his DNA."

"That can't be right," Darmstedt scoffed.

"And look at the retinal scan results! The guy's got some outrageous readings: range, peripheral, differentiation—"

"Wait just a nanosecond," Sergeant Valdosta blustered. "You mean that our new BDA is telling us that there's a Lizard Man down there with X-ray vision?"

"It's got to be a glitch or something," Darmstedt said worriedly, leaning closer to the screen.

"But Baby BAD's doing the right—uh—thing," David insisted, having already picked up on Darmstedt's term of endearment for the BDA. "It's giving the readouts, analyzing the results, and announcing the anomalies. If the bioscan were malfunctioning, the self-diagnostics would make Baby announce that."

"I'm just kind of loitering around here, guys, while you wonder about Son of Pterodactyl down there," Fong announced crossly. They'd been making wide circle passes of the galloping horses, and Deacon Fong just hated to cruise slowly. "Do you want another pass, or can I fly on?"

"Fly on," Captain Slaughter ordered. "Darmstedt can analyze the raw data when we get back to base. Then, if we have to, we'll get some tech-heads to look at the BDA."

"Not my Baby," Darmstedt grunted. "I can fix her myself, if she needs fixing."

Sergeant Mitchell was still lost in wonder, and spoke so softly the helmet comm almost couldn't pick it up. "He heard us. The horses didn't. But even in the middle of that—that stampede, he looked up, because he heard us."

They felt the helo pick up speed, though the sound was still much like that of a purring Rolls Royce engine. Vashti asked Captain Slaughter if she might open the bay doors again; she loved the air of the desert at night, even when it was rushing by at 220 miles per hour. She and Darkon took their seats on the floor again by the open doors—cautiously this time, making certain they sat close to the gunner's straps for handholds in case of sudden stunt flying by Lieutenant Fong again.

Though the day had been sweltering, the night was cold, the stars distant and crisp. There was no moon, and no lights shone in the desolate land below. Vashti still caught whiffs of the desert perfume: the smell of hot sand and the nostril's sting of cold, thin night air.

"What's that?" she asked, sitting up straight and pointing.

"Kingman, Arizona," Captain Slaughter answered. "At least, it was Kingman, Arizona. Now it's Quadrant XJ2199 of the Shortgrass Steppe Biome."

"Can we do a quick flyover?" Vashti asked.

Slaughter was silent.

"I'd like to see it," she insisted.

"There's nothing to see," he said in an arid voice.

"We could try the BDA again," Vashti said slyly.

"All right, Colonel Nicanor," Slaughter reluctantly agreed. "We aim to please."

They flew over Shortgrass Steppe Biome Quadrant XJ2199. Once a thriving desert town of close to twelve thousand people, now it was a shabby ruin, with sagging power lines, abandoned homes, empty streets, and darkness.

David Mitchell ran the BDA, more expertly this time. It read out rabbits, coyotes, snakes, lizards, and two North American jaguars.

But there was not a single man or woman left in Kingman, Arizona.

———

Vashti made hot tea for Darkon Ben-ammi. It was the only semblance of servitude that she ever acceded to, and she only did it because she had such great respect for her comrade in arms. She would have done it if she were a man, she told herself, and that made her feel less uncomfortable with the taint of wifeliness. Of course, Darkon Ben-ammi had been happily married for thirty years to a woman who was Vashti's direct opposite—soft, feminine, acquiescent.

But Vashti Nicanor wasn't masculine—far from it. She was graceful in her movements, but not in an affected, flouncy way. At thirty-two, she was grateful she had the same body tone and curves she'd had in her twenties. The military uniforms she wore were severe, of course, but she wore them with a certain womanly dignity.

"Hot tea," she announced, setting a motley collection of crockery that passed for a tea service in her quarters at Fort Carson. Actually, the officers' quarters were luxurious by Israeli standards. It was just that Americans had never known how to do tea. "I had to use six of those little paper bag things," she groused. "The first time I made tea I tore them all open, but there's not a single tea strainer in this fort!"

"They call it a 'base,' Vashti," Darkon said, squirting lemon extract from a foil packet into his steaming cup. "It was a fort a long time ago."

"It's still named Fort Carson," she argued.

"But they don't call it that in general conversation."

"Just like Americans. They name it something, but they don't call it by the name they give it."

Darkon took an appreciative sip, set the cup down with great deliberation in the exact center of the mismatched saucer, and commented precisely, "It is not like Americans, Vashti. They are not that devious."

She deflated a little, then smiled. "No, they're not, are they?"

"The tea is very good. Thank you." He never failed to thank her for doing him this small service, and it never failed to embarrass her.

"It was nothing; I wanted some tea, too," she mumbled. "Why don't you tell me your impressions of our first reconnaissance with real Americans?"

"I'm not certain that these elite soldiers can be called real Americans—or at least, representative citizens," he mused. "But I do say they're more real than those Tyvek cutouts we've been talking to for the last month in Washington."

"So true!"

"But I would prefer that you give me your impressions first, Vashti," he said.

"So I can make a fool of myself?"

"Not at all," he said sturdily. "I find your point of view, and your observations, both refreshing and intelligent. You know that."

"I didn't do very well with Sergeant Mitchell. I thought he was going to be so easy . . . he seems like a simple every-American boy."

"I think you mean 'all-American.' And do you now think he is? Simple?"

She thought for a few moments before answering. "No, not at all. In fact, of all of them, he is the least—the least—"

"Discernible?"

"Yes. Discernible," she repeated carefully. They had decided to speak only in English while they were in America, to polish their language skills. It didn't matter much, with the RS voice scrambler on, no one could possibly electronically overhear or record their conversations. "There's much more to learn about Sergeant Mitchell, I think."

"Did you know that he's a hard-line Christian?" Ben-ammi asked casually. "Perhaps that might alter your tactics."

"It certainly does, and no, I didn't know that. How did you know? Don't tell me they've all been coming to your quarters and telling you their secrets already, Rabbi!"

He shook his head. "No, he just casually mentioned it while we were at the cafe this morning. I had breakfast with the noncoms."

"I should have thought of that," Vashti fumed. "Officers just talk about their planes, their helicopters, and their weapons."

"True. Perhaps you will join me in the morning for breakfast in the cafe?" Darkon asked gallantly.

"It's called a cafeteria," Vashti corrected him, with some triumph. She had no idea that Darkon had been using the wrong word on purpose, to allow her a small win.

"Ah, yes, of course. The cafeteria. So, tell me, Vashti. What have you learned so far?"

It was a long time before she spoke. Darkon waited patiently, as he had waited for people to talk to him for the last twenty years.

"I think," she said, with slow care, "that the soldiers hate what's happened to this country with this insane population redistribution, and this bizarre nature worship." She hesitated, and again Darkon waited. When she went on, her smooth brow creased darkly. "I just don't understand it, Darkon. I don't think we ever will. What's happened to these people? They have more land, more riches, more beauty than we could ever dream of. And what do they do? Shut themselves off in ugly titanium-and-glass cities, and refuse to even look up at the sun, or grow a tree? How can we ever understand such insanity?"

Darkon sighed heavily. "We have to, Vashti. We must come to some kind of—grip—hold—on what's happening here. It's so important to us, to our country." America was still Israel's staunchest ally in a hostile world. But the United States' peculiar insularity had filled the Israeli government—and people—with doubt and insecurity. Yes, Americans still generously supported Israel through billions of dollars in aid, the sharing of all sensitive technologies, brisk trade, and support in the United Nations.

But *where* were they, the Americans? They were here, hiding, between their deserted shores, refusing to look up or around at the world anymore. The Israelis had sent ambassadors, diplomats, writers, poets, and spies to try to figure out what Americans were *thinking.* And so far not one Israeli could comprehend America's mind-set, not one iota of it. It was a dark and frightening mystery to the tiny country that stood so alone in a hostile continent.

Darkon prodded Vashti again: "And what about the soldiers?"

"I think that they are highly trained, exceedingly intelligent, skillful and courageous men who have nothing better to do than play with billion-dollar toys. They have no higher purpose than that of a ceremonial marching band—and they know this too well. And I think they are afraid."

"Yes? Of what?" Darkon asked alertly.

She took her time again before answering. "Of what America has become, and of what will happen when the time comes for the price of their folly to be paid."

THREE

——◆——

THE DYING APACHE LAY as still as if he had already crossed over into the other life. His face had a marmoreal quality, almost like marble, but there was life behind the coppery visage.

Cholani lay with his eyes closed, the light from the window illuminating his face, now shrunken so that it resembled an ancient mummy's. His skin was creased with fine lines, the signs of a difficult life and much trouble. Beneath the thin, faded blanket his body had lost all the firm muscle and tone that had been his up until the sickness had taken him. Even wandering in the shadow land between waning life and looming death, his mind went back to the time when he led his people as chief and had been stronger and faster than any of the other young men. Now all that was past and he stood on the brink of passing into that for which he longed.

Leaning over him was a young woman with the blackest possible hair braided down into a single long braid that came below her waist. She wore a pair of faded jeans, a T-shirt stretched to capacity by her full figure, and a pair of dusty, worn half boots. She was no more than twenty and was not a beauty. Strength was in her face, however, and in her dark brown eyes, well-shaped and well-set in the sockets and widely spaced. None of the grief that flooded her heart was allowed to show. Her grandfather had been her anchor, and seldom had a day passed since she was born that she had not spent time with him.

Leaning close, she studied the still face of the one man she had found to be faithful in all the world. Only the faint stirring of the thin chest beneath the blanket gave evidence that he was still alive.

His eyelids moved slightly. Leaning over close, she whispered, "Grandfather . . . ?"

For a moment she thought she had been mistaken, but then the eyelids opened to reveal the obsidian eyes that had observed her whole life's passage. Little Bird squeezed his hand. "Can you hear me, Grandfather?"

"Yes." His lips worked and quickly Little Bird leaned forward to catch the words. "Yes. I am going. It is time for me to meet God."

At the mention of the word *God,* Little Bird restrained a look of doubt. Her grandfather's eyes were on her face and she knew that even in his present condition he was capable of reading her thoughts. All it took for Cholani to know the thoughts of man or woman, so it seemed, was one single look. It was as though his dark eyes bore into the brain and lay bare the secrets of anyone who faced him. Little Bird had learned as a child that there was no point in trying to conceal her thoughts. Once she had lied to him; instantly, and gently, he had laid bare her deception. Since that time Little Bird had been able to say whatever was on her heart, no matter how dark or how shameful, to her grandfather. She had had a hard life, for she was set in the modern world of 2050. But her grandfather's mind and heart were firmly rooted back in the Old Time, and she had done her best to be there with him.

"What can I do for you, Grandfather?"

Cholani stirred slightly. He felt the warm touch of Little Bird's hand, he smelled the thin soup that was cooking on the stove across the room. He could smell Little Bird's scent; faint woman, shampoo, perfume, and machine oil. He was aware, too, of the sounds of the rat that was burrowing in the stucco wall, and had been for many days as he had lain there dying. From outside came the sound of two dogs barking. He knew their names and remembered when they were but pups. The sights and sounds, however, were filtered, as if covered with a thin layer of gauze. The room was dark, except for a single lamp with a twenty-five watt bulb on a makeshift table, and the hot light that filtered through the dirty panes of the single window.

But there was another light that the woman who leaned over him could not see. It seemed to grow from a deep well far off, a golden light that was becoming stronger, he knew, every moment. It had begun over a week ago and as soon as he had seen the first faint aura he had known in the way of his kind that his time on this earthly plain was approaching an end. Now it seemed to be more luminous than ever, with a piercing quality that he had never seen from sun or electric light or star.

"Go—bring me Him-Who-Touches."

The eyes of the young woman narrowed slightly. "Do you think if he touches you, you will live, Grandfather?"

"Go. Bring Him-Who-Touches. I must . . . see him before . . . I make my journey. Hurry, Little Bird."

For one moment Little Bird hesitated, then she said quietly, "All right, Grandfather. I'll bring Him-Who-Touches."

A faint flicker of something like humor came to the veiled eyes of the dying Apache. "I will wait here for you."

Little Bird wheeled and moved quickly out of the cabin. It was not yet noon and the sun was ten degrees from being exactly overhead. As she moved there was something of the movement of the wolf or the cat. She wasted no movement and the smooth muscles of her body worked like oil and machinery. Leaping from the porch, she ran to the shed and the door creaked sadly as she opened it. Pulling the tarpaulin off and throwing it to the side, she stepped astride the ancient motorcycle that said "Harley Davidson" in faded letters on the side. Adjusting the controls, she pulled her body up and rammed her foot down. The machine coughed and grunted, protesting at the usage, and then startled the owls in the rafters with its deep-throated roar. Little Bird pulled a pair of goggles from a nail, slipped them over her eyes, and then with one twist of her wrist shot out of the dilapidated shed.

Little Bird left the yard, littered with cans and trash, throwing a plume of dust behind her. Reaching the road, she skidded in a half-circle, using one foot as a fulcrum. When she straightened, she opened the throttle. The single braid stood out behind her and she leaned forward, the stiff breeze flapping at her cheeks as she skillfully wove a pattern to avoid potholes and debris. The approaching death of her grandfather had done something to Little Bird that she had not anticipated. It had opened up a great gash of grief in her, an almost unmanageable sadness. Although she had not wept, even as she shot along the dusty pathway that was once a road but could hardly be called that anymore, the sorrow grew much more powerful than any she had ever known. She swallowed hard, drew her lips into a thin line, and urged the Harley Davidson on even faster.

As Jesse Mitchell reached into the hip pocket of his faded overalls, a pain shot through his shoulder and he grunted involuntarily. "Be still there!" he commanded the pain, and reaching up with his free hand, rubbed it for a moment. The pain subsided and now he easily burrowed into the hip pocket and came up with a small cylinder. Ordinarily he would have opened it at once but for some reason the old man simply stood there, holding what was an ancient silver snuffbox between his thumb and forefinger. It was past three o'clock now but the sun over the desert was still brilliant and he kept his eyes almost shut to protect against the brilliance.

Jesse had never known a time when he had not had the snuffbox, and he knew its history well. It had belonged to his great-great-great-grandfather—with, perhaps, a few more "greats" thrown in. Jesse was not quite sure about that. He recalled clearly how his father had given it to him when he was only twelve years old, saying, "This snuffbox belonged to your great-great-grandfather Lafayette. He was a Confederate, and fought all the way from Bull Run to stack his musket at Appomattox. And when he came home from the war minus a leg, he became a metalworker. He made this snuffbox and carried it until he died. He left it to his oldest son in his will, and then it came down to me, and I'm giving it to you, Jesse."

Jesse remembered that his father's light blue eyes had seemed to glow as he spoke of his ancestor, long buried in the hills of Arkansas. "They didn't give medals out much in those days, but he was a good soldier, and did his duty. Every time you hold this, you think, *The Mitchells come from brave stock.*"

A faint sense of pride stirred within Jesse Mitchell as he stood rubbing the worn surface of the silver box. It was his prized possession, and next to his .410 single-shot Remington he was more careful with it than anything else that he owned. Now his mind went back as he thought of that ancestor of his who had died so long ago and then he thought of his own father and of others who had crossed over. At the age of eighty-eight, Jesse had passed that stage where one thinks mostly of this world. Much of the time his thoughts and his reveries were spent on the past, the long-ago world he had once known. There had been warm flesh, loud laughter; the odors and the touch and the sights of those gone over were very real in his mind. He thought of his twin brother, killed at the age of twenty-nine in a hunting accident, and even as he held his great-great-great-grandfather's silver snuffbox, he murmured, "Won't be long, Jake, before we'll be back together."

A shadow, quick and darting, crossed his face and he looked up to see a hawk sail by in the magically effortless way that he'd always admired. He watched the hawk wheel, muttering, "You'd better stay away from my chickens, Mr. Hawk, or I'll teach you a lesson from which you won't soon recover!"

Stepping forward between the tall, fragrant rows, Jesse moved carefully, examining each of the green ears. He was a small man, no more than five feet five. Though he'd never had much size, he had always been sturdy, and was still wiry and strong. He could see as far as ever, too, although he needed the glasses a bemused pharmacist had finally found and dusted off to give to this odd little man who refused free vision-corrective laser surgery. Jesse Mitchell read his Bible, and the small store of books that he guarded carefully. His hair was silver and that tint was matched in the sweeping, broad mustache that drooped over his mouth. His eyes were hazel. There was a sharpness, an alertness about him, unusual in one his age. Beneath the faded overalls—he'd had two real cotton pairs of overalls for twenty years, as he despised Tyvek-cotton fakes—he wore a plain white cotton shirt worn thin as silk from countless washings. On his feet were a pair of deerskin Indian moccasins—illegal, though Jesse didn't know it—made by one of the San Carlos Indian women. Before the plague had decimated the San Carlos tribe, this country where he now lived had been filled.

But now it was empty and desolate with only a handful of the Apaches still hanging on to life.

Each ear of corn was examined painstakingly. Jesse had not looked at more than ten of them when suddenly he stiffened. Yanking the green shucks back, he whistled between his teeth. "There you are, you imp of Satan!" He was staring at a worm that was burrowed comfortably between two rows of the plump kernels. Flicking the snuffbox open, he tilted it and doused the worm with the tobacco. He had grown the tobacco himself and used it as a pesticide to kill, for he himself did not use the weed.

"Lord, kill this evil worm," he said comfortably, and then began moving down the row. As he did, he thought of the many years he had grown a crop of corn on this very spot. They had melded into one another, those years. He had been a young man when he and Noemi had come to this place all the way from the

Ozarks to minister to the San Carlos Indians. With a quick grin, as the past came to him clearly, he recalled that he had preached for nine years before he had seen a single convert. *I always was stubborn,* he thought. *I don't know if I could wait nine years for another convert now.* But he could have, and he would have, if that's what the Lord told him to do.

Reaching the end of the row, he turned, pulled the worn black Stetson off of his head, and wiped his forehead with his sleeve. He studied the flotilla of crows beating their way across the sky and said conversationally, "Lord, I sure do appreciate all this good corn." It was a way he had of praying, as if he were speaking to a friend standing right at his elbow. There were times, certainly, when he would cry out loudly to God, and weep, but those were times at night in the cabin with only Noemi to hear.

A sound came to him then and he looked up to see a plume of dust rising across the desert. The sight of it made him smile, for he knew that this was Little Bird coming on her Harley Davidson. Jesse's best friend on earth was Cholani, chief of the Apaches. What was left of them, at least. It had taken Jesse Mitchell nearly forty years to win the chief to his own faith in Jesus, but he felt that it was time well spent. He had said once, "Some things take longer to grow than others, Noemi. If you want to grow a weed, it goes up right now. A pumpkin takes three months, but a good sound oak tree takes many years. That's the way it is with Cholani. He's slow growing but he's strong."

As the red motorcycle crested a hill, he admired the way the young woman rode. It was not a horse, but it was the next best thing to it, he secretly admitted. Now as she applied the brakes and swung the back around so that the Harley came to a stop, he moved forward to greet her warmly, though a warning was sounding somewhere in his mind. Little Bird often came to see him, but rarely without her grandfather. "Come in out of the weather, daughter."

"There's no time. Grandfather says for you to come."

Jesse stood stock-still. He had been anticipating this moment for a long time, but now that it was here the reality of it struck him. The young woman didn't move. Jesse lifted his faded eyes and said, "Is it his time, Little Bird?"

"Yes. He says bring Him-Who-Touches." She hesitated for a moment, and then said bitterly, "He's dying. I know you can't do anything to stop that."

Jesse Mitchell did not answer. More than once in his life he had seen death rebuked and forced to wait for God's timing. He had no thought that this might happen with Cholani; he felt in his soul that it was, indeed, his old friend's time to die. But he knew that Little Bird would be angry, for she was a hard young woman. She had been misused and maltreated, by others and by herself. But now was not the time for Jesse to minister to Little Bird. Now he said only, "I will come. Let me hitch up the team."

"There's no time. You'll have to ride with me."

"All right." Jesse turned and walked quickly to the house, stuffing the silver snuffbox in his hip pocket. He stepped inside the door and saw that Noemi had turned from the sink, where she was peeling potatoes. She was a small woman, ten years younger than he, and had sharp, far-seeing brown eyes. "Is it Cholani?"

"Yes. I've been sent for."

"He wouldn't have sent for you if it weren't his time."

"I think that's right. Well, Noemi, I'll do the going and you do the praying." He moved over to the rough old kitchen table that served as dining room, study, conference table, or for any other necessary activity in the small house. Picking up his Bible, he went to his wife and patted her shoulder affectionately. "I'll be back as soon as I can."

"You're riding on that infernal machine?"

"Yup. I wish it was a horse."

"Go careful, Jesse."

Jesse left the house, pulling the drawstring of the black Stetson tight under his chin. Hopping over the seat, he put both arms around Little Bird's waist, holding the Bible right over her stomach. "Let her rip, daughter."

With a cacophonous roar the Harley shot out of the yard. Jesse felt the strong body of the young woman tense and his hat was snatched off to blow behind him, held on by the rawhide thong. His eyes were almost shut as the landscape flashed by. He was already praying for wisdom to speak to his friend, the chief of the Apaches.

———————

As soon as Jesse entered the room, he walked over and sat down on the rickety straight-backed chair by the simple cot that was Cholani's bed. Jesse's face was covered with dust and he licked his lips and found them gritty. He was aware that Little Bird had entered after him and was now standing behind his back.

Leaning forward, he placed his hand on Cholani's brow and asked, "How is it with you, my brother?"

"It is well."

"I have come," Jesse said simply. "You'll be in the presence of our God soon."

"Yes. It's time to cross over."

The two men were quiet then. Jesse felt the life of the Apache flickering like a candle, waxing and waning in a wind. They said nothing for a long time, but he sensed that Cholani had held on to that brief flickering spark of life merely to see him. Leaning forward, he asked, "What is it, Cholani?"

"I go to my God—and to your God." The voice of the dying man was so faint that Little Bird, for all her acuteness of ear, could not hear it. Jesse put his ear down almost to Cholani's mouth and listened carefully. "God has spoken to me and I have a word for you." The words came out haltingly and grew fainter. Jesse didn't speak; he held his breath. Then he heard the words, "Go back to the hills where you first breathed the air. The good Father—He says He will go before you. Go back to the hills that gave you birth. That is the word of God for you, He-Who-Touches."

Jesse heard truth in the dying man's words, and calmly he said, "Yes, I'll go. You've never failed to hear the truth from God, my brother. And now you must go to our God, the Lord Jesus Christ. And I will be obedient to the command that has been given me."

Suddenly Cholani's eyes opened wide and he stiffened. With a strength that none of them could imagine was left in his aged, wasted body, he pulled himself upright. He reached out his hand and Little Bird came and took it. He said, "You have been true, Little Bird. You are bitter now, but God is good. You will find Him."

Those were the last words of the last chief of the Apaches. He turned his eyes upward and gave one loud cry of victory, a faint echo of the triumphant war cries of his ancestors. Then the strength left him and he fell back. His chest heaved twice and then he was still.

Jesse stood up and bent over Cholani to fold his hands and gently close his eyes. Quietly he said, "We will bury him in the old way." He saw that this pleased Little Bird, for though she disdained the old ways, she had honored her grandfather's belief in them. "He was a good man, the best I've ever known," Jesse said sadly.

"Yes. He was good," Little Bird sighed. "We will bury him in the old way . . ."

———

"Well, Jess, is he gone?"

Jesse came in and tossed his hat on the table. He pulled the cane-bottomed chair out and slumped down in it, for he was weary. The funeral had taken two days; he and Little Bird had tried to gather the remnants of the tribe from the nearest co-op cities of

Albuquerque and Santa Fe. Many of them couldn't be found, and most of them wouldn't come. Finally he, Little Bird, and just eight other Apaches had buried their last chief.

Jesse had slept little and the wild ride back on the Harley had felt as if it were dislocating his bones. He sat there, a shadow in his eyes, as Noemi hurriedly prepared a quick meal. He ate absently but drank the coffee thirstily, holding his mustaches back until he lowered the cup.

"Cholani had a word for us, Noe."

"I guess I'm not surprised. He was strong, Cholani was, and of the Lord's mind."

"So he was. What he said always was truth, you know. You remember in the Bible it says you know a prophet if what he says comes to pass." He leaned forward, put his pointy elbows on the table, and held his chin for a moment. Weariness made his old muscles weak, his eyes were gritty from lack of sleep. He stared blankly at the wall covered with pictures of old friends, mostly those with coppery skin. "He told me to go back to the hills, Noe. Back home to the hills . . ."

Noemi Mitchell was a strong woman, though at seventy-eight she suffered from some arthritis. Even the touch of her husband and his anointed prayers had not taken it all away. She was a smart woman, too, and had learned many years ago, with only a little rebellion, that when God spoke to Jesse Mitchell that ended the argument. Now she sat down beside him and studied his weathered face. She saw the truth, and the end of the argument, there right now. "So when will we be leaving, Jess?"

"Tomorrow, I think."

It came as no surprise to Noemi that Jesse would act so promptly and surely. "David's going to worry. Especially since we're not sure exactly where we're going." David was their grandson who was stationed with the 101st Airborne (Air Assault) at Fort Carson, Colorado.

"I know; you'd better write him a letter, Noe. Tell him that as soon as we get settled we'll send word."

Noemi Mitchell turned in a slow circle and said casually, "I don't care about most of this stuff, but I'd like to take my mother's chair."

"'Course you would, you've had that all your life. So you write the letter to David, and decide what you want to take. I'll take a little nap. When I wake up, we'll get packed."

"All right, Jess."

Jesse went to take a nap, which turned out to last the rest of the afternoon and most of the night. He woke up with a start. Beside him Noemi, immediately awakened when he was, said, "You were just too tired, Jess, so I let you sleep. We can still get on our way today."

They were eating breakfast, and the sun had not fully risen over the western hills, when they heard the unmistakable growl of a Harley Davidson approaching. Little Bird, dusty and sad, appeared in the open kitchen door. "Hello, Sister Noemi; hello, Brother Mitchell. May I come in?"

"Of course, daughter. You know where the plates and cups are. Join us."

She shook her head, the gesture weary and defeated. She did, however, sit down in one of the cane-bottomed chairs. "I got you a flight out of Santa Fe tonight at eight-thirty. Did you know that you and Sister Noemi both have over *eight months* of diversionary time accumulated?"

Jesse laughed. "No, I didn't, and I was kinda hoping that the old red-eyed monster everybody worships nowadays had lost us, or forgotten about us." Jesse had never had a Cyclops in his house, and never would.

"They don't lose or forget anyone, Brother Mitchell," she said, slumping down and staring blankly into space. "It is kind of funny, though. You're still recorded as living in Santa Fe. The address is the old Mission House. That thing hasn't been standing for twenty years."

"Then just leave it be, daughter," Jesse said complacently. "The less that old Cyclops knows about me and Noe, the better."

Little Bird shifted uncomfortably in her chair, and focused on Jesse Mitchell's aged face, his white hair and sweeping mustache. "You're still bent on doing this? It doesn't make sense to me. I don't think it's too smart to let the wanderings and wonderings of a dying old man upset your whole life." She spoke defiantly, with the hard edge of a voice veiling tears.

Noemi Mitchell patted Little Bird's gritty brown hand. "The Lord Jesus Christ is our whole life, Little Bird. And your grandfather was a man of God, who often took on the mantle of a prophet. He spoke God's word, and God's truth. We wouldn't be happy—in fact, we couldn't live if we didn't obey God's word."

Little Bird refused to meet Noe's eyes as she spoke. When Noemi finished, Little Bird said carelessly, "Well, anyway, you know you could only get permission for a two-week visit. If you wanted to relocate, that could cause some real problems. Especially to Hot Springs, Arkansas. Evidently that's on the edge of a biosphere, and the Sixth Directorate is trying really hard to clear it out, get everyone moved to Little Rock, which is the nearest co-op city."

"I don't understand all that," Noemi sighed. "It's so hard to understand how a television could decide where we live or how long we vacation."

"What's a television?" Little Bird asked, with dull curiosity.

"A long-dead and gone machine," Jess said quietly. "Now we have Cyclops." He got up and went to his satchel, in which his Bible and some of his favorite books were already packed. Pulling out a map, he laid it out on top of the table and pointed, showing Noemi. "Look, Noe, you see the color coding? This is an ecosphere map, put out by the Man and Biosphere directorates. The vice president paid for every American citizen to have one of these nice maps," he said, barely concealing his disdain. "Anyway, you see the little white dots? Those are the co-op cities. They're the places where the directorates want to move everyone."

"Looks like a lot of wasted space to me," Noemi remarked mildly.

"Would seem so," Jess responded shrewdly, "but then I guess it's a matter of who you think is a waste of time and space. If you think animals and plants and air and rocks and dirt are more important than people, then I guess you don't think the space is wasted. The green parts, that's for all of nature to live in. No people."

Noemi pursed her lips, an expression of disapproval, as she studied the map. "So we're going here, Jess?" She pointed to Hot Springs, which was just on the edge of a big green blob.

"Yes. At least, that's where we'll start from."

"But where are the mountains your family is from?"

With a gnarled old finger he made a light circle on the map. "Right here. The Ozarks." Little Bird sat up, now alert, and frowned.

Noemi looked up at him. "But that's all colored green. Didn't you just say the vice president doesn't want anyone to live there?"

Jess grinned, his eyes sparkling like stars. "That may be what the vice president says, but that's not what God said. God told me to go back to those hills. So I guess the vice president will just have to put up with me and you being right in the middle of his little green things." He sat back down with finality.

Little Bird looked first at Jess, then at Noemi. "You're loco," she said succinctly. "You'll never make it, and you'll probably get picked up by the commissars for trying."

"Maybe so, maybe so, daughter," Jess said cheerfully. "But— *Though He slay me, yet shall I trust Him.*"

Little Bird dropped her head, shaking it with evident disgust. But what Jesse and Noemi Mitchell, for all their wisdom, did not know, was that she was hiding scalding tears in her wounded brown eyes.

Gently Jesse said, "Wake up, Noemi. Look out the window. We're flying over the Ozarks."

Below the jet, the Ozarks looked much like they had on the map: a vivid green swatch of earth, rising and falling in gentle peaks.

Noemi blinked several times, then said tentatively, "I just had a dream."

Jesse was surprised. He was the one that usually had dreams. "What was it?"

"Nothing much. Just a house."

"The old house? On the reservation?"

"No. It was a house I've never seen before. I could see it, sharp and clear, though."

"Tell me about it, Noe," he said intently.

"It wasn't fancy, and it was old. Just a shotgun house with pine trees in the front and in the back, but it was up high, because I could see glimpses of a valley below. There was a chimney on the west end of the house. On top of the chimney was a brass weather vane shaped like a rooster. It was all turned green from the weather." She thought for a minute, closed her eyes, and then resumed dreamily, "It was painted white, and even though the house is very old, the paint looked new. The windows were framed in green. It had flower beds all around, and the flowers have run riot . . . but they still bloom. Petunias, lantana, four-o'clocks . . ." Noemi hadn't been able to have a flower garden in New Mexico. The topsoil they brought in to mix with the red sand outside their stucco hut had of necessity been used for the vegetable garden.

"Doesn't sound like any place we've ever been," Jess said thoughtfully.

"No. Oh, well, it's probably nothing, Jess. You know my dreams—when I ever remember a minute of them—are usually just a jumble of nonsense."

The two sat quietly for some time, staring out the grimy window at the verdant hills below. Finally Noemi said quietly, "But it sure was a pretty house."

FOUR

⬥

QADDAR SQUIRMED FORWARD ON his belly, his mouth as dry as the fiery sands beneath him. He had lost his canteen, and *wadis*, little catches of life-giving rainwater, were almost nonexistent in the southern reaches of the Syrian Desert. Far ahead, shimmering in the hadean heat, the sea of sand broke up into a jumble of small, coarse rocks and undulating dunes with dark splotches along the ridges. Qaddar thought the splotches might be wild caper shrubs, or perhaps desert gourds. Fruits and buds of the caper would be delicious. Gourd flowers would be even better. The wound he had taken in his right calf seared him, and he was lame, so he crawled. He knew that the wound was infected, but there had been no medic, no hospital. All had been blasted out of existence by the deadly Tornadoes of the Luftwaffe.

A slight movement to his left caught Qaddar's eye. He froze; he was face-to-face with a serpent, not two feet away. The small, dark, beady eyes locked with his, the forked tongue flickered rapidly. The snake was in a coil, his neck posed in the "S" of the striking arc. Cold fear rushed through Qaddar, energizing him, but for only a few moments. He was spent, used up, his mind darkened with confusion. Three days of incessant battle had robbed him of most of the rational parts of his mind. He tried to think, he tried to plan, he tried to judge the distance the snake could strike . . . but it all seemed too large a task, and too wearisome. Lassitude swept over him and Qaddar embraced it, for it was a sort of release. *If he strikes me, at least it will be all over,* he thought, eyeing the venomous serpent with only mild curiosity. He didn't know what kind of snake it was, but it had a fat triangle behind its nose, so Qaddar knew it was a type of pit viper. He himself had been raised in the cities and knew nothing about the ghastly man-killing desert.

Qaddar had been snatched from his home, the gentle city of Samandagi on the shores of the lovely Mediterranean Sea. Pressed into a makeshift army at the last minute to stop the onslaught of the ravaging German army and the sky-terrors of the Luftwaffe, Qaddar had made a pitiful soldier. He was no mujahedden—freedom fighter—thrilling to die for a jihad. He was a farmer, a simple wheat farmer, with a small square of rich earth, a cozy house, a wife and a son. Still, Qaddar had not run away. He had stayed on the field of battle, until the Syrians were defeated beyond all hope. Uncaring whether a German shot him or a Syrian officer—if there were any left alive—executed him for desertion, Qaddar had started crawling away when it seemed everyone on the blood-soaked desert was dead except for the Germans.

And so he had arrived here, at a crossroads in the desert, with death behind him and death before him. So it seemed Allah had willed it for the wheat farmer from Samandagi by the sea.

The snake began weaving from side to side slowly, rhythmically, as regularly as a metronome. Qaddar stayed completely still, whether from courage or weariness he didn't really know. Only his eyes moved, following the deadly, sinister dance of the serpent.

Thoughts of home drifted airily to him, visions of his young wife and son, and bitterness welled up in his mouth as sharp as quinine. *What does this war have to do with me? What does it all mean?* he thought dully. He had never really understood how his country had incurred the wrath of the Germanic Union of Nation-States and brought the hordes of merciless, steely-eyed Germans and their other Nordic brothers of war to crush them. None of the men who had been his comrades understood, either. They couldn't find any-one to explain it to them, and most of them had died without knowing why.

His wife's voice came to him, and then that of his small son, as he lay there, contemplating his last enemy, the snake. Qaddar, time and time again, had conjured up their faces and their voices as he fled the battlefield. He had crawled across dead bodies, already half rotted under the fierce sun, covered with the torturous mites and flies and vermin of the sands. Still, he hadn't exactly connected the grisly remains with men, or with breath, or with living. Life had ceased to have any meaning three days ago.

The deadly black Tornadoes, swarming like a pestilence, had first swatted aside the Syrians' few cheap little Mirage 3000 fight-ers. Then the Luftwaffe, at will, had bombed the Syrian ground forces, blasting brigades, tanks, command posts, field hospitals, and single soldiers into annihilation. Then the bombing had ended, and now the fearsome panzer divisions had come, their great Leopard 5 tanks and Marder APC's rumbling across the desert like prehistoric monsters. Thousands of *Infanteristen* swarmed behind them, marching in a deadly cadence, even though they were unopposed. The few Syrians left alive were sitting blank-eyed, emptied arms at their feet, waiting for the first German to arrive to receive their surrender.

The snake suddenly became still, then raised his head alertly, with the peculiar grace that serpents have had since the beginning of time. As if he had grown bored with Qaddar, he flattened out on the sand and slithered off.

Qaddar felt weakness overcome him, and again, he didn't know if it was from relief or the stuporous effects of fatigue. He had reached that point where humans, at the last ebbing of hope, give in to a numbness. Death and pain had been Qaddar's world for three solid days. He could no longer receive or feel or think in the old logical ways.

With a groan, Qaddar got to his feet. Fiery pain shot through the calf of his leg, but he ignored it. He took a few drunken steps, his eyes and mind on gourd flowers ahead. But he fell, first to his knees, and then rolled into a shallow, rocky gully. It wandered a little, but it led in the general direction of the promising ridges ahead, so he kept moving.

The terrain grew more irregular, with more scrub and pebbles and coarser red sand mixed in with the fine golden sands of the heart of the Syrian Desert. The land began to rise and fall somewhat, and was crisscrossed by more of the gullies, some of them as deep as Qaddar was tall. He kept walking, staggering, cursing the pain in his throbbing leg. As happened to so many men in the desert, the distance to the dunes with the green vegetation was farther than Qaddar had thought, for he was not a man with eyes for the desert. Still, he finally stood at the base of the ridge and looked up uncertainly. The top of the ridge—he could see the tantalizing crimson of wild caper buds—was ten feet above him, and the ascent was slightly undercut. Wearily Qaddar decided to go around to the other side of the dune, to see if it might be easier to climb up.

He rounded the first small rise—and found himself looking square into the eyes of a German Infanteristen. For one moment Qaddar was paralyzed. The German, his blue eyes widened in surprise, was slow to react. Fumbling a bit, he raised his G12, the compact and deadly rifle of the German army.

Without thought, Qaddar threw himself forward, snatching the knife from his belt, the only weapon he had left. He hit the German's chest, and it was as if Qaddar had thrown himself against a stone pillar—but he felt the bigger man stumble, waver, and then crash heavily to the ground on his back. The rifle was still in the German's hand, but he'd lost his grip on the stock and trigger.

Qaddar, his eyes locked with the German's, stabbed him in the heart.

The man grew still, his face went blank, and still he looked at

Qaddar. Trembling, nauseous, Qaddar moved away from him and sank into a huddle on the ground. At least now the German was only looking up at the hard blue sky.

Finally, with a shudder, Qaddar crawled back to the dead man and grabbed his rucksack and canteen and drank greedily of the warm but sweet-tasting water. He found no food in the rucksack, but he pulled a wallet from it. Suddenly clumsy, Qaddar finally managed to open it. He sat there, dully staring at the holograph of a young woman embracing two small children. She had blonde hair, as did both of the children, one a boy and one a girl. Across the bottom names were written in a childish scroll.

Qaddar, suddenly angered at the stupidity and bestiality of it all, growled, "It could have been me dead instead of him—and then my wife and my son would have been without a husband or a father. Allah's curses on these dogs! I wish I could kill every last German pig on this earth!"

He fell silent, his head bowed, clutching the picture of the pretty blonde woman and the fair children in one grimy hand. It seemed that he sat there a long time, looking at the picture of his despised enemies' loved ones, cursing the dead man and his family, too.

He heard something. The muted roar of the spent battlefield was a continual hum in the background, but this was a distinct sound, a single sound . . . a close sound. As soon as Qaddar identified the sound, the fury rose in him, galling and bitter. He grabbed the German soldier's foot and dragged him around to the other side of the ridge, dumping his body into a small ravine. Then he scrambled to the top of the dune, crawling on his belly. As he crawled he checked the load of the German's rifle; the pig hadn't fired one shot. All eighty rounds in the magazine were intact.

Qaddar of Samandagi, who might, perhaps, have something of the mujahedden in him after all, waited.

The Vulcan's diesel engine had a gutsy roar. The German version of a military utility vehicle, the Vulcan was made by Mercedes-Benz and had a certain ascetic military elegance. This one was painted the tans and yellows of desert camouflage, and the top had been removed. A stylized wolf's head was painted on the doors. On the rear flatbed a recoilless 100 mm cannon, capable of stopping the middling T-90 Syrian tanks, was mounted.

A man sitting in the passenger seat stood up to stare into the harsh setting sun over the windshield. He had stars on his shoulders, the mark of a general. The eyes, sometimes a glacier blue, sometimes a shroud gray, were as cruel as the grave. No dross of mercy or kindness diluted his adamantine features.

General Tor von Eisenhalt sat back down, frowning. Taking out his pistol, he ejected and checked the cartridge, shoved it back into the grip, and reholstered it, deliberately leaving the safety flap unsnapped.

Major Garant Stettin, squinting into the blinding sunset, risked a quick glance at Eisenhalt. In profile the general was a handsome, distinguished-looking man at his peak. Eisenhalt's raven-black hair had wings of silver at the temples. His eyes, direct and unflinching, were hauntingly intent. Fair of complexion, Nordic of feature, Tor von Eisenhalt was the kind of man in whom even other men could see masculine good looks. He stood at exactly six feet and weighed a fit one hundred eighty pounds, without a decimeter of fat. He had never been touched by sickness in his life, this soldier-general, and he had difficulty in understanding it in others. "Do you see something up ahead, *Mein General?*" Stettin asked anxiously.

"Yes and no, Major," he answered shortly. "I'm ready for either."

Stettin was accustomed to such obscurities from his general. After all, Tor von Eisenhalt was a genius. Such men, who dwelt in planes above other, weaker men, often couldn't be understood by mere mortals like Garant Stettin.

Eisenhalt, as if he craved the touch, took his pistol out again. After staring down at it for a moment, he gripped the top milled knobs and pulled the breech back. It made a dangerous metal sound as it chambered the first 9 mm cartridge. Stettin glanced at the gun, then quickly averted his eyes. He was curious about that pistol. It was old, though it shone as though it had never been dirtied by use. He had always thought it curious that Tor von Eisenhalt carried a gun that was almost 150 years old.

"This is the finest pistol ever made, Major. The 9 mm Luger, the Parabellum model of 1908. It has been used in two world wars by my ancestors, and it has never failed the Eisenhalt name." Eisenhalt's voice was rich, and Stettin was glad to know that he hadn't offended the general by his curiosity, no matter how veiled. Eisenhalt stroked the smooth barrel of the weapon. "I call it Balmung."

"What is that, General?"

"The sword of Siegfried. You should know the history of our fatherland better, Major."

Major Stettin was an older man, at fifty-five he was almost fifteen years older than his commanding officer. Still, he did not resent this; Tor von Eisenhalt was a leader of men, and Garant Stettin was not. It was that simple. Also, Stettin knew very well of the *Nibelungenlied*, the epic poem that related the heroics of Siegfried, son of Sigmund. Nothing, however, would induce him to say this to his general. After all, he hadn't known the name of Siegfried's sword. "Balmung . . . ," he repeated thoughtfully. "You're right, sir. I should read the *Nibelungenlied* again. I haven't read it since I was a boy."

"Norse mythology . . ." Eisenhalt pulled a silver flask from his inner pocket, drank two swallows, then replaced the cap. He suddenly gestured with the flask toward the sinking sun. "It was believed that night came first, followed by day; but day had to be preceded by darkness. The night was the ruler, the creator of the day."

Flattered by the general's uncharacteristic sharing of retrospection with his driver, Stettin chuckled. "All German boys—and most German men, I suppose—dream of being one of the old gods. Thor, god of thunder. Vidar and Vali, Odin's warrior sons. Ull the Magnificent . . ."

Still staring unblinkingly into the harsh glare, Eisenhalt said with deceptive softness, "Thor the thickheaded, Loki the sneak, Balder the weeping beauty . . ."

Stettin couldn't stop a quick sidelong glance of surprise, and he muttered, "But, sir, I thought—forgive me, I had understood that you were a student of German history, both real and mythical."

"I am. And that is why I have only contempt for our so-called gods."

"But, sir, surely you are aware that your men take great pleasure in comparing you to the ancient warrior kings? Far from meaning disrespect, they see you only as a sort of—of symbol of what we once were . . ."

Stettin's voice faded out as he turned to see Tor von Eisenhalt looking at him with narrow-eyed concentration. From a man such as Tor von Eisenhalt, this could mean either that he was giving you the honor of his full attention—which was good; or it could mean that General Eisenhalt was angry—which was definitely not good. Stettin wondered if his general was considering his words, or considering whether to strike him for his insolence. Staring straight ahead with alarm, Stettin said gutterally, "Forgive me, sir. I meant no impertinence."

"I know that, *Herr Major*."

The general sounded indulgent, almost warm, so Stettin decided to take a chance on Eisenhalt's good mood. "So, sir, you don't wish to be promoted to the status of Odin by your armies?"

Stettin was again taken aback by the brooding seriousness in Eisenhalt's answer. "I would never wish to be a motley god such as Odin. Part warrior, part poet, part prophet, part artist. There is no purity there, no clarity. No, I would wish to go farther back, back in the shadows of time, before the weak and frail gods ruled, when the night birthed the day . . . to Wode. Wode, who gave us the word *wüten*, for *frenzy*. Wode of the Wild Hunters . . . the god that mortal man never knew, only his frenzied horde of hunters, who rode across the sky leaving traces of flame and no living being behind . . . the stern ruler who disdained jeweled breastplates and golden helmets . . . just a dark horseman whose only battle dress was a long cloak and a broad hat, so no one ever looked upon his face . . . sometimes he rode upon a black horse, sometimes upon a white . . ."

"But—but I thought that Wode and Odin were actually the same," Stettin ventured.

Tor von Eisenhalt looked at him with a trace of what appeared to be pity. "Oh, but you're wrong, Major Stettin. You're very wrong. Wode is a much older, much purer god than the half-mortal, ever-dying Odin. And I believe that in the Ragnarok, the Twilight of the Gods, in the last great cataclysmic battle when the world will end, that Wode will stand when all others fall . . ."

As the general spoke, Stettin somehow was lulled; his lips and mind felt a little numbed. Were they speaking of the world, the real world, this world? No, no, that was the Syrians—that was the war, the great battle that had just taken place . . . why, then, did Tor von Eisenhalt speak of ancient myths as if they lived and breathed and walked this earth, this desert, this lonely desolate road?

The answer was hidden in the enigma of the man himself, General Tor von Eisenhalt. Raised by his father and tutors, well-traveled, sophisticated, erudite—and rugged, mystical, and ruthless. He was a man who could be stern, passionate, humorous, vicious, and seemingly comfortable with any one of them. At times he ran hot and cold, both extremes ruled and shaped, it seemed, by a cruelty that was curiously impersonal.

Tor von Eisenhalt and his father, Count Gerade von Eisenhalt, and their fathers before them, were ancient Prussian nobility, the last of the Junkers, sons of the supermen of the *Reichswehr*. The Eisenhalt noblemen, with their vast estates and Balkan battlements, had ruled for centuries in the mist-shrouded, mystical lands east of the Elbe. Even in the dark years of the last century, after the last great war, when Eastern Germany had been ruled by the barbaric Soviets, the Eisenhalts had emerged unscathed, seemingly untouched by time and circumstance.

He is extraordinary, but he is just a man, Major Stettin thought nervously as the general again caressed his pistol. *But something about Tor . . . what is it? Is it the ringing voice, the compelling authority he carries so easily . . . or is it something in his eyes, something rarely seen in mortal men? A core, a spirit of fearlessness, no, more than that—of disdain, arrogant disdain of fear . . . of death?*

The weary major settled down more comfortably in the hard seat of the armored car, casting furtive glances at his commandant. Behind them the sergeant manning the cannon stood, his face blank, his youthful eyes staring far away into nothingness.

Neither of them had occasion for last words.

Close-range weapons fire, so fast the sound was a continuous noisome hum rather than a rattle, sundered the cooling twilight air. Major Stettin did not even have time to think, never knew he was dying. The 4.7 mm rounds from Qaddar's stolen German rifle pierced his heart, then his throat, and his mind had died before the blood stopped pumping from his torn jugular.

The sergeant had time to jerk the heavy gun around to aim at the Syrian soldier who stood above them on the low ridge. But Qaddar was still firing hot bullets from the massive 80-round magazine; the twenty-year-old rifleman died within seconds as a train of bullets moved upward stitching him from gut to face, the last bullet entering into his right eye and shredding his brain.

Tor von Eisenhalt suddenly exploded. With one smooth, catlike motion, he leaped from the still-moving Vulcan. He ran and he fired his beloved Luger.

He had no awareness, no conscious thought—only fury. He saw nothing but an enemy, a faceless, meaningless thing whose only reason for existence was to be killed. His vision was filtered with glaring crimson light. His ears heard nothing but the slow explosions from his ancient pistol. He was without breastplate or armor, as wild as a wolf or dog; he had embraced and become one of Odin's most feared warriors, the *Berserksgangr*.

Tor von Eisenhalt ceased to exist. Even this—the strong legs pumping up the hill, his hand, unshaken, holding the old pistol steady at eye level, the heart rhythmically pumping blood to give iron to his muscles—even this body no longer belonged to him. He was filled with a wild and magical frenzy; he no longer belonged to himself, and he embraced the other, Wode of the Wild Hunt, the gleeful animal fury, with savage joy. Nothing could stand the force of the Berserkirs. In them and through them, forces were unleashed that only magic, secret and dark, and ancient sorcery, could evoke.

One bullet burned its way along von Eisenhalt's neck, another struck the side of his belt, but did not touch his skin. He heard the slugs as they screamed by and at the same time he emptied his Luger, standing full upright and tall, running at full speed.

He smashed into Qaddar, who was standing, frozen with horror, his hands shaking and weak, staring at the maddened savage who was descending on him with such fury. Tor von Eisenhalt, disdaining the impersonal kill of a bullet, smashed him in the face with the butt of the Luger. Qaddar fell backward, uttering one garbled scream. Then Tor von Eisenhalt, with brutal joy, killed him, beat him to death, with his bare hands.

Staggering to his feet, Eisenhalt stood, breathing hard, his face as cragged as ancient runes, his eyes like bellowed coals. Slowly the red haze lifted from his eyes, and the shroud of savagery from his mind.

I'm alive, he mused, with a certain slowness as his reasoning righted itself. *I'm not even in pain . . . How could I have walked through forty, maybe fifty rounds of G12 rifle fire?*

Looking down at his chest, Eisenhalt saw two holes in his gray tunic. He stared, bemused, meditative. *I have been shot.* Finally the thought filtered down deep into his consciousness. With hands that were not entirely steady, he opened his tunic and ripped his shirt aside.

There were two large bullet holes in the tunic, the rims of the holes blackened and burned. There were two bullet holes in his white shirt, also with burned edges. There were two red marks on his chest, directly corresponding to the trail left in his tunic and his shirt.

Eisenhalt knew the striking power of a G12 assault rifle. It could drive the 4.7 mm slugs through a lightly armored tank.

Again, within the space of only a few minutes—or was it eternity?—something changed in General Tor von Eisenhalt. He remembered the dreams he had, of which he spoke to no man; dreams, like his ancestor, Bismarck, of *Weltanschaung*, blood and iron. He was, in that eternal moment, visited by thoughts of love and other, darker beings and tools and weapons—not of the frail human body—but of the darkest secrets of the spirit. He recalled his visions of ancient and mysterious Wode, of whom he only half jested, and the Wild Hunters. He remembered his obsession with Fenrir, the ravaging wolf who bit off the hand of Tyr and the killer and eater of Odin. He remembered how he had chosen the wolf as his ensign, his standard. He stared with fierce triumph at the broken, bleeding body of the man at his feet, and brought to mind the killing lust of the *Berserksgangr* that had lived in his mind, sucked his air, quickened his blood . . .

And now he knew why all of these things were visited on him.

As Wode the Wild Hunter, as Fenrir the ravager, as the Berserkirs, he killed men, and neither fire nor steel could prevail against him. His enemies were struck blind and deaf in battle, as were the enemies of the Beserkirs, their limbs paralyzed with fear. As with Fenrir the wolf, no man-made weapon could prevail against him. And as with Wode the Wild Hunter, he breathed the love of war, of death and fire and blood, into the hearts of men.

But Tor von Eisenhalt stared again at the red marks on his chest, already fading. He was more than even the most ancient ones. He had more than they, he could have more power than any man, or even powerful ancient deities, could have.

For now he knew; Tor von Eisenhalt would not die.

"I cannot die," he said to the corpse at his feet. It was an oddly calm and sure tone for such an insane declaration.

The last arrow of the dying sun shot over him, heated him, dyed him a crimson as lurid as the blood-soaked thing at his feet. Tor, unafraid, looked straight into the sun, his arctic blue-gray eyes wide and harsh.

He heard the voice clearly, and at first he thought it was his father's voice, clear and commanding, but then again, he knew it was not his father, Gerade. Then, with a sort of gibbering gladness of recognition, Tor knew: It was his spiritual father, the father of darkness and of death, and hell followed with him. Tor von Eisenhalt fell to his knees and embraced them both.

He heard the chant three times before he fell to the ground, senseless, biting his tongue, black blood oozing from his forehead and bubbling from his mouth and his nose. It was a sound not made of blood and muscle and tissue, but of fire and earth and air:

"Night is coming."

"Night is coming."

"Night is coming . . ."

FIVE

———•———

THE TWELVE-INCH-THICK TITANIUM steel elevator door slid upward quickly and silently, and all twelve commissars in Level One of SS Biome Lab XJ2197 jumped to attention. Alia Silverthorne marched into the circular room, flanked by her two bodyguards. She gave the fist-pound-heart salute to the men and women standing stiffly, and they relaxed a bit, but not much; she was, after all, the third commissar and their supreme field commander. Aside from that, she was a woman that didn't appreciate military interference in her biosphere, and her unexpected arrival presented a possibly sticky situation.

"My Commissar—" began the unfortunate woman who was lead commissar on this shift. This was her first week at XJ2197, her first shift lead, and her first meeting with Alia Silverthorne. Her name was Bennie Mays, and she thought that it was just her luck. She was standing in the middle of a circular console in the center of the round room, and couldn't get to Commissar Silverthorne in time.

Alia, still striding quickly to the lab elevator, tossed over her shoulder impatiently, "Yes?"

Commissar Mays hurried to intercept Alia, stammering uncomfortably, "My Commissar, perhaps you would care to use the north elevators? I believe these are occupied."

Alia stared at the woman, who happened to be taller than she was, although Commissar Mays was making a valiant effort to appear shorter. "What are you talking about, Commissar"—she glanced at the silver name patch—"Mays?"

Commissar Mays swallowed hard. "I—I—"

But it was too late. The elevator made the soft neutral chime alert, and the door disappeared upward. Alia turned to see two "brass monkeys"—high-ranking military men—standing in the roomy mirrored cubicle, along with six aides.

Everyone froze in an odd tableau. The two generals, one two-star and one four-star, stared at Alia. Alia stared at them. Commissar Mays stared at the floor. Alia's two bodyguards stared neutrally at the back of Alia's head, which was a full foot below their eye level.

Alia didn't move to allow the military men to step out, and they didn't move to allow her to step in.

Impasse.

"Good afternoon, General, sir, General, sir," Alia said in a frosty voice.

"Good afternoon, Commissar Silverthorne," the four-star said with equal coolness.

The holographic insignia on her beret and on her left shoulder—a leaping jaguar—clearly denoted her rank. They were supposed to call her "My Commissar," the title address used for the chief commissar and all second and third commissars. Secretly Alia thought the personal form was a little melodramatic, but at this moment she felt outraged that the brass monkey hadn't accorded her the same greeting of professional courtesy she had accorded them. Alia's temper rose a few degrees higher as her voice grew colder.

"If you and your men are finished riding in it, may I use my elevator, General?"

"Of course. Please excuse us, ma'am," he said with exaggerated deference, as he and the rest of the men brushed by her. She stood unmoving.

She didn't enter the elevator until all of them had cleared out. Then she took two marching steps, whirled, planted her feet solidly apart, and crossed her arms. The two bodyguards stood facing her on each side.

The elevator had no buttons, no panels, no controls. All four walls and the ceiling were mirrored, and the floor was of white tile. "Red," she growled. They had no sensation of movement, of falling, because of the air hydraulics, but still Alia felt a familiar stifling feeling that made her lungs compress slightly. She only felt this way when entering this lab. She knew the schematics of XJ2197 very well, and it was shaped exactly like an enormous bottle with a very thin neck sunk into the ground. Perhaps that was why it gave her slight claustrophobia—not the fact that it was so far underground, but because there was only one way out. No soldier likes those odds, and in spite of her conscious disgust with anything military, Alia Silverthorne was wrought just like a soldier.

They reached Red Level in a few seconds, and Alia hurried to Niklas's lab without comment to her bodyguards. She was still uncomfortable with twenty-four-hour guards, as this had only been instituted for all high commissars last month. The second commissar of the Fifth Directorate had died mysteriously at a Diversionary Facility in Virginia, and the rumor was that he'd been assassinated. An even darker rumor was that he'd been assassinated by a militant religious group hiding out in the Smoky Mountains, and the Sixth Directorate had no idea that they even existed, much less where and who they were. The Sixth Directorate had doubled the contingent of commissars in the area, and were combing the mountains. If there was even one dunkhead (so called because of some of the Christian groups' odd rituals of dunking people underwater as a sort of rite of passage, as Alia understood it) in Virginia or any of the surrounding states, they'd find them.

All this had taken place shortly after she'd last seen Niklas, and she'd combed the files of the three thousand men and women under her command to select her team of personal guards. The corner of her firm mouth twitched. Niklas would be surprised, and a very small part of Alia hoped he would be jealous. She'd picked the eight most handsome commissars she could find as her constant companions. Might as well have something pleasing to look at if they were going to be in her face all day and night. Alia really didn't know whether they would be good guards or not, and she didn't care. She was her own best defense against anything.

She stood in front of the shiny steel door to Niklas's lab and said, "Access Silverthorne."

Incredibly, the door was unmoved.

"Access Silverthorne," Alia said loudly.

It still didn't move.

With quick, impatient movements, Alia pulled a hair-thin wire that was laced around her right ear to position it in front of her mouth, pushed a single button on the flat SATphone on her belt, and waited. Niklas didn't pick up the phone, so she pushed another button and said with great deliberation, "Niklas, I'm standing outside the door. It won't do you any good to hide, I'll just use the TC override." The third commissar could open any Cyclops II–controlled access in their entire biome.

The door slid open.

Niklas didn't look up as she came in. As an affectation, Niklas still wore white lab coats, actually made of real cotton instead of the Tyvek coveralls that everyone else in the lab wore. Now his coat, usually immaculately cleaned and pressed, was wrinkled and stained. His long hair was unkempt, and his eyes were bloodshot. Sitting in front of a complicated apparatus that he called a Genome Cross Analysis Tabulator and Alia called the Hairy Spider, he looked up and said dully, "Hello, Alia. I'm really busy right now, as I'm certain you can see, now that you've broken into my lab."

Alia wanted to retort angrily, but she felt her temper oozing down into a sort of warm puddle, as it always did with him. "Niklas, you look ill. What's the matter? I'm sorry I interrupted you, but—you've completely forgotten, haven't you? We're supposed to be going to Perdido Key for the weekend."

"I forgot," he said absently, tweaking one of Hairy Spider's antennae expertly and staring into an eyepiece. "I'm busy."

"So I see." He hadn't even noticed the bodyguards. She turned and said quietly, "Leave us." They disappeared out the silent door, which would open automatically to let people out but not in. She turned back to watch Niklas uncertainly, frustrated at how off-balance he could make her feel. No other man—no other person—could unsettle her as he could.

Tentatively she said, "I'd like to stay for a while, maybe have a coffee with you. Couldn't you take a short break and at least say hello?"

"And then good-bye?" he asked pointedly without looking up.

She sighed. "Maybe, if I can't talk you into coming to the Key with me. Eighty-two degrees and sunny today, Niklas."

There was a long silence as he stayed perfectly motionless, his eye still pasted to the slender tube. "Sunny? No rain?" he finally asked in a neutral voice.

"No rain there, or anywhere near, the Key."

Another long silence, then: "I need to work. I've got a big problem here."

Alia took a moment to gauge whether Niklas really wanted her to wheedle him, or whether he meant what he said. She decided that he was serious, because he sounded regretful. He really did want to go to the Special Diversionary Facility at Perdido Key, Florida. The six condos set aside were sumptuous, and were nowhere near the DF's for the general public. The special DF's were limited to second and third commissars and second and chief ministers of the directorates. Even Niklas, influential and well-respected scientist that he was, couldn't go to the special DF's. As if to reinforce her musings, and his decision, he muttered to himself, "No, no, I've got to fix this, I've got to figure this out."

"Then I think I'll stay the night," Alia said with elaborate casualness. "You've got to stop playing with your bugs sometime."

"Suit yourself," he said carelessly. "But I don't know how late I'll be working."

"It's all right," she said rather lamely, upbraiding herself for not saying something like: *It's my lab, my biome, and you may not work for me but I could order you, as third commissar, caretaker of the Shortgrass Steppe Biome and all its facilities—including human assets—to cease and desist working right now until you are rested.*

Instead she said, despising the pleading note in her voice, "How about if I make us some hot tea? I'll go get some real honey and cream from the kitchen, none of that fake stuff in ugly little foil packets. It'll refresh you, the caffeine and sugar lift, I mean."

He looked up in surprise. Alia rarely offered to do anything at all like this for anyone, even him. "That sounds good, love of my life," he said, suddenly wishing very much for a break and someone to talk to.

Niklas had been surprised how much he'd missed Zoan in the last month, since he'd disappeared. It had been a shock when Niklas realized how he'd gotten into the habit of talking to the young man—or at least, talking out loud to himself when Zoan was in the room. Zoan, of course, never responded in any way and couldn't have comprehended one phrase of one sentence concerning Niklas Kesteven's work. Still, Niklas had found that the amusing exercise had come to be sort of an outlet for him, a mind-cleaner-and-straightener, to talk to Zoan. And it just wasn't the same, talking out loud to himself, though Niklas had tried it repeatedly.

Suddenly he was struck dumb by a concept: *I wonder if that's how he charmed animals? If they somehow felt a special level of communication with him, even though it wasn't exactly in their language? That's how it was, wasn't it? I got something back, something in return, on some level, when I was droning on and on to him . . . At the time*

I thought it was like talking to a blank slate, writing ideas on it, then collating them, arranging them, pushing them this way and that and then placing them just so, in the right order and the right time . . .

But what if it was Zoan who was doing the collating all the time?

"Nonsense," he growled. Abruptly he noticed he was once again trying to argue with an empty room. Alia had left, and turning his mind away from the ephemeral, he licked his lips and hoped she hurried with the tea.

"So it's your ohm-bug that's giving you trouble, is it?" Alia asked lightly. They were on their third cup of tea, and Niklas was showing signs of uncoiling from piano-wire tensile level.

"That's a dronehead phrase for it," Niklas said lazily. "It's not an 'ohm'-bug. An ohm is the unit used to measure electrical resistance, and is not an accurate representation of what *Thiobacillus chaco* does."

"But you've called it that yourself," Alia said lightly. "You told that boy, what's his name again? Zoan?—you told him that at least 'ohm-bug' was better than 'ampere-bug' or 'kilowatt-bug.' I heard you."

"Yes," Niklas admitted grudgingly. "Zoan gave *Thiobacilllus chaco* that silly nickname. For some reason, he recognized the symbol for 'ohm' in some of my documents and labeled *chaco* the 'omega-bug.' I explained that the Greek symbol he was seeing was actually for 'ohm,' and it sort of got shortened to the ohm-bug."

"Where is he, by the way?" Alia asked carelessly. "He's usually somewhere close around you, drooling and staring into space."

Niklas almost retorted angrily, *No, he's just quiet and unobtrusive, virtues you wouldn't understand, Alia.* But he controlled himself at the last moment, and bit off the angry retort. He did feel a strong reluctance to tell Alia that Zoan had disappeared. The vision of her and her storm troopers, dressed in their all-black paramilitary garb, swooping down on Zoan in one of those ugly black Vindicators, repulsed him.

"He's around here somewhere," he answered. It wasn't a lie; though Zoan had never disappeared before, Niklas was certain that he'd be all right out wandering in the desert on his own little quest, or whatever it was. And Niklas was sure he would come back to the lab. After all, it was the only home Zoan had ever known. And what could possibly be out there in the world for a being such as Zoan?

"About the ohm-bug," Niklas said quickly. "You're not going to believe what it's doing to me."

Alia jerked upright, a spasm of fear contorting her face. "Doing to you—you mean—"

"No, no, Alia," he scoffed. "I keep telling you, it's not the kind of bacteria that infects humans."

She relaxed a little. "Well, I know you've got some nasties down here somewhere. I saw some brass monkeys leaving when I came in, and I just know that they were down here petting some of their doomsday bugs."

Niklas shrugged. He never visited the biochem weapons labs, didn't know anything about biological or chemical weapons, and he didn't want to know. There was just no percentage in developing them, or any superweapons, since no one would be interested in buying them except maybe some crazies in the Mideast. Besides the American military crazies, that is. And they didn't pay much. "Well, my ohm-bug isn't one of those, Alia. I've told you over and over again, it's a life-form that could be one of the most important organisms ever to benefit mankind. At least, it could be. Except that it's playing the old Cinderella game. Without my permission," he added dryly.

Alia sighed. "I don't understand, Niklas. As usual. What game are you talking about?"

With exaggerated patience, he replied, "I call it the Cinderella game. It's a type of point mutation of the coding sequence of DNA nucleotides. It's called 'slipped mispairing.' Get it? Cinderella—slipped mispairing—slipper mispairing?"

Alia looked utterly mystified.

"Never mind. I would have thought you, of all women, would know the Cinderella story," Niklas said with a touch of malice. "Forget all that. My nice little ohm-bug, my beautiful blue light of heaven, my multimillion-dollar electrical conductor, is now a mutant monster electricity-eater."

"It's—mutated? Into an electricity eater?" Alia repeated with difficulty.

"Yes. *Thiobacillus chaco* has spontaneously decided to change its DNA coding, and now, instead of possibly making the world a better place, all it does is eat electricity and make billions of other little *chacos*."

Alia grew very intent. "Explain it to me. What do you mean, it eats electricity? Do you mean it—it—"

"I mean that it absorbs the unstable electrons in an ionized atmosphere, just as it always did. Only now, instead of conducting them like a circuit, it chemically throws off negatively charged ions to offset the positrons. It negates electricity. Nullifies it. Makes it go away."

"I get it, Niklas," she said with a touch of impatience that took him aback. Alia never responded to him so sharply, and it upset his equilibrium. Before he could regain it, she jumped up and started pacing the laboratory, her eyes, unseeing, on her laced-up black paratrooper's boots, her hands clasped tightly and neatly behind her back. "Can you control it?"

"In what way?" he muttered.

"In any way. Its rate of reproduction, the span of its effective life, its dispersal, its rate of intake—"

"No," he said a little sulkily. "I've just been trying to get it to either voluntarily cancel the mutation or add the same conductivity capability the earlier generation has."

Still she paced, deep in thought, obviously listening closely to him but not looking at him. Finally he asked, "Alia? What are you thinking about? I'm the one that should do the thinking in this partnership, you know."

The weakly cajoling joke didn't work, and the offhand reference to a "partnership" didn't either. Niklas hadn't been aware until now exactly how intense Alia could be. "Listen to me, Niklas," she said in her commissar's order tone that Niklas despised. "Don't destroy all of the ohm-bugs that have this electricity nullification property yet. It has possibilities. It definitely has possibilities."

He eyed her warily. "I guess you can have all the little mutant beasts. I've still got plenty of the original strain to work with."

"Where are they?" she demanded. "I'll take them now."

"No, you won't," he snapped, finally getting impatient with this Alia, this imperious, take-charge Alia. He wanted his old Alia back, the pliable, lusciously weak Alia. "This is my lab, Madam Third Commissar, and no one takes anything out of my lab without my permission."

She stopped, whirled, and her strong features were set in granite. But then she softened and said, "Of course, Niklas. I just meant that there's someone I know who might be interested in such an organism, for a variety of reasons. Of course, if any recognition is ever due for any kind of use of *Thiobacillus chaco*, I'll make certain that you receive it."

"Forget recognition," he grumbled. "But if there's any money in it I'd better get a hefty cut."

"I promise," Alia said, then walked slowly to him and slithered into his lap. "Well, since you won't allow yourself to be kidnapped, I suppose I'll have to make do with just staying here tonight. But I promise I'll do my best to be more interesting than your old bugs."

He pulled her close, and she kissed him long and with much promise. "I believe," he said heavily, "that it's time to take a long break. I've been working much, much too hard."

———

At about two o'clock in the morning, the door in Niklas's laboratory leading to his private quarters opened and a shadowy figure silently slipped into the darkened lab. The halogen light above Niklas's cluttered worktable was switched on, and Alia Silverthorne hurriedly starting thumbing through the crumpled papers piled helter-skelter on the desk. She looked surprisingly young and soft and small; she was wearing a powder-blue satin night shirt with a matching robe carelessly pulled on over it, and she was barefoot. The small queue at the nape of her neck had a tiny blue ribbon tied in it.

Impatiently she stared at this paper, then that one. It was incomprehensible to her that Niklas still did much of his work with expensive wooden pencils on rare yellow notepads; it was another ostentatious quirk of his that he would only use imported notepads of virgin paper, not recycled. He said that recycled U.S. paper had the finish of a piece of particleboard (Alia didn't even know what that was) and it smelled like cheap glue.

He certainly uses it without worrying about the cost, she reflected as she tried to arrange the papers in some sort of order. *Of course, he can afford it . . . I know that the directorates would never buy real pencils and paper for anyone, not even the great Dr. Niklas Kesteven . . .* She realized that Niklas's notes were nonsense to her, she wasn't even really seeing them, much less comprehending them. With an impatient movement she went to Niklas's Cyclops II, switched off the audio-vox response module, arranged the SATphone earpiece and microphone, and called her shift lead bodyguard, Kev Jamison.

"Where are you?" she whispered. "No, everything is fine, Commissar, I just don't have my intracomm unit with me."

Then: "Which one of you is most Cyclops-literate? All right, then come to Dr. Niklas Kesteven's lab immediately. Be quiet."

She gathered up the papers, then remembered that neither of her bodyguards had been vox-scanned for universal entrance. "Not a very smart move, if they had to get to me quick," she muttered darkly.

It was really her fault; they couldn't, alone, initiate the security process that gave them the same access she had. She had to make their security and access arrangements. Alia thought now that maybe it wouldn't be a bad idea to stop treating her guards like her personal show drones and maybe show them a little respect, give them a reason to have pride in their position.

"Access," she whispered to the steel door leading out into the hallway, and was surprised to find Kev Jamison already standing there, dressed in his uniform, waiting. He didn't even look sleep-stupefied . . . surely they didn't actually stay awake to take shifts to guard her, did they? The realization that evidently they did—and that she hadn't been aware of it—galled her. A coppery blush flared on her pronounced cheekbones, and Commissar Jamison stared at her with surprise, and something else—appreciation?

Suddenly flustered and self-conscious in her nightwear, she whirled and spoke much more sharply than she intended, though she kept her voice low. "Commissar, I want all the information you can find in this laboratory about a bacteria called *Thiobacillus chaco*. Or it might be denoted as the ohm-bug. That's o-h-m. Download all pertinent files to the Cyclops II at my residence. Here's the access code. Also, take these papers, and any others you can find lying around, and scan them in. Don't try to organize anything, just create a dump file called—called—"

"Blue Satin?" he suggested, deadpan.

He was really devilishly handsome, and did his dark eyes glint with appreciation? Alia swallowed, then managed to say, "Fine. Just encrypt it using RS/SAT."

"I can't access that without your code, My Commissar," he said.

"No, no, of course you can't," she stammered. Her fingers moved over the Cyclops II keypad . . . she stumbled, made an error, and was glad she'd turned off the audio. Did he notice? She cast a quick glance up at his face, but he was pointedly looking away from the keyboard as she entered her code. No low commissar was supposed to have access to the Radio Static Satellite encryption program. At least he had sense enough to show he knew that. "Done," she muttered, stepping back.

"This will take me a while," he said, already cyber-thumbing through Niklas's database, which was named simply "Chaco." "Maybe an hour or so, with the scanning."

"That's all right. When you finish, go back to base mode." She hesitated, then said thoughtfully, "There's something else . . ."

"What?" he asked alertly. "I'm sure either I or Evans can take care of it for you."

"Some samples. Bio samples. I'll bet they're here." Moving to the wall just past Niklas's desk, by the two easy chairs and black acrylic table that still held their litter of afternoon tea, she felt along the concrete wall, then pushed a button that was unnoticeable unless one were looking for it. A panel slid open, a soft overhead light in the hidden cubicle came on. In the small square partition were several bell jars and sealed flasks. With relief she saw that none of the samples were connected to biofeeds; they must be absorbing the growth medium inside the containers, and the atmosphere must be sustaining them. For the samples in the bell jars were alive, no doubt about it; soft blue ribbons of light danced in them. Kev Jamison, forgetting he was just a dronehead, whistled softly. "We named them right, didn't we? Looks like blue satin. Living blue satin lights . . ."

"Perhaps," she agreed dully. "But I think we want the samples that aren't so pretty." The Erlenmeyer flasks had no visible organism in them, only the growth medium as dirty puddles at the bottom.

"Check the files for the codes of the mutations. These are all labeled. We don't want the original strain, the ones that look like blue lights."

"Yes, My Commissar." Kev disappeared into the robotic face again.

Alia stood for a moment, watching the hypnotic blue lights as they whirled and swirled. Abruptly she jabbed the button to close the partition and turned to Kev. "Find out which samples we need, and how to safely transport them. Then go ahead and take them to the helo. Get Evans to help you if you need it."

Without waiting for his reply, she moved close, accessed a SATphone code again (noticeably jerking when her hip brushed against his shoulder), then hurried to the farthest corner of the lab.

"Alia Silverthorne, Third Commissar, Shortgrass Steppe Biome," she said in a soft but clear voice, then waited. After a long hesitation, she spoke in a deferent whisper. "Minden? Minden, I'm sorry to have awakened you, but I think it's important. Yes, important for you and important for me . . . and important for America. Can I come to Washington tomorrow and meet with you? Good. No, I'd like to come to your residence, if possible. Good. I'll be there at 0800 hours. All right, 0900. Thank you, Minden, and good night."

Without another word, Alia went to the interior door and slipped through it into Niklas's personal quarters.

Behind her, dronehead Kev Jamison, low commissar lead bodyguard, was wondering what in the world was going on, but he knew he'd find out as he transferred this data to Alia's residence Cyclops II. He'd get some idea, anyway. As he performed clerical setup duties, he idly wondered, *Could that have been Minden Lauer, the Lady of Light, that she was talking to? The vice president's consort? Is that possible, that Alia Silverthorne is personally acquainted with the most famous . . . and maybe the most beautiful . . . for certain the most powerful . . . woman in America?*

Kev realized that his personal guard stint wasn't up for another seventy-two hours, and he also realized that meant he'd find out for sure if it was Minden Lauer by ten o'clock in the morning, eastern standard time.

Suddenly this job didn't seem half bad. And Kev was really, really glad that he'd drawn this particular, and peculiar, shift guarding Alia Silverthorne in the dead of this night.

SIX

———✦———

IN PUBLIC, IT SEEMED THAT Minden Lauer, the "Lady of Light," and the vice president of the United States, Aristide Luca Therion, were the immaculately perfect couple in an imperfect world. Aside from their youth and vitality, and the pleasing antithesis in their looks and demeanor, they seemed to epitomize pure and true love. When together, they were always arm in arm, and gave each other small signals of affection through half-smiles, eye-twinkles, and light touches that were magnified a hundred times by the unblinking eye of Cyclops.

In private, however, they were very different.

The vice president was sitting hunched over a stack of papers that he shuffled and reshuffled, picking one up and poring over it, placing it here just so, filing another beneath it, and so on. He sat on one of two antique Venetian sofas, covered in brocade with real gold thread. Between the facing sofas was a long mahogany coffee table, polished so highly it looked as if the top were glassed. The furnishings were carefully centered on an enormous and priceless Persian carpet. Dozens, perhaps even hundreds, of potted plants and small trees hovering around gave "Luca's half" of the vast studio room the atmosphere of a secluded arbor.

By contrast, "Minden's half" of the room was severe, though graceful. The long expanse of oak flooring was polished to a rich patina, and was bare. A spidery-sleek architect's table and a high

stool, centered in front of the eastern glass wall, were the only furnishings. The entire western wall, except for an inset six-foot by
six-foot Cyclops II unit, was a mirror. Minden Lauer was standing,
watching a recording of her last live comm broadcast, pausing it,
and turning to practice gestures and facial expressions in the mirror.
Often she would stop the tape after a particular phrase or sentence,
and repeat it over and over again in her throaty, hypnotic voice,
trying different ascensions and descensions and timbre and emphasis.

The two might have been on different planets.

A heavy black lock of hair fell over onto Luca's forehead, and
impatiently he brushed it back. He had a finely shaped brow
crowning a thin face, intense brown eyes, a long nose, and a
woman's full mouth. Slender and graceful, he moved like a male
ballet dancer. He seemed the most aristocratic of men, even though
his father had been a farmer in what had once been Nebraska, and
his mother was a nobody from Atlanta, Georgia. He hadn't cultivated his aristocratic demeanor, not consciously, anyway. Even as a
child he'd been thin and sensitive, passionate and eloquent.
Studying his innocuous-looking papers of columns and tables and
graphs, he was as focused as if he were seeing his future in a diviner's
enchanted mirror. As, perhaps, he was. At least he believed so.

"Did you know," he muttered between gritted teeth, "that the
estimated number of squatters in Texas actually increased last
month?"

"No, I didn't, Luca," Minden responded politely. She always
paid strict attention to everything that Luca said, no matter how
disruptive to her own thoughts at the time. And she took great care
to respond to him in an intelligent manner. "Can you tell why it's
happened? Do you think it's those arrogant cowboys riding the
ranges again, or do you think the Sixth Directorate is slipping?"

Turning lightly, she struck a pose in front of the immense
mirror. Raising her arms high above her head, she concentrated on
arranging her fingers in the most graceful pose possible, and

repeated the little choreography twice more. That was it. It was looking very natural, very graceful now . . .

Luca frowned, concentrating, and shuffled a few more papers. "I just can't tell. It would seem that the Sixth Directorate is stretched a little thin in the Konza Biome. It's so vast, and those Texans are boron-headed people. They just refuse to understand. That's all. They just refuse to."

"I know, Luca, I know," she sighed, practicing sweeping her arms out to the sides in an all-encompassing love-the-universe gesture. "It's such an oddity, too, since the rest of that biome is so easy to manage. Nebraskans and Kansans beg to be assigned to the co-ops, and never wander out into the biosphere."

She liked that particular finger arrangement, and she'd hit it by chance. With concentration she gestured until she captured it again, and then practiced until it became easy and unthinking.

She really was a lovely woman; even she saw it clearly. Her platinum hair was incandescent, her skin was like purest milk, her body shaped like every man's dream. Her features, though surgically enhanced, were as near to perfect as a human being's could be, and Minden had never been afflicted with that tight-edged, unreal look that some unfortunate women developed after extensive corrections. Minden had even had her jaws broken and reshaped when she thought she could discern an asymmetry in her full-face shots on Cyclops. She was satisfied with her looks, for now, at least, though it might be time for another touchup around her neck and under her chin before long. She was twenty-eight, looked twenty-two, and intended to stay that way for a long time.

"I'd better meet with the chief commissar tomorrow," Luca said heavily. "We need to gain control of this situation before it gets out of hand. I'll see what the Sixth Directorate needs to keep those renegades out of the biosphere areas. The First, Second, and Third Directorates are about 85 percent under control, except for those obnoxious little pockets of militants in Texas. It's imperative that we keep the West, at least, under control while we're struggling so hard in the Fourth and Fifth Directorates." The Fourth and Fifth Directorates were the overseers of the Man and Biosphere Project in the eastern half of the United States.

"How long, Luca?" Minden sighed tragically. "How long before all of our beloved land is whole and free of this terrible plague we've inflicted on her?" Minden exuded such an earthy and a sensual power, she was one of the few persons in the world who could speak with such melodrama and be wholly believable. Millions of women wept, and many men got a lump in their throats, when listening to her live comms every day.

Even Luca was bewitched by her passionate pleas. Throwing down his papers, he stood and walked to the north windows to view the street below. It was empty, for it was only a little past dawn on a Tuesday morning. Of course, in this exclusive section of Virginia, with such a sparse population remaining, the century-old streets were never crowded, anyway.

"I don't know, Minden," he murmured. "It seems that we can never get a firm grasp on it, can we? We lose our direction, our life's determination, our driving force, and get lost in the tables and charts and live comms of the day. We need a—a significant event. We need something stirring, something life-altering. An impetus, a mandate, that people can see as clearly as a torch on a mountaintop."

Minden grew very still and finally turned away from her enchanted reflection. "What do you mean, exactly, Luca? I know you aren't thinking of just another approach to the education, or more funding for the project, but I can't . . . do you mean, an inspiration? A spiritual change in the hearts of these blind and ignorant humans who are so befouling our loving earth? But how? How can we make them see?"

He turned and gave her a grave smile. "You do it every day, My Lady of Light."

"You're so kind to me . . . ," she murmured.

"Not at all. I merely answered your question. You do it, Minden, by the force and purity of your beliefs and the spiritual strength that you've gained from them. But no one else seems to be able to touch people the way you do, and even you have limitations. Sometimes people must be shocked out of their complacency, or their ignorance, or their deliberate blindness."

"But how?" she asked plaintively. In her deepest heart she wanted the blind to see the truths that it seemed sometimes only she and Luca truly understood.

"I don't know, I just can't think of a way, or a method, or a tool, or even a beginning. Sometimes I think that the earth must do it herself. She must avenge herself for the terrible wrongs done her. Sometimes I think only a tragedy, grinding hardship, or terrible loss will bring people to a place where they can understand that we must stop killing this earth, now, not tomorrow, not later, not someday!"

He was on the verge of rage, and with his deeply ingrained politic self-control he made himself calm down. Luca was always a little surprised at how very deeply he felt about the earth, about each and every part of it, from the air to the soil to the wild animals to the rocks. The depth of his anger at man's trespass on the earth, and man's criminal ignorance of the power they disdained in it, amazed him sometimes. But he never analyzed his rage too closely. He had decided, long ago, that such close dissection might be a psyche-damaging thing to do to himself, when his mission was pure and far from finished. Luca comfortably decided that he needed that righteous anger for the agonizingly difficult task he must accomplish: the saving of the earth herself.

Minden had become intent, standing still and motionless, a faraway look on her perfect face. Finally she roused and came over to Luca's luxuriant half of the room. Sitting on one of the gold-brocade sofas, she patted the seat beside her. Like a loyal terrier, Luca sat down close, his eyes burning as he listened to her every word, relished every nuance.

"Early yesterday morning," she began in a reverent voice, "I had a visit from a friend. Alia Silverthorne, the third commissar of the Shortgrass Steppe Biome."

"I remember her," Luca said thoughtfully. "Young woman, well-suited to the commissary. Dedicated member of Earth's Light."

"Yes," Minden said modestly at the mention of her enormous "church." "And a dedicated friend to me, too. She brought me some news of a new earth-being, a new life-form, Luca. I've been meditating on it ever since. It was a sign, I knew it then, but I couldn't exactly divine the portent. But I knew it was a strong sign, a vivid sign, that it would be a source of power to me. To us. For our sweet Lady Earth."

Luca's voice was hushed with awe. "A new life-form? A special sign to us? How can you be certain?"

She smiled a Madonna's smile. "The name of the new life form is *Thiobacillus chaco*. 'Chaco' means 'children of light.'"

Luca said nothing; he merely swallowed hard, his face drawn with passion, his eyes blazing with dark fires.

"This morning, just now, I have seen what this portends, Luca. I've seen, as you yourself said, that the earth herself is defending herself. She's given us, her most dedicated guardians and lovers, the tool."

"Tell me."

Minden nodded and took a few moments, both to decide how to begin and for dramatic effect. Then she began in a more prosaic tone, "Forty years ago, Luca, you know very well that the military establishment in this country had diminished in power, in size, in appropriations, in respect—in every way."

"Yes," he responded with a hint of puzzlement.

"And then what happened?"

"Libya. Those stupid, accursed savages. The aborted missile attack. On American soil!" He felt gall rising, bitter and strong, in his throat. It wasn't because the Libyans had dared to attack his country; it was because they had dirtied his ocean (even though Luca had only been two years old at the time).

The missiles had been deployed from an ancient and half-functioning Russian Typhoon-class submarine that some Duma member, probably, sold to an insanely fanatical—but oil-wealthy—jihad militant group. The old sub just stumbled through the SOSUS net, and was detected by the U.S. nuclear sub *Dalton*, prowling the coast of Newfoundland. Mostly it was sheer blind luck, considering the unreadiness of America's defenses, particularly the lack of naval defenses of its own coastal waters. The first strike fell short—luckily—and all four shabby and rusted Mako missiles fell into the southern Labrador Sea. *Dalton* blasted the Russian sub with Harpoon missiles, and the two five-hundred-pound warheads practically dissolved the craft and, of course, all of its submariners, most of whom were mercenary Russians. The debris of the aborted missiles and the oil slick, which was all that remained of what was found out to be named *Allah's Thunder*, had polluted the waters off Newfoundland for two years. Canada had grown exceedingly irritated, not with Libya, but with the United States, for dirtying up their Labrador Sea and Gulf of St. Lawrence.

"Yes, it was terrible for the coastal Atlantic ecosystems," Minden agreed, "and that's the only viewpoint I've had of it—until now. I'm sure you, however, realized the far-reaching effects of that attack on American culture."

"Of course," he said impatiently. "It resulted in America's insistence on the deployment of the Strategic Defense Initiative, and then the Galaxy Guardian satellite defense systems. Expensive toys the military concocted there. But I must say, it's an unrivaled defense mechanism that has allowed us as a people to turn to other, more important things," he admitted grudgingly.

"Yes. But the missile strike had one more important, long-lasting effect. Even now, forty years later, the results are still with us," Minden prodded him gently.

"Of course, the sharpening and polishing of the armed forces and advancement in weaponry," Luca said with an edge to his voice. "And you're right. It's been forty years, and still we spend money on our military as if we were on the verge of a world war. It's absurd. No one would dare attack us, ever again, with SDI/GG systems. Finally we've matured as a nation, so that we're not nosing around in every little flare-up in every little corner of the world, like the Germanic Union. Let Tor von Eisenhalt and his Goths fight in every meaningless little argument that erupts in piddling little nations. At least we've moved on to a higher spiritual meaning in America. Anyway, it's obvious that even such a relatively small military presence, in our homeland, is unnecessary and redundant. But still, the American people hero-worship the military, and for some reason that I can never quite fathom, they're proud of their hateful high-tech weaponry systems."

The American people had, indeed, come to a very odd polarization in their culture, and the conflict had gelled to a curious impasse between the military and the vast and powerful Man and Biosphere Project bureaucracy.

Most Americans had supported the MAB Project, at least in theory, in the beginning. When it started, of course the average person didn't understand that the end result would be a massive population shift—which was effected by a loss of property rights and civil liberties. But as the program advanced, the federal government quietly began to offer them exactly what they wanted: programs to take care of them, such as nationalized health and food credits; programs to shelter them, in MAB Project–subsidized housing at very low cost; blanket provisions for each person of a multimedia computer, Internet, telephone, fax, and most important, entertainment, in the form of the Cyclops system, which was standard in every MAB home in America. Still, Americans seemed not to realize the high costs of such coddling. The tax rate was more than 60 percent for most upper-middle-class and prosperous

Americans. And there was no accounting for the loss of personal freedom and self-determination.

At the same time, Americans loved their shiny toy soldiers. They were young, they were highly intelligent, they were fit and strong and dedicated. They were a small, elite force, as the standards for military service had been raised high, mostly as a result of the technical expertise involved in the advanced weaponry and the lack of need for a sizable force merely to guard America's borders. The American people paid these men and women well, too.

"But you do see my point, do you not, Luca?"

Minden's throaty, insistent voice penetrated the fog of antimilitary resentment in his thoughts. "No, I'm afraid I don't, love," he answered with a touch of impatience. "The Libyan attack had far-reaching effects on the American people, of course. And ultimately it strengthened our defense capability."

"And it gave the people a vision, it changed their hearts and minds, Luca," Minden continued softly. "It was a significant event. It was an impetus. It was a mandate. And it made the people *worship* their soldiers."

He stared at her as if he were trying to see inside her head, her mind, her thoughts. "But the missile strike was deliberate—an engineered event."

"That artificial event resulted in a spiritual transformation. If certain circumstances came about that furthered our cause, that would get the people to see, to leave the forbidden places of wilderness and move to the co-op cities, then their hearts would follow them."

His thoughts wandered; he admired her heavy-lidded dark eyes, such a startling contrast to her glowing hair and skin. He reflected how luscious her mouth was, and how voluptuous she was, like the richest of velvets.

He wondered if she was suggesting high treason.

He decided that she was, and one small part of his mind was appalled. But he quickly stifled that. After all, it was all for the most noble of causes: the re-wilding of the earth. And just as cauterization might be painful, so does it stop corruption, and any human would finally, ultimately, be grateful for the suffering in order to save the earth, and thereby attain a higher spiritual plane.

"As usual, my lady, you have shed some light on a dark and difficult terrain," Luca said in a low voice. "What's in your mind and heart, Minden? What do you see?"

"I see people weeping, afraid because they've offended our mother. I see people, many of them, lost, because they are blind, and ignorant, and have no love for this earth. I believe, Luca, that we can change that."

"How?" he demanded.

She cocked her head to one side, an assessing pose, as if she were measuring him. At length, she spoke in a more matter-of-fact tone, all fey Lady of Light gone. "The 'children of light' is a sign that we're nearing the source of all power. But we must be strong, and not look to the left nor the right, and stay the course."

"I will," he said hoarsely. "I'll do anything, Minden, for this power. So few could wield it with meaning and purpose. But I could, with you at my side."

Secretly Minden thought it more likely that she would wield power with him at her side, but that could wait. Now she pressed in. "Then I will begin it, Luca. I'll call Alia, and then I'll call Gerade von Eisenhalt."

"Why him? Why the Germans?" Luca asked rather petulantly. Count Gerade von Eisenhalt and his son, Commandant Tor von Eisenhalt, were central figures on the world stage. Luca resented this, as he was still very much in the shadow of his chief executive, President Bishop Beckwith.

Minden answered soothingly, "We must have help, and friends who are with us and can offer us the support we need. And Luca, surely you understand that we can't involve the president, or any of his military monkeys in this."

"No . . . no, of course not."

"We must look to other loyal followers of the Earth's Light. Since Gerade von Eisenhalt has become the director of the UN Trusteeship Council for international oversight of the Man and Biosphere Project, he's been our staunchest supporter. And you do recall that he is one of my distant kinsmen? Very distant, to be truthful, but he has honored me by recalling our kinship often. He will help us."

"All right," Luca said decisively. "Let's begin. Set up a meeting with Count von Eisenhalt in six weeks. Get all the information on this new life-form, our newest child of earth."

"I would also like to make the information available to Count von Eisenhalt's German team of eco-scientists. They are so much more dedicated than American scientists. I think they'll be able to apply the information on the 'children of light' in a way that will be more beneficial to us, and to our loving earth."

"You're right. Very well, send them all the data. And you're certain of Commissar Silverthorne's loyalty?"

"Absolutely."

"Then we shall use her and a team of her own choosing as security. No military men."

"Good," Minden said approvingly. "Very, very good. I have begun this journey, Luca. But we both will finish it, you and I. We will triumph, no matter the cost."

"No matter the cost," he repeated as if in a trance.

One day he would recall those arrogant and foolish words; but on that day, he would be unable to repent of them, and so they would bind him forever.

———————

Dancy Flynn Thayer shot the commissar. Bright blood and gore spurted from his gaping chest wound, and Dancy's grandmother, Tessa Kai Flynn, said in a sweet voice, "Wonderful shot, darling!"

"Mother, you should be ashamed of yourself. It's bad enough that you encourage Dancy—but now you're actually playing those awful games?" Victorine Thayer admonished them.

A soft rustle behind them, she passed by their modular control chairs and snapped open the heavy drapes. Agonizingly bright sunlight struck them with a tangible warmth. Victorine pushed a control button on the wall, and the glass doors slid silently to the side. The sound of a lazy summer surf, the smell of salt and sand, and the jangling crowing of seagulls drifted in.

Turning to her sixteen-year-old daughter, Victorine put her hands on her hips and said with exaggerated patience, "And you, Miss Dancy Flynn Thayer. How many times have I explained to you how awkward it's going to be if a commissar sees how you've altered the—those—"

"The Evil Horde of Ungol," Dancy said gravely.

Victorine refused to be amused, outwardly at least. "—the wicked soldiers to look like commissars. And Dancy, really. Even without my glasses I can see that woman looks exactly like Third Commissar Silverthorne! We'll probably be managing public amenity facilities in a Structured Dependence Zone if she sees that!"

"She won't, Mama Vic, I promise I'll zap it before she gets here tomorrow," Dancy argued. "Besides, no self-respecting Cyclops operator would ever take a second look at this ancient, rickety game! The players, they aren't even real! They're—they're like—dumb drawings, or something."

"They're called cartoons," Victorine said with exaggerated patience. "And they're real enough for those gory games you play."

Suddenly smiling brightly, Dancy jumped up and threw her long arms around her mother's neck. "I know, Mother, I love you, **and** I don't care if you don't let me play the Cyclops Ultimate Reality games. You know I don't."

Victorine immediately softened, and reverted to her vaguely anxious look again. She was not an unattractive woman, but she was untidy sometimes. Especially when she was preparing for a visit from the commissars. The chief and second ministers weren't so bad, but the commissars were nerve-racking to cater to. They were arrogant and demanded outrageous services such as cooking for them, and then still seemed resentful that Victorine and her daughter and mother were there in their biosphere area to manage their Diversionary Facility.

Their resentment worried Victorine, for in the last ten years she'd seen people lose their homes without even that much of a reason. The worry made her absentminded, and she became a little frowsy and windblown when she was worried. Her hair was tangled and half of it was pulled back with an old tortoiseshell comb. Her glasses were hanging around her neck with a plastic cord that had broken, and was tied in a messy knot in one place. Her Tyvek-cotton pants had smudges at both knees.

But Dancy knew that by tomorrow, her mother would look so polished and dignified that she could calm even the gruffest of commissars. Her mother was a relic, yes, but in one way it was to her advantage: She was an intellectual, a truly intelligent woman who clearly knew a vast amount of things. Not all of them were particularly useful, but somehow her certainty of her intellectual superiority—though never arrogant—seemed to intimidate other adults in a manner that Dancy had never quite comprehended. When she grew older, she would recognize the qualities: They were called dignity and self-respect. All except the most brutish of beasts responded, however reluctantly, to these traits in a human being.

"Have you seen my copy of the Tang poems, Dancy?" Victorine asked abruptly, searching around the room as if to see them flying there, tucking a stray strand of hair into the lopsided comb.

"As if any normal human would steal those dry, incomprehensible things," Tessa Kai, a spirited Irishwoman, replied to her daughter. "Of course Dancy doesn't have them, Victorine, you've lost them."

"I haven't lost them, I just can't find them," Victorine replied somewhat distractedly. "They were right there, with those socket wrenches . . . who could have taken them?"

Well, she is very intelligent, Dancy amended her previous thoughts of her mother with amusement. *She's just a little disorganized at times . . . But people like her, they enjoy her, they like to be around her . . . except that awful Alia Silverthorne,* Dancy thought fiercely. *Why does she resent my mother so much? It doesn't make any sense! She's never been rude to me or to Grandmother Tessa Kai . . . why is she so hateful to Mother?*

Behind them, the Cyclops gave a soft chirp and a robotic male's deep voice intoned, "Victorine, you have a live comm coming in."

"From whom?" Victorine asked impatiently.

"Third Commissar Alia Silverthorne, from an unknown location in the Shortgrass Steppe Biome."

Victorine touched her messy hair self-consciously, then pulled her glasses from around her neck and hid them. Hurriedly she smoothed her clothing, took a deep breath, and sat down in Dancy's chair. "Go," she said to Dancy, who obediently scooted into the bedroom, followed by her grandmother. "Put her through, please," Victorine said hastily.

The screen changed from the old toy war game, and Alia Silverthorne filled it. "Thayer, I'm canceling my scheduled diversionary weekend there tomorrow. None of my party will be there. But I want you to block out the sixth weekend from now; a large party will be coming. I'll let you know the details later."

"Yes, My Commissar," Victorine said, wishing that she didn't look as though she'd just come in out of a typhoon. Alia Silverthorne, as usual, had the hard sheen of a highly polished blade. "How many units do you wish blocked off?"

"All of them."

"All of—but, My Commissar, how can I refuse if another high commissar or some of the ministers—"

"Send word to my personal Cy II immediately if anyone reserves that weekend," Alia said sharply. "Do you understand?"

"Yes, My Commissar."

"Do you still have my personal access code?"

"Yes, My Commissar."

"Good. Remember, let me know immediately."

"Yes, My—" But Alia Silverthorne disappeared abruptly, and the enormous flat screen filled with the frozen image of the cartoon commissar sprawled on a cartoon desert with cartoon blood and guts coming out of his chest.

"I must go apologize to Dancy," Victorine mused to herself. "And maybe I'll ask her to teach me to play this game."

The library of a luxurious beach cottage
House Island, off the coast of Maine

A fevered storm was brewing in Casco Bay, and the wind shrieked imprecations and beat at the old wooden shutters, making them shiver and crack. President Bishop Beckwith liked it. He liked storms; he admired their power, he reveled in their Gothic mystery, he responded on a deep personal level to their challenge. If he had been at the cottage alone, he would have, in defiance of all convention and common sense, gone for a walk along the wild and deserted shore.

But he was not alone. Men were with him, grave men, somber men, and there was much work to be done and difficult decisions to make. Beckwith, with a last, longing look at the wildness outside the shadowed and smoky room, turned his attention back to the man who sat in the wing chair to his left .

"So Therion's meeting with some Germans in six weeks? Him and his witch? That doesn't seem so ominous to me, my old friend. Remember, the Germans are our friends!" *He spoke with caustic heartiness. Beckwith was a bombastic, colorful man who left a strong impression on people, and even imprinted rooms. He was a big, barrel-chested man, with a rich roar. His hair was thick, luxuriant, the color of purest silver. He had a tan that had been engraved on his skin in countless dawns and days and late afternoons as he had soldiered for thirty straight years. People loved him, hated him, despised him, worshiped him, feared him, but they never forgot him.*

The man on Beckwith's left—an older man, weary-looking, with rounded shoulders—leaned up so that he could speak clearly to his friend. "Sir, you know as well as I do that Germany appears to have managed—again—to rise to superpower status, and has a standing in the world today that is equal in many ways to our own. If he is meeting with influential German officials, the vice president should announce if it is a state visit, or even if it's purely a personal diversionary weekend. Certainly these days no one would care about that, as long as it's just an orgy or something. But he didn't. It's the secretiveness of it that's telling."

Beckwith took a long time to reply. He did that. He could appear to be a hearty blabbering fool when it suited him, but in serious talk with men he trusted, he never insulted their intelligence in such a way. "Yes, you're right. And as far as meeting on American soil—their military presence here is so integral, there would appear to be no reason to have to arrange a meeting in secret. They have—how many is it now— eighteen air bases?"

A man sitting in a nearby armchair, dressed in a khaki Marine uniform with a slender row of single ribbons but with two stars on his epaulets, nodded slowly. He was staring into the fire as it hissed and sizzled. The rain had begun. "Eighteen Luftwaffe bases, sir, and they have begun negotiations with the Commerce Department for another three."

"They pay good money, and they mind their own business, and they never miss a chance to express their appreciation at our allowing German pilots and soldiers to train here," Beckwith said heavily. "So why should Therion keep it a secret if he wants to meet with the lot of them?"

Beckwith stopped talking, but the four men present, and even the splendid Marine guards who unobtrusively stood at attention at each of the two doors, knew that it was a rhetorical question. Beckwith was just organizing his thoughts.

"It's got to be that bloodsucking MAB Project," he finally growled. "Gerade von Eisenhalt talks a good game in the chambers of the UN. He's especially helpful and supportive when America wants to do something stupid."

He stood, a towering, intimidating figure of a man, with a power that did not come from just being tall and muscular. He emanated strength, raw and barely contained, even at fifty-five years of age. He had never had any corrective surgeries; he openly scorned them. He had a daily physical workout regimen that would have stunned an ox.

"So what can they possibly do?" he asked, striding to the fireplace, grabbing the poker, and stoking the fire so savagely that the other men hoped the entire old cottage didn't catch fire from the sparks. "Nothing. In the first place, Therion can't hope to get any kind of legislation through without my knowledge; that's ridiculous. He can't issue any executive orders that I can't cancel. He's tried that before, remember? Sneaky little red-eyed rat."

"You're absolutely correct, sir," his old friend in the wing chair said. "So. What is he doing? Something that must be kept secret, that's what, and that means nothing good. And there's something else that my sources managed to gather, sir. He's using commissars for security. No Marine guards."

Beckwith swore. He had requested, as a personal favor to him, that Therion always use U.S. Marine guards, as did he. Neither of them disdained their pervasive Secret Service protection, of course. But Beckwith felt that since he had to mealymouth those absurd earth platitudes all the time to assuage that slice of America, so Therion could tone down his Green fastidiousness and have a decorated and shining marine or two standing behind him as symbols of the nation's military guardianship. Beckwith and Therion, the two men, despised each other, and each was incomprehensible to the other. But they had managed, in their seven years of office together, to make certain concessions to one another. Their peculiar blood and water had mixed to America's taste, so they were generally careful to give the other every consideration possible—in public, at least.

"That little weasel and his cartoon SS troopers!" Beckwith grunted. "I hate 'em! Prancin' little toylike soldiers, rounding up stray cattle and counting gophers and running good God-fearing people off their land. How did we come to this? How could this have happened—to Americans? What's happened to our country, our people?" He shook his head, a curiously helpless gesture, jarring in such a forceful man. "But

I'm wandering, aren't I? I do that a lot these days. My time's growing short, isn't it, my old friends? And I haven't made one whit of difference. Not a whit."

All four men, spoke up, protesting, but Beckwith stopped them with an impatient cutting gesture. *"So Therion's taking the storm troopers with him, huh? Well, let him. In fact, good riddance to him. I don't much like the idea of any of my boys being cooped up with that dreamy-eyed witch for a long, cozy weekend, anyway. She's trouble, and I don't mean a little, either."*

"People love her, sir," Wing Chair said neutrally. *"You don't want to go around saying things like that too much."*

"I know, I know, but I've just about had it. For the night, anyway. I think all of you are getting your shirttails untucked for no reason. Let Therion go off dreaming his little Green dreams with his dainty little whore. If the Germans want to waste their time bowing down to rocks and worshiping bushes and kissing prairie dogs, that's their crisis. I'm going for a walk—before my wife gets here. Because she wouldn't let me go if she knew."

He marched to the two Marines guarding the door. They were in dress blues, swords intact, brass shined to mirrors. *"You little boys sure look pretty,"* he boomed. *"Guess if you get wet you'll melt into sweet little puddles of goo, huh?"*

"No, sir!" shouted his two *"boys."* All soldiers were Bishop Beckwith's *"boys."*

"Ready to go and guard my precious body from the nasty raindrops, then?"

"Sir, yes sir!" they responded in unison.

"Let's go then, little boys, if you can keep up with the old man. And keep a sharp eye out for my wife's helo. We'll have to run and hide for sure when she shows up."

Beckwith, in private, got a positive delight in calling his second wife his wife, with emphasis added. It galled him to have to refer to wives and husbands as *"partners,"* so as not to offend the adulterers and *homosexuals and who knows what other weird pairings that seemed to make up a lot of America these days. But there it was; it was a compromise he'd had to make, and one of the smaller and less consequential ones at that. Still, it was one of the most irritating for this straight-talking and straight-shooting man's man.*

Stamping to the mud room, he pulled on a thick sou'wester and jammed the hat on his head, shadowed by his "boys." As he flung open the door and let the raging wind snatch his breath away, he decided that he was going to tell the world, on Cyclops, during the very next stupid speech he made, how proud he was of his wife! He didn't care if he made every sensitive pervert in America cry when he did. He was out, anyway, in just a year. They could all go hang.

Back in the darkened library, the mood was not so exultant. The uniformed men looked to President Beckwith's oldest friend, his closest adviser, and the savviest internal intelligence officer that had ever been a silent shadow in Washington. He looked troubled. "He just can't make himself care anymore. Bishop's tired, you know. He's sick of it all. He's fought valiantly and courageously, and he's lost so many times. His victories have been few and small, and most of them unknown by his people and unappreciated when they did know. Oh, he won't stop, he'll keep on fighting until the last day, the last minute, his last breath. But I think he's really glad it'll all soon be over."

The sad old man in the wing chair never knew how prophetic his words would prove to be.

PART II

FULL SUMMER

Now learn a parable of the fig tree; when his branch is yet tender, and putteth forth leaves, ye know that summer is nigh: So likewise ye, when ye shall see all these things, know that it is near, even at the doors.

—MATTHEW 24:32–33

From Nineveh the silk that made the sash
She wore about her. On it played the flash of splendid gems.
When Brunhild saw, she wept.
—FROM *NIBELUNGENLIED* (*THE SONG OF THE NIBELUNGS*)

But at my back I always hear
Time's winged chariot hurrying near;
And yonder all before us lie
Deserts of vast eternity.
—ANDREW MARVELL, FROM *TO HIS COY MISTRESS*

SEVEN

———◆———

L IKE AN ENORMOUS TIDAL WAVE, the Black Death scythed over Europe in the fourteenth century and slew nearly a third of the people in three years. The cry "Bring out your dead!" was echoed in every city and village, and the inhabitants of the royal castle died as quickly and as terribly as did the serf in his straw hut. During the height of the plague a song was sung by children:

Ring around the rosy,
Pocket full of posies,
Ashes, ashes,
All fall down!

The "ring around the rosy" was a description of the sign of the plague—a raw skin eruption encircled by a red ring. The doctors were helpless, and the common way of attempting to ward off the plague was to deck oneself with flowers—"a pocket full of posies." "Ashes" referred to the great funeral pyres of corpses that burned—at first. Later, attempts at cremation were abandoned, as the dead seemed to outnumber the living. The final line sung so lightly by countless children all over the Western world for centuries to come—"All fall down"—was the grim fate of most who were infected.

Although the plague that struck the Native American population in the summer of 2028 never was given a popular label, some called it the Red Plague. "Red" referred not to any physical symptom, but to the fact that only Native Americans were susceptible to the disease.

Prior to the onslaught of the plague, Native Americans had secured generous federal lands and protection for their tribal homes. They grew proud and disdainful of the white race, and determined to be set completely apart from them. As a result, they became very insular, and interbreeding with other races, even other tribes, was rare. All tribes secured rights to have gambling casinos in order to develop their tourist trade.

The U.S. Man and Biosphere Executive Council decided to leave the Indian reservations intact for a period of another ten years, without redistributing the inhabitants, as they began doing with the population at large, particularly in the western half of the U.S. The MAB Project executives saw an opportunity to make the best of the "misuse" of the lands that the Indians owned: they designated most of the Indian reservations' casinos and hotels as Diversionary Facilities, and most of the working population in the West rarely got to go to any other part of the country. That way, the populace at large were receiving their two-week designated vacation under the Worker's Perquisites Act—and the Indians were getting enormous amounts of tourism in their casinos.

These factors were fated to be tragic for the Native Americans. The interbreeding of relatively small tribal populations resulted in a weakening of the genetic strains, much as happened in European royal families. And once again, Caucasians, coming in huge droves to their lands, carried a disease to them that Indians could not overcome.

The first wave of the plague struck without warning in the Nez Perce reservation in the panhandle of Idaho, in the summer of 2028. An Indian child was stricken with a mysterious liver ailment and died within a week. His mother and father, and then his sister, contracted the same disease and died within a month. That spring the plague swept the Nez Perce reservation, with a mortality rate of 68 percent; as always, children and the very old were more likely to die than the young and strong.

On the Nez Perce reservation, the illness (which later came to be called by the medical community hepatitis-X, or hep-X) peaked in April, then diminished. But before the end of May, hep-X had made an appearance at three other reservations. The national health authorities, who had assumed that the liver disease was localized within the Nez Perce tribe, now frantically tried to find a genetic shift, such as a common-denominator trauma to Indians for some difference in their melanin (which is the pigment that produces the particular color of each race's skin). They did thousands of tests on Indian blood (such sweeping and meticulous analysis of this race had never been done before), hoping to find a racial defect similar to blacks' susceptibility to sickle-cell anemia.

But they were looking at the wrong end of things. The explanation was much simpler. Caucasians had developed a peculiar antibody resulting from generations of vaccination for hepatitis. Indians, secure in their isolated culture, scorned the vaccination program that was mandatory for all other Americans. This antibody, slowly and unnoticeably, mutated very slightly. The antigen shift was unnoticeable in Caucasians, and the only physiological result to them was a slight change in the bacterial composition of excretions. However, it proved highly contagious and infectious to Indians when exposed to saliva or sweat or even the oxygen molecules expelled in breathing. Most of the initial cases literally caught it from breathing the same air as white people. Then they caught it from one another.

Because of the heavy tourist traffic at all of the Indian reservations, the plague swept through the Native American populations quickly, causing initial high mortality; later, because of the decline in infectious population, the mortality rate slowed down but the disease itself thrived. Finally in 2032 a successful vaccine was discovered, but by that time America no longer had enough "indigenous peoples" to rate a population percentage in the census. Though the fittest survived, almost the entire population of children and infants died, and because of simple mathematics the Indians never regained their numbers.

The MAB Executive Council, expressing great sorrow at the tragedy, offered to integrate all Indians into the co-op cities, in the finest homes, and stipulated that in deference to their terrible loss, no pure-blooded Native American would ever have to work again. America would support them, give them homes, food, luxuries.

That killed most of the rest of them off.

Some of the Indians of the northern forests and high, cold deserts managed to settle into American mainstream life and lived, usually marrying and integrating with whites. Many of the Indians of the hot deserts (the Hopi, the Navajo, the Apache) could never seem to adjust to the cold glass and steel of the co-op cities, and many of them died out. But some of them wandered the deserts, living a nomadic existence; generally even the commissars left them alone. There were so few of them, and they were a lost and forlorn people.

Most Indians, because of the high rate of death among the elderly, lost all sense of heritage in the plague. Some of them weren't even certain of their tribal designation any longer, for since the numbers were so small, the tribes who stubbornly stayed on their native lands huddled together and intermixed. They were still a race, but they had no history.

But heroic figures at times spring from unlikely roots. A crude, homely rail-splitter can become the greatest of presidents, born or fated to be the hinge on which history ponderously swings. A simple village maiden can hear the voice of God and become a warrior followed by generals and kings. True enough, at times these roots out of barren ground who transform history can be dangerous. A paperhanger named Hitler can almost destroy the world and a French corporal named Napoleon can fill the earth with graves.

During the darkest hour of Native Americans, whispers of a full-blooded Apache named Cody Bent Knife began to be heard. He had no honor among his own people, for he was not a descendant of famous chiefs. Born in 2031 in Las Vegas, his father was a blackjack dealer and his mother a cocktail hostess. According to reports, both were shallow and greedy, drinking and abusing the now-legal recreational drugs and trading "partners" with monotonous regularity.

They named their son Cody Tabor, but when he was still in his teens the boy appropriated his own Indian name—Cody Bent Knife. He was what Herman Melville called an "isolato," one who isolates himself from others. By the time the boy passed out of adolescence, he had come to believe that he was one of the last true Apaches, one of the last warriors, and as the weapons of his people had disappeared, so he was flawed and mocked—hence the name Bent Knife.

When Cody was sixteen, he abruptly left home to go on a vision quest as the ancients had done. Wandering the desert, he fasted almost to the point of starvation, drank very little water, and stared into the heat-shimmers and dreamed. Cody Bent Knife, the lost and last Apache, finally had a startling vision. He saw an empty land, with no people, no children, no life at all, except animals and cactus. A magnificent jaguar, the fiercest predator of all, dominated Cody's vision. He saw that this killer cat, though it once had almost been driven to extinction, had multiplied and grown numerous, with no predators and an unlimited food supply. But in Cody's dream ugly green worms grew plentiful, and grew stronger, and began to kill the jaguar's meat: the prairie dogs, the gophers, and finally even the elk and antelope. So the jaguar, brought down by the meanest of creatures, died, and the land was overrun by green worms and noxious rats and beetles and spiders.

Cody Bent Knife made that vision the center of his life. As he explained it to his followers, "The jaguar, he is the Indian, and the worms are white people. We cannot win a war against the whites. Just as the jaguar couldn't kill and eat poison, so we can't hope to erase the white men from the earth. It is a warning; we must find another way to survive."

After more meditation, Cody Bent Knife began to see his destiny, and that of his lost people. His message, and his deliverance, was simple: "The whites have grown to fear the spirits of the earth. They have run from them, hidden from them, tried to separate themselves from them. They will eventually die, for no man can live apart from his land and the love of it. But we, the true people of this land, will live and love the earth again. We will flourish and one day, as in the old times, we will rule the plains and mountains and deserts."

The gathering of Cody Bent Knife's followers was as simple and as complex as the source of a wind. Although Cody Bent Knife made no appeals, one by one or in small groups, they came to the Four Corners, so called because it was the only spot in America where the borders of four states meet. This conjunction is marked by a circular plaque, and if one got down on all fours, he could be in Colorado, Utah, New Mexico, and Arizona at the same time.

Most of those who filtered into the desert to join Cody Bent Knife were refugees from a world they had not made and which they despised. Nor did any of them understand what force it was that drew them to Four Corners. The first lesson that Cody greeted newcomers with was this: "The white people, they have tried to put this vast and unknowable desert into squares, and they name it Four Corners, as if it were a little room. But I say to you that it is a circle, an ancient and mystic circle, as our ancestors, the Anasazi, lived and breathed and flourished here. Here we will learn to live, and watch the whites die."

It would seem that Cody Bent Knife had borrowed his symbolism from one of the old ones, Black Elk, an eloquent martyr. But Black Elk's words had been lost and forgotten for generations, and Cody Bent Knife only spoke from his heart, as had the warrior of old:

> The white man made us to live in little square houses, which is bad, for there is no power in a square. All of our lives once were formed by a circle, because the Great Spirit never works in squares, but always in circles. Everything in nature is round, for it is the way of life. The sun is round and the moon and the stars. The seasons move in a circle, as does the life of every man. The life of a man is a circle from childhood to childhood. In the days of our fathers, all our power came from the sacred hoop of the nation. As long as the hoop was unbroken, we flourished. All of life was good as long as we observed the sacred hoop. We lived in round tepees and always in our camps we set them in a circle. In those days we were strong, but now we have been forced to live in square boxes. The Great Circle has been broken, our power is gone . . .

EIGHT

———◆———

THE SMALL BROOK BEGAN WITH a mere trickle from a hidden spring higher in the sandstone hills. It wound in a serpentine fashion, leisurely feeling its way to lower levels, gently wearing down the soft, sandy rock. In a country blistered by the sun and baked by torrid summers, the stream created a green passageway sought out by animals both day and night. It was a winding oasis that clashed with the heat-baked desert and one that Zoan had learned to love. Often he found himself at a small pool that had been formed where the brook banked against a rising crest of ready stone that doubled back and changed directions. In this rock elbow was the hidden pool. When he put his hand into it, the water leaped over his knuckles with a delicious coolness.

The sun was dropping down into the west, sending dusky crimson slants of light down into the narrow gorge. The pool itself was still, so clear that Zoan, as he knelt and peered down, could see the silvery minnows as they moved in unison like a tiny flotilla. He was fascinated at how they could remain motionless—then suddenly, as if at the alarm of some sort of unseen trumpet, could all wheel instantly and shoot away in perfect order. It was as if a single brain were connected to every one of the argentine bodies and Zoan never ceased to marvel and delight in this spectacle. What Zoan didn't realize was that all of it—the pool, the stream, and especially the fact that fish had somehow been transplanted into it—was a mighty miracle in the midst of a barren land. To Zoan the minnows' organizational cleverness was phenomenal enough for childlike wonder.

Though he glanced at the minnows, his attention was riveted on the shadowy form of a large fish that lurked underneath a shelving bank, a darkly shadowed crevice worn by the patient passage of the water. Only the sharpest eye could have seen the trout, and Zoan, who had remained in the same position for over forty-five minutes, did not so much as flicker an eyelash.

He had learned that stillness was the essential quality for this sort of fishing. Now he knelt, his body immobile as a statue. Zoan moved no more than did the impastoed rocks that formed a semi-circle around the elbow of the creek. A thought flitted through his intense concentration on the fish: *I wonder if men fished here long ago when there was life in this place?*

Zoan often mused about the past, for since he had come to Chaco Canyon he had been alone, and in his stream-of-time-and-consciousness way of thinking, the shadows of the past were much the same as the reality of the day. To him, ghosts had the same reality as the living, for neither was with him, yet all had left an imprint. For now, Zoan mentally shifted to pay strict attention to the fish. At the same time, however, his heightened instincts made him totally aware of everything that went on about him. The four vultures that circled above him were mere dots in the inverted bowl of the sky, yet he knew they were there. Deep down, he even had reflected that the great birds were actually the dramatic California condors, not the half-crow, half-buzzard types of common vultures that were so plentiful in the deserts. If Zoan had so chosen, he could have placed himself, made himself into a condor, in the inexplicable way he had of becoming like an animal. He could have soared lightly on the hot wind, staring down at the seared land below, hungrily assessing the still figure of the human beside the stream.

Zoan also, in this deep sublevel of knowledge, was aware that by his left knee a group of red ants was struggling to convey the carcass of a dead grasshopper. There were only four ants; one had evidently been to the wars for he lacked one feeler and one of his legs was sheared off at the joint. Moving the dead grasshopper was a monumental task for these tiny creatures, but for the past half hour they had succeeded in dragging the grasshopper along over a slight rise. They labored without rest and evidently without weariness. Zoan wondered what it would be like to be trapped in the tiny body of an insect.

The sounds of expulsion of breath from a deep hot-blooded chest barely touched his ears. Zoan was intensely conscious of the jaguar that he called simply "Cat." Without looking up, Zoan knew that the half-hooded green eyes of the beast were fixed on him. Zoan loved Cat. The jaguar had become his constant companion since he had been so completely cut off from humans. He knew that if he looked up he would find the attention of the magnificent animal focused on him in the remotely interested, slightly aloof manner that felines have of communicating affection.

The silvery shadow underneath the moss green ledge suddenly moved, quicker than thought. Like an arrow the streamlined form of the fish shot out, mouth open, to snap up one of the minnows. At the same moment Zoan's hand moved. Scarcely ruffling the water, his arm shot under and he felt the scales of the fish as his fingers closed like talons. With a swift motion he threw the fish back so that it landed on the sandy soil.

Zoan was pleased, as always, that he had achieved a goal, no matter how small. He looked over and smiled. "Supper, Cat." Picking up a stone he struck one quick blow, and the silvery fish lay still. Zoan had once tried spearfishing with a sharp stick, but somehow he felt it was cruel. Despite his mystical affinity to all animals, Zoan was not a soppy fool; some creatures were food, and that was their reason for being there. No need to grieve, but no need to be cruel, either. A single blow killed the fish quickly and mercifully, and so Zoan had honed the more difficult skill of fishing with his bare hands.

Proudly Zoan held the big fish up high. The jaguar's pupils, which were dilated to needle slits, opened fully, then she exhibited a feline grin, grimacing to expose the white, needle-sharp fangs. "Your favorite meal, Cat," Zoan said with satisfaction. He moved over and pulled a burlap sack that was tied with a leather thong to one of the saplings that grew along the edge of the pool. Opening the mouth of his rucksack, he slipped the fish in with the others, then continued to follow the meandering brook. Cat padded along patiently behind him.

The sun seemed to drop even as he watched and he picked up his pace a little. Leaving the ribbon of ravine cut by the little stream, he scrambled out onto the crust of one of the jagged hills that brooded over his home. Carefully he worked his way down the sandy, rocky decline, his silent and ominous companion steady at his heels. Soon they arrived on a small plateau that overlooked a generous expanse of golden sand. Zoan and Cat half slid, half jumped down onto the floor of the mesa and turned due east, walking along the base of the craggy line of hills.

The mesa was covered with horses, a great herd of wild mustangs. Alertly, and as cleverly as the minnows, as one they lifted their heads as the man appeared. They did not bolt, however, as they had done when Zoan had first come to this place. First they had become accustomed to him, and now they were familiar with him.

Zoan could have walked straight through the herd—if he had been alone. He often did mingle playfully with the wild herd. It gave him pleasure to move among the mustangs, to reach out and stroke them, to rub their noses and feel their coarse coats and untamed manes. Zoan had become so familiar to the horses that the small foals, ordinarily fearful of everything that moved, would watch him with curiosity. Once he and one of the yearlings had even played an odd game of tag. Or perhaps it was hide-and-seek. Zoan was not sure, for no one had ever actually played either of the games with him. Dr. Kesteven had just told him about them.

But now the mustangs realized that the man was not alone. The lead stallion snorted angrily, then uttered a shrill neigh, a warning. Rearing, tossing his head, then wheeling, he led the stampede. The thunder of hooves shook the mesa as the herd swept away from where the man stood watching. Zoan turned to smile. "You scared them, Cat." The jaguar yawned, bored with the spectacle. Gliding forward, she nuzzled the sack. One broad paw, with the terrible claws sheathed, batted it.

"Hungry, are you? So am I."

Once again Zoan started, this time breaking into a trot. As he moved through the great flat expanse, a slight change, a mixture of feeling and knowing, came over him. He looked up to the darkening sky. *It may rain.*

The thought pleased him, for it had rained only twice since he had been in the canyon. He missed the rain; he had always loved to stand out in it and let it run down over him. To Zoan, it was a uniquely cleansing experience, different from bathing. Slowing again to a walk, he looked around speculatively at the flatness of the terrain.

"This could be farmed," he mused aloud. "I could grow corn here." He searched the manganese violet-colored twilight shadows. Zoan's long night-eyes could easily see the distant herd, which had dramatically stampeded—for about half a mile. "Nothing for you, Horses. You can't eat fish," he murmured. "But you could eat corn if we could grow some."

As he approached the massive lift of sandstone that was swallowing the sun, his mind was on farming. He knew farming—how to plow, how to plant, how to take care of crops, and how to harvest. That had been the good part of his life on the surface above the laboratory. But here there were problems for there were no neatly humming electric tractors with plows and disks and sodbust attachments. He stared blankly, concentrating. *No water. How could I get water here? Maybe—what's that word?—irrigate. Bring a ditch down from the creek from where it rises in the hills.* But he had no shovels, and besides, it would take a single man a long, long time to dig a ditch like that.

Now Zoan considered his new home—the great stone edifice that was so integrated with the rising cliffs that it seemed to have been carved out of them. A huge D-shaped structure, it covered nearly three acres and reached as high as five stories in places. When Zoan had left the lab, his trek had seemed aimless at first. But somehow he had ridden the grisly old stallion right into this canyon, to this ancient place. As soon as he had seen it, he knew this was where he was supposed to stay.

And now, as he had so many times, he studied it again, marveling anew at it. Two large plazas dominated the center of the lower level, with great dark echoing openings yawning in them. Zoan had a dreadful fascination for the circular holes. He knew that they had been underground chambers at one time, but time and weather had stripped away the roofs.

Behind and to one side of the plazas rose the ruins that had once been the homes of an ancient people. Now only stubby brown grass and tough mesquite shrubs lived there.

As Zoan often did, whether through effort or gift, he had a vison so vivid it was like living and walking and breathing the reality of the once-thriving civilization. He saw the fields, not exactly lush, but they did thrive with orderly rows of corn and beans and squash. He heard the muted splash of streams running down from the hills and cliffs, cutting deep into the stone that still bore the trail but not the life-giving water. People were there, people Zoan could see and hear clearly, as they moved across the community plazas, calling out greetings and pausing to visit neighbors in the doorways. High cries of children, running and playing, sounded in the golden air. From the windows high above, faces peered out. It was a live place, of color and light and sound and heart.

Suddenly Zoan expelled his breath, realizing he had been holding it. He knew little about the people who had built this magnificent place so long ago. In the way of odd connections Zoan had, he recalled Dr. Kesteven talking to Alia Silverthorne about "the children of light," and a place called Chaco Canyon, and the *Anasazi*. The word meant, Dr. Kesteven had said, "Enemy ancestors." At the time the conversation had been nothing to Zoan but another indelible, and unfathomable, imprint on the map of his memories. But when Zoan had found this place, he had, in his peculiar way, recognized it, and had recalled Dr. Kesteven's explanation. About the Anasazi, Dr. Kesteven had known but a little. They were wanderers, the Anasazi, he had told the woman. They learned to plant corn and had built fine communities here and in Arizona and Colorado. They were a peaceful people, good at making exquisite pottery. Niklas had frowned, then muttered, "No one knows what happened to them. They just left their homes, and then they disappeared into the mists of time . . ."

It was almost fully dark, so Zoan entered one of the apartments on the first floor that he had made into a home for himself. It was a spartan place. A sleeping bag lay against one wall. On a shelf carved out of stone were a razor, two bars of soap, which he hoarded carefully, a toothbrush, and a brush and a comb, which pretty well summed up the total of his toilet articles. He had also brought a small store of supplies: some basic cooking utensils, needle and thread, small tools, two electric lanterns, a few packets of dried beef and vegetables, two five-pound bags of rice. But the only personal things Zoan had brought were two books that he had found, lost and forgotten, in the well-stocked lab library. One was a Bible and the other a book of poetry by a man named George Herbert. Sometimes at night he would sprawl belly-down by the fire and read from the two books.

Zoan understood little of the Bible and even less of the poetry, but he had read it so often that it had become imprinted in his mind, and had somehow soaked into his understanding. During the days when he roamed the barren plateaus, bits and portions of his books would come to him. In his solitude, his books had come to form a great deal of his thinking. One conscious analysis that Zoan had was that he liked the poetry; even just the sounds and rhythms gave him light pleasure. But the Bible he loved deeply, an emotion that Zoan hadn't known he was capable of. Especially he loved the last book, even though sometimes it made him feel a little bit of dread, much like the times he mystically knew of Bad Things to come. Slowly, however, Zoan was coming to understand that the book told of terrible happenings, yes—but also of victory.

Efficiently, Zoan made a fire using the old flint-and-steel method. He had one piece of steel and flints were abundant. He kept punk from dead trees and shrubs so that when he struck a spark it caught eagerly; a tiny lick of flame and a thin wisp of smoke wavered in the cold desert night. Patiently he blew on it, adding more of the punk until finally a small blaze kindled. Nourishing it with small twigs, gradually adding larger ones, he soon had a cheerful fire snapping and crackling, a homey sound that gave Zoan a feeling of peace and security. Outside Zoan cleaned the fish. He fed one to the jaguar, one to the old dingo, and one to two twin brindled cats that had mysteriously appeared out of nowhere to adopt Zoan and the dog. Even the jaguar put up with the two cats, who were only half grown. It would seem that some confusion would have resulted from their joining the community, for Zoan called both of them "Cat," too. Happily, Zoan wasn't confused because he knew who he was talking to, and neither the big cat nor the two little ones cared because they only paid attention to humans—even special ones like Zoan—when they wanted to anyway, regardless of what they were named.

Moving back inside, he pushed a green stick through the white meat of the other fish and held it over the fire. When it was cooked he ate hungrily, singeing his fingers pulling the meat off. It was white and flaky and delicious. "Could use some salt. I'll have to see if I can find salt somewhere," he spoke aloud.

He took a drink out of the ola that he had discovered down in the circular caverns. He had gone down into them—steps were carved out of the walls—a few times, but only in the daytime. The ola was a small but beautifully designed clay jar with geometrical designs painted in reds, yellows, and blues. The water was tepid, but Zoan was accustomed to that. He picked up the smaller book and turned the page to one of his favorite poems:

> A broken Altar, Lord, Thy servant reares,
> Made of a heart, and cemented with teares,
>> Whose parts are as Thy hand did frame;
>> No workman's tool hath touch'd the same.
>>> A heart alone
>>> Is such a stone
>>> As nothing but
>>> Thy power doth cut.
>>> Wherefore each part
>>> Of my hard heart
>>> Meets in this frame,
>>> To praise Thy name:
> That, if I chance to hold my peace,
> These stones to praise Thee may not cease.
> O, let Thy blessed Sacrifice be mine,
> And sanctify this Altar to be Thine!

He read the words aloud, pleased with the way they appeared on the page, more pleased by the mere sounds. He murmured the line, "A heart alone is such a stone as nothing but Thy power doth cut," many times, not understanding it in his brain but stamping the sentiment deep in his spirit.

Going back outside, Zoan stood for a long time, just watching the millions of stars and marveling at the silence of the desert at night. His mind went back to the time when the Voice had come to him in the laboratory, in a dream and in music. The Voice had told him to leave the lab, to go out alone, and he had been afraid . . . but the Voice had spoken truth.

So he had been obedient to the Voice, and since he had been isolated, alone with his thoughts and meditations, in this quiet place, Zoan had learned two things with absolute certainty.

One was that the Voice he had heard, and knew so well, was God.

The other thing that Zoan was sure of was that he had been brought to this place for a purpose. Zoan still wasn't clear exactly what his purpose was; that is, it was not a formal plan laid down in neat compartments in his mind. It was something of an inner surety, a visceral comprehension, and the beginnings of a vision. But Zoan was not the kind of man to be bothered with hurry. He would know, and see, at the right time.

Finally he went back into his home of old stone and snuggled down in the sleeping bag. The nights were cold, and his sleeping bag kept him wonderfully warm. His acute hearing caught the sound of heavy pads. Without looking up, he knew that the jaguar had come inside the ruins of the house to stretch out in the doorway. "Good night, Cat," he whispered. He got no answer but he could hear the animal's deep breaths as he dropped off to sleep.

Dawn came—and with it a sense of urgency. Zoan scrambled to his feet, slipped on his boots, and hurried outside, still unsure of what he was sensing but knowing it to be a true instinct. The jaguar was gone. The old stallion, Zoan's sometime friend and sometime mount, was outside, stamping impatiently and tossing his head. His eyes rolled, showing white.

"What's wrong, Horse?" Zoan murmured. He watched the agitated animal for a moment, then suddenly he knew that someone was coming. Without hesitation he broke into a lope and left the ruins. He ran to a distant cliff, a great fault break where the floor of the mesa ended in a jagged drop down to a scrub valley below. Standing at the edge of a precipitous undercut cliff, his sharp eyes picked up a group of people, far away but moving toward him. Some of them were mounted, some walked. They had several pack animals. He studied them, his eyes narrowed but his unusual pupils rounded into full black disks, even in the brightness of the morning. Finally he lay down on his stomach so that they could not see his outline against the sky.

As the band came steadily forward, Zoan turned his full attention on the man who was obviously their leader. The young Indian sat his horse easily, in the timeless natural manner of his people. His dark eyes were deep and glinted like obsidian stones set in the copper glint of his skin. His mouth was wide, but not full, and was now closed into a thin line of determination. A tall man, he was lean, wiry, sinewy. Long gleaming black hair hung down his back in a thick braid tied with a leather thong and a single tan feather. He was dressed in a pair of old, loose buckskin trousers, and wore a leather vest with no shirt.

Something about the Indian fascinated Zoan, drew him. Of the few people Zoan had known in his life, Dr. Kesteven had been the only one with whom Zoan had had a human relationship—and it was a rather shallow and one-sided one at that. Now, as he studied the face of the man who rode the bay stallion, Zoan suddenly felt a kinship. It was inexplicable and beyond reason, but Zoan was not a man who moved and lived according to reason.

Now, Zoan thought, *I'm not going to be so alone anymore.* He knew, somehow, that this young Indian, whoever he was, would be inextricably entwined with Zoan's life. Silent and unmoving, he watched the group as they came plodding forward. His eyes moved from point to point, noting individuals, but always his eyes returned to the lithe form of the leader. "I don't know your name," he whispered, "but I'll come to know you well."

Ever since the death of her grandfather, Little Bird had been unhappy and lost. Perhaps if the Mitchells had stayed in the West she might have found some sort of place for herself, or some sort of peace in herself, but they had left. For weeks she had restlessly prowled the countryside, unhappy and aimless.

More grief came when she blew the engine of her Harley Davidson. The motorcycle had been a means of escape for her, but now it was past fixing. Little Bird had no money. It didn't matter, anyway, for there were no parts available for such an ancient machine, and no one who knew how to make them work anymore.

Now as Little Bird pulled her horse up close to the leader of her bedraggled little community, she reflected on how she had heard a rumor of a man in the desert who was turning back to the old ways of his fathers, the Apache. Little Bird had always been impulsive, but since the death of her grandfather and the loss of her only close friends she had become thoughtless and reckless. Blind and uncaring she set out to wander, telling herself she wanted to know what truth lay in the rumors. As she had roamed the southwestern mountains and plains, she had encountered other Indians, lost and uncertain as she was. Finally a small group of them had found the elusive Cody Bent Knife, as he called himself. She had watched him daily for weeks. She was drawn to him, and at the same time disdainful of his beliefs and the hope for the future that he offered.

Abruptly Little Bird taunted, "You've gotten us lost, Cody."

Cody turned his deep gaze on the young woman. As he studied her, he saw the strength in the firm body, the determination in the dark brown eyes, marked the pure Apache blood that was revealed in her burnt coral skin and the jutting planes of her cheekbones, high and prominent. "What makes you think I'm lost?" he asked.

"Because we've wandered all over this desert for weeks now, and all your fine talk about going in circles is just that—going in endless and useless circles. We don't have anything to eat and everyone's sick of it."

Cody pulled his horse to a stop and let him lower his head. There was weariness in the animal, he felt, as there was in his own body. He looked back over the small group that was strung out behind him and saw that the hard traveling had planed away all excess flesh. His eyes went from person to person, for he had learned to know them and see them as he had never known people before. His gaze rested on the oldest of the party, the seventy-year-old Benewah Two Color. Here was the one man whom Cody trusted, and the one who had caught the vision that had driven Cody himself to the desert. "Two Color, Little Bird says I'm lost."

The old man's hair was still black except for the white streak at the left temple. He had been born with that odd white mark, which was the reason for his name. There was something of the prophet in him, this old man. He had spent his life watching his people fade away and die off and turn away from their history until now, he saw with profound grief, there was almost nothing of the American Indian left.

Yet still there was, behind his jet-black eyes, the hope of things not seen. He was a man who knew what it was to have visions, for he had both welcomed them and cursed them at different times in his life. Now time had pared him down in body, but in strength of heart he was as determined as his young friend Cody Bent Knife to learn of the truth of these terrible times.

Now Benewah Two Color's jet-black eyes settled disapprovingly on the young woman, but his rebuke was gentle. "You are too forward, Little Bird. Your grandfather would not have approved."

Little Bird flushed. She was wearing a pair of faded jeans and a thin, cheap white man's shirt. Her feet were shod with worn half boots and her black hair was tied carelessly behind her back. She wore a floppy brown hat with a wide brim. Rather sulkily she retorted, "My grandfather would never have come on a wild-goose chase like this."

"I think he would have," Two Color said mildly. "It's just the sort of thing we talked about when we were young men."

Actually Little Bird knew that the old man was right. She had grown up listening to her grandfather's stories of the old days, and he had always insisted that there would come a time when the tribes would return to the old ways of living in closeness with their lands. Of course, after he had become a Christian he had modified his visions, hopes, and dreams somewhat.

Now Little Bird looked around at the dusty, travel-weary crowd and felt the same old impatience she'd had time and time again with her grandfather. "I've heard enough Messiah talk for a lifetime. What I want to know is when are we going to stop some-where and set up a real camp where we can get some rest?"

"And something to eat." The speaker was a man in his early forties with the name of Bluestone Yacolt. His father was Apache, his mother Blackfoot. He had been born with bright blue eyes, which was inexplicable to both his parents. They had never changed, and from them he had been given his name. Pulling his horse up beside Little Bird, he wondered, again, what exactly he was doing out with the bunch of dusty visionaries. He couldn't explain it. Now his eyes were flashing the color of turquoise. He had been a gambler and a drunk and had learned to hate all con-nection with anything Indian. He had married a Nez Percé woman and she had borne him a child that Bluestone had named Sunstone, but Sunstone and his wife had died in the plague.

Bluestone had wandered aimlessly, always weary but never stopping. For some reason that was unfathomable to him, he was out in the desert with what he considered a bunch of deluded, and possibly dangerous, weirdos. But part of Bluestone Yacolt's rebel-lion was to stay far away from the grave dignity that was evidenced by the Old Ones such as Benewah Two Color, so now he said in a lazy voice, "I'm starving to death, Cody. Hey, could you maybe do a rain dance, get us some nice cold water? And while you're at it, do us a T-bone steak dance, with maybe a potato chant on the side?"

Cody Bent Knife was accustomed to this sort of outburst from Bluestone, and he never let it bother him. "We're not lost, Bluestone, and we'll eat. With that little paunch you've got going there, you'll live for a while longer."

"Cody, I'm tired, I'm hungry, and I don't see anything around here except cactus and mesquite scrub. I don't want to be so much like the Old Ones, and eat beetles and grubs and things. You sure you can come up with something a little more appetizing for all of us noble tribesmen?"

A murmur went through the others, some twenty of them, who had now caught up with the leaders. A big Navajo named Ritto Yerington stood watching carefully, listening with a surly look on his face. He was a tremendously strong man who could be mean and savage. Most of the time he just ignored Bluestone Yacolt's foolishness, but he was getting tired of the way the man was nagging at Cody Bent Knife. Ritto had no idea how, exactly, nor why he had come to view himself as Cody's personal body-guard and defender, but there it was. He was it. His one other blind and undying loyalty was to his younger sister, Layna. She was totally dependent upon her brother and now came to stand quietly beside him, looking up at him for reassurance.

The argument, mild as it was, was very short, for Cody had learned that argument would not move people. Those who had come to him had been sent, he felt, and were a part of the puzzle that was a constant maze in his mind. He knew that somehow he had been brought to this place, this enormous plain of deserted and barren land. He knew that this small group that followed him had been chosen also.

For what he didn't know.

Now, since he was weary and dusty and a little forlorn, he went over the questions he had repeated so often to himself that he was almost driven insane: *Chosen—but chosen for what? Why are we here? Why this place?*

As if in answer to his question, a voice suddenly broke the uneasy silence.

"Hello."

Instantly Cody whirled and the eyes of all the travelers were fixed on the man who suddenly stood there before them. He was not armed, which was the first thing they all looked for, but stood quietly studying them out of deep-set eyes. He was a plain man, simply dressed. The very stillness of his stance and his smooth, unremarkable looks were precisely what made him seem so unearthly, so flagrantly unusual, appearing out of nowhere in this barren and forsaken place.

"Who are you?" Cody challenged him.

"My name is Zoan."

"I'm Cody Bent Knife. What do you want?"

"Nothing. I just thought you might want to stop here and rest and eat."

"Stop—here . . ." Cody was disoriented; he kept searching around for a frame of reference for this odd young white man. "Are you alone here?"

"Yes."

The answer was brief but there was nothing churlish about it. Little Bird suddenly clapped her horse's sides, pushing him forward. "You said you have something to eat?"

"Well, there are things to eat. We could catch some fish. I have some rice. If you want to come with me, you can have some."

"Come where?" Cody asked cautiously.

"Over there. There's a place over there, an old place. You'd like it, I think, Cody."

Suddenly a grin transformed Cody Bent Knife from the grim

wanderer into what he really was: a tired and hungry nineteen-year-old. "You're telling me that you live in Chaco Canyon, Zoan? In the old Anasazi ruins?"

Zoan blinked, then answered with his customary brevity. "Yes."

"You're right. I know that place well, and I like it."

"Me, too."

"Well, it sounds good to me," Bluestone interrupted. "I must be really hungry to have a mouthwatering episode for rice and fish."

Benewah Two Color moved his horse with a touch of his heels. He brought the animal directly over Zoan. Zoan looked up and the gazes of the two men locked. Finally Two Color found something in the simple features of Zoan that seemed to please him. "My name is Benewah Two Color."

Zoan, never having been taught the niceties of social introduction, responded, "My name is Zoan."

Two Color exchanged a sly wink with Cody. "So I heard. Cody, I think we should stay, talk to this man. I believe he has words that we need to hear."

Cody was startled. Very rarely did the old man say such things but Cody had learned to trust Two Color's instincts. "All right," he agreed.

Zoan's eyes were roaming hungrily over the horses; to be more precise, he was looking at the blankets that they all had, instead of saddles. "You have lots of nice blankets."

Amused, Cody agreed, "Yes. They are. Our people made them for many years, and we've kept them."

"Can I have some of them?"

Little Bird asked suspiciously, "What do you need with so many blankets?"

"Because I'm going to have friends here this winter and I worry about them getting cold. I don't want them to be cold."

"Friends? What friends? Who?" Ritto Yerington demanded.

Cody exchanged a quick glance with Two Color, gave Ritto a slight shake of his head to signal quiet, then turned back to Zoan. With an intentness that belied the mundane conversation, he said, "We'll trade you some blankets."

"Trade?"

"Yes, trade. You know what that means, don't you?"

"No."

"The little guy's just a simpleton, Cody," Bluestone Yacolt grumbled. "What are you wasting time on this silliness for?"

Patiently Cody addressed Bluestone. "He is not a simpleton, Bluestone. Look at him, watch his face, see his eyes. He's something more. Anyone with eyes to see would know it. So would you please just give me a chance to talk to the man?" Turning back to Zoan, Cody observed that he had ignored this very personal conversation concerning himself. He was stroking the horses' noses while keeping his oddly deep eyes fixed on Cody Bent Knife.

"So, Zoan. Trade means that we give you something and you give us something in exchange for it. What do you have to trade?"

Zoan's face assumed a puzzled expression. "Everything here," he swept his arm in a wide, all-encompassing gesture, "belongs to God and to His people that are coming. So if you are His people, it already belongs to you and you can take anything you want." He thought for a moment, then added, "If you're not His people, I guess you'd better leave everything here."

An unpleasant discomfort came over Cody Bent Knife. He sensed something about Zoan that was certainly unworldly, but was also something deeper, something alien, something—unearthly. In his life he had met men and women, cruel, dishonest, who had broken every law of God and man, and whose spirits were unearthly, all right, because they were twisted and distorted and sickened. But that certainly wasn't the case with Zoan. He had a strong spirit, this one did—in spite of his tiresome belief in the white man's God.

"Oh, grief, a dunkhead," Little Bird grumbled. Then her dark eyes narrowed and she challenged Zoan, "Do you mean commissars are looking for you? Who are these people that are coming? Why are they coming here?"

"Don't you know?" Zoan asked in wonder. "I thought everyone knew."

"Knew what?" Little Bird repeated impatiently. Like Cody she felt a touch of the surreal when talking to this young man.

"It's God's children that are coming. This is their last home."

"What do you mean? Are they going to die?" Cody harshly demanded.

Zoan's face grew troubled. He sought Cody Bent Knife's gaze and something was exchanged between the two. Zoan knew that this was a man that he could trust. He had a sure and certain knowledge that the two of them, as different as they looked on the outside, were alike. The others he was not sure of, but he knew that he could speak the truth to Cody Bent Knife.

"I don't know what's going to happen," he said softly. "But I know it's going to be winter soon. It'll be cold . . ." He fell silent for a moment and not a soul spoke.

Zoan took a deep breath and finished in a stronger and surer voice, "I know that the darkness is coming. And I know that we are the last children."

"We—you and I?" Cody asked in a slightly choked voice.

Zoan answered simply, "We are the Omega people."

NINE

————

"I FOUND SOMETHING YOU might like," Tessa Kai said nonchalantly.

"I know I will. You always 'find' good things for me, Grandmother T. K.," Dancy said enthusiastically. "Where is it?"

"In my bag, Dancy, but let me come in and sit down first. And I want some coffee. And don't tell me I can't have any; I'm an adult and you're just a child, and I'm not going to allow you to start acting like the horrible pint-size tyrants that people raise these days."

"I'm not pint-size," Dancy said indignantly. "And I'll get you some coffee, but you'll have to tell Mother that you made me."

"Tyrant," Tessa Kai said affectionately. She eased herself onto one of the bar stools at the generous kitchen counter. Tessa Kai Flynn was a small woman, only five feet two, and she had to tiptoe to maneuver into the tall chair. When she finally got situated, she swung her legs back and forth in an endearingly childlike way. That was how she was: At sixty-six years old, she was a mixture of outspoken Irishwoman of bedrock common sense, and fey dreamer from a misty faerie-land, childlike in joy and wonder at life. A bereaved and grieving widow, mischievous girl, loving mother and grandmother, Tessa Kai had been bemused by her grave and somber daughter Victorine, but she had been overjoyed by her granddaughter Dancy, who was much like her. *Only prettier, lovelier,* she thought. *I always looked like a sly little elf, but Dancy looks like a water sprite, maybe . . . How odd that she resembles no one in the family . . . except in her hard looks, sometimes. Reminds me of her grandfather. And her mother.*

"Here's coffee," Dancy said, setting down a mug of coffee with heavy sugar and cream. "Now where's my present?"

"Right here, Dancy-doodle," Tessa Kai said indulgently. Reaching into her voluminous black leather bag, she pulled out a bright square of pink and blue. "It's a scarf. It's very old, darlin', but I've either forgotten or never knew whose it was."

"Oh, it's gorgeous, T. K.!" Dancy breathed. She caressed the filmy fabric.

Tessa Kai wrinkled her pert nose. "Well, I don't know about gorgeous. The artwork is a little blurry, isn't it?"

The scarf was hot pink bordered in white. At each corner was a likeness of a ballerina, with a blue tutu, white tights, blue satin shoes, black hair, and a blue comb.

"It's not blurry, it's Impressionistic," Victorine told them as she came out of her bedroom on a cloud of delicate scent. "Have you seen my silver earrings, Dancy? The ones that look like little arrowheads?"

"They're in the blue porcelain bowl in your bath, Mother," Dancy replied. Victorine whisked back into her bedroom and Dancy called after her, "What's Impressionistic mean?"

Victorine called back something unintelligible. Tessa Kai shrugged, then laid the scarf out on the smooth acrylic counter, running her hands over the delicate fabric. "Well, to me they look like blobs; I'm not too impressed with Impressionists," she maintained caustically. "But it does feel nice, doesn't it?"

"It's—so soft and gauzy," Dancy agreed. "What is it?"

"It's called rayon. I used to love to have clothes made of rayon," Tessa Kai said dreamily. "Even though it never was a very practical fabric. It unravels easily and doesn't wash well."

Dancy sighed. "I wish we could afford to buy stuff like rayon.

I hate Tyvek fabrics. I wish we still could get real cotton and silk and satin."

"I wish we could afford real food," Tessa Kai grumbled, taking a sip of her coffee. "I hate Proto-Synthesis. Them and their fake food. Proto-Syn cream, Proto-Syn green beans, Proto-Syn meat, Proto-Syn bread, Proto-Syn coffee. At least the sugar is real, only the good Lord knows why we still get that."

"I know, especially the green beans, they taste like amalgam paper"—Dancy shuddered—"even though they look real. It's just like the clothes. Ty-cotton looks like cotton, Ty-silk looks like silk, but they feel just like Tyvek. Ick-stick. They're just not the same, are they? But then, I guess I'd never know the difference if you didn't spoil me so much, always puddling around in your mysterious boxes and 'finding' me things like this."

Tessa Kai was a dedicated pack rat. Her condo, except for the living-dining-kitchen area and her bedroom, had every space stuffed with boxes and trunks. Sometimes she let Dancy look into a trunk or a big box, and Dancy thought it was just like nesting dolls; boxes inside of boxes, and when one got to the smallest, always a treasure inside: old buttons, or gold pieces, or old paper money, or feathers, or rocks, or thimbles, or silk flowers.

"Well, darling, I know the ballerinas aren't very good, I don't care what your mother says," Tessa Kai staunchly returned to important matters. "But the colors are so wonderful for you, and I thought you might be able to fold it, you see, and maybe wear it around your neck, tucked under one of your jackets—"

"No, no, I like the ballerinas, T. K.!" Dancy insisted. "They're the quirk!" She took the scarf, folded it into a triangle, and fastened it around her waist, so that one ballerina showed at her hip.

"The quirk?" Tessa Kai repeated, bewildered. "So—that's a good thing?"

Dancy merely laughed and hugged her.

Victorine came back in, fastening an earring, frowning a little.

"Dancy, are you going to wear that when our guests arrive?" Dancy was wearing a white shell with cut-in shoulders, a short pink skirt, and white Ty-leather boot leggings.

"Sure, Mother Vic. Why not?"

"It's the quirk," Tessa Kai said airily.

"Oh," Victorine said uncertainly. "I suppose it will be all right. No reason for you to have to look like a mortician, as I do." She was wearing a long black cheongsam made of Ty-poly that still managed to flow a bit. The tunic had a mandarin collar and slits up the sides to the hip, with black pants underneath, black hose, and flat black shoes. Her hair, which she kept unfashionably long and full, was pulled back into a severe chignon with two silver hair sticks. Her only other accessories were the small silver earrings.

"No, Mother, I think you have true zazz," Dancy said stoutly. "Really."

"Is that good?" Victorine sighed, smoothing her already-immaculate hair.

"Better than quirk," Dancy said solemnly.

"All right, I'll have to take your word for it, my love." Victorine hesitated, biting her lower lip. Dancy and Tessa Kai watched her, puzzled; usually by now Victorine was in seamless chatelaine mode, unruffled and serene. The helicopters would arrive at any time now, and Dancy would barely see her mother until the "guests" left.

Since Dancy had reached sixteen and overnight had turned into a bright and vivacious—and lovely—young girl, Victorine had managed to keep her away from the arrogant male commissars. She had tried to accomplish this, hoping Dancy didn't notice too much, as Victorine didn't want to frighten her. Dancy, of course, knew and understood it all too well, but she never gave any hint to her mother.

Victorine kept watching her daughter and mother with an uncertainty and reluctance that were odd for her. Finally she stammered, "I—I don't know how many guests we're having, or how long they're staying. Commissar Silverthorne never let me know the final plans. I expect that it's going to be more work than usual though, considering the circumstances, so Gerald is coming to help me. Perhaps it would be better, Dancy, if you went home with Tessa Kai. I know I'll be late with dinner tonight, so why don't we make plans to have breakfast together?"

"That's fine. I'm going to drag out a bunch of boxes and paw through them," Dancy said, giving her grandmother a sly look.

"No, you're not. You might get to look through one box, but you will most certainly not paw through it, Miss Fit." The pun was one of Tessa Kai's favorite nicknames for her granddaughter, and it usually made Dancy giggle. But now she stared at her mother, with an understanding and concern far beyond her years.

"Mother, why don't we all pray before they get here?" she asked. "We haven't done that in a long time."

Victorine was surprised, then a little embarrassed. Dancy was right, the three of them always used to pray together before any of their difficult guests arrived. When had they stopped doing that? Why had they stopped? Victorine really didn't know. "All right, that's a good idea, Dancy," she said quietly, stepping forward to stand close.

The three joined hands and bowed their heads, and without hesitation Dancy prayed, "Dearest Father, we ask for Your protection, Lord, for me and Grandmother Tessa Kai. But right now we especially ask for protection for my mother, as You have set a table before her in the presence of her enemies. Walk with her, speak for her, see for her, hear for her. Amen."

Victorine was astounded by Dancy's odd prayer, and exchanged startled looks with Tessa Kai. But Dancy seemed not to notice, as she grabbed her grandmother's hand and teased, "I'm going to run on over to your condo, T. K., and start in that first spare bedroom."

"You wait for me, little girl. And I despise this trend in young people addressing their elders by their proper names—or worse. So don't call me 'T. K.'"

"O-K, T. K." Dancy retorted merrily.

Tessa Kai, struggling to climb off her "high chair," opened her mouth to reply, but the sonorous voice of the Cyclops sounded from the wall in the open living room.

"Victorine, autos are arriving at the gate. Switching to camera one."

Victorine whirled in astonishment. "Autos?"

"Confirmed," Cyclops said, not being able to distinguish a rhetorical question from an interrogatory. "Three autos confirmed arriving at the gate." The great screen showed the live shot of three long black cars pulling into the condo's front parking lot.

Dancy asked, "Grief, are those old fossil-fueled autos?"

"No, darling, they're electric, but one hardly ever sees such luxurious ones—" Victorine answered.

"Confirm alert," Cyclops insisted.

"Thank you," Victorine said hurriedly, then turned back to Dancy.

But the Cyclops wasn't through, and said neutrally, "Is the alert of three, that is three autos, confirmed arriving at—"

"Acknowledged," Victorine almost shouted the code word to shut Cyclops up.

"He's such a drimp," Dancy said impishly. Then she took her mother's hands. "Don't worry, Mother. I know this is upsetting, because the commissar trolls are sneaking in and not telling you anything. But I know that the Lord protects us, always, and I believe that now He'll be especially watching out for you."

Victorine stared down at her daughter, this woman-child with her flashes of knowledge that surely were not borne of human intelligence. It seemed that Dancy had been doing, seeing, knowing this kind of thing often. But Victorine knew this wasn't the time to contemplate her daughter's psyche, so she took a deep breath, nodded, and made herself relax. "I love you, Dancy. You're a treasure. All right, are we ready? Let's go down and do our curtsies."

"What's that?" Dancy asked curiously.

"You don't need to know," Victorine answered calmly. "And by the way, stop calling them trolls. It's going to jump out of your mouth in front of a high commissar one day, and we might just find ourselves in a mud hut in the Fargo, North Dakota, co-op. And I mean you, too, Mother."

"That's not what I call them. That's nicer than what I call them," Tessa Kai muttered under her breath, but Victorine chose to ignore her.

Victorine's unit was on the top corner, a luxurious penthouse condominium that her father had left her. Together, she and her mother had bought the other top corner unit for Tessa Kai after Victor's death eleven years ago. It had taken almost all of Tessa's and Victorine's cash after settling Victor's estate, but it was a necessity. The MAB Project Fourth Directorate, which managed the Gulf Coastal Plain Biome that included all of Florida, had put a time limit on private purchase of any housing on the beach that was to expire the same year that Victor died. If they hadn't bought the condo for Tessa Kai, she would have been assigned to a co-op, probably Miami. Then they worried about how to support themselves, when all beach areas, including the keys, were being brought into MAB compliance—which meant moving the humans out.

Victorine, through a year of hard study and apprenticeship work and sheer stubbornness, had taught herself how to manage a condominium, and had secured a position as a Diversionary Facility Hospitality Manager for the Fourth Directorate. She had been the guiding force behind getting their condominiums, the Summer Sea, in first-class shape so that they were designated as suitable for high commissars, MAB ministers, and high government officials.

Her exalted title was deceiving, however, for Victorine did everything from maid work to interior decorating to grounds maintenance to inventing impromptu cafés and doing the cooking, too. But Tessa Kai helped a lot with that, and Dancy was a quick and efficient maid, though, like most teenagers, she had to be prodded quite a bit to help out when Victorine got overwhelmed. All three of them were grateful to have the work, because it meant that they were some of the very few people who actually got to continue living on the beach, and were even allowed to keep their own homes.

Now they went to the outside scenic elevator, a glass cylinder that floated down the center of the building and offered a panoramic view of the bay just across the street from the beach. Victorine smoothed her hair again, made sure that all two dozen tiny fabric-covered buttons of her tunic were done, checked to see that her shoes weren't dusty, took a deep breath, and moved to the front of the elevator to look down at the arriving guests.

The cars, though electrically powered as all vehicles were now, were a vintage design: long, sleek black limousines with black-tinted windows. They sat in a row, directly in front of the building, as if in a phalanx. Then, as Victorine watched, the doors came open on all three cars and people began getting out. Victorine's eyes widened, and then she frowned. She had been expecting Alia Silverthorne with her friend Dr. Niklas Kesteven, and maybe a larger-than-usual contingent of commissars. Unconsciously, she touched her hair again; Dr. Kesteven, the first time he had come with Commissar Silverthorne, had impudently stroked her hair and murmured something about how thick and beautiful it was. Alia Silverthorne, who sported the man-cut of all women commissars, had shot Victorine a look of pure menace. She'd resented Victorine ever since, and never bothered to hide her dislike.

But Victorine forgot about the wolfish Dr. Kesteven. Alia Silverthorne was, of course, here, with a full twelve-man squad of commissars. In the second car a man, dressed in a dark suit and wearing dark glasses, was helping a lady out. The woman, whom Victorine assessed only quickly, was dressed in flowing white. It was the third limousine that worried Victorine.

Six German soldiers had poured out of it. They stood facing into the light sea wind, as if at attention, staring up at the elevator as it descended. Hastily Victorine stepped back, which was silly, since the entire elevator was glass and they could see all occupants perfectly well, no matter where they stood.

Turning to Dancy, Victorine felt a small frisson of fear. They had only rarely had German military men stay at the condos, and then only one or two at a time, as guests of some chief or second minister, usually. But Victorine's experience with them wasn't very reassuring. Besides being arrogant, they seemed to treat women— perhaps it was American women—with a marked lack of respect.

Even though Victorine was thirty-eight and thought that she looked and dressed as if she were fifty-eight, they still leered at her and made crude remarks when she walked by them. True, most of the time they made their vulgar jokes in German, but Victorine understood German, because she'd studied it for fun, as she had accumulated much knowledge. She didn't actually speak German because she'd never practiced. But she could understand it well enough to recognize lewd comments. Now she cringed inwardly as she stared at her young, innocent daughter. Dancy was like a flower in delicate first bloom, with clear blue eyes and thick sandy-gold hair and girlish curves.

Victorine put two fingers under Dancy's chin and lifted her face. Keeping her voice calm and neutral, she said, "Dancy, when you are introduced, keep your eyes down. Don't look the German men in the eye, don't smile directly at them. Just nod and smile in a very general way. Do you understand?"

Dancy smiled up at her mother, a sweet but knowing smile. "Better than you think, Mother. Don't worry, I won't flirt."

"I'm serious, Dancy."

"I know. I promise; it'll be all right."

Victorine had to be content with that.

The elevator floated to a stop, and Alia marched forward to stand in front of her squad, her jaw square, her eyes hidden behind dark glasses. "Thayer, I hope your preparations are adequate. These are important guests, and will require very special attention."

"I'm certain we can make them comfortable, and competently attend to everyone's needs, My Commissar," Victorine said smoothly.

"Better be more than competent. You better be real good, Thayer," Alia grunted. "Now, the scenic elevators hold six? The inside ones twelve?"

"Yes."

Alia turned and went to the couple, who were standing with two Germans. They all returned to the scenic elevator.

As they neared, Victorine received another shock. She hadn't looked too closely at the couple, as she had been worrying about the Germans. But now, as they neared, she recognized them.

The man was Aristide Luca Therion, the vice president of the United States. The woman was Minden Lauer, the Lady of Light, the leader of Earth's Light. Victorine's indrawn breath was ragged. Behind her, her mother and daughter were whispering furiously. Victorine hoped they would be quiet and circumspect; obviously this was some sort of secret meeting, and she was certain that the vice president didn't want to be remarked upon under the circumstances.

It did seem that was the case, at first. Alia walked by and took her station in the elevator, her head moving around alertly, as if on lookout. The vice president followed her without a glance at Victorine or her mother and Dancy.

But the lady in white hesitated.

She was Minden Lauer, no doubt about it. She was wearing an ankle-length white sheath of three filmy layers, with white shoes. A long white scarf was draped over her silvery hair and wrapped around her elegantly long neck. The long ends of the scarf, as filmy and insubstantial as ghosts, floated in the gentle breeze behind her. She wore large dark glasses with white square rims. What little of her face showed was perfect, however, with her trademark translucent skin and a perfect wide bow of a pink mouth. She stopped, and Victorine couldn't tell what she was looking at behind the dark glasses.

Without speaking to Victorine, Minden glided past her and came to stand directly in front of Dancy. Victorine's heart plummeted with fear, though she was unsure why. She whirled, saw that Tessa Kai had a decidedly disgruntled look on her face, and gave her mother a severe frown-warning. Tessa Kai almost, but not quite, made a face at her in return. But she said nothing.

It didn't matter, however, as Minden completely ignored Victorine and Tessa Kai. They might not have even been standing there.

Long, elegant fingers, the perfect oval nails painted a delicate shell-pink, caressed Dancy's face, and she looked up, narrowing her eyes a little against the bright morning sun. "What a lovely child," Minden murmured. "What is your name, little water sprite?"

Dancy swallowed hard, but her voice was calm. "Dancy Flynn Thayer, ma'am."

Minden laughed, a tinkling bell sound lost on the wind. "How quaint! 'Ma'am.' Most people don't use that word much anymore, Dancy. And most people call me 'My Lady.'"

"Yes, ma'am," Dancy murmured, bemused. "I mean, My Lady."

Minden, her fingers still on Dancy's cheeks, stared down at her. She was motionless, and Dancy obediently kept her face upturned, unflinchingly staring into the dark glasses, which only mirrored her face.

Finally Minden spoke again, in a voice so low that Victorine almost couldn't hear. "Dancy Flynn Thayer . . . you haven't joined us in Earth's Light, have you, darling? No, I can see you haven't . . . but you must, Dancy. Because you're special, aren't you?"

Dancy said nothing.

Minden nodded once, affirming herself. "Here, I want you to have this. It's so much better than that old one you have . . ." She untied the scarf from around her neck, then with a graceful movement, pulled it free. It fluttered, flying high above her head, and she held it out to Dancy.

For one moment Victorine was horribly afraid that Dancy would refuse it, but finally Dancy reached out slowly and took the long white piece of the most delicate of silks. "Thank you, ma'am. I mean My Lady."

Minden smiled again, then said, "You, Dancy, may call me Minden. I'll see you again soon, won't I? Good."

Serenely she floated into the elevator, where the vice president of the United States and two severe-looking German soldiers waited patiently for her to play out her surreal scene. Victorine, feeling as if she'd received a stunning blow to her head that had numbed her brain, stepped woodenly onto the elevator and mumbled, "Six."

The elevator rose, and no one spoke a word. But Minden Lauer turned and leaned far over to wave at Dancy's tiny little form far below.

TEN

O BERSTLEUTNANT RAND VON DRACHSTEDT eyed the twenty-
eight dripping candles with narrowed, almost colorless
hazel-brown eyes. Raising his fine crystal goblet to his
lips, he took a small sip of burgundy to hide a contemptuous smile.
*A perfect symbol of the American weak mind . . . They shudder in hor-
ror at misusing the earth's natural resources, while burning pure
beeswax candles simply for ostentation . . .*

The German colonel, a craggy, severe man of fifty, deliberately
shut out his dinner companions' light laughter and polite conversation that would last until the hospitality manager and her assistant cleared away the remnants of the evening meal. Rising, he
moved to the great expanse of glass that viewed the Gulf of Mexico.
No outside lights burned, so he couldn't see the gentle surf below.
He listened to the rhythmic cresting of waves with their with-
drawal echoes. Drachstedt disliked the sea. Born in the dark and
fir-scented shadows of the Black Forest, the sea was alien to him,
and therefore hostile. He much preferred impenetrable depths of
misted woodlands, or soaring mountains and stringent air and the
bite of snow. This lazy semitropical paradise, to him, was uncomfortably warm, the humid air oppressive and somehow decadent.

Turning, he made slight adjustments to his evening dress uniform so that it would be perfect. *My commandant is a shrewd man,*
he reflected proudly. General Tor von Eisenhalt had ordained new

uniforms for the Joint Task Forces of the Germanic Union of Nation-States. That was just a nice-sounding euphemism for the combined military of seven countries that represented the mightiest armed forces the world had ever seen.

A lilting voice, full of laughter, interrupted his reverie. "Colonel Drachstedt, you must convey my compliments to my kinsman Tor for his choice in the Joint Task Force military uniform," Minden Lauer said. "Oh, they are so handsome, so dashing. So much more striking than American military uniforms."

She's never seen it before, Drachstedt thought with grim amusement. *No one, except obscure military historians, perhaps, and they are nearly extinct!—would recognize it.*

Then Drachstedt was taken aback for a moment. He thought he saw the serving woman—what was her name? Victoria? The Thayer woman looked shocked at Minden's bubbly foolishness. And did she give the Germans a quick glance of recognition, of comprehension? *Surely not, she looks so—normal. She must be like all the rest of these fat slugs of Americans . . . sitting in front of their Cyclops, their brains turning to gray slush . . . She couldn't possibly recognize the uniform, or make the connection . . .* Drachstedt dismissed the "serving woman" from his mind.

The uniform was distinctive. The cap was visored, and still all men—even Commandant Tor von Eisenhalt—took out the rigid crown spring and crumpled the cap. The uniforms were olive drab, the gray-green color of lichen. The jacket was a tunic, with a wide leather belt and a shoulder strap. The tunic had front flap pockets, with discreet collar insignia and cuff flashes and shoulder boards. Tor had, without comment or explanation, decreed that a dagger, a plain silver one with brown leather scabbard, be an integral part of the uniform. Drachstedt and his men, in evening dress, wore the dagger suspended from a silver ring at their left tunic pocket instead of on their left side, at their belt. The breeches were jodhpurs, and the footwear was knee-high black jackboots.

Only the red armband with the black broken cross was missing.

Hitler was a madman, Drachstedt reflected bitterly, turning to the darkness again. *But Tor von Eisenhalt is not. It was wise of him to give us these uniforms, an unmistakable identification with the fatherland, a defiant reminder that we are still a proud people, and that not all German leaders are deluded egomaniacs . . . But I would be willing to bet that no one in America ever has, or ever will, connect this dress to those long-ago, long-forgotten fallen millions of the Waffen S.S. . . .*

He turned slightly to survey the room. It was a combination kitchen, dining, and living area; large, he supposed, for the cramped quarters that Americans had built so extensively in the last century on their beaches. It seemed small and suffocatingly severe to him. Drachstedt hated the angular and hard-edged modern furniture of black, silver, and glass. The dining table, where his dinner companions still sat as the serving women cleared, was a long, glaring expanse of glass, with uncomfortable black minimalist chairs. Drachstedt preferred a long-lost, almost forgotten style of the burnished gleam of wood and dull, aged brass and heavy brocades and luxuriant lines. For such an ascetic man, his taste in rooms and furnishings was quite baroque.

The colonel noted, with approval, his two bodyguards, hard-edged, silent men, formerly of the grim *Kommandos Spezialkréfte,* standing in the shadows. Though they took care to remain—in physical distance and in demeanor—removed from the principals, Drachstedt could see the vigilance in their stances and in their eyes as they swept the room, the doors, the windows, assessing and watching him and his assistant, Oberleutnant Jager Dorn, continuously. They were professionals, men to be depended upon, guardians who would gladly die for Commandant Tor von Eisenhalt. As their commandant had ordered them to be ready to die for *Oberstleutnant* Rand von Drachstedt or *Oberleutnant* Jager Dorn, Drachstedt knew that nothing would touch him or his assistant as long as these two grim soldiers lived.

With disdain he glanced at the vice president's bodyguards, the commissars. The two men and the woman were careless in their watch, too avidly listening to the conversations, too interested in the food and drink and party. The woman—Commissar Alia Silverthorne—was more guarded and professional than the two men, Drachstedt begrudgingly admitted to himself. However, she was the team leader, so the two male commissars were under her authority, and therefore their shortcomings were her shortcomings. They slouched against the wall behind the vice president and his woman, grinning at jokes, sometimes even impudently laughing out loud, talking in low voices to each other, both of them obviously smitten with Minden Lauer. Minden continually gave them barely hidden seductive glances and slyly made delicate gestures of inclusion toward them.

Again the colonel took a sip of the rich burgundy wine to disguise his contempt. Distilled to its finest essence, his judgment of the vice president of the United States of America and his consort, the Lady of Light, Minden Lauer, was this: *Fools.*

———————

"I am a soldier, and I am a simple man," Drachstedt stated. "Normally, I don't serve as a diplomat, or an adviser, to men such as you, Mr. Therion. My only credentials to offer you are that I have been fortunate enough to be in service to both Count von Eisenhalt and Commandant von Eisenhalt for many years. They entrusted me with so important a mission as to serve you and your country in this matter. I hope that will be sufficient reference for you to trust me and, of course, my aide-de-camp, *Oberleutnant* Dorn."

"Of course," Luca Therion said cordially. "We understand that the leadership complexities of the Euro-German alliances are much less straight-line than American governmental officialdom. I would like to clarify one thing, however, Colonel Drachstedt. Under whose direct authority are you, and to whom will you directly report? In whose name, exactly, do you speak?"

Drachstedt drew himself up ramrod-straight. His shadow, in the lurid flicker of the candles, looked like an immense Reaper. "I speak in my commandant's name, Tor von Eisenhalt," he intoned in a harsh voice. "I am under his authority. Surely you don't question that?"

"No, no, of course not," Luca responded hastily, averting his eyes. "It's just that I'm unclear about the connection, sir. Here, in America, as I'm certain you're well aware, our military is not sympathetic to our cause. Count Gerade von Eisenhalt, as Director of the United Nations Trusteeship Council of the Man and Biosphere Project, has been our staunchest ally in the entire world. But I've had very little dealings with his son, your commandant, and until now I've worked very hard to—er—minimize connections between the Man and Biosphere Project and the military—er—establishment," Therion finished lamely. He still didn't meet the German's eyes.

In a slightly mollified tone, Drachstedt said, "Of course, I understand, Mr. Vice President. As you say, the relationship between our armed forces and our governing executives is much more intertwined than your American model. Once you understand that, I'm sure you'll see that although you contacted Count von Eisenhalt with your difficulties—and it has remained in the strictest confidence at the highest levels—the count is a very busy man, with a multitude of concerns. My commandant, Tor von Eisenhalt, is currently in the process of relieving his father of his heavy responsibilities. Commandant von Eisenhalt offered to help his father—and you, and your country—in the matter we are here to address. The count gratefully accepted his help, and we hope that you will, too, sir."

"Of course, we are honored," Minden said graciously. "Luca is not as close to the Eisenhalts as I am, Colonel Drachstedt, and he is by nature a cautious man. Certainly you can understand that, and approve of it, particularly concerning such sensitive matters of state."

"I do. So—if we are all comfortable with my credentials and those of Lieutenant Dorn, then I must assume that we all trust one another explicitly. Therefore, I would like to speak freely and openly." Drachstedt, still standing in the exact center of the glassed wall, stared pointedly at the three commissars who remained after the hospitality staffers had cleared out.

Luca looked back at his bodyguards, then—a significant sign, in Drachstedt's opinion—stared uncertainly at Minden. She bit her lower lip, her eyes narrowed as she considered the two handsome commissars, then murmured, "Alia, we have no physical threat here. Dismiss your men; I'm certain they would like to have some dinner, too. You may stay." Turning back, all coquettishness gone, she said, "Now, Colonel Drachstedt. Please feel free to speak openly and directly."

Drachstedt thought: *She dismisses her own protection, yet does not dare question my men. That is good; that is a definite tactical advantage . . . hardly a triumph, though, is it? To intimidate this fey fluff of a woman? But then again, it does seem that the power of the United States of America—or at least a good deal of it—is centered on her . . . Are these people stark raving mad? How could a powerful man such as the vice president of America—in fact, an entire nation—be so lulled into such a foolish, self-destructive deceit?* Bitterly, then, he recalled the history of his beloved Germany in the first half of the previous century, and the thought helped him to comprehend the bizarre and surreal politics of American culture.

He waited for the commissars to leave and close the door securely behind them. Then, playing for time and effect, he hesitated for a long moment before speaking. Alia Silverthorne, Minden Lauer, and Luca Therion were watching him with an almost tangible hunger. Drachstedt was gratified to see that his young aide, Lieutenant Jager Dorn, was relaxed and at ease, but was avidly watching and gauging the Americans. Young, heart-breakingly handsome, and masculine, Dorn had been mildly flirting with Minden Lauer all night. She had responded so openly, so aggressively, that Drachstedt again had doubts about Vice President Luca Therion's sanity. How could a man—especially one as besotted as he obviously was—allow his woman to act like a pernicious harlot right in front of him? Then again, Americans and their supposedly open and free sexuality . . . but that was not his problem, not this night.

Brusquely, his voice an abrupt growl in the eerily shadowed room, he said, "As my commandant sees it, Mr. Therion, you have two problems. One problem is that you have goals you cannot accomplish because of factions in your government that hinder you. The other is that you have discovered a possible tool—or weapon, if you will—that could be of great value to your cause, but you have no idea how to utilize it."

Luca winced. "I—never quite—looked at it in such a blood-less manner."

"That's because you are a visionary," Drachstedt said with uncomfortable gallantry. "To shape a vision, a high and noble goal to achieve, is the job of statesmen and philosophers. To calculate the shortest and most effective route to achieving that goal is the work of soldiers. That is why I am here, Mr. Therion. That is why Commandant von Eisenhalt believes that it is time for the simple soldiers to go to work."

Luca and Minden both took on a look of far-eyed vision, of not-quite-subconscious martyrdom and nobility.

Drachstedt went on, "Your organism, your *Thiobacillus chaco*, is unique. Our scientists have found that it has most interesting capabilities. Commandant von Eisenhalt has designed a program that utilizes this tool in a way that will help you to achieve your ultimate goal."

Minden, her blue eyes glowing, nodded and asked silkily, "So, Colonel von Drachstedt, it is true that you, and Commandant von Eisenhalt, and your leaders do comprehend our desire to bring America to her utmost and highest achievement: a final and complete unity in harmony with the earth?"

"Oh, yes, we understand it completely, My Lady," Lieutenant Dorn said smoothly, with a woman-slayer smile. "We have all worked very hard to create a program to assist you. Our scientists have designed some valid dispersal methods of the organism under tightly controlled conditions. They have discovered a way to impose a time limit—a biological fail-safe, if you will—on its effects. Commandant von Eisenhalt and Colonel von Drachstedt have formulated a model that will allow you to release the organism at strategic points, and it will affect only certain areas for certain periods of time. This will allow you to impose this sanction, if you will, on the areas of your choosing, for the time allotment that you deem to be necessary to redistribute the population."

Luca and Minden glanced at each other, unsure of Dorn's exact meaning. Truth to tell, they had been so engrossed in the spiritual meaning of the discovery of the "children of light," and the supernatural plane that they both longed to dwell in, that neither of them had any practical or clear idea of what they were embarking upon. Alia, who stood behind them listening with cold calculation, grew restless. With a wary glance at Drachstedt, she stepped up to whisper furiously in Minden's ear.

A beatific smile came over Minden's lovely face. "So, Lieutenant Dorn. Let us, as your colonel said, speak directly. You are saying that you have a way for us to release the organism into the parts of the United States that have stubbornly and blindly refused to voluntarily participate in the Man and Biosphere Project. Those areas will be without any electrical power for a period of time that we can designate?"

"Yes, My Lady of Light," Lieutenant Dorn answered in a

caressing tone. "And I may add that using the 'children of light' is a much better strategic tool than simply shutting off parts of the power grid on Cyclops. You would have to involve too many people; and someone would diagnose it and correct it almost immediately, I'm sure. This way, using our team, full knowledge of the situation is certain to stay within our small circle."

"Our children of light," Minden said dreamily. "So your team will release the organism. We—that is, the Sixth Directorate—will declare a national emergency, and we will move everyone to the co-op cities. Then, in a time of our own choosing, and to an extent that we feel necessary, we can reintroduce the power for such things as critical factories, Diversionary Facilities, Directorate Centers, Commissaries, and buffer zones for guardian care of the biomes?"

"That, My Lady, is precisely what we are saying," Drachstedt rumbled. Minden was gratified to hear him use her title, for the first time. "I must stress to you, once again, that Commandant von Eisenhalt himself, because of the great respect he has for your country and its place as a world leader, and because his heart is bruised for your turmoil, has been the guiding force behind all facets of this plan." *Do they really believe all this drivel?*

Evidently they did; they regarded Drachstedt as besottedly as if he were the angel Gabriel, arriving to save them. Once again struggling to hide his incredulity, Drachstedt continued, "So that solves one tactical problem, Mr. Therion. We have made your *Thiobacillus chaco* a useful tool. Now, concerning your other problem: the opposition."

Luca shifted restlessly, his sensitive features drawn in bitterness. "For once, Colonel Drachstedt, I will use the military terminology that you obviously are striving to avoid in deference to me: I say that they are our enemies. They are ignorant, destructive men who have no comprehension of the forces they are fighting against. They would insult, and war against, and injure, the very earth herself, the origin of their life and breath. They must be stopped; they must be utterly defeated."

Drachstedt nodded soberly. "Yes, you are right, Mr. Vice President, and my commandant is in perfect agreement with you. It is our understanding that your military—unlike our alliance forces—actually strives against you and the International Man and Biosphere Project. They oppose you in every way, except with actual force, that is."

"Yes! And I believe the military establishment would be insane enough to use actual force if they—if they—"

"Knew of your plan?" Drachstedt said with great smoothness. "Let me assure you once again, Mr. Vice President, that these plans have been handled at the highest levels of confidence within the Alliance—and that is why *Thiobacillus chaco* is such an excellent top secret device. Your military has no knowledge of it, and they will have no counter for it. And Commandant von Eisenhalt has had the foresight to make plans that will blunt any attempt by your military to interfere."

"Really?" Luca asked, childlike. "How is that?"

"Lieutenant Dorn has all the logistical details for you," Drachstedt answered. "It's merely an extension of the plan to exert a short-term control over your general population. In a very limited capacity, you can utilize the organism to render key military bases ineffective for a short period of time. Not, of course, the strategically important ones, such as NORAD or the Pentagon; but only those few locations that might, for instance, have the capacity to deploy soldiers to assist the public so that they wouldn't feel it necessary to relocate to your co-ops."

"Yes . . . yes . . . of course," Luca agreed dreamily. "There are only a few bases—mostly in the South and East—that would need to be neutralized . . ."

"Neutralized, yes," Drachstedt repeated, with such aridity that his more devious aide gave him a warning glance. In a more agreeable tone, he went on, "So that problem has been solved. The only facet of this project that you must deal with yourself is the problem of how to effect such a massive population redistribution."

To everyone's surprise, Alia Silverthorne spoke up in a strong and decisive voice. "That is my area of responsibility, Colonel Drachstedt. That is what the Sixth Directorate does. We do it well. This project will be, for the Commissary, an opportunity, not a problem. I could have all assets—men and material—in place in a short period of time."

Drachstedt made a stiff half-bow, apparently a tribute from one professional soldier to another. "That is good to hear, Commissar Silverthorne, and I commend you. As we understand your passion and desire to achieve your noble goals, Mr. Vice President—and My Lady—we have formulated a time frame for the project so that it can be implemented relatively quickly."

Luca Therion frowned. "I appreciate that, Colonel Drachstedt, but surely you are aware that there is no possibility of implementing the project while Bishop Beckwith is president. I believe wholeheartedly that within a year I will be president, and I intend to put the project in place soon after my election. But it's simply not going to be possible, not as long as Beckwith is president."

Drachstedt, for the first time that night, smiled. It was a cold expression, without humor but full of dark amusement. "Our last gift to you, Mr. Therion, is a personal assurance from Tor von Eisenhalt. He personally will intercede with your president, on your behalf, and on the behalf of the American people. And my commandant is certain that President Beckwith will finally—see the light."

Luca stared at the German, his eyes burning with passionate intent. Hoarsely Luca said, "I am forever indebted to Commandant von Eisenhalt."

"Yes, you are," Drachstedt agreed in an uncharacteristically mild voice. So such moments of eternal decision sometimes flow

by, with courteous and grateful words and the warmest of solic-
itudes.

Raising his goblet, Drachstedt said in a low voice, "My commandant bestowed upon me the honor of naming the project, and
I would like to borrow your wise words, My Lady of Light. I name
this noble endeavor: Final Unity."

Heavy goblets, filled with thick red-blood wine, were raised.
"To Project Final Unity."

━━◆━━

Was I off the grid this time, Victorine reflected bitterly. *These
Germans haven't given Dancy a second look . . . they're like cyborgs, or
something. But that woman! "Lady of Light," my pinky finger! How
creepy, pseudo-psychic mystic can you get? More like the Wicked Witch
of the West, as if anyone besides me remembers her anymore . . . I hope
I can keep Dancy out of her claws until they leave . . .*

Victorine cleaned furiously. She was always quick and efficient, but for this contingent visiting her Diversionary Facility, she
refused Dancy's help, and also tried to keep her mother with Dancy
as much as possible. That left her and her friend Gerald Ainsley,
who came sometimes to help Victorine when she had a large
group. He managed a nearby Diversionary Facility for the general
public, and he was a wonderful cook and hard worker. It was all
but impossible for Victorine to do all the cooking and cleaning and
housekeeping for a group any larger than six. Victorine and Gerald
were just managing this group of twenty-one, as long as they both
worked furiously all day and half the night. And Victorine was
determined to keep Dancy away from Minden Lauer, no matter
what she had to do.

In spite of Victorine's earthy thought-opinions of Minden
Lauer, the woman had disturbed Victorine on a much deeper level
of cognition. Victorine was a Christian, but she prided herself on

being a practical person, one who faced the problem of the moment without flinching, one who tackled and solved difficulties head-on. She had spent years honing this stubborn determination. She saw no need in addressing any deeper trials of the spirit. To Victorine, if one looked after the mind and the body, the spirit would take care of itself.

As she finished the last polish and shine in the kitchen, the voices of the two German soldiers who were breakfasting out on the balcony drifted in through the open glass doors. They were laughing and talking, and as an idle brain exercise, Victorine listened to them to see if she could still comprehend the language. Her German studies had ended two years previously, when she had suddenly become enamored with the Roman Empire, and had switched to Roman historians.

As she polished the acrylic counter to a high sheen, she frowned. The two men were talking about Minden Lauer, who evidently had entertained the young *Oberleutnant* last night . . . Victorine had known this, because Jager Dorn had arrogantly answered Victorine's knock at Minden's door that morning and had brusquely ordered her to return later, as the lady was still asleep. *Evidently everyone knows it . . . even the vice president?* she wondered, then sighed. *Even as old as I am, and as long as America has been sliding down into this corruption, I still get shocked by such careless debauchery. Even though my own husband . . .*

With stubbornness Victorine blocked all thoughts of her former "partner," Dancy's father. He had had a "life shift" at forty—which was society's polite excuse for a midlife crisis—and had left Victorine and the seven-year-old Dancy to live in a Structured Dependence Zone in Miami. The drugs were free in the Zones, the life-styles outrageously decadent, and the responsibilities few. They were kept there, of course, by the toughest of commissars, so they lived in a hazy and drugged prison. But they chose it voluntarily, even gladly, and rarely did anyone who had checked themselves into a Dependence Zone ever want to leave. Though Victorine had not heard from Indie Galloway, her legal partner, for eight years, he had written her with an unspeakable and cloying buoyancy, telling her how happy he was in the Zone with his two new consorts. Victorine had felt positively nauseated at the Cy-mail. She'd destroyed the file and had told Dancy that she'd never heard from her father. It was much better that way.

Visibly shaking her head as if to rid herself of a noisome insect, Victorine fiercely concentrated on polishing the already-gleaming acrylic expanse, and turned her entire concentration on laboriously translating the German words that rolled into the room.

The two men were no longer laughing and making coarse jokes about Minden Lauer; now they were somber, their voices cold and intent.

What was that . . . I know that phrase . . . Projekt Schlußenheit. That's Project—End?—Last?—no, no, it's Final. Final Unity. Project Final Unity.

She didn't try to guess the meaning, only enjoying a small satisfaction at understanding the rather difficult phrase. As she listened further, both men repeated a phrase that she couldn't even envision in her mind, much less translate. She grew very still and listened harder. Both of the soldiers had deep voices, and some of the conversation was lost in the never-ceasing song of the waves, but she could tell they were talking about dates, times, the future . . . ?

" *. . . Tagundnachtgleiche herbstlich . . .*"

She stood still, repeating the difficult phrase in her mind. She'd finally visualized it, though she didn't know what it meant.

"*Sprechen sie Deutsche?*"

The harsh question, barked behind her right ear, made Victorine jump. Whirling, she looked up into Rand von Drachstedt's eyes, which were narrowed to tight slits with suspicion.

"No, *Herr Oberstleutnant,* I don't speak German," Victorine answered calmly.

He stared at her, and she stood, unflinching, serenely returning his heated gaze.

After what seemed like a very long time to Victorine, the colonel almost imperceptibly relaxed, though he seemed reluctant to dismiss Victorine. "Your accent, it is very good for someone who doesn't speak German, madam."

Victorine nodded gracefully. "I try to address my guests properly, sir. It's a matter of courtesy."

After only a moment more of hesitation, he nodded brusquely. "Don't allow me to interrupt your work, Madam Thayer."

"I am finished, *Herr Oberstleutnant,* if you will excuse me . . ." Quickly gathering her cleaning supplies, she left the condo. Though she felt Colonel Rand von Drachstedt's suspicious gaze burning into her back, she managed, with a great effort, not to turn around.

Hurrying to her own unit, she went into her bedroom. Two walls were lined floor-to-ceiling with bookshelves. Victorine, without fumbling, put her hand right on her German-English dictionary. *"Herbstlich* . . . That's autumn, isn't it? . . . yes, autumn, or autumnal . . . the other word—of course, it's a compound word." Grabbing a pen and scribbling on the back inside cover of the well-worn dictionary, Victorine wrote:

Tag—day
und—and
nacht—night
gleiche—same

She looked up, comprehension dawning on her still features. "'Day and night same' . . . it's the equinox. The autumnal equinox."

Project Final Unity—whatever that ominous-sounding thing might be—was to take place in less than three months.

Without warning, a shard of a Scripture popped into Victorine's head that made her draw a sharp, ragged gasp of breath:

. . . pray ye that your flight be not in the winter . . .

ELEVEN

AS JESSE MITCHELL STROLLED DOWN Main Street, it occurred to him that Hot Springs, Arkansas, had been designed not by a human architect but by two lakes—Lake Catherine and Lake Hamilton. These two bodies of water pushed and nudged at the city, stretching it out at times, at other times squeezing it into a ridiculously narrow girth. Jesse was rather surprised that the Man and Biosphere Project had changed the city so little. Perhaps physically it could not be changed, for the traffic plan was simple enough. Central Avenue ran just as he remembered it, the length of the city, and Grand Avenue crossed it at right angles. If anyone cared to go anywhere on either of those streets, there were possibilities. Otherwise it was a matter of searching down one of the twisting, winding streets that changed names sometimes as often as they changed directions. The main feature on Central was a thoroughbred racetrack. It had not been used for many years, but Jesse remembered visiting there long ago and thinking how strange it was for people to watch horses run around in circles. Now, of course, people thought that it violated the horses' rights to make them run races. Jesse thought that was very odd, too; it had always seemed to him that thoroughbreds really liked to run. He wondered, now, if there were any thoroughbreds left in the world, for that was the only reason people had had them, to watch them run.

He found the city depressing, and he had had enough. Reversing his steps, he made his way back down Grand Avenue and entered the double doors of a six-story building. It was an old hotel, and the lobby had a sad aura of lost grandeur. The floor and great staircase were of marble darkened with age and careless use and grimed with years. Slowly he climbed to the top story and went down a dark hallway lined with ancient and blackened wooden doors, and entered into Noemi's and his room.

She was standing in the tiny cubicle of a kitchenette, cooking. Without looking up she said, "Hello, you. Thought maybe you'd decided to take a grand tour, see all the sights."

"I saw all I needed to see. More than I wanted. Smells good, Noe."

"Here's fresh corn bread. Don't know how I managed it in that little nothing of a pretend kitchen, but maybe it's edible."

Jess sat at the ugly chrome and glass table for two and eagerly pulled over the pan of corn bread. Cutting himself a generous slice, he crumbled it up into an old stemmed goblet of half-inch-thick glass. His goblet and Noe's iron skillet were two of the few things they'd kept through their lives. When his glass was crammed full of the corn bread chunks, he poured the milk over it, then bowed his head, holding the spoon in his right hand. "Lord, thank You for this prime corn bread," he said. Dipping his spoon into the glass, he scooped the rich mixture into his mouth and chewed with delight. Talking around the mouthful, he said, "Edible! You know you're just talking nonsense. Nobody can make corn bread like you can, Noe."

"I ought to know how. I must have made ten million pans of it for you."

The old couple sat without speaking, the kind of easy, warm silence that only many years of love and dedicated companionship can produce. The only sound was Jesse's enthusiastic smacking as he ate the corn bread and the scraping of the spoon on the glass. When he finished, she asked, "More?"

"Not right now. Might have another helping just before bed."

Moving rather slowly, Noe got up and picked up the glass and the spoon. Quietly she washed and dried them and put them into the single cupboard. Now her kitchen was clean.

"Why don't you read to me, Jesse?" she asked, coming to join him in one of the two ugly armchairs in the living room.

Jesse Mitchell reached over and pulled the well-thumbed Bible with the faded black leather cover toward him. "I think I'd like to read a little in Hosea today," he announced.

"I always liked Hosea. He was a good man."

Opening the Bible, Jesse began to read. It was obvious, however, that he scarcely needed the printed page before him. For the last seventy years he had done little else but read the pages of the Bible. He had a phenomenal memory, and if he had been stranded on a desert island with nothing but a pen and tablets, he could probably have re-created nine-tenths of the King James Version of the Scripture. Noe had asked him once, "Why haven't you learned all of it?"

"Can't see any sense in memorizing Numbers," he had scoffed. "It's mostly a list of the names of the tribes and the heads of the tribes and the children of Israel. Doesn't hurt to go back and look all that up."

But if he was weak in the book of Numbers, he was strong in the Minor Prophets of the Old Testament. It was a time in which many people barely even knew exactly what the Bible was, but to Jesse Mitchell and his wife the old book had been the very heart and center and foundation of their entire lives. Jesse had even made a translation from English to Apache, an accomplishment that gave him great satisfaction.

For a long time Jesse's voice broke the silence while Noe sat leaning her head back, her eyes closed. When Jesse finished the book and looked up, he saw that her mouth was drawn together with a hint of tension. "Your hands hurt?" he asked quietly.

"Oh, I feel all right," Noe said quickly, lifting her head to smile at him. She never complained, but she never deceived him, either. They had lived together for so long that they could practically read one another's thoughts.

Running his hand over the worn cover of his Bible, Jesse sat quietly for a time, staring into space. It was difficult for Noe to tell if he was praying or simply thinking, for he was, at times, prone to go off into long silences. This had never disturbed her, and she never bothered him when he was in such deep introspection, no matter how long it lasted. Sooner or later he would talk to her about whatever was on his mind.

After a long while he reached over and covered her gnarled, blue-veined hand with his rough one. For a moment he ran his thumb over the plain gold wedding band, then he smiled. "I remember the day I put this on you."

"So do I. Even though it was—what, about a hundred and ten years ago?"

"Seems like. I thought you were the prettiest thing I'd ever seen." Jesse grinned and squeezed her hand. "I still do." He patted her hand, then leaned back in his chair and finally said what was on his mind. "I've got an uneasy feeling, Noe."

"I knew something was bothering you."

"Ever since we've come to Hot Springs, I've felt like something was wrong."

She asked thoughtfully, "Wrong . . . you mean that we've done something the Lord didn't will us to do? Or that we've made a mistake or something?"

"No, no, that's not what I mean. It's something else." He shifted in his chair, ran his fingers through his thick white hair in a gesture of frustration. "It's sort of odd—and hard to explain—" He stopped, then blurted out, "I've got the feeling that someone's looking at me."

Blankly Noe responded, "Looking at you! What does that mean? What—who would be looking at you?"

"I know it sounds . . . strange."

"Well, yes, it sure does, Jess. You mean—you feel like some-body's stalking you like—like they do those Cyclops people or famous people?"

"No. Not like that. I don't know how to explain it to you." He was obviously frustrated.

Noe studied him, frowning. "Do you feel it now?"

"No, no—not really. It comes over me, sort of, when I'm alone." Jesse went into the kitchen and poured himself a cup of coffee. Returning to his armchair, he held his mustache back and sipped it noisily. His strange mood clouded his hazel eyes, and frus-tration tightened the lips almost hidden by his sweeping mustache. "You know how sometimes we've laughed because we're so used to being together that we talk to each other, but we turn around and no one's in the room?"

"Yes . . . ," Noe said hesitantly.

"But that feeling—that certainty—you get that I'm there, right in the room, you're just so sure I am that you start talking? You know how that feels?"

"Sure do. I just know it. That's why it's so funny that you're really not there."

Uneasily Jesse said, "Well, that's the closest way I can think of to explain it—only with this, it's not funny. I'm just sure, in the way that humans have, that someone's there, watching me, looking at me. But I turn around, and there's no one there."

Shifting restlessly, Jesse took another sip of the coffee. He dropped his head for a moment and then looked up at her with pain, and a touch of fear, etched across his face. Noe hadn't seen her husband look like that in—forever. It had never entered her mind or thoughts or prayers that Jesse Mitchell could ever be frightened of anything again.

With great calm and assurance, she said, "Well, Jess, whatever it is, you know that we'll find the truth, and the answer, in God's

Word. Now, it doesn't sound to me like this—experience—is in any way a godly one. Right?"

He focused on her intently. "No. No, it's not God's presence I feel."

"So if it's not some kind of communication from God, then it could only be one other thing."

He grimaced. "That I'm going out of my mind?"

"Jesse Mitchell! You know better than that! You have the mind of Christ!" she staunchly asserted.

Instead of looking chastised, he grinned at her, and looked twenty years younger. "Times like these I recall just why the Lord gave me such a gift as you, Noe. You're a treasure."

She smiled, pleased, then prodded him, "Don't try to charm me, you rascal. We're going to work through this, with the Lord's guidance. Now, tell me, if it's not the presence of the Spirit of our Lord you sense, what else would it be? Evil, of course. Pure and simple."

Jesse, now sober, sat back in his chair; his eyes searched a far distance again. Noe waited patiently; she had told him of her knowledge, but Jesse was the prophet. He would, she knew well, in the end have to deal with this himself. She would never leave his side, but God had required much of Jesse Mitchell, much more than He had of her or of most of His children. Following and upholding Jesse on his difficult path had been both Noe's greatest joy and her hardest tribulation. But always, in the end, Jesse had to stand alone with his God.

The church that Jesse and Noe had been attending while in Hot Springs was located on a side street two blocks west of the long, narrow strip of downtown. The church was old, built in a time of lavish monies spent for Gothic cathedrals. Built of dusky gray sandstone, the tall needle-pointed spire rose to heaven. Jesse had said when he had first taken Noe there, "I remember seeing this church when I was a little boy. Then I was young and foolish, and I wished we could go to this fancy 'High Church' instead of the little country churches my father always took us to. Turned out I was just a 'Low Church' kind of man, after all."

"People and their foolishness," Noe sniffed. "High church, low church. We're all God's people."

Now as the couple sat six rows back and directly in the center, Jesse studied the auditorium, which was at least three-quarters filled. On this cheerful Sunday morning light streamed in through the stained glass windows, casting effulgent brilliant colors on the faces of the worshipers. The ceiling rose to a sweeping arch by hammered beams and lent an air of spaciousness to the building.

Jesse's eyes were still trained upward; he was thinking that this church looked like the sort of place where angels might be flitting around the rafters.

Noe poked him lightly in the ribs and whispered, "Jess, you still haven't told me what you think of this pastor."

"I've not made up my mind yet."

To Noe this was a rather strange response, for Jesse was ordinarily quick to discern people. She understood his reticence, for Tybalt Colfax was unlike any preacher either of them had ever seen. The couple had spent so many years in the desert under primitive conditions and with a people that lived in a world out of time. It seemed that the world of theology had whisked by them, as had the style in preachers. Both of them remembered in their past poorly dressed, rough-hewn men weathered and beaten by the elements and by struggles simply to get by. But the man who pastored this United America Church was nothing like that.

Reverend Colfax was a fine-looking man in his mid-thirties. He had a pair of sharp blue eyes and was roughly handsome. He was articulate, even eloquent, but Noe found her mind wandering.

She shifted her eyes to Mrs. Colfax, the pastor's wife, who sat on the front row. At twenty-seven, she was eight years younger than her husband, and although Noe was not sophisticated enough to realize it, even as young as Galatia Colfax was she had already had several corrective surgeries. Her hair had been color-corrected to that glowing platinum blonde that was a rage since the Lady of Light had grown so popular in the religious world. Galatia's eyes were a dark brown, which clashed slightly with the platinum blonde hair, and a hint of melancholy touched her pleasant features even though she kept a smile on her face. She kept her eyes fastened on her husband in such a way that Noe Mitchell suddenly thought, *I'll bet she's had trouble with that man of hers. He's too nice looking for a preacher. Women go after preachers so much anyway, what the poor souls are looking for I've never understood . . . but I'll wager that they must have been after that one a lot.*

Jesse had somewhat of the same idea but he was trying to concentrate on the sermon. It troubled him. The words of the minister were smooth and the delivery fluent, and it was certainly scriptural. Still Jesse felt uneasy.

Finally he realized, *He knows a lot of theology, but it all seems to be coming from his head.* In all truthfulness, Jesse Mitchell loved preaching, regardless of quality or articulation or intelligence, that came from the heart. In his younger days, he had mistaken volume for this quality and had sought out preachers who had rattled the windows with thunderous voices, or roved across the platform and even into the audience like raging lions, shaking their fists, the veins in their foreheads swollen with blood. But Jesse had passed through that stage and had come to realize that the voice of God often came in a small whisper rather than in a thunderous blast of words. The catch was not the method of delivery, but the content of His Holy Spirit. Reverend Colfax certainly was not a shouter nor a Bible-thumper and he certainly did have a graceful and smooth delivery. But still, Jesse decided that his words came from intellectual resources, not from the throne of grace.

One of the sure tests for Jesse Mitchell of a preacher's power was his ability to keep the attention of his listeners. In spite of his determination to pay attention to what the man was saying, Jesse found himself thinking of other things and he also found that his eyes were wandering over the congregation. He couldn't help himself from wondering, with a bit of dread, how so much had changed, and he hadn't been aware of it for so many years.

For one thing, this church was a United America church, and apparently that was about all that was left. Somehow over the years the government had managed to phase out the tax-exempt status of many of the big denominations. The heavy monetary burdens imposed upon them, plus the legislative restrictions placed upon them, had forced the different denominations to align themselves with this organization. The government had designated the United America group as a true nonprofit organization, and it and the Catholic Church—and, of course, Earth's Light—were the only religious groups that had tax-exempt status.

That didn't bother Jesse Mitchell too much; over the long years, denominations had ceased to be of much importance to him one way or the other. After all, no denomination could give a man new birth and the Holy Spirit and eternal kinship with the Lord Jesus Christ.

But what did bother him was these commissars.

On the first Sunday they had attended, Jesse had been greeted heartily by a couple, Merrill and Genevieve Stanton. In the way of brothers in Christ, each recognized kindred spirits in the Lord, so Jesse had spoken openly to Merrill Stanton. "Why are these commissars here? It's kind of plain they're not what you'd call dedicated churchgoers."

Merrill Stanton's kind face grew grave, and he dropped his voice to almost a whisper. "Times are hard for the church, Brother Mitchell. That woman and her group of tree- and rock-worshipers . . . it seems like they've not only taken over people's souls, but they've taken over the government, too. There's been lots of ugly talk lately, talk about how the right-wing Christians are all troublemakers, dissidents, and fanatics—dangerous to the culture, dangerous to Earth's Light, dangerous to everyone."

Unexpectedly, Jesse grinned. "Well, I would say that might be true in a manner of speaking. The love and the power of the Lord God Almighty can be a dangerous thing."

"Well . . ." Stanton dropped his eyes to study his worn brown loafers. "Anyway, the commissars started attending all the United America churches last year. They're just watching, and listening, I guess—to make sure that no one preaches about overthrowing the government or assassinating the president."

"How about preaching about that woman and her would-be church being a bunch of adulterers and idolaters and devil-worshipers?" Jesse asked cheerfully.

Merrill Stanton looked pained, and even a little afraid, though they were standing alone out on the walk in front of the church. "Brother Mitchell, I don't know what would happen if someone were to try to preach that out loud in public these days. I just really don't."

Now Jesse, his mouth unconsciously set with distaste, studied the commissars. They wore their black uniforms, a kind of paramilitary garb with combat boots and berets that they didn't bother to remove in church. At least they weren't wearing their pistols. Some of them sat right on the front row, slouching and openly bored. Some of them stood against the wall, a cold, calculating glare in their eyes.

But at least one of them was different. She was a young woman who sat directly across from Jesse and Noe, and she had taken off her beret. As Jesse was considering her, she abruptly turned her head to look at him. He almost looked away, but something in her eyes drew him and he sat there exchanging a long glance with her. Almost imperceptibly she nodded, then turned her attention back to Reverend Colfax.

With amusement Jesse thought, *At least she doesn't look mad at the world and determined to make everyone pay for it.* Suddenly slightly ashamed by his wandering attentions, he made himself concentrate on the sermon again, dismissing the woman commissar from his mind.

As soon as the service ended, Jesse was ready to go, as Merrill and Genevieve Stanton hadn't attended the service, and they hadn't really met anyone else they felt comfortable talking to.

"Let's go, Noe," Jesse muttered, and the two started down the aisle. The crowd shuffled along in front of him and Reverend Colfax had taken his position at the front door. When he shook Jesse's hand, his grip was firm and he had a warm smile. "I'm so glad to see you again, Brother Mitchell. I hope you'll consider becoming a member of our group. Have you relocated here?"

Conscious of the commissars loitering around, Jesse stammered, "I—we're here, we're sure here, yes, sir, Pastor Colfax." He felt that was close enough to the truth to get him by without lying outright, but he felt strange as they moved away. It didn't really matter, anyway, for Ty Colfax had already shifted his attention to a woman behind Jesse and had dismissed him. No one else was paying the least attention to the little old couple.

Jesse and Noe, hand in hand, walked outside and down the walk. They had only taken a few steps, however, when Jesse stopped dead still, and pulled Noe to an abrupt halt.

The woman commissar, the one whose gaze Jesse had touched on in the service, was standing farther down the sidewalk, alone. She'd put her beret back on, and she stood, tight-lipped, arms crossed, watching the people leaving the church. As soon as she saw Jesse and Noe, her eyes widened slightly, and she didn't take her gaze away from Jesse.

Jesse, under the heat of a commissar's direct gaze, felt a small shudder of dread. He had so hoped that he wouldn't have to have any dealings at all with those people.

Suddenly, as he and his patient wife stood in the middle of the walk, stock-still, staring at the young commissar, Jesse clearly heard in his spirit: *The Lord is my light and my salvation; whom shall I fear? The Lord is the strength of my life; of whom shall I be afraid?*

When Jesse Mitchell heard the Lord's voice, it was almost an audible sound, and through his long journey with God he had come to enjoy an art of personal conversation with Him. Now, after hearing the Word, Jesse said in his soul, *Yes, I know that, and sure I'm not afraid of that poor little lost girl, no matter what she's wearing or who she serves, Lord. I'll just go say hello to her.*

Noe Mitchell, with a long-suffering sigh, saw the intent look on her husband's face, and his peculiar stillness, and knew exactly what was going on. With resignation she went to sit on one of the stone benches that lined the walk. Jess didn't notice. But Noe was accustomed to that.

In fact, Jesse had almost taken a step toward the commissar, but it seemed that the conversation was not over yet. As pure as sound, as clear as water, he heard, *No, Jess. Ask her.*

Jesse's eyebrows shot up, and he was motionless once again. Now the commissar was watching him with curiosity. Jess really wasn't seeing anything, he was so absorbed in his conversation with God. *But—but ask her what?*

Ask her for help.

Now Jesse Mitchell balked, just a little. It had been many, many years since he had hesitated to obey what he knew in his soul was God's command . . . but this was different. With a taint of mulishness he thought, *Ask her for help? But she's one of them, Lord. You know, one of those secret police people!*

The silence was deafening.

To his credit, Jesse's small rebellion lasted only a few short moments. With one last dry observation—*No, I suppose You didn't make a mistake*—he swallowed hard and marched.

Still she watched him, a woman in her early twenties, Jess

thought, with plainly modeled features and level gray eyes. She had dark brown hair, shaved in the man-cut of the commissars. Though she was not a muscular or chubby woman, she was sturdily built. As he neared her, he was aware that he was crushing his old gray Stetson in his hands, because he was nervous. That was of no importance, though, because God didn't care about the deceits of emotion; He cared about obedience, and Jesse Mitchell was an obedient servant.

Finally he stood in front of her. She did not speak, nor did Jesse for long moments. Jesse was aware of the hum of voices, but it came as from a far distance. It was as though he and the woman were surrounded by a bubble and everything else faded away. He swallowed again, then said, "Hello there, ma'am. My name is Jesse Mitchell."

"I'm Xanthe St. Dymion."

"It's a pleasure to meet you, ma'am. Well, ma'am, you may think I'm crazy but I was wondering—" He broke off, not because he was losing his determination but because he simply couldn't think of what to say.

St. Dymion studied him. "Wondering—?" she prodded.

"Wondering if you might help me." Now that it was out Jesse felt ridiculous. He hoped that this commissar wouldn't arrest him outright for talking like a crazy man. "Help me and my wife. She's over there. Her name's Noemi."

The gray eyes were shadowed, unclear. Suddenly Jesse Mitchell grew impatient with himself. Hadn't the God of all creation Himself given him the words to say? What difference did it make what this woman thought or did? "Ma'am, I'm a Christian, and I was just now praying. The Lord told me, I'm certain of it, to come over here and ask you if you would help us."

Instead of the shock or puzzlement or anger that he half expected, he saw that her eyes lightened and once again her clear gaze focused on him. She even nodded, ever so slightly.

Encouraged, Jesse asked directly, "So will you help us?"

For a long time the woman did not move. She had clear, unmarred features and there was an air of strength about her; yet at the same time, at the present, she seemed vulnerable, unsure. "I—I—it's a strange thing, you asking me for help."

"Yes, ma'am, I'm more aware of that than you realize," Jesse said, with the barest hint of exasperation.

Suddenly Xanthe St. Dymion seemed amused. "Maybe I do realize, Mr. Mitchell." She took a deep breath, then continued soberly, "What could I do to help you?"

Once again Jesse was disconcerted. Now that he had asked the question and—miraculously—the woman had agreed, what help did he need? Instantly the answer came. *She'll show you the place, Jesse.* Ramming his hand in his inside coat pocket, he took a deep breath and pulled out a piece of plain white paper folded into quarters. Carefully he unfolded it. "My wife and I, we want to go into the mountains. We don't have a photograph of the place or anything, but I drew this picture of it." It was amateurish, endearing in its childlike simplicity. But it clearly showed the house, the distinctive rooster weather vane, the pine woods to the north and west, the mountains behind and to the east.

She took the picture and stared at it for a long time. Glancing up at him, she asked, "This place, is it yours? I mean, was it yours before the relocations to co-ops?"

Jesse shook his head. "No, ma'am, I grew up in the Ozarks, but I don't know exactly where this place is."

"But you want me to help you find it."

"Yes, ma'am, I'd certainly appreciate it. And I'm in the way of knowing that God would have a special blessing for you, too, if you'll help us."

Suddenly Jesse thought he saw a glint of tears in the steady gray eyes. Xanthe's smooth features crumpled a bit, as if she felt pain. Her lips trembled slightly as she whispered, "Yes, Mr. Mitchell, I can help you. Not only will I find this place for you, I'll take you there."

"You will, ma'am?"

"Yes. Meet me early in the morning. Do you know where the big fountain is in the park?"

"Oh yes, ma'am. Go there nearly every day."

"Be there at dawn."

Jesse swallowed hard and nodded. "Yes, ma'am. We'll be there."

———

Jesse and Noe stood in the semidarkness beside the fountain. The water gurgled and made a pleasant sound, and true to the name, it was a hot spring, so a thick mist rose from it. In the east, a faint gray had begun to light the tops of the near hills.

"Stop fidgeting, Jesse. She'll be here," Noe said calmly.

Jesse nervously shifted his feet. All night he had slept only in fits but had awakened to wonder at the encounter with Xanthe St. Dymion. Now he shrugged his thin shoulders. "She said to be here at dawn."

Noe responded, "Well, that wasn't a very precise time to set for this big secret meeting. After all, that sun takes a few minutes to rise over those mountains. So maybe she meant the end-dawn instead of the beginning-dawn."

Jesse smiled broadly. "How come you know so much, Noe?"

He had no sooner finished this sentence than the sound of a diesel engine chugging near caught his ears. He watched as a low, wide vehicle came to a stop directly in front of them. Xanthe leaned over and called out the window, "I'm sorry, but I must ask you to get in the back."

Jesse helped Noe in and then climbed in beside her. "This is my wife, Noe. This is Miss—um—I'm afraid I can't say your name right."

"Just call me Xanthe." As she pulled the Humvee around she said, "I think it'll be best if you get down and pull that blanket over you."

Jesse obediently pulled the gray blanket over his wife and then himself. Calmly Xanthe instructed them, "Don't talk and don't move, please, until I tell you."

Jesse felt the powerful engine of the Humvee rumble and he held Noemi's hand tightly. Both of them felt out of sync, somehow, and oddly surreal. They found it hard to believe that this was the United States of America, and here they were, two harmless old people, having to be smuggled into the mountains as if they were some kind of dangerous criminals. *Which we are, I guess*, Jesse thought with a sudden relieved amusement. *Fancy that, at our age.* He squeezed Noe's hand gently, and in the way of people who have loved each other for decades, he knew that she, too, had become slightly amused at the absurd melodrama.

The Humvee made its way through the deserted streets of Hot Springs until they came to a highway just west of the city that was still open for the techies to go study the Ozark Plateau Biome. It did have a checkpoint, however. She slowed down and a tall, gangling guard with a mop of red hair ambled over, giving her a sloppy little patting salute to his chest. "Hello there, Commissar," he said. "Making a little trip?"

"Short-range photos of a condemned highway about twenty miles up here, Commissar," she answered, waving a complex-looking camera. Bored, he waved her through.

She drove hard until they were clear of the city. After about ten minutes of silence, Jesse and Noe heard, "You can come out now." Xanthe waited until they threw aside the smothering blanket and got settled comfortably. Then she handed a color 8 x 10 photograph back to them.

"It's on Blue Mountain, in the range called the Ouachitas. Years and years ago, it was called Blue Sky Farm."

It was an aerial photograph, showing a dusting of pine woods crowning the high slopes. Almost to the top was a generous shelf, and on that shelf sat a cabin, the white paint still gleaming, the weather vane clearly outlined against dark pines and firs. The photo was so good, so clear, that Noe Mitchell could pick out the vivid blob of lantana blooms—golden yellow and glowing orange, growing on the same bush—in the tangle of weeds and shrubs surrounding the cabin.

"Where'd you get this picture?" Noe breathed with delight.

"It's an aerial surveillance photo from the CID, Fourth Directorate module on Cyclops II." This was like speaking Swahili to the older couple, she saw, so she simply shrugged, saying, "I found it with the computer. As you can see, Mrs. Mitchell, the cabin is still standing and looks good. But the Ouachita Mountains have been deserted for thirty years so there's no telling what kind of condition it's in."

Jesse said dreamily, "It's a good little cabin, solid and sturdily built. The floors are made out of hard pine, last forever. It's tight to keep out the winter wind, and there's a well, laid solid and fine in the mountain stone, just outside the window."

Xanthe glanced in her rearview mirror and met Jesse Mitchell's far-seeing hazel eyes. Still, however, she didn't speak, and the couple were content to just look out the window, hungrily searching the thick green woods after years of harsh desert glare and unforgiving seas of sand.

They drove steadily for more than two hours, saying little. The road grew steadily worse, as most of the roads in the biome had either been destroyed or simply allowed to deteriorate to a "rewilded" state. Finally it turned into more of a wooded trail than a road. Calmly and efficiently Xanthe forced the powerful Humvee through the underbrush, pushing down saplings and considering her map and compass from time to time. She had taken exact markings on an enlargement of the map and had two good checkpoints because two sharp, naked ridges pointed up toward the sky exactly on the east and west of the old cabin.

Finally with a lunge the Humvee broke through and came into what was now thick meadow; once it had probably been a plowed field. The grass had grown waist high, and there were shrubs but no saplings in the cleared square. Just on the other side of it was the cabin.

"It's just like I dreamed," Noe breathed. "Oh, thank You, Lord."

Jesse felt as if he had come home, which, in a way, he had. "There's the well," he said with satisfaction. "Just like I said. I'll bet you that water's the sweetest and coolest in the world."

Xanthe watched as the old couple got out and made their way toward the cabin. It was obviously a private moment, and she gave them a few minutes alone. Then she got out and picked up their pitifully few belongings, which seemed to be in one threadbare suitcase and an old crate that said in faded stencil, "TYVEK-POLY SHEETS—DO NOT OPEN WITH SHARPS."

Jesse and Noe were inside, standing in the center of the room, turning slow circles and looking around. "It's still in good shape," Jesse said. "It needs a little work but it'll do fine."

"I think it's lovely, Jess," Noe said quietly. "It's just perfect."

The cabin was a simple two-room box with a tiny front room. The kitchen consisted of a sink, a wood-burning stove, and a rough wooden counter with two homemade cabinets above it along one wall. Through a door at the back of the small room was the bedroom. The door was open, and Xanthe could see white humps in the shadows. While Jesse and Noe were still admiring the windows and the old stove and the native-stone fireplace, Xanthe slipped into the back. In one corner of the tiny single bedroom was the smallest water closet she had ever seen. The white humps were, as she suspected, pieces of furniture. There was an old iron bed, dismantled, the ornate head- and footboards leaning against the wall. She saw the iron bedsprings covered by canvas sheets, horribly rusted. At Xanthe's merest touch, they squeaked in protest. There was also a rough-hewn square table for two, four plain wooden chairs, a scarred and slightly uneven washstand. There were also three rocking chairs, lovingly and securely covered by canvas, the ends neatly tucked under the curved bows of the rockers.

"That's real nice," she heard Noe say behind her. "That one looks kind of like my mama's rocker. Teach me to worry about leaving behind stuff that's just—things. The Lord is good. Two nice rockers for us, Jess, and one for a friend."

Xanthe stood up, dusted her hands, and frowned. "This cabin is surprisingly clean, and this furniture looks in much too good condition to have been here for thirty years. I hope this isn't some kind of meeting place, or hunting cabin, for squatters."

Jesse and Noe looked at each other uncertainly. This woman had helped them, yes. But they still hadn't talked to her enough to understand why she had brought them here. And now she was looking, and talking, and acting, much like every other commissar they'd ever seen . . .

"No, no," Xanthe said hastily, stepping close to them. "I didn't mean—that. I'm just concerned about you two being here alone."

With a relieved smile, Jesse said, "But we're not alone, ma'am. God has prepared the way for us, and He's prepared this place for us. He's always with us. We're never alone."

Xanthe blushed and averted her eyes. "Yes, of course," she said uncomfortably. "I—I brought you some things. I'll bring them in."

The back of the Humvee was filled with boxes. Xanthe had brought dried and canned food, blankets, towels, socks, a clever little toolbox with fitted slots and grooves for all the tools, a set of acrylic dishes, and a pot and pan and kitchen utensils. One box even contained some commissar pants and blouses, without the insignia, of course.

As soon as she had brought everything in, she said awkwardly, "Well, good luck. I'll be leaving you now."

"But daughter, of course you need to tell us why you've helped us," Jesse said gently. "Please."

Xanthe was already halfway out the door. Without turning, she stopped. Her head dropped, and awkwardly she brushed her hand against her face. Jesse and Noe exchanged knowing glances;

she was crying, and they knew exactly why. They'd seen it so many times before.

"We were assigned to go to the churches, you know," she said in a trembling voice notably unlike her own assured tones. "I went, because it was my duty. And I listened . . . and I found that instead of hearing hate speeches and incitements to rebellion and militant fanaticism, I was hearing about the love of God. And then . . . and then . . . I started hearing God Himself."

Jesse and Noe moved to stand on each side of her. Noe took Xanthe's hand, which was shaking, and stroked it.

"God is dealing with you, my daughter," Jesse said quietly. "You will be a handmaiden of the Lord. You will dream dreams, and you will see visions."

Xanthe St. Dymion, the woman she had always been, changed at that moment. She felt the old couple's hands on her shoulders and suddenly a strong hand was laid on her forehead. The prayer that she heard was like nothing she had ever heard before, and she felt strength flowing into her, and her shoulders shook as a storm of weeping took her. She had not cried since she was a very young girl and now she felt as if, indeed, something had broken inside. But, contrary to all human wisdom, it was not a bad feeling, it was a blessed relief, and the beginning of a cleansing. As she wept, she prayed out loud, her words awkward and stumbling, but with pure and simple faith she asked Jesus to save her soul, and come into her heart.

When Xanthe finished praying, and her tears had stopped, Noe retrieved her purse. She pulled out a brooch, a very old but beautiful brooch. It had a smooth mother-of-pearl stone in the center surrounded by delicate silver filigree. Two horses, cunningly wrought, reared and pawed the air on both sides of the stone. Again Noe took Xanthe's hand, and placed the brooch in it. "I want you to have this, Xanthe. It was my mother's and her mother's before her. But I never had a daughter to give it to. I want you to have it."

Xanthe closed her hand on the brooch and held it to her breast, merely nodding. "I—I don't know—what I'm supposed to do now."

Jesse Mitchell answered, "Don't you fret, ever again, about your future, daughter. You are safe in the everlasting arms of the Lord, and He will carry you wherever He wills. Now, I don't have anything to give you but my thanks, for your courage and for your obedience to the Lord. But I do have a word of light and a word of warning for you.

"The word of light is that when you give a child of God a drink of water, no matter what your reason, that blessing will be returned to you a thousandfold. Daughter, you have given us a great gift, and I know it was a dangerous thing for you to do, but God is going to bless you mightily for it."

He hesitated, then continued in a somber tone, "And the word of warning. Take care of yourself and keep watch. For I see . . . I can see . . ."

Swallowing hard, her gray eyes troubled, Xanthe breathed, "What?"

Sighing, Jesse murmured, "A darkness. A great darkness is coming . . ."

Shortgrass Steppe Biome
Outside Lab #XJ2197

For some reason that he couldn't quite fathom, Dr. Niklas Kesteven was outside. At night. Alone.

"Guess I'll have another drink," he said loudly. As he brought the silver flask to his lips, he considered the sound waves that emanated from his mouth, how far they would travel, how there was no possibility of them reaching another human's ears, since he was out in the middle of the great empty western desert. "It's like that old conundrum about the tree falling in the forest. Since no one's ears are receiving my sound waves, therefore there must be no sound, therefore I must not be talking. There's an existential concept for you."

The esteemed and acknowledged genius, Dr. Niklas Kesteven, was sprawled spread-eagled on the hood of a Humvee outside the ranch house that squatted directly over SS Biome Lab XJ2197. The Humvee's engine was still cooling, ticking loudly, and that was the only other sound in Niklas Kesteven's world.

He was a little drunk, and he knew it, but he didn't know why. Niklas Kesteven wasn't a very introspective man, never had been. His main interest in life had always been assuring that whatever was inside him was comfortable and happy and satisfied and sometimes satiated. Why he needed the things he did wasn't his problem. Only getting them was.

He stared up at the sky, the eons in visual. In the vast darkness of the desert, no "light pollution" dimmed the brilliant canopy. To really look at the night sky and the millions upon millions of stars and worlds and galaxies was truly breathtaking.

"I wonder why . . . ," he muttered, not finishing the thought out loud. He tried to recall why he had forbidden Zoan to sleep "up top," as they called the crust of the earth from the depths of the lab. He just

couldn't remember why he'd told Zoan he had to stay down in the lab. It seemed that he had a perfectly good reason at the time . . . but right now he couldn't remember any reason at all.

"I miss Zoan."

He deliberately spoke the words out loud, but it still came out in an ashamed whisper. He couldn't even say it properly now, even though there was not a single soul to hear.

"And that brazen hussy Alia," he muttered to himself, partly angry, partly amused. "Fancy her stealing my chacos and disappearing in the middle of the night! Wench!"

Niklas, in the honesty of this hypnotically beautiful night, admitted to himself that he wasn't angry about Alia stealing his organism. "Wasn't really Thiobacillus chaco, *anyway. Was that useless ohm-bug. Now what did she want to do with that, anyway? An organism that could knock out electricity is useless, except for military applications. What's she gonna do, conquer Fiji or Tambora or something? Not hardly, not My Commissar. Not the way she feels about the military and their lost dreams of conquest.*

"Would seem to be that she feels the same way about you, Kesteven. She just melted into the night with your ohm-bug, without a good-bye and without a word since. That's loyalty for you, huh?"

But it wasn't exactly loyalty that Niklas was missing, or that he had thought he shared with Alia. It was something much more akin to love.

At least, he had thought that Alia had loved him.

"Wench," he grumped again. He wasn't going to think about that, not even on this revelatory night.

"At least she's shrewd enough to align herself with some powerful people," he muttered. "The vice president of the United States, and the Lady of Light, now that's some exalted circles, Alia girl. Power to you." Niklas had been seeing Alia on Cyclops at least twice a day, either with Minden Lauer in Earth's Light broadcasts, or working with the vice president's security team. He lifted his flask high over his head in a

salute to her. Squinting upward, he saw a spiky black form blotting out the stars.

It was a helicopter, as slender and ominous as a wasp. It made no sound.

"Apache," Niklas said fuzzily. Raising his flask higher, he pledged a toast: "To my lost friend Zoan. To Alia, once My Commissar. And to silent black helicopters in the lonely night."

TWELVE

———◆———

CAPTAIN, WHY DO WE HAFTA invade a bunch of rocks?"
Captain Con Slaughter, in his throaty half-whisper, intoned into his helmet comm, "We aren't invading the rocks, Darmstedt. We're covertly inserting ourselves in the midst of them, and then we're covertly extracting them. One rock each. Guard them with your lives."

Colonel Vashti Nicanor and Colonel Darkon Ben-ammi exchanged amused looks. In an affected Middle Eastern accent, Ben-ammi trilled, "Yes, yes, we are veddy mean, we are veddy bad, Colonel Nicanor."

Deadpan, Vashti crashed her small fists down on Darkon's giant shoulders and grunted, "Air Assault, sir!"

Ben-ammi, unable to resist the drill, growled, "Huu-ahh!"

First Lieutenant Ric Darmstedt grinned at the spectacle, and Vashti Nicanor, who had been transformed—albeit reluctantly—into an enthusiastic member of Fire Team Eclipse, returned one of her enigmatic half-smiles.

After observing Darmstedt coolly for six weeks, Vashti had seen that the big, goofy American was actually extremely intelligent, and was truly a good-natured man. He was the only male soldier she had observed who honestly tried to help the female paratroopers. There were very few women in the 101st; even though they were highly skilled technicians, and each member of the small division was required to get a helo rating, each trooper still had to be a jumper. That meant—aside from the stark fact that they had to jump out of moving airplanes—that they had to be able to load down with, and efficiently manage, more than 170 pounds of gear. Very few women, no matter how strong their desire and how determined they were, ever could accomplish a full combat drop. Vashti had found out that Ric Darmstedt helped them; he often designed personal regimens in strength training for the few women who survived basic training. Finally Vashti had sidled up to him and hinted around until he offered to "illustrate" some physical training techniques he used to help out the women.

Within a month, Vashti Nicanor, at thirty-two years old, was in better physical shape than she had ever been. Vashti knew that she'd never be on a fitness level with a twenty-year-old paratrooper, and she had no intention of trying combat parachute drops. But Darmstedt had taught her how to rappel. Vashti was amazed to find that not only was she good at it—she actually liked it. Ric Darmstedt had never taken advantage of the situation in any way; he always treated her with the utmost respect and courtesy.

Vashti had decided that she liked Ric Darmstedt very much. In fact, she and Darkon Ben-ammi both had formed close relationships with all of the members of the team. Somehow, in the weeks that they had been acting as "advisers," Vashti and Darkon had become constant companions of this one team, had started participating in all of the team's activities, had accompanied them on all their "missions," and then, slowly, they had begun to participate in the missions, as members—if unofficial—of the Fire Team Eclipse.

And so now they were preparing to invade a bunch of rocks.

Captain Con Slaughter ordered, "Pair off. Check your gear."

In the course of things, Vashti and Darkon had gotten in the habit of pairing off with other members of the team besides each other. Vashti immediately started a check with Ric Darmstedt, while Darkon and Sergeant David Mitchell started muttering together in low tones, with each appearing to "pat" the other down as they double-checked their equipment.

IAF Colonel Darkon Ben-ammi, two weeks previously, had stalked into the 101st Brigade Task Force commander's office and demanded that he and Vashti be issued all the equipment that any paratrooper of the 101st Airborne had. His justification was that he and Vashti wanted to be able to give the Israeli army and air force the most accurate information possible on the exact functioning of the new, tightly constructed smaller fire team units. Strictly speaking, that didn't exactly mean that he and Colonel Nicanor needed to have their own T-10 parachutes and M-20 rifles and night vision goggles and all the rest of the paratroopers' cutting-edge gear. But the brigade commander, with an internal shrug, indulged his Israeli "adviser."

So now Vashti and Darkon, along with their comrades in Fire Team Eclipse, checked for at least the tenth time their rappelling ropes, their NVG's (night vision goggles), their M-20's and ammo, their Beretta M9 personal defense pistols, their Genesis body armor, their Spectra-Lite PASGT helmets . . . and so on. Each of them was weighted down with approximately fifty pounds of equipment, and at that they were traveling light, for they were rappelling out for a simulated covert insertion-extraction mission, instead of a full combat parachute drop.

Slyly Vashti cut her dark eyes up to Darmstedt's friendly blue ones and murmured, "Too bad we can't advise you on how to do a covert insertion-extraction of a real person or persons, instead of rocks. I, too, am a little disappointed, Lieutenant Darmstedt."

"Yeah, well, guess there's no one needs extracting anymore," he lamented. "Just like there's no one needs killin' anymore. Makes our job a real bore, huh?"

"Darmstedt, you want an exciting job?" Slaughter inquired. "How 'bout packaging MRE's, counting bullets, that kinda thing? Heard they need a clerk in Receiving."

"Aw, that's too kind of you, sir," Darmstedt sighed. "But I just couldn't bear to take a job away from some dedicated little drone-head. But, hey, Captain, I got a recommendation for making this job a little more interesting. Permission to speak?"

Con Slaughter's sigh was audible over the helmet comm. The Apache was, indeed, so quiet when in silent running that they could hear each other's whispers. "I'll listen to your recommendation, Darmstedt, but I warn you that I intend to stay a captain for a while. I know you don't care if you get busted down to bullet-counter, but I'm not going to pull any stunts that'll get me in trouble."

"No, no, what I'm thinking is, Cap'n, that we need to *seize the initiative*," Darmstedt said enthusiastically. "That's our prime directive, isn't it? It's in all the books, you know."

"Uh-huh," Slaughter muttered cautiously. "Seize the initiative."

"Yes, sir. And I think that instead of trying to conquer a pile of rocks, we ought to try a for-real—well, not a real for-real, but a more for-real covert approach to something besides some rocks."

"Uh-huh," Slaughter repeated. "Approach to what?"

"People?"

"What people?"

"Like German people, maybe? Like maybe the 66th Luftwaffe Fighting Squadron?"

"What? At Holloman?"

"Well . . . yeah. I mean, yes, sir. I mean, come on, think about it, Captain. We're halfway to Holloman anyway. We could just do a quick flyover, see if they notice us. I mean, that's a better test of the stealth features than sneaking up on a pile of rocks. If they do catch us, we can just kinda wave and say Hi, and then chop on off into the night. If they don't, well, we could just sorta . . . you know, test our covert insertion technique."

"Not our covert extraction?" Slaughter asked with feigned surprise. "You don't want to try and kidnap the commandant or anything?"

"Maybe his daughter?" Darmstedt suggested innocently.

"Yeah, I've heard enough," Slaughter growled. "Darmstedt, sit down and shut up."

"Huuu-ah, sir," Darmstedt said cheerfully. He winked at Vashti, and the team sat down in their small pull-down seats.

No one spoke for a long time.

With elaborate casualness, Slaughter asked the pilot, Deacon Fong, "Deac, what's the incremental flying time to Alamogordo?"

Fong pushed a couple of buttons on his NavStar/LORAN keyboard, then pointed to the numerical display. "There you go, Captain. Additional 20 minutes, 12.2775 seconds from the original drop coordinates."

"Check the weather," Slaughter grunted.

Fong said with impressive professionalism, "No cloud cover, ground temp 66 degrees, temp at 10,000 feet, 42 degrees, light southerly wind, no chops."

Another long silence ensued.

Slaughter said to the group in general, "This is a black-ops exercise, you know. No team-to-base communication."

"Yes, sir," Darmstedt sang out. "That means we wouldn't even have to tell the brass we spied on our little German friends."

"Darmstedt, I thought I told you to shut up."

"Yes, sir, you sure did, sir."

"Fong, head for Alamogordo."

Someone snickered; Vashti was fairly certain that it was David Mitchell, but when she looked at him, his face was set in his usual angelic innocence.

Slaughter growled, "Darmstedt, if I have to tell you one more time to shut up I'm going to show you a new rappelling method I've been working on. You know, the one where you don't use a rope?"

David Mitchell found something very interesting to look at on the helicopter's low ceiling, while Ric Darmstedt looked tragically hurt. "Yes, sir, Captain Slaughter. I'll try to keep it down."

"Okay, people, let's do the makeup job. Colonel Nicanor, Colonel Ben-ammi, I would advise you not to let Sergeant Valdosta assist you with the camo face makeup. He always gets it in your mouth. Sergeant Mitchell would probably be best."

Vashti sniffed. "At last," she declared, "I've found something that a woman can do better than you men. Give me that tin, Lieutenant Darmstedt. I'll show you how to put camo makeup on so that your own mother couldn't find you in your backyard."

The human eye, in spite of its shortcomings in some respects, progressively developed in all people; even children and people with poor vision. The eye aligned itself with the brain in such a way as to recognize faces at very long distances, and even under poor light conditions. A person who couldn't see a bus at fifty paces at midnight and without their glasses would still see a face peeking around the corner of the same invisible bus. So Fire Team Eclipse, with Vashti Nicanor's expert advice, applied the green and gray and black matte paint to their faces in patterns that broke up the normal outlines recognizable as a face.

Darkon Ben-ammi refused, declaring, "I am a pilot and I have never seen any valid reason for jumping out of a perfectly good aircraft. I'll stay. That is, if Lieutenant Fong would do me the honor of allowing me to copilot for him." In spite of his declared condescension for helicopters—he called them "potato mashers"—Darkon Ben-ammi had been taking lessons from Deacon Fong and was secretly enjoying learning how to fly a helicopter. At any rate, he was a little too old and a little too meaty to safely rappel or parachute. Vashti nodded to him with understanding, and moved to Sergeant Rio Valdosta, ordering him to sit down and stop complaining so she could put makeup on his face.

Darkon Ben-ammi reflected, as he watched the men of Fire Team Eclipse, how very much he'd learned from them. This mission, tonight, was an encapsulated example of the American military as a whole. Their orders were to test the stealth features of their

Apache AH-64D; they were to go out into the desert, decide and navigate to a landmark, and practice their covert insertion-extraction technique. That was about as detailed as their orders were, Ben-ammi knew, for Captain Con Slaughter confided in him pretty openly about military matters. Ben-ammi had intuited that the higher command always worried about how, exactly, to keep their elite fighting units at top condition, at maximum readiness. The military phrase for it was "optempo," or "operational tempo." It was always a problem to keep soldiers at an optimum state of readiness without burning them out. It was an especially delicate problem when they weren't in actual combat—or ever likely to be.

And so, Ben-ammi had observed, the units that were especially well-tuned, such as Fire Team Eclipse, often had great latitude in their training mission orders. In other words, their commanders often kept them stimulated and at an acceptably high operational tempo by giving them expensive toys to play with, and then assigning them a loose set of testing parameters, or a hypothetical tactical situation with rather vague outlines, and let them devise their own missions, rather than a line-by-line set of orders to follow. Such discretion of command worked well with these smaller four- or six-man teams, when they obviously wouldn't work with a less closely integrated company or squad.

Everyone, including Con Slaughter, knew that while he might get a dressing-down for temporarily kidnapping his new Apache and harassing the Germans, there would be no real serious consequences. In fact, the brass probably would secretly admire the team—especially if they could pull it off without the Germans ever knowing. The Luftwaffe airmen in America were considered fellow soldiers, and there was a sort of stilted camaraderie, but still there was a fierce competition between them and the American forces. One-upping them with the Americans' new stealth helicopter would make up a little for the fact that the German F4 Tornadoes were about the meanest thing flying these days, though they never actually, statistically, beat the army's FA/20's or especially the FK-120 stealth penetration strike fighters. It was just that the Tornadoes *looked* so sleek, so streamlined, so ominous. They were flashy jets, all black, with the Iron Cross outlined in blood red. Arrogantly disdaining any pretension to stealth, they had a high-pitched, nerve-shattering scream that clearly announced their ground-hugging 900 mph bombing runs. The Air Force hated them.

As they neared Holloman Air Force Base, Deacon Fong whistled. "Man, what is it, German New Year or something?"

"Germans have the same new year as we do, Fong," Darmstedt grumbled as he re-tied his paratrooper's high boots. "I mean, everybody's been on the Gregorian calendar for a coupla thousand years now."

"Not everybody," Fong retorted smartly. "The Chinese have their own new year. Have had for more thousands of years than Julian has."

"Well, the Germans have the real one. The one everybody else has."

"Just keep it down, people, this is supposed to be a covert mission, remember? That means that people four or five miles away shouldn't be able to hear us arguing," Slaughter ordered. "Sergeant Mitchell, get Baby BAD heated up, check to see if they might have outlying sentries. Lieutenant Fong, I want a slow circle at 21,000. Keep out about a mile from the base perimeter."

"Uh, Captain, I gotta tell you, with that high-intensity glare over the base, one mile might not be far enough out to keep somebody from spotting us on simple visual," Deac Fong maintained. "What is going on down there, anyway?"

"What's the deal?" Sergeant Valdosta finally demanded, moving to lean over into the cockpit so he could see out the canopy. "Great grief! What're they doing down there?"

"Could someone give us a hint?" Lieutenant Darmstedt complained. "I mean, if we're gonna jump into it, I'd kinda like to know what it is. A glare? What is it, a bonfire? UFO's? Candlelit dinners?"

"It's lit up, all right," Slaughter answered. "The whole base. Looks like they've even set up their air searchlights, but they're not searching the air, they're lighting up the grounds."

Darmstedt shrugged. "Oh, well, that'll just make a close insertion easier. If you're standing in front of bright lights, you can't see past 'em."

"That's true," Slaughter agreed. "Okay, Sergeant Valdosta? Is your rappelling team in order?"

"Yes, sir!"

"On the ready line?"

"Yes, sir!"

"Then let's drop, people. Sure you don't want to tag along with us, Colonel Ben-ammi?" Slaughter asked respectfully.

The big man grinned. "No shinnying down a rope for this old man, Captain."

"All right—Deac?" he said into his helmet comm.

"Yes, sir?"

"You and Colonel Ben-ammi land this bird a kilometer due north of the insertion point. The team and I will rendezvous back with you on the ground. While we're out here flying by the seat of our pants and just kinda doin' whatever feels good, we might as well work a simulated combat pickup."

"Heard, understood, acknowledged, sir."

"Whatever the devil in this galaxy are they *doing*?" Rio Valdosta exclaimed. He spoke in a normal tone into his small walkie-talkie. Besides being harshly lit, Holloman was noisy.

"I don't know," Slaughter answered with frustration. "But I want to figure it out. Any ideas, Mitchell?"

"Not an idea in my head, sir," David Mitchell answered, clearly mystified.

Five black figures, unseen except when they moved, lay belly-down at the far end of Runway L6 of Holloman Air Force Base. Normally, at 0130 hours, this end point of the base would be dark and deserted; it was the longest runway, and only used for the great transports like C-140's or C-5's. The Tornadoes didn't need nearly this much room to swat down from the skies.

But on this night, it was as garishly lit as if it were a Broadway stage. Great searchlights had indeed been positioned everywhere, but instead of pointing long light-fingers into the sky, they were trained downward, lighting every square inch of the base. It seemed as if every piece of equipment that the Germans had was dragged out onto the runways, onto the grounds: Jeeps, motorcycles, autos, trucks, helicopters, airplanes, portable generators, communication equipment, and weapons were everywhere, making a strange surreal techno-landscape architecture. Hundreds of men, dressed in head-to-toe loose silver jumpsuits, were spraying a fine mist onto every inch of every piece of equipment from great barrels with no identifying markings.

"Those look like Level 5 bio-suits," Mitchell said, worried. "We might be in danger of exposure, Captain Slaughter, and we don't have chem-gear, sir."

"No, look, Mitchell. Over there, at the—uh—what are those monsters, anyway?"

"Those are Messerschmitt-Kawasaki BK 2000's, sir," Sergeant Valdosta breathed enviously. "They're sort of the Rolls-Royce models of helos. Usually used as a fast but relatively luxurious transport for their chancellor and ministers. They're not really military aircraft. And I've never seen any in the States. They usually keep those limos close to home."

"Yeah, well, anyway, see there, Mitchell? Two men, civvies, standing over there talking. No protective gear. So what are the guys in the Jupiter suits spraying?" Slaughter muttered.

No one answered, for no one knew.

Mitchell lifted his head, then sniffed. "Smell it? What—it's not paint . . . what is that smell?"

Vashti, sniffing delicately, whispered, "Captain Slaughter, I do some artwork, and I've done some of my own mounting and framing. I'm not sure . . . but I think it's a spray mount. Like an aerosol glue? It's very weak, though. It's not nearly the concentration of the sticky kind of spray mount one buys in art stores."

"That's it, it does have a very faint glue smell," Slaughter agreed. "But why would anyone want to spray glue all over such delicate equipment? It's insane!"

No one answered that, either, though they all agreed with him.

They watched for a long time without speaking. The men just kept meticulously spraying the fine mist all over everything. David Mitchell noted that they ensured complete coverage; they were methodically spraying a small area with vertical strokes, then covering the same small area with horizontal strokes.

Ric Darmstedt saw that, although they were spraying the exteriors, they were being very careful not to spray the interiors of the autos, the helos, and the jets. Sergeant Valdosta also pointed out that there were two teams going around, checking the Tornadoes and the helos, and sealing some parts of them up with a sort of grout. Rio speculated that when the sprayed substance dried, or took, or whatever, the grout could be removed.

"But what the deuce is the grout for?" Slaughter growled. "So they're spraying perfectly good machinery—with something that they have to protect it from? I just gotta figure this out, people. Something's up here with the Goths. Something's definitely up."

David Mitchell said slyly, "Sir? I think what we need to do is get a sample of the spray. We can take it back to the base and get it analyzed."

"Yeah," Slaughter said slowly. "I'd like to have a sample. But I don't think anyone needs to try to get in any closer. I know they'll never hear us, with the roar of all those pressurized hoppers and with the helmets they're wearing. But we're really too close; they could see us if they just happened to scan the ground right here. If it weren't for them being in those moon suits, and those zillion-kilowatt lights, I wouldn't have come in this close."

"Whatcha gonna do, Mitchell? Volunteer to be a sprayee?" Darmstedt asked.

"No, just thought we oughta complete the mission," Mitchell replied. "Look over here, Captain. Just to my right, about fifty feet. Right under the left wheel. See it?" A Tornado, a phantom black shape hulking in the bright lights, was just to David Mitchell's right.

Slaughter lifted his binoculars, and his teeth, titanium white against his mottled gray-green-black face, showed in a reluctant grin. "Yeah, I see it, Mitchell. Think you can snake up there?"

"Yes, sir, sure do. He's on the other side now anyway. It's gonna take him until next Tuesday to get that side covered."

Slaughter nodded once. "Okay, it's a go, Mitchell."

Just like a snake, David Mitchell belly-crawled, torquing his slender body along in the grass by the runway. He was clearly visible in the harsh light shining down on the jet, if someone had happened to look right down at the ground where he was. But as soon as he crossed into the jet's knife-edged shadow, he became invisible. Within moments he was squirming back toward the team.

"Sir, I would like to report that I have successfully completed the mission," Mitchell intoned.

"What's going on?" Vashti hissed.

Captain Con Slaughter turned slightly and held up a bulky brown object. "Sergeant David Mitchell just completed a successful covert extraction of a rock."

"It's been a week, Captain Slaughter," the 101st Airborne (Air Assault) Brigade task commander growled. He was a short chunk of a man, with a square head and face and no neck. He was Lieutenant Colonel J. P. Nix, and though everyone called him "Nixie" behind his back, no one—not even generals—called him that to his face. Only his wife did. Now he was staring at Con Slaughter, chewing and talking around a stub of a cigar. "You boy geniuses got any better ideas what the Goths were up to? Anything else you can tell us? Anything at all?"

"No, sir," Con Slaughter answered rigidly. "We've been over and over it again among ourselves, sir. We haven't been able to come up with anything more than we gave you in debriefing." He was sweating profusely, because he had just finished his Punish Run with his "disgraced" fire team. Of course, the fact that almost everyone on the base had sidled up to them to secretly congratulate them on sneaking up on the Goths at Holloman had softened the punishment somewhat. But Colonel Nix still looked grim, so Captain Slaughter took care to stand at a handsome and crisp "at-ease" in the B. C.'s office. "But sir, Fire Team Eclipse would like to volunteer to make another covert surveillance of Holloman. We're ready at a moment's notice, sir."

"Aren't you though," Nix said dryly, removing the sloppy stub from his mouth and surveying it with great interest. "Or even without a moment's notice."

"Yes, sir," Slaughter sighed resignedly.

Nix shook his head and averted his face slightly to hide a grin. "Sit down, Slaughter."

"Thank you, sir." Con Slaughter sat in the wooden straight chair in front of the brigade commander's desk about as comfortably as he had stood "at ease."

"Relax, son," Colonel Nix said, with a touch of unusual warmth. "I didn't call you in here to hand down more punishment. By the way, how's the daily five-mile PR going?"

"Excellent, sir. My team has tackled it like troopers. We're clocking some good times."

"I've noticed that Colonel Nicanor and Colonel Ben-ammi are running with the team."

"Yes, sir."

"They volunteered to do that?"

"Uh—they just sort of—did it, sir. We didn't really talk about it, actually." Hastily he added, "I certainly never tried to impose the punishment on them, sir."

"No, guess not—*Captain*." Colonel Nix harrumphed. The Israelis were colonels, after all. "But how are their times?"

Slaughter's golden-brown eyes focused smartly on a point just beyond Colonel Nix's left shoulder. "Their times are fine, sir."

"Uh-huh. Everyone still keeping up with the other PT and weapons and tactical training?"

"Yes, sir!"

"The entire team?"

"Yes, sir!"

"Including your Israeli advisers?"

"Yes, sir!" Slaughter replied snappily.

Nix was relieved—even glad—to see no hesitation in the fire team leader's backup of the two Israelis. If ever there was a time to complain about having two outsiders—one a woman, and one an older man—tagging along with a tight young team, Nix had given it to Slaughter now. If Slaughter had any gripes, he sure didn't want to air them with his commanding officer. This was interesting; evidently Slaughter himself had come to regard Colonel Vashti Nicanor and Colonel Darkon Ben-ammi as an integral part of his team, and defended them, just as a good leader always did for the men under his command.

"Good," the colonel said quietly. "The reason I brought you in here, Con, is because we got the results back on the rock from Fitzsimmons Medical Center labs."

Slaughter's eyes lit up alertly. "Yes, sir?"

Nix stuck his cigar back in his mouth and chewed contemplatively for a few minutes. Then, picking up a single piece of paper, he read—with a pronunciation that would have been amusing if he hadn't had the power of life and death over Con Slaughter—"Trichloroethane, isobutane, cyanoacrylate ester, and some dioxane thrown in there. And here, lookit these jobs—how do you read these things?"

Obediently Slaughter looked at the line Nix pointed to on the piece of paper: $NaCl$, $MgCl_2$, KI, NaF, $CaCO_3$, $BaSO_4$, KCl. He looked up at his commander and said evenly, "I don't know how to say them, sir, and I sure don't know what any of it means."

"Me neither," Nix growled. "Blasted tech-heads. I called 'em and told 'em to give it to me—the English translation." He eyed Slaughter speculatively, then said, "It's a sticky spray that has a high concentration of sea salt in it."

Slaughter stared at him in disbelief. "Sea salt? Sir, is there—could there be some mistake at the lab?"

"Yeah, I told 'em there must be," he said dryly. "Told 'em to do all their fiddlin' and faddlin' all over again. They ran the tests again, twice."

"So—the Germans are spraying multimillion-dollar equipment with—with—salt?"

"Looks like it. In a sticky spray. At least, it has a very light adhesive quality, but it also has elements of a polymer sealant. The tech-heads said it would stick to whatever you sprayed it onto, but the salt wouldn't actually—uh—be touching the surface you sprayed. It's like a separate layer."

"Like—like—" Slaughter was so dumbfounded, he was struggling to organize his thoughts. "You're saying it's sort of like a protective coating, but it has sea salt in it?"

"I ain't sayin' it. If I said it, you might think I was stupid," Nix grunted sarcastically. "The lab techies are saying it. Swearing it."

"But sir, that doesn't make any sense!"

Nix nodded, contemplating his stubby cigar again.

They were silent for a few moments, then the colonel spoke, and it was as if he addressed the cigar he was holding instead of Captain Slaughter. "So that leaves the big question. So far nobody can answer it—not the techies, not you, not your high-flyin' team, not me, not the whole bloody brass band." His puzzled brown eyes settled on the young captain.

Slaughter, forgetting protocol, whispered to himself: "Why?"

THIRTEEN

The seventy years that Count Gerade von Eisenhalt had spent building his life had not drained his vitality. His towering six foot five inches of height lent him an air of majesty, and the fortitude that had brought him to the helm of the Germanic Union still burned brightly. He was the perfect example of dramatic Prussian manhood of the old school, even to the saber scar on the right side of his aristocratic face. The strength and vigor of the count emanated almost as a physical force, and now he was, some believed, the most powerful man in Europe, if not in the world. He was the chancellor of the Germanic Union of Nation-States—which included Germany, Switzerland, Austria, Sweden, the Netherlands, Denmark, and Norway. He was also first minister of the Western European Alliance, and the expanded European Union that covered the continent like a carpet.

Count von Eisenhalt was by nature a stern, proud man. Leaning back in his nineteenth century "gentleman's chair," his glance swept critically over his son. Tor von Eisenhalt, commandant general of the German *Bundeswehr*, commandant in chief of the Joint Task Forces of the Germanic Union of Nation-States, sat on the other side of an enormous fireplace in another Louis XVI chair, staring blankly into the roaring fire.

Gerade's gaze roamed over the room where so many critical and historic decisions had been made. Years before the count had ordered this small *jagdschloss* built at Waldleiningen. *Halle Eisenhalt*, farther to the east, was too isolated for Gerade to comfortably shuttle back and forth to Berlin. Waldleiningen was far enough away from the capital that he could retire to ponder his schemes for making Germany the premier nation in the world, yet close enough for him to fly to Berlin by helicopter in less than forty-five minutes.

The room itself was a marriage of German gothic and neo-classic English. The ceilings were twenty feet high, dramatically adorned with white plaster, and bordered with a frieze made of intricately carved walnut. The windows were high, admitting the amber light that fell upon the dark crimson carpet. On this rainy and dreary day the thick dark green embroidered curtains were half closed. The baldachin was a rich medieval fabric of silk and gold. The furnishings were eclectic, some brought from Paris, others from Berlin. A massive chandelier made of black iron studded with jewels of every hue hung over the large teakwood library table that dominated the room. Around the walls, bookcases rose as high as the first tier and above that niches were framed with Gothic arches pointed at the top. One end of the room, where Gerade and his son sat, was dominated by a massive fireplace of neo-Gothic design. All of the furniture was upholstered with dark oxblood leather. It was a man's room—a strong man's room at that—bearing the mark of its designer. Everything was striking and bold and dramatic, which accurately described Count von Eisenhalt himself.

The door opened and a thin, pale-faced man with iron gray hair entered carrying a square bottle and two balloon glasses. He had eyes the color of spit and not an emotion flickered across his face as he set down the tray and poured a generous two fingers of amber liquid into the glasses. Without a word, he slipped back out through the double black oak doors.

Count von Eisenhalt took one of the glasses and motioned toward the other. He watched while his son picked up the glass.

Still silent, the two men caressed the glasses in their palms, swirling the fine old Napoleon brandy to warm it slightly. They sipped at the same time. "It is still fine," Gerade commented, "even after three hundred years."

Tor murmured a muted assent, then meticulously dusted an imaginary speck from his mirror-polished jackboots. His uniform was the same style he had decreed for the Joint Task Force personnel; plain blouse, belt, shoulder strap, dagger, jodhpurs, boots—only Commandant von Eisenhalt's was solid black instead of brown. He also had a peculiar four-leaf-clover design for his insignia that no other soldier wore. The dramatic uniform molded to his body, outlining the deep chest and the natural power of his build. Tor was not as imposing physically as his father, at first assessment, anyway. When in company with his father, however, Tor definitely irradiated an aura of power with an underlying ruthless strength.

Tor had been ill only once in his life, when he was eleven years old. The cook at Halle Eisenhalt had served him a day-old stew, which had given him a mild case of food poisoning. Tor recalled how his father's face had grown scarlet with anger. Gerade had beaten the man with a riding crop until the servant cried for mercy. Tor had never seen the cook again; his name had never been mentioned. It was a vivid lesson that Tor had filed away in his mind on how to deal with ineffective people.

"Open the window. The fire is too hot; it's stifling in here," Gerade commanded. There was no graciousness in his voice. He had long since forgotten how to do anything but command, if indeed he had ever known. He watched as his son moved with feline grace to the windows and threw the long double panes open. A smell of rich wet turf and the chill of evening wandered into the room. Tor breathed deeply, staying at the window, staring out into the deepening twilight and the gray mists curling sinuously up from the spring-warmed earth.

Gerade studied him, then said, "You look sunburned and stripped down to sinew and ligaments."

Dryly, Tor said, "I'm well; thank you for your concern, Father."

"Tor, come back here and sit down. I can hardly hear you. You're mumbling out the window."

In spite of his father's brusque command, Tor did not sit down. He circled the room slowly, looking at the titles of the books. He had endured a hard, vigorous apprenticeship under this man who had all the strength of manhood with few of the graces. After the death of Tor's mother, the two of them had traveled extensively, but not for pleasure. Gerade had always treated Tor as a student who was slightly backward, and had gruffly demanded an impossible perfection from his son. Count Gerade von Eisenhalt was never satisfied with anything his son had ever achieved.

Tor ran his hand over the leather covers of a line of books, caressing them roughly. "*Denwald's Geometry.* I remember this book," he said. He pulled it out and as he opened it a faint smile relaxed the corners of his stern mouth. "I remember it well. Almost every page of it." He walked back toward his chair and stood for a moment leafing through the pages. "I remember this problem." He turned the book so that his father could see it. "I failed to solve it in the proper time and you gave me a thrashing for it."

"I don't recall that," Gerade said evenly.

"I do. I remember it well."

"And it made you angry."

"Of course it did. Did you think an Eisenhalt could endure a thrashing without being angry?"

The remark amused the old man. He took another apprecia-tive sip of brandy. "I had to thrash you. I was molding you into the future chancellor of Germany. You don't make a chancellor with a feather duster."

"You never mentioned that while I was growing up."

"I thought you had sense enough to know it."

"I was intelligent enough, but maybe I needed more. You never told me I was a man of destiny."

"A man that has to be told that he has a high destiny doesn't deserve one."

Abruptly, Gerade's stern features wavered, distorted, like a man's face seen underwater. Pain flickered into his eyes and involuntarily his hand moved to his stomach. It was a gesture and an expression that his son did not miss. "Getting worse, isn't it?" Tor asked neutrally.

Eisenhalt did not like anyone to refer to his illness; indeed, as was so common in people who had a dark and secret fear, he ignored it except in the deepest depths of his subconscious. Count Gerade von Eisenhalt's terrible raw ulcers had started producing cancerous cells that were eating away at his intestines and stomach. Gerade had not consulted his physician about it, so it had not been diagnosed, and he pretended to himself that he didn't know it. His closest realizations of the fact that he was dying came in the form of nightmares. Still, Gerade had taught himself to regard illness as a weakness, and all of his life he had despised weakness in any form, and had denied any manifestation of it in himself.

Now he replied curtly, "No, as a matter of fact I've been much better." Regaining his cold manner, he went on, "At any rate, Tor, I'm aware that you had a hard childhood. But I knew what was facing you, and I believed that you must not be coddled."

Tor sat down and closed the book, running his hand over the worn cover. He precisely placed it on the table, picked up his glass, and sipped lightly. "I've never complained and I don't now. You did what you had to do. We just missed something along the way."

"Missed what?"

"Why, the usual closeness between father and son," Tor said, with an irony as cold as frozen steel. "You never came to my soccer games even when our team won the national championship."

"I was a busy man, with very important matters to attend to. Germany was my interest, not games."

"Of course. Well, I have survived and so have you, Father."

Gerade was somewhat shaken by his son's words. He did not know how to handle these personal references, indeed he never had. Now he drained the last of his drink and set the glass down too hard on the tray. Almost inaudibly, he murmured, "I attended your championship game."

Tor's glacier blue eyes flickered. "I never knew that. You never told me."

"I didn't want us to get involved with a sticky, sentimental relationship. But I was proud of you. That last goal you made, it was the finest achievement I ever saw on an athletic field."

Tor stared at his father, feeling no sudden rush of gratitude nor sympathy. He could clearly see death in his father's face. *He gets weaker every day, but that's only in the flesh. His mind and stubborn will are as strong as ever.* The old man might be sick, even unto death, but he was still as dangerous as a coiled snake when he was crossed.

Coolly Tor shrugged, dismissing remembrances, now irrelevant, of a cold and loveless past. "Why did you want to see me, Father?"

Gerade's eyes narrowed. The blue had faded somewhat with age, but they still looked out on the world with the same penetrating calculation and barely disguised arrogance. "I was concerned about you, of course. What happened in the Syrian campaign?"

Tor laughed, an ugly sound that made Gerade flinch inside. "You were concerned about me? You mean you were concerned about replacing the commandant in chief of the forces."

"No. I was concerned about you, Tor. You are my son." It was the closest Gerade could come to expressing warmth and affection.

Shrugging one shoulder carelessly, Tor leaned back into his chair, swirling his drink in hypnotic circles. "Yes, you are my father, and it would seem that you, the only person on this earth who is of my blood and bone, would be able to comprehend what happened to me in Syria. But I know beyond all doubt that you never will."

Gerade was growing impatient. "Just tell me, Tor. You disappeared for nine days! Surely you do have an explanation, and I assure you I still have the mental acuity to understand it."

"Mental acuity, yes. Spiritual depth, no."

A sharp pain, like a fire-heated dagger, ripped through Gerade's gut. With almost inhuman control, he didn't grab his stomach, but his faded blue eyes darkened to indigo. Stoically he waited until the torrid waves of pain subsided. With only a slight coarsening of his tone, he said, "Don't be melodramatic, Tor. Of course I possess a soul. I would think that would supply any credentials I need to understand your spiritual journey, or revelation, or whatever it is."

"Ah, yes, the soul. The inner spirit of a man. The seat of all mystic knowledge and understanding. Let's talk about your soul, Father. And then, perhaps, I will tell you about mine."

Abruptly, Gerade was exhausted. A weariness, of age and debilitating sickness, coursed throughout his body like a fever. His mind seemed to sag, like a rotting curtain at a window looking out only on darkness. A bitter taste invaded his mouth, and with a grimace he swallowed hard. "My . . . soul," he grated. "I have lately been considering the state of my soul more than I ever have in my entire life. I have been thinking about God."

A spasm—whether of shock or distaste—flitted across Tor's roughly handsome features. Gerade thought he might have imagined it, however, as only a moment later Tor looked quite as smoothly intent as he had when they began this odd conversation. "Another subject that never came up between us. What conclusions have you reached, Father, about the state of your soul and God?"

Gerade dropped his eyes. His answer was oblique. "Your mother was a Christian, you know."

Tor was so stunned, it was almost a physical sensation. Jerking upright in the chair, he leaned forward, his eyes fiercely brilliant.

"You've never said a word to me. You never showed the least interest in Christianity."

"I may not have shown it, but no man could have known your mother without feeling the power. Her power."

"Power!" Tor almost choked. "She died. What power is that? And you—you taught me that there is no power, unless it is exerted over other men. Power is only to control men: their health, or their decisions, or their minds, or their will, or their money, or their life and death. You taught me that!"

Gerade finally met his son's enraged gaze and still refused to answer him directly. "I loved her, you know. I have never loved anything on this earth as I did your mother. If she had lived I might have been different."

"You might not have been chancellor of Germany," Tor argued heatedly. "You know how debilitating a woman's influence can be."

"So I once thought. That is why I did not allow you to have women . . . I taught you to despise them as the weakest of all creatures . . . but I may have been wrong about that." It was the first time in his life that Tor had heard his father admit to a possibility that he might have been wrong.

Tor jumped out of his chair, went to the fireplace, and crashed his fists against the great marble mantelpiece. Gerade waited, watching his son with an expression that might have been pity in a man of more human compassion.

After a long and loaded silence, Tor asked gutturally, as if the words were forced out of his mouth against his will, "What was she like?"

"She was a strong woman, as strong as I. No, she—she was stronger, inside. In her will, in her spirit, in the depth and breadth of her courage. You've seen her pictures. You know what a lovely thing she was, how fine, how delicately made. But inside she was iron, strong and pure."

Tor whirled, and Gerade was taken aback at the tight fury

marring his features. "And now, after forty years, you have decided to tell me, old man, that she believed in the Christian God?"

Tor's fury merely made Gerade more distant. "Yes. She made no show of it, but I knew it before I married her. But I, who had already conquered so many enemies, failed to conquer the spirit that was in your mother. I also failed to conquer the love I had for her. When she died it broke my heart, and almost ruined me as a man."

"That must have surprised your enemies who thought you never had a heart. It certainly would have surprised me, if I'd been old enough to understand," Tor remarked coldly.

Anger flared through the older man. "What possible use can there be in this maundering, Tor? You've had a classical education. You know that a man is more than a body and more than a mind. One of the old English poets wrote: 'I tune my instrument here at the door.' He spoke of going to be with God."

Tor, with measured steps, returned to his chair and sat. Crossing one booted ankle over his knee, he said in a curiously flat voice, "And now, just at this time, you have decided to contemplate your mortality and the disposition of your soul. How very odd."

Gerade ignored his son's peculiar demeanor and words and continued with the thoughts that were just now surfacing in his mind. "I have always thought that Christianity was very foolish, just a weak man's excuse for silly delusions of grandeur after he died, when he didn't have the courage to rise above mediocrity and stupidity and timidity on this earth. But sometimes . . . more often now . . . I wonder if it is real, very real, perhaps the only truth." He smiled faintly. "I'm like the old Roman emperor—which one was it? He had done all he could to stamp out the Christian church but failed. When he died, his last words were, 'Galilean, Thou hast conquered!'"

In a voice so quiet Gerade could barely hear him, Tor said, "Never. Not in the past, not now, not forever." His eyes burned.

Gerade was shocked and bewildered . . . but he lost the thread and the ominous foreboding of the moment, for the infernal pain racked him again. His sculpted features washed out a sickly gray, while the cruel saber scar was a ropy worm of red. He leaned back in his chair, his body stiffening with the unbearable pain. It was so appalling this time that not only could Gerade not hide it, he could barely keep from wailing.

This time his son offered no solicitations. In an odd, surreal dream-tone, he began to speak. Gerade could hardly hear him for the shrieking of blood in his ears, and he could barely see him, for in his agony his eyes were not focusing clearly.

"You're dying, aren't you? It's odd. I always thought that you would live forever, that you were so strong and invincible that nothing would ever weaken you or kill you. As it has turned out, however, I am the one who has triumphed, Father. I am banishing my enemies; I have won over the hearts and minds and even the very souls of tens of thousands of strong men; I never waver in my determination or my purpose. But most important, Father, I have triumphed over *you.*"

Sweat, chilly and clammy, was moistening Gerade's forehead and upper lip. With a shaking hand, he brushed above his eyes. Tor watched with clinical interest. "What—what—" Gerade stopped and licked his lips, then began again. "What are you bleating on about, Tor?"

Anger, raw and savage, turned Tor's features into something alien and terrible. "Don't ever speak to me in that manner again!" Gerade flinched, and suddenly Tor calmed down, his face assumed its normal cast. "I'm merely telling you, Father, as I promised. You told the story of your soul. I heard you. Now that you are dying, like an ignorant and superstitious peasant woman, you're considering crawling on your belly, drooling and sobbing, to the Christian God. It would be amusing if it weren't so pathetic."

Count Gerade von Eisenhalt's eternal fate—as it had for ages and for countless men and women—hinged on the next few moments. Tor waited, his eyes burning with a secret dark glee, as his father struggled with terrible pain, with great grief, with horrible loss, with fear and loneliness and longing for God—and also with the enchanting and seductive vision of dying an invincible and proud icon of man's power.

Gerade dropped his eyes, took a ragged breath, and said hoarsely, "I am getting older, and I contemplate eternity as any thinking man must do. It does not mean, Tor, that I am ready to be turned into a sniveling, low church hymn-singer."

And so his eternity was sealed.

Tor smiled, and if Gerade had seen it, he might have been truly afraid for the first time that night. When his father looked up, however, Tor's features were impassive. With mild emphasis, Tor said, "I cannot die, Father. I know that this triumph, in particular, had nothing to do with your supposed begetting of me. But I offer it to you as a sop . . . of vinegar, if you will," he said, with mild amusement.

Gerade had no idea what he was talking about; the pain was subsiding, but it had left him weak and a little disoriented—and vastly relieved and hugely grateful. To whom, he did not know nor care.

"He shot me twice, you know. Point-blank, in the chest. Today not even a small crimson mark remains," Tor said conversationally. "Poor fellow; he couldn't kill me, though it certainly seemed that he should have. And then he died, rather badly. It took a long time, it seems . . . but I'm not too sure of that. I was a bit distracted at the time by other matters."

Obviously struggling, Gerade stammered, "Tor—Tor—are you saying that you were *shot*? In the chest, twice? And no one even *notified me*?"

"You might say that I didn't notify anyone," Tor said, with bizarre humor. "The bullets did not touch me, Father. They couldn't harm me. Nothing, and no one, on this earth can harm me ever again."

Gerade stared at his son, his eyes round with surprise, and something close to alarm.

"You believe me, don't you?" Tor asked, with a certain quiet menace.

Gerade swallowed hard; he couldn't look away from Tor's heated gaze. Finally, he managed to croak, "Yes. Yes, I believe you."

"Yes, you do," Tor agreed, a clear threat. "I wandered the desert for nine days. No food touched my lips, no water quenched my thirst, not a drop of my blood was spilled . . . and I saw no man. For nine days."

"What—what did you see in the desert, Tor? What happened to you?"

He rose and stood over his father, his presence and strength suddenly terrifying to the old man. "I saw no *man*," he repeated with urgency, "but I saw the truth in the form of my spirit-father, and I saw my destiny, and I saw myself. *I saw no man.*"

He began to pace, his steps hard and pounding. "I am going to rule this entire world, Father," he said in a thunderously deep voice quite unlike his own. "I have conquered much of Europe. When this old and decrepit continent is subdued, Asia, including that most accursed Middle East, will know my fury. But first"—he smiled, a terrible grimace—"first of all, I will have the pleasure of turning our mightiest and most despised enemy of all into a barren and forsaken wasteland. Only worms and poisonous plants and vipers will thrive there. I have set my plan in motion. It will begin soon, and it will end quickly."

Gerade struggled to breathe evenly; he was gasping with sheer shock. "Are you—are you talking about America?"

"Of course."

"Tor—Tor—are you mad? Are you insane?" Gerade recovered some of his strength in fury. "I have worked for years—decades!—to isolate that accursed country, in her laziness and weakness and cowardice! And I, almost single-handedly, have succeeded! Now she is nothing but a fat slug, slopping up the world's goods and paying for them with *the only money that has any worth in this world*, you fool! Don't you understand what it will do to the global economy if America is decimated?"

Tor turned to face his father, and the exasperated amusement on his face convinced Gerade, more than ever, that his son had gone irretrievably mad. "Do I understand?" Tor mocked him. "Of course. Do I care? I do not."

Gerade started choking. His face, which had been a pasty shade of gray, started turning a dire warning red. When he managed to swallow the bile rising from his horror and uncontrolled fury and regain his breath, he gasped, "You—you can't do this, Tor. You will not do this. It's . . . insane! I forbid you, and I will fight you as long as I live!"

Tor cocked his head slightly to the side with detached interest. "Too bad. Father, you look very ill. Here, let us have more of General—or should I say Emperor—Napoleon's brandy, and calm down and discuss this like the intelligent and civilized men that we are. I think we both might be a little overwrought."

Gerade was mollified slightly by Tor's calm reasonableness, and jerkily he nodded. "Yes, yes—please—a drink would help . . ."

Tor went to the low marble table between their chairs, maneuvering so that he stood in front of his father. He stared down at the bottle, at the two graceful glasses, at the amber liquid that was so precious it could not be priced. He saw nothing, however, but a dark gray shimmering light, like a candle shining through black gauze. He felt as though he were standing on the very edge of a precipice; one wrong step . . . no, one wrong move . . . he would fall, and fall, and fall, and forever . . .

I cannot die . . . I cannot be killed. I have power, I learned power, in those stark days of unforgivable exploding light in the desert, and those dark and whispering cold nights . . . I learned of you, from you, Father, my real father, my father of blood and iron, of weeping and terror and

gnashing of teeth, of power such as this world has never seen before . . .
this pitiful little shamble of a man behind me is not my father. He is
merely a pothole in my Roman road, a chafe in my skin, a bone that
could catch in my throat and choke me . . .

He dies, Tor! Now!

For a breath-stealing moment, Tor thought that the death
curse had been said aloud; he even wondered if he had said the
words. But in the next breath, Tor surrendered to all of the power,
knowing full well the terror and the weeping and the blood and
iron that followed.

He poured two fingers of brandy into each of the balloon
glasses. Slowly, with precise and cautious movements, Tor thrust
his forefinger into the heavily fragrant golden liquid. On this, his
left forefinger, was a heavy beaten-silver ring, curiously wrought,
with the four eternal circles crowning it. The brandy moved,
slopped, and three golden rings radiated outward to rise high
against the side of the glass. Then it was still. Tor handed the glass
to his father, then picked up the other one and raised it high.

"To my father," he said in a low voice.

Gerade barely noticed; he longed for the coarse burning
warmth to numb his fright and his pain and his overwrought
mind. He took a long drink.

Tor stood rigid, watching as his father's light blue eyes
widened, then distended, seeming to strain out of their sockets. A
wisp of smoke, bearing a noxious odor, rose from between Gerade's
twisted lips.

"They called it Prussian blue—or iron blue. The color, you
know," Tor whispered. "Because it was invented by one of our
esteemed ancestors—a Prussian of high family, Heinrich de
Diesbach. And from Prussian blue they made hydrocyanic acid . . .
it is rather fitting, don't you think?"

Count Gerade von Eisenhalt could not answer; his tongue and
lips had burned away, leaving a horrid stench on the air. He was,

unfortunately, still breathing. Obviously he wasn't listening to Tor; perhaps in those last seconds of life he was crying out to the Galilean he had scorned only a few short minutes before.

But Tor thought that unlikely. Drinking Prussic acid, though a quick way to die, was hellishly painful.

Tor continued, "I might have chosen for you to die like a man, like a true Prussian soldier, or a Junker nobleman . . . but he wouldn't allow it. My real father, my spirit-father . . . do you understand?"

Gerade von Eisenhalt, mercifully, was dead.

Count Tor von Eisenhalt thoughtfully sipped his fine Napoleon brandy, and reveled in glorious visions of his destiny. It awaited him, soon, so soon . . .

America One

Washington National Airport, Washington, D.C.

Though America had by choice become a weakened country, she was still viewed as a dangerous, though sluggish, giant by the rest of the world. In the same cautious analysis, her president was still considered to be the most powerful man on earth.

President Bishop Beckwith stood at the door of America One, the titanic C-6 Ajax that had been outfitted as palatially as any luxury hotel, posing for the Cyclops live comm of his and his family's departure for the West Coast. Though he waved and cheerily smiled, his thoughts were dwelling upon this irony—of his great power, and the near-impossibility of wielding it.

Unconsciously his arm tightened around his wife. Josephine Beckwith was a rather insignificant woman, only modestly pretty and rather shy. She adored Beckwith with all of her heart. She was only twenty-eight and was pregnant with his fifth child, her first. Behind them were Beckwith's four children by his first wife, who had died: his two sons, proud U.S. Marines, and his two daughters, one in junior high and the other in high school. It was an excellent photo op, for they were a photogenic family.

Beckwith's wide smile, when seen up close, looked hot-glued onto his face. "Come on, I think this is enough."

The family went inside, followed closely by an army of Secret Service men, aides, staff, and of course, Beckwith's beloved Marine honor guard. As soon as they were out of the reach of Cyclops's prying eye, Beckwith loosened his tie, took off his coat, and settled down to talk to his wife privately for a while, which was a rare and welcome interlude for him. He felt the power of the engines throughout his solid body as the enormous aircraft began lumbering along the landing strip.

Jo sank gratefully into the seat beside him, holding a tomato juice.

She was rarely without a glass of it these expectant days; in spite of the fact that medical technology had established that pregnant women's cravings were psychosomatic, Josephine Beckwith wanted tomato juice day and night, and whatever the first lady of the United States wanted, she got.

They stared out the window as the green grass of the runway turned into a long verdant blur. "Jo," Beckwith said in a low voice, "I've come to a decision about how I'm going to spend the rest of my term."

Jo studied him with serene blue eyes. "This sounds important."

"It is. Right now it's just kind of an intention. I haven't really got my tactics in mind, but I do have a strategic goal."

Secretly amused at her husband's habit of the military way of thinking, she merely asked, "Can you tell me about it?"

He looked directly into her eyes and smiled gently. "I can tell you about it, Josephine. Always."

She returned his smile with a Madonna-like one of her own.

Encouraged, he said in a very low tone, "I'm going to figure out how to dismantle this accursed Man and Biosphere Project. It's an atrocity. It's like a tumor. Shoving Americans into little boxes in twenty-something cities! It's—it's criminal!"

"But Bishop, it's such a well-entrenched project. The bureaucracy itself involves thousands of people. And you know very well that the Executive Council has gotten control of almost half the economy since they took over Cyclops and Proto-Syn and Earth's Light."

"I know all that," he growled. "It doesn't matter."

"But how can you—one man—possibly do such a thing?" Jo asked, distressed.

He turned to her, then took both her slender hands in his. His steel-colored eyes glinted with cold fire. "Jo, this is the United States of America, the most powerful, the wealthiest, the most blessed nation the earth has ever seen. I still see it—and I don't care how silly and fatuous it sounds—as the land of the free and the home of the brave. And

I'm the leader of this nation. I can lead her to a better and nobler future, as our past was."

She stared deeply into his fevered gaze for long moments, and then she whispered, "Yes, Mr. President, I know you can. And, Bishop, I love you very much."

"Jo, I love you, too."

The words were certainly not the worst ones to have on your lips at the moment of death. The plane cleared the runway and turned upward in the familiar sharp ascent. The cabin dissolved in a burst of phosphorous white flame. The last breath that President Bishop Beckwith took cooked his lungs, but he never knew it. He died instantly, along with every human being on America One.

The camera had recorded the takeoff and all of the cameramen blinked stupidly at the huge ball of flame that vaporized the C-6 Ajax. One of them finally gasped, "It's gone! The president—he's gone!" His horrified gaze fixed on the mile-high black-and-white explosion of flame, he could think of nothing else to say. "He's gone—he's gone!"

One moment of time, one fiery blast.

All the hopes and dreams of America, the land of the free and the home of the brave, died in that moment, too.

PART III

AUTUMNAL EQUINOX

And they shall look unto the earth; and behold trouble and darkness, dimness of anguish; and they shall be driven to darkness.
—ISAIAH 8:22

"Lord," answered Lecanius, as pale as a wall, "the whole city is one sea of flame; smoke is suffocating the inhabitants, and people faint, or cast themselves into the fire from delirium. Rome is perishing, Lord."
—HENRYK SIENKIEWICZ, QUO VADIS

*And we are here as on a darkling plain
Swept with confused alarms of struggle and flight,
Where ignorant armies clash by night.*
—MATTHEW ARNOLD, DOVER BEACH

FOURTEEN

T HIS DAWN BEGINS A DAY of strength through unity.
   "Today is the autumnal equinox. On this magical day all
   of the spiritual forces from which we draw our strength—
the earth, the moon, the sun, the stars—are in perfect harmony.
Each of you, if you will meditate on our Lady Earth, and the high
and noble spirits of all of her wonders, will gain knowledge and
wisdom and dominion from her . . ."

Oberstleutnant Rand von Drachstedt turned from the window
to glance at the great Cyclops screen for a moment. The picture
was a breathtaking view of dawn at sea. A fingernail moon faded to
a mere ghost in the lightening sky. A sliver of vivid orange signaled
the rising sun, and the placid ocean's horizon line glowed a rich
plum. Minden Lauer's voice overprint floated, interweaving with
the colors and the light and the whisper of waves.

Frowning, Drachstedt turned to study his aide-de-camp,
Oberleutnant Jager Dorn. Dorn was seated at the small worktable
in his plain barracks room, staring almost slack-jawed at the
Cyclops. Seeing his assistant's obsessive attention to Minden
Lauer's Earth's Light broadcast, Drachstedt restlessly turned back
to stare out the window at the spotlessly clean street below. It was
Officers' Row, the smallest street on Patrick Air Force Base, which
for the last three years had belonged to the German Luftwaffe 99th
Air Wing.

Beyond the street and a generous expanse of green parade ground, Drachstedt knew that men were still working feverishly, spraying the eight great C-6 Ajax transports. Since President Beckwith's death—still unexplained—in *America One*, which was an Ajax, the Americans had superstitiously shunned the enormous planes. The Germans had bought six of them for half their cost. The polymer spray with its sea salt content was the only sealant that would keep out this dreadful organism that actually reduced one of the elemental powers of the universe to nothing but a germ's offal. *So bizarre . . . all of it is unsettling . . .* , Drachstedt reflected uneasily.

Even as he had turned his eyes and attention away from the Cyclops, he felt a mental tug, a nagging imperative to watch the broadcast and especially to direct his hearing to absorb Minden Lauer's husky, erotic voice. *I thought she must use subliminal messaging . . . that is the only explanation I could think of for the—the urgent command, the irresistible pull one feels to attend to her broadcasts.*

But then Colonel Drachstedt had found out that Minden Lauer only did live broadcasts, with real-time audio. She had even admitted, with amusement, that no one could explain—including she herself—why recorded broadcasts were not watched and received nearly as avidly as her "live communications." Contributions for recorded broadcasts were always about one-third of the contributions for her live comms.

It had disquieted Colonel Drachstedt when the Lady of Light had told him this. Now he felt even more repelled by the throaty urging of her voice that was so hard to blot out.

"*Oberleutnant* Dorn, if I am not intruding too much on your time, I would like to go over the plans for Project Final Unity again," Drachstedt said, much more sharply than he intended.

"Hmm? Oh . . . oh, yes, of course, sir," Dorn responded with some confusion. He touched a button on the remote control, and the Cyclops screen changed from Minden's lovely form on some high rooftop to the Cyclops red eye logo. "I'm sorry, sir, I didn't realize that you required my attention. I was just . . . just . . ."

"Yes, I know," Drachstedt said gruffly. Turning away from the window, he eased himself into the uncomfortable straight chair at the desk by Dorn. He hesitated a moment, then said as casually as he could manage, "She is enchanting, I must admit. Is she quite so—absorbing in private?" Drachstedt had never asked Jager about his private time with Minden Lauer, and Dorn had never mentioned it to his superior officer.

But now the handsome young lieutenant answered readily, though his smooth brow furrowed. "She is an extraordinary woman. Of course, you've seen that she's quite beautiful, and very—uh—eager. But I'm not sure . . . it's somehow just not the same as when she's doing these live comms . . . it's like she—Minden—is just sort of a—an imitation of the Lady of Light. A very good imitation, an excellent likeness . . . but still not nearly as . . . haunting and entrancing as the Lady of Light. I'm sorry, sir, I know I'm not making much sense, but I can't think of any other way to explain it."

Drachstedt shook his head, a dismissive gesture. "Never mind, Jager. You understand that I don't care about your private life. It's just that she's such a pivotal part of this complex plan that I feel I ought to understand her better than I do."

Again Lieutenant Dorn was perplexed. "Of course, sir. But I can't help you much with that. I don't understand her strange sorcery either."

Drachstedt thought that the word *sorcery* might be much too accurate a description of this situation. Ever since the night three months ago when they'd met with Vice President Luca Therion (who was president now) and Minden Lauer and Commissar Alia Silverthorne, Drachstedt had been apprehensive about many events surrounding Project Final Unity: about the ease with which they'd deceived the vice president; Count Gerade von Eisenhalt's untimely heart attack within a week, and President Bishop Beckwith's death the next day; about the way their German scientists had, in such a short time, been able to shape and design the *Thiobacillus chaco* to be of such phenomenal, and favorable, use to Germany.

The chain of events had seemed to Drachstedt as if there were some forces—elemental and inexplicable forces—that he could neither account for nor control. Being a pragmatic man, Drachstedt attempted to dismiss what he viewed as irrational fears. It had been difficult for him to ignore his deepest instincts, however, as his apprehensions had grown, instead of diminished, as the time for Project Final Unity had neared.

It was all very troublesome to a staunchly rational man like Rand von Drachstedt. He didn't mention his misgivings to his assistant, however. He just felt compelled to go over the final plans—again.

"All right, Lieutenant Dorn. Step-by-step, explain to me what you and the technical team have told the Americans," he ordered brusquely.

Dorn let a small sigh escape him, though he took care not to let his harsh superior officer see it. But they had, after all, been over the finalized plans hundreds of times. In just a few hours Project Final Unity would begin. Even if his commander found a fatal flaw, it was too late to do anything about it. Still, he obediently began, "We have told the Americans, and we have offered them authoritative documentation as proof, that tonight at approximately five o'clock, the organism will be inserted into the output coils of key step-up and step-down power transformers. This will isolate the crucial 'pockets,' the small areas that the vice president— I mean, the president—indicated for blackout. We have further told them that the insertion of the ohm-bug will not actually affect electrical production; only small segments of the distribution lines."

"What did you call it?" Drachstedt asked abruptly.

"Sir? Oh, yes, the 'ohm-bug.' That's what Commissar Silverthorne calls it, sir. I assume it's from Ohm's law, a measure of electrical resistance. Georg S. Ohm, one of our nineteenth-century kinsmen, invented the calculation, by the way, sir."

"It would appear that we always have been ahead of them, would it not?" Drachstedt said dryly. "Yet we've never been able to best this country in any way."

"Until now," Dorn said arrogantly.

"Perhaps," Drachstedt replied in a neutral tone. "It still appears to me that they have only defeated themselves; we are only incidental bystanders, so it is an empty triumph to an old soldier like me. Continue, please."

"Yes, sir. The ohm-bug, we have assured them, will travel only in the direction of the flow of the electrical current. That means it will not back up into their production plants."

"And they truly believed this—meaningless technical babble," Drachstedt rumbled with disbelief.

"We had most convincing charts, graphs, algorithms, logarithms, and detailed maps, sir," Dorn assured him. "Our technical team performed miracles."

"Haven't we all," Drachstedt growled. "Including our genetic engineers. They've actually engineered this organism to die out, practically upon command. That I do find amazing."

"Yes, sir, they have. It's just that we've altered the exact extinction rate in what we've told the Americans. We've shown them projections of exactly what they wanted; Site A ohm-bugs to die out within a month and Site B bugs within three months."

"But actually, all of the organisms are supposed to die out completely within a six-month period, correct?" Drachstedt asked cautiously. "That is certain, is it not, Lieutenant Dorn?"

"Yes, sir, our genetic engineers assure us that the organism will quite simply starve to death within six months."

"They'd better," Drachstedt said darkly. "This vast and rich country won't do Germany a whit of good if we can't produce any electricity here."

"I can't believe Commandant von Eisenhalt wouldn't realize that, sir," Dorn said evenly. "Naturally, the genetic engineers understand that if their extinction rate is not accurate, they would have to answer to him."

Drachstedt nodded with more certainty. He, and Lieutenant Dorn, the genetic engineers, and everyone else under Count Tor von Eisenhalt's command understood what a grave thing it would be to displease him. One simply did not do that.

Finally Drachstedt said thoughtfully, "And if I understand it correctly, the actual project will be launched much as we have represented to the American Final Unity Team. The organism will be inserted—initially at least—exactly as you told them, correct?"

"Yes, sir. At five o'clock this evening. By seven o'clock, the areas that the president and the lady chose will be without any power at all."

"And within eighty-four hours, it will begin to spread uncontrollably?"

"That's correct, sir. It is calculated that by then the geometric growth rate will reach saturation in the initially infected areas, and it will begin spreading to other areas. Also, three days from now, more of the organism will be released in the West, so as to ensure complete coverage of the United States in four days."

"Four days," Drachstedt murmured gutturally. "The most powerful nation the earth has ever known will fall, and be utterly destroyed, within four days . . ."

Of all the places in the United States of America that had been so wrenchingly changed by the Man and Biosphere Project, there was one sanctuary that had not. The Oval Office, the hallowed seat of power in this most powerful of nations, had changed little since the nineteenth century, when it had been completed.

The room was elegantly furnished, with pieces that had centuries of history behind them. The president's desk was made of wood from the HMS *Resolute*, a British ship that sank in American waters during the 1850s. Americans had salvaged her, and Queen Victoria had graciously shown her gratitude by ordering a desk made from its oaken timbers. Behind the desk was a brand-new chair, custom designed with Kevlar-Genesis armor in the back for a brand-new president. The desk was curiously bare; normally the president did have mementos or photographs on it, the only personal touches in the formal room.

On this day, however, the polished ancient oak expanse was bare except for a single silver tray. On the tray were three heavy and obviously old silver goblets, curiously wrought with ancient runes. Beside them was a tall bottle, pitted and pocked with age, its neck misshapen as it had been blown in an age when only human hands could form the magic of glass from sand and fire.

The tray, the goblets, the old bottle, and the liquor were all gifts from Count Tor von Eisenhalt to President Luca Therion, and his two closest associates in Project Final Unity, Minden Lauer and Alia Silverthorne.

The three were standing in a loose semicircle at the edge of the desk, their eyes frozen as they stared at the three-hundred-year-old grandfather clock. Today, for the first time in centuries, the bass chimes had been reconnected to sound. The small hand majestically moved to one minute before five o'clock with a tiny *snick* that seemed loud in the soundless room.

Luca turned, uncorked the bottle, and poured thick golden liquid into the goblets.

"It is mead, the drink of the gods and goddesses, Tor said," Minden whispered reverently, and took the cup to caress it between both hands.

Alia took hers and glanced down into it; she had never seen mead before. It smelled bitter, but it looked sweet.

Luca kept his eyes on the majestic old clock.

Five deep, sonorous notes sounded.

The president of the United States lifted his heavy silver goblet high. "To Project Final Unity."

Alia Silverthorne, newly appointed chief commissar of the Sixth Directorate, raised her curiously wrought silver goblet. "To Project Final Unity."

Minden Lauer, the Lady of Light, the consort of the most powerful man on earth, raised her goblet with both hands. "To Project Final Unity. To our most high goddess, our Lady Earth. And to our beloved and loyal friend, Count Tor von Eisenhalt. May he live forever."

"May he live forever," Alia and Luca intoned, and then drank.

FIFTEEN

———◆———

THE STORM WAS ENORMOUS. Great, glowering charcoal-colored clouds billowed across the Gulf from the south. They seemed to move entirely too fast for their bulk, the sullen lightning flashes in their secret parts like whips beating them onward.

"Ugly storm," Tessa Kai murmured. Her short, coarse red-gold hair blew straight back from her face.

Victorine said nothing. She had said very little all day.

Dancy popped up between them, leaning far out over the iron railing of the balcony. "Look, a sand-devil," she cried, pointing down to the beach.

"Dancy, don't lean out so far, please," Victorine ordered. Her voice was calm, but her eyes as she stared at the coming fury were narrowed to two sharp black lines.

Dancy looked at her mother curiously, but she did pull herself back from leaning so precariously over the railing. Something was wrong with her mother, she knew. Something had been bothering her all day. Normally Dancy knew exactly the things that upset Victorine, but today she had been as mystified as Grandmother Tessa Kai. Finally Dancy, in her own little straightforward way, decided to stop wondering about it and just ask. Most of the time that worked with her mother. "Mama Vic, what's wrong?"

Victorine gave her a short sidelong glance. "Nothing, Dancy."

"Are you sure? I mean—you're not mad at me, are you?"

That did it. Turning, Victorine gave her a quick hug. "No, of course not. I'm just a little tense, I suppose. Probably because of the storm. It's well documented that the onset of storms can affect people and animals."

Dancy studied her solemnly, but Victorine had again turned away to watch the tempest.

She knows . . . and I've tried so hard to hide it all day. Today is the autumnal equinox . . . Projekt Schlußenheit . . . What does it mean? What's going to happen? Oh, Lord, how glad I will be for this day to be over!

For months Victorine had agonized so much over the coming of the equinox, and Project Final Unity, that she had almost driven herself insane. She had considered all sorts of disasters, including nuclear war, gigantic asteroids destroying the earth, plagues, tidal waves . . . all things fearful and horrible. But as summer drifted by, and days and then the months had passed after the meeting between the vice president (now the president) and the Lady of Light and the Germans, no alert had been announced, no warnings, no instructions, no word at all had come from the government.

Victorine did consider—and tell herself over and over again—that "Project Final Unity" sounded like some kind of Man and Biosphere Project that could be anything from a Save the Gophers program to a new tax burden. It really didn't have the stirring ring of some sort of military alert or a natural disaster plan.

Still, Victorine had been dreading this day.

Then finally, at dawn this morning, she had been somewhat reassured. Minden Lauer's live comm had featured some live shots of the sun rising on Perdido Key, for Victorine had seen the camera crew a few hundred yards down from the condos and had then quickly turned on the Earth's Light broadcast to see the shots on Cyclops. Minden herself had been in Virginia, on the rooftop of her vast mansion that had been built two centuries before. She had installed a soundstage, and often broadcast from there.

If Minden Lauer was still on the East Coast, then Victorine was certain that whatever Project Final Unity was, it was not a widespread natural disaster or a sweeping military alert. Nothing that affected the eastern United States, anyway.

She had celebrated—her sort of devious defiance—by buying real T-bone steaks for their dinner that night. It had cost her forty food credits, when three Proto-Syn steaks cost only eight. Still, it had been well worth it, for her mother's and Dancy's delight. Victorine herself, in spite of her strict self-instruction to stop fretting about nothing, had had very little appetite.

"Thanks again for the real steaks, Mom," Dancy was saying. She grabbed her mother's hand and squeezed it, then held it.

"Yes, Vic, it was so generous of you, thank you," Tessa Kai said warmly.

"You're welcome, both of you," Victorine said. "It's little enough, it seems . . ."

In the blink of an eye, their whole world changed.

But Victorine and Dancy and Tessa Kai didn't know that—yet.

"Drat-rat," Tessa Kai said. "The power's off."

Victorine sighed. "I'm not really surprised, with the storm. It must already be inland, up west. You know where the candles are, don't you, Mother?"

"No, I thought we used them all for that last blowout with the trolls and Goths," Tessa Kai tossed over her shoulder, turning to go back inside Victorine's condo. "All those candles, it looked like a coven or a cathouse or both."

"What's a—" Dancy began.

"Never mind," Victorine said hastily. Tessa Kai had just taken a few steps inside and they heard a thump and then a muffled, "Mmph—ouch."

"I'm coming, Mother," Victorine called. "Just stay where you are."

"Gladly," Tessa Kai muttered. "I think my shin's bleeding. Stupid coffee table right in my way."

"I know, the impertinence of it," Victorine said dryly, skillfully negotiating her way around the memorized path of her furniture. Her eyes adjusted quickly, and she went to the pantry in her kitchen, knelt down, and put her hand right on the flashlight on the left corner of the bottom shelf. "That's odd . . . the flashlight's out. I thought I checked the battery recently. Dancy?"

"Yes, ma'am?" She was a slight shadow by Tessa, leading her to the sofa.

"Get Tessa Kai settled down out of harm's way, and then come put a new battery in this flashlight while I light some candles. Odd," she muttered. She could have sworn she'd checked that flashlight just a few days ago; she'd checked all of them in each condo. Victorine had a schedule for things like that and she never missed anything on her schedule.

She fumbled until she found the box of all the candle stubs she'd saved from the candlelit dinner three months ago. Pure beeswax candles didn't drip, and burned very slowly; even a two-inch stub would burn for hours. Quickly she found the matches and some candleholders, and lit three candles. "Here, Mother, just stay right there." Hurriedly Victorine went to close the glass doors to the balcony. The wind was growing fierce, making the feeble little candle flames bend and struggle.

"Mother, I—I guess this battery's dead too," Dancy said helplessly. "This thing still won't work."

"That's impossible," Victorine scoffed. "It was a brand-new one, dated two years from now. You must have put it in wrong, Dancy. Here, give it to me." Victorine was the type of person who, deep down, thought she could do most things better than anyone.

Resignedly Dancy handed over the flashlight. Actually it was more accurately called a lantern, for it had a four-inch-square light-box with a 9-volt battery. Victorine unloaded the battery, then loaded it again. "You didn't confuse the old battery with the new one, did you, Dancy?" Victorine asked.

"No, Mother. I threw the old one away before I opened the new one."

"All right. Maybe it's the bulb. I don't think I have any new ones. I'll just go over to 703 and get that flashlight."

"Why don't you start up the generator, Victorine?" Tessa Kai asked impatiently.

"Because it's noisy and it smells," she answered shortly, "and probably the power will be back on in a few minutes. I'll be right back."

She grabbed her great round key ring and bustled out the door. The wind caught it and blew it back against the wall with a crash that made Dancy and Tessa Kai jump. Victorine grabbed it, muttering, and with some difficulty pulled it shut.

Dancy said in a small voice, "Something's wrong with Mama."

Tessa Kai swallowed hard, but her voice was light and natural. "Yes, she's a great grump, is what's wrong with her. You come over here and sit by me, Dancy-doodle."

Carefully shielding her candle, Dancy came to sit close to her grandmother. "You know she's been—upset, or something, all day," she continued.

Tessa Kai stared hard at Dancy; the girl kept her face averted, and picked at her Ty-denim jeans. "I know she's been quick and crisp, yes," Tessa Kai said slowly. "But I'm not sure she's upset, exactly."

Dancy looked up at her grandmother, startled. "But Grandmother Tessa Kai, don't you know? Don't you understand? When Mama's upset, she's all pin-striped and focused, like she is when the commissars are coming. When she's relaxed and happy, she's—you know, kind of absentminded and—weird."

Tessa Kai didn't laugh, as she might have under different circumstances. And Dancy wasn't trying to be amusing, not at all. "Yes . . . yes, she has been very much the proper pro today, but I'm not sure she's what you'd call upset, or anything bad, Dancy. I don't think it's anything to be worried about, little girl."

Dancy dropped her head again. "But I do worry, Grandmother. Because I don't think she's upset, either. I think she's afraid."

Tessa Kai shifted restlessly, then picked up Dancy's hand. It was cold. "Afraid of what, darlin'?"

But Dancy never answered, for the door again burst open and Victorine ran in, her strained white face a blur in the deep shadows. Slowly she said, "For some strange reason, the flashlight in 703 doesn't work, either . . . and neither does the one in 705. I'm going to go downstairs and start the emergency generator." She turned and hurried back toward the door, but stopped and said in as normal a tone as she could muster, "Don't worry, you two. I buy all of the batteries for the emergency flashlights in bulk. I'm certain it's just a bad batch or something."

"Mother, wait," Dancy said, jumping to her feet and holding out her hand in a beseeching gesture.

Victorine said calmly, "Now, don't worry, Dancy, everything will be all right. You just stay here with your grandmother and keep her from bashing her other shin, or worse."

"Be . . . careful, Mother," Dancy said tremulously. "It'll be dark in the stairwell."

"I know, I'll be careful. I'll be right back."

Again she had to fight the door to close it. The wind was like a cavalry charge now, stampeding first this way and then the other way. Victorine, from decades of habit, turned left to go to the elevators. After a few steps she stopped, grunting with disgust at herself, and turned around. The exit to the stairwell was directly across from her front door.

For a moment she was afraid she wouldn't be able to get the door opened; it was a three-inch-thick metal fire door, and the wind was charging up the stairwell, fighting Victorine. Then the wind grabbed it and temperamentally tossed it open, and the metal clang sounded like a car crash. Victorine flew down the first six steps. But at the first landing she slowed a little and grabbed the rail. The wind was fitful, slashing her face with stinging fine sand. Almost blinded, she made herself walk carefully. "That would be a nice touch, if I fell down six flights of stairs," she growled to herself. Of course, she wouldn't. There were only six steps, then a landing and turn, and then another six steps to each floor.

At each landing was a three-foot-square open porthole, for which Victorine was glad. If it hadn't been for even the little ambient light from the outside, it would truly be ink-black in the stairwell. Abruptly she stopped and stared upward. Dancy had been right, though how she'd known was a mystery . . .

The emergency lights weren't on.

They were supposed to switch on as soon as the main power source went down.

But Victorine was a practical person, so she added this to her mental list of problems, and started down the stairs again.

When she reached the fourth floor, she stopped and threw herself against the wall, her eyes wide, her heart banging painfully against her chest.

Was someone in the stairwell with her? She thought she'd heard . . . something . . .

She heard it again; it was like a shrieking insane laugh—

"Uhh . . ." A tiny little moan of fear escaped her, and Victorine pressed against the gritty cold concrete wall as if she could plaster herself into it.

It . . . can't be . . . there can't possibly be anyone there . . . I'm just—just—imagining things . . .

She stayed still, straining with every muscle in her body, as if that would help her to hear.

But now all she heard was the wind, beginning as a low groan, rising to a frantic wail; now a banal howl, then an ominous growl . . .

Victorine swallowed, and it was like trying to eat sand, for her mouth and tongue and throat were parched and gritty with fright. "It's just the wind," she said loudly. "It's just the storm!"

The echoes of her voice were lost in the din.

Victorine wrenched herself away from the wall as if she were physically attached to it and started down the stairs again. Her eyes stung, watered, and her skin crawled, and she was panting shallow little desperate breaths. She felt as if someone . . . or some *thing* . . . would any moment lay a hand, clammy and chilling, on her shoulder. Wild and panicked, she ran down the stairs, sling-shotting herself around the corners.

But finally her stolid common sense and her strength of will took over, and Victorine stood still on a step. Though her mind cried out to, she refused to look behind. Straightening her shoulders and grasping the railing hard, she walked with dignity down the last flight of stairs.

As soon as she opened the ground floor door and stepped outside, she lifted her head and gratefully took deep breaths, even though the savage wind tried to snatch them away. Her hair was wild, like thick whips about her face and neck. Impatiently she shoved it back and went to the maintenance room.

The maintenance room was, indeed, flat and impenetrable black, for it had no windows. Victorine struck a match, and was shocked to see her hands shaking as if she were palsied. With a great effort of will, she made them stop trembling, and then lit the candle she'd brought. On the workbench were two small flashlights. Victorine grabbed them and tried first one, then the other. The measure of her confusion and disarray was evident when she was astounded that both of them actually worked. They were cast-offs, cheap plastic lights, and the batteries in both were weak because the lights were blinky and dim. Still, they did work.

But the generator didn't.

It was a keyed-ignition gasoline generator, old but in good condition, for it was used very little, and Victorine serviced it regularly.

But now it had no spark of life, none at all. When Victorine turned the key, it was utterly silent.

"What is going on?" she muttered.

Another small rebellion: She switched off the small flashlight as she stood still and made herself think. *Not going to scare me, not going to get me . . .* , winged by in the back of her mind, but she quickly dismissed such foolish defiance of imaginary terrors.

She stood, concentrating, for perhaps ten seconds. Then, moving deliberately, she switched the flashlight back on and went out to her car. It was a small, beat-up Smith-Deal, ten years old, and it sounded like an ancient sewing machine.

Without even bothering to get in the car, she leaned over to insert the key for manual start.

It was dead.

Her movements slow, she shut the door and leaned against the little car, staring blankly at the boiling clouds above. Three fat raindrops splatted down onto her face, but she didn't notice.

Could it be solar flares? I know that if they are a certain magnitude, they can disturb electrical fields . . . But for how long? Seems that I read it could be for days . . . maybe even months?

Is that what Project Final Unity is? Some—program to deal with the effects of solar flares . . . if it is this strong, if it even affects 9 volt batteries . . . it must be powerful, and the effects must be widespread . . .

But that doesn't make sense! If they knew it was going to happen, and they were formulating some sort of disaster plan . . . why hasn't it been publicized?

As if an immense bucket had been overturned in the heavens, a fierce torrent of rain started.

Victorine jumped as if she'd been stung. Her eyes were wide with alarm. But it wasn't because of the sudden flood of water soaking her.

She ran, her steps hard and frantic, to the stairwell.

It was a terribly hard climb, up seven stories. Victorine ran the entire way, but when she finally reached the condo, she could hardly talk.

Throwing open the door, she stumbled inside. She was soaked, and she was gasping painfully and clutching her side. Hoarsely she shouted, "Water! Now! Fill . . . the tubs . . . and anything you can . . . find! Hurry!"

The water ran for about ten minutes.

And then it, too, died.

Sixteen

———◆———

NIKLAS KESTEVEN WAS A MAN who liked his comforts. He
spared no expense when something appealed to him aes-
thetically, and now as he leaned back with his heavy-
lidded eyes half closed, the feel of the honey-colored leather under
his body pleased him exceedingly. It had cost him four hundred
credits, but now as he ran the tips of his fingers over the material,
a sense of satisfaction came to him.

"This chair, sir," the representative had told him smoothly, "is
covered with leather from cattle grown in a secluded area of
Argentina. The cattle are kept in open fields without any barbed
wire, which would scratch and mar their hides. This gives a perfect
material, none like it in the world." Somehow the idea of cattle
being grown in another hemisphere kept by stock riders for no
purpose other than to give him pleasure was most agreeable to
Niklas. He also got a furtive pleasure from defying the mandates of
the MAB Animal Protection Trade Protocols.

But if the leather-covered chair that gave with each motion of
his body pleased him, the program that he had been watching for
the past hour on the Cyclops did not. Niklas was an accomplished
musician, playing the violin, the flute, and the piano with equal
skill, and had looked forward to the program that was a historical
survey of the history of music in America. The first part of the
program had dealt mostly with theory, for, unfortunately, only old

tintypes existed of the earlier musical genius of America. And of course, none of the actual sounds that preceded the invention of the phonograph had been preserved. He had been clinically interested in the sounds of the first recordings and had been mildly amused at the awkward methods of recording a symphony by a small orchestra. Since there was only one microphone, the musicians had been forced to rush forward, getting themselves as close to the single mike as they could in order to get on the wax tube. Niklas had laughed aloud as players on the woodwinds stampeded forward at the same time, trying to keep the tempo as they crowded around the microphone—and then had made a clumsy retreat as men wagging trumpets had come to take their place. "A barbaric system," he muttered. But at least he had found this segment of ancient film amusing.

When, however, the program had reached the 1960s, Niklas's disgust had begun. He had watched with a scowl as a young man with long side burns, heavy eyelids, and a sensuous face twisted and contorted on the screen of the Cyclops. He was singing a song whose lyrics—as well as his music—made Niklas wince. "You Ain't Nothin' But a Hound Dog" was apparently the title, and the gyrations of the young man were more gymnastic than graceful. The fruity-voiced commentator had said, "Elvis Presley quickly became known as 'Elvis the Pelvis,' and the adulation that young people heaped upon Presley brought a sense of despair and fear to parents throughout America."

Niklas poured himself another drink from the half-empty bottle that sat on the table beside him. He drained it quickly, braced himself for the jolt, then shuddered. "Elvis the Pelvis!" he muttered. "Now *there's* an abomination for you!"

He continued to watch for a time, growing more and more dissatisfied. He watched as a group called the Beatles, according to the commentator, changed the history of the Western world. Again the lyrics and the music seemed to Niklas abominable. And as the rapturous commentator gushed on through hard rock, metal, soft rock, hip-hop, rap, salsa, shock rock, snuff rock, tribal, synthesised, computer-created, and finally Ultimate Reality Self-Expression, his musings evolved from disgust to alcohol-enhanced anger.

What does any of it have to do with music? Niklas ranted to himself. *There's been no real music made for two hundred years!* As he poured another drink, he realized that his movements were slow and unsteady. Draining the half-full glass, he let it drop to the table, and when the sound of it falling seemed muffled and far away he knew that he was, indeed and again, drunk.

In slow motion he reached out, picked up the remote, and switched the Cyclops video off. He then tried a sequence of keys—three times—and finally the sound of a piano filled the room. It was Chopin, Opus Number Ten from the Twelve Etudes. Closing his eyes, Niklas lay back and let the chair embrace him. As the music filled his mind almost like wine filling a bottle, he found peace for a time. He hated all the new music, particularly the artificial and meaningless sounds of the Cyclops-generated self-expressionists. As a student of history, he felt that something had gone wrong; he knew that music, like painting and drama and fiction, had taken a wrong turn somewhere in America. Something close to ecstasy filled him as the recording continued. At least the Cyclops had sound systems of excellent quality. With his eyes closed, he could almost picture Chopin himself playing the melody. Of course, Niklas felt that he himself was better on the piano than Chopin. This streak of egotism touched Niklas in almost every facet of his being.

For a long time the music went on, and he drifted into a coma-like sleep. He came awake with a start and a feeling of vague discontent. Rolling out of the chair, he shut off the music that had gone to Berlioz's "Harold en Italie," a symphony based on an English poet, Byron's *Childe Harold*. Unsteadily he stood up, holding on to the arm of his fine leather chair, waiting for the room to stop revolving. *I drink too much—and I don't sleep well.* He made a ridiculous sight, a big shambling man much like a shaggy bear, sleepy and bewildered. Niklas had always looked more like an illiterate wrestler than he did a physicist and a scientist, but behind the dark brown eyes lay a brain that was almost never inert.

Staggering to the bathroom, he switched on the light, then leaned forward, putting his weight on the lavatory. Staring into the mirror he was filled with disgust at the bleary, bloodshot eyes that stared back at him. "I'm drunk," he muttered. His mouth formed a petulant curve and he snarled, "All right! So I'm drunk! So what? I'm a better man drunk than any other man is sober . . ."

A searing pain struck him over his right eye and nausea rolled low in his gut. He stood shakily, holding on to the lavatory, until the stabbing pain dulled somewhat and the nausea subsided. He filled the lavatory with cold water and splashed his face. Then, with jerky movements, he turned on the shower and the small bathroom steamed up quickly. It was almost too hot to bear, but it felt good to Niklas, who suddenly realized he couldn't remember when he'd last taken a shower. He was letting his personal habits slide, too, and that was an even worse sign than his drinking. With a brush he scrubbed himself all over, even his face and head, until he felt almost raw. Finally he stepped out, shaking his shaggy hair like a wet dog and drying himself briskly. Dressing in clean khakis and a shirt made of old, soft denim, he felt much better.

His stomach rumbled, and he wondered what time it was. Blearily he thought that he didn't even know, down in his steel cocoon, if it was day or night. He headed toward the kitchen, already grimacing, thinking that he had nothing appetizing in his quarters. Then a bland, metallic voice came over his Cyclops: "Attention, please. As of 1900 hours, all Man and Biosphere Directorate facilities in the Shortgrass Steppe Biome are on a Code Yellow Alert. Repeat, Lab XJ2197 is now on a Code Yellow Alert. Unauthorized personnel are to remain in their quarters. All personnel are requested to remain in their directorate facility until all clear on Code Yellow Alert is signaled. Next notification will be at 1950 hours. This Code Yellow Alert is authorized by Chief Commissar Alia Silverthorne."

A red flush crept up the neck of Niklas Kesteven and he cursed eloquently. "Chief Commissar Alia Silverthorne," he grunted. "You, little girl, have never, and will never, tell me what I can and cannot do!" If Niklas had faced it, the depth of his anger and resentment toward his former lover was telling. He flatly denied to himself that he cared for Alia at all, or that he missed her, or that he regretted that he'd lost her. Staunchly he told himself that she'd treated him badly by taking his *chacos* and disappearing like that. Then, after she'd joined the exalted circles of the president and the Lady of Light, she'd snubbed him. So he hated her.

So he told himself . . . sometimes a dozen times a day.

"Stupid commissar drills," he rasped, stamping impatiently into the small cubicle kitchen. "Think they're like real soldiers with real jobs. Idiots." He was like a huge bear that had been confined in a cage and now was being poked by the sharp, pointed sticks of those above him. Rage contended in him, for he was not a man who could bear being controlled. He mimicked the inhuman voice. "No one will be permitted to leave . . ." He cursed again, then grinned ferally. "We'll see who will be 'permitted' to leave . . . !" He lurched toward the door and struck it with a blow as he passed through, leaving his apartment.

Gildan Ives prepared the injector while humming a tune from her childhood. The show had been called "Farmland," and it was the direct reason that she'd eventually decided to become a veterinarian. Gildan had loved the show, with its quirky animals that managed to come up with an amazing problem to solve every week for their viewers, which were many and worldwide. Even Gildan's mother had liked watching the show with her.

She gently picked up a brown and white guinea pig that was very tame and did not struggle. This was the part she hated still, even after twelve years of treating animals. "You trust me enough to let me pick you up, then I do this," she told the pig regretfully, boosting the serum into the meat behind its right shoulder. The guinea pig twitched but made no sound. Setting it back into the open-topped cage, she said, "If it makes you feel any better, it's for your own good, believe me."

Humming the "Farmland" theme again, she hesitated before reaching for another guinea pig. How old had she been when she'd lived to glue herself to the Cyclops and drink in the show? Seven? Eight? And now . . .

"Thirty-two years old today," she spoke aloud, then quickly looked around, relieved that no one was in the lab to hear this confession. She had heard the announcement that no personnel would be permitted to leave their quarters and in a way was relieved. Not that there was anywhere to go, but one of her supervisors, a tall, leathery-faced man with greedy black eyes had been giving her some problems. He was unappealing in every way, at least ten years older than Gildan, which would not have mattered, but he had a sort of oily insinuation that offended even her.

If even I think he's creepy, he must be a real toad . . .

Gildan sighed at the thought, for she had long ago faced the fact that she was not very bright, and was particularly dense about men. She never seemed to be able to figure them out, what they meant, what they wanted, what they intended . . . and she never seemed to learn.

Now her birthday was a depressing weight on her mind. Her thoughts, flinching, flickered back over her life to the series of men with whom she had allied herself over the years. She was rather glad that she could not remember their names or faces very well. The dim memories gave her very little pleasure.

Gildan was one of those intentionally blonde women who were beautiful in youth and adolescence and carried it even into her late twenties. But just this morning she'd studied her face in the mirror and noticed the beginnings of tiny crow's-feet around the eyes—not laugh lines, as she'd tried to tell herself before, but *age* lines. It had depressed her on a day that was supposed to be special. Her hair at the present time was not blonde but a brilliant cherry color, and she'd wondered if there was any gray there beneath the gaudy dye.

Her figure, delineated clearly by the green Ty-nylon jumpsuit that she wore, was that of a young girl. Her body was, in fact, a triumph of body sculpture. Everything had either been planed down or pumped up. Her face also was a tribute to the Beauty Masters. Nose, chin, throat, skin, all were formed into the current fashion of beauty. But she didn't feel pretty. When she inspected her face and body she always found something lacking or something sagging or something less than perfect. Today it was the tiny, fine skin around her sad blue eyes.

She picked up another guinea pig and this time, lost in thought, she injected it without the usual pathos. Suddenly, thirty-two years old seemed *ancient* to her. It struck her that her *mother* had been thirty-two when she'd given birth to Gildan—how was that for old? At that moment, she had to hold herself tightly in hand. She was not a woman given to hysterics, but this penumbra, this shadow that she recognized as fear of the future, had been haunting her more often of late. And now on her birthday it seemed to be more potent and virulent than she had ever known it could be.

The sudden sound of a door hissing open interrupted her frightening thoughts, and she turned quickly to see Niklas Kesteven enter. He was not wearing a white smock uniform as he usually did, but a pair of khaki slacks and a floppy denim shirt. Her quick eyes took in the ruffled appearance, the bloodshot eyes, the shambling gait, and she realized that he was half-drunk. That was an odd thing about Niklas. He never seemed completely drunk, but lately he'd never been dead sober, either.

"Hello, Gildan."

"Hi, Niklas." Sudden hope flared in her. Did he know it was her birthday somehow? Did he bring a gift? No, no, a gift didn't matter—just a "Happy birthday" would suit her just fine. She didn't realize just how lonely she was until that moment.

"What are you doing?" he asked idly.

Gildan held up the injector. "Giving shots. You have to get in line, though."

"Nah, I don't believe in waiting for my turn." Niklas took her arm, his eyes glittering. "Let's go up top to the ranch house, Gildan."

"But we were ordered to stay in our rooms. Speaking of which, why are you out wandering?"

He grabbed her and kissed her roughly. "Looking for you, of course. And you worry too much about rules, rules, rules. Come on." He tugged her toward the door, barely giving Gildan a chance to put down the injector.

"But, Niklas, the commissars—they'll stop us at—"

"They'll *try* to stop us."

Gildan allowed him to lead her to the elevator. She liked Niklas very much, despite the arrogant coolness he exuded most of the time. He was, in his rumpled way, strangely attractive. He wasn't handsome, but Gildan had known her share of good-looking men. There was just something about Niklas that drew her to him. He'd always been friendly to her in that slightly insinuating way, but he'd never tried to seduce her.

In the elevator, Niklas tried to kiss her, but she held him back. "Stop it, Niklas! Not here."

"Why not?"

"I don't like these mirrors. I think it's for the commissars so they can see who's in here."

"You think?" Niklas said carelessly. "Hello there, *Unterscharführer! Sieg Heil!*" He stabbed the air with his open hand.

Gildan had no idea what an *unterscharführer* or a *sieg heil* was, but she gamely giggled and said, "Today's my birthday."

"Really? Then how about a birthday kiss?"

Gildan pouted, petulantly pushing him away. She really didn't want to spend this night alone, but she craved at least a *little* tenderness. Then she thought, *I'm with the wrong man for that.*

Niklas saw her disappointment and said solemnly, "Happy birthday, Gildan. It will just make this night more special."

Gildan smiled her thanks just as the door opened to Level One. Four commissars waited warily outside the doors. One of them, a burly man with a scar near his mouth, challenged, "What are you doing out of your quarters, Doctor Kesteven?"

Niklas barely gave him a glance as he led Gildan toward the ranch elevator. "To get a breath of fresh air."

"Hold it, Doctor—" The big man moved to block their way. "We're on alert and you know it. You know the rules."

Niklas grinned at Gildan. "There's that word again." To the commissar, Niklas directed the full force of his size and authority. "Yes, I'm well aware of your rules. But are you aware that a certain *friend* of mine—I believe her name is Alia Silverthorne—is now Chief Commissar of the Sixth Directorate? Were you aware of that small fact?"

The commissar hesitated, licked his lips, then said, "Yes."

"I'm sure the Chief Commissar is very busy, wherever she is, and wouldn't like to be disturbed over a matter so trivial as this. Do you agree?"

Looking over at his comrades and not getting any help from them, the commissar seemed to shrink in size before their eyes. "I don't . . . I mean, it wouldn't be—"

"Oh, get out of our way. Or shoot us," Niklas growled as he shoved past the man. Gildan expected another warning or threat, but the commissars said nothing more.

When they emerged into the ranch house, Niklas promptly used the same tactics to order the two plainclothes commissars who occupied the house as cover for the biome lab below. After consulting by radio with the cowed commissars on Level One, they promptly took their leave.

Niklas led Gildan toward one of the bedrooms. "Now, here I am, finally, all alone with the birthday girl."

Gildan smiled weakly, but resisted. "Can't we just talk for a while?"

"Talk about what?" Niklas asked roughly. The drinks had loosened his reactions and he was really not in the mood for anything more than a distraction from his bothersome thoughts. "What would you want to talk about?"

"Anything. Tell me what you did when you were a boy."

Seeing that he was going to have to pay for Gildan's favors, not with money but with attention, Niklas sighed inwardly and went to the kitchen to fix them a drink. This was shaping up to be one of those nights that only ended up in *cuddling*, for crying out loud.

Gildan seated herself on the horseshoe-shaped sofa in the living room. When Niklas handed her the drink, she only sipped at it and then left it untouched. He sat beside her, seeing her expectant look. "Why do you want to hear about my childhood?"

"I don't know. I just do. Just think of it as my birthday wish."

Niklas sighed and shook his head, then began speaking. Strangely enough, after he had talked for a time rather perfunctorily of his boyhood, he found it comforting. He reflected that telling Gildan was like speaking down a well. She didn't interrupt, didn't ask questions or make mindless comments. She just listened, with that wide-eyed, rather blank look she had. He found some sort of satisfaction in relating how he had grown up, and as he did so he was brought through the remembrance of how lonely his childhood had been. His parents had abandoned him early to paid nannies and keepers, anyone to take the responsibility off their shoulders. He had been diagnosed early as having an astronomically high IQ and had thrown himself into his studies with a fervor that pleased all of his instructors. "I missed out on a lot growing up. No sports, no hobbies—nothing but study."

Gildan stared at him for a moment before speaking. "That's very sad, Niklas. It sounds so . . . barren and impersonal."

Niklas shrugged. "It made me what I am."

"But it sounds like it was so *hard*."

"Yes it was. But you can't go back. You can never go back."

"But you can look ahead," Gildan said. She reached out, put her hand on his cheek, drew him to her, and kissed him. He reached for her and was surprised at how welcome, and somehow comforting, her softness and unquestioning yielding were to him.

Though the Cyclops in the room wasn't actually on, it was of course in standby mode, and it made the small alert chimes for a broadcast. Both of them turned to see the red eye.

A bloodless male voice intoned, "Attention, please. Code Yellow Alert has been upgraded to Code Green Alert in the Olympic Biome and the Stanislaus-Toulomne Biome. All Sixth Directorate facilities are on a Code Red alert; all other Man and Biosphere Directorate facilities will remain at Code Yellow at this time. Unauthorized personnel remain at your facility. Lab XJ2197, all personnel are restricted to quarters until further notice. Next notification, twenty hundred hours."

"What does all that mean, Niklas?" Gildan asked plaintively.

"I don't know, and I don't care. The Sixth Directorate thinks they're the KGB, the CIA, and the ISS all rolled into one big ball. The devil take all commissars." He jumped to his feet, pulling Gildan with him. "Come on, Gildan. I need you . . ."

SEVENTEEN

———✦———

EVER SINCE LITTLE BIRD HAD come into young womanhood, she had been aware of the attraction she had for men. Some men she had flatly refused. Some of them she had given her body to, some her friendship, some her love, and one man had completely stolen her heart.

All of them had left her, sooner or later, with one excuse or another, so Little Bird had also become wary and taught herself to keep to herself. That didn't keep them from trying, however, and ever since she had met Cody Bent Knife, she had been trying to prepare herself for the moment when he would reach out for her. It was difficult, though. For the first time in a very long time, she didn't want to push a man away, and she could get no satisfaction from anticipating the control she would finally be able to exert over him when she repulsed him.

But as the days and the weeks progressed and Cody showed no attraction to her, Little Bird became first puzzled and then a little annoyed. More than once she had looked in the small mirror that she had brought, studying her features, although she knew them well enough. Little Bird's pure Apache blood gave her no pretensions of soft prettiness; her features were as sculpted and still as the eternal rock faces of the desert. Her dark eyes were bottomless, fathomless pools, giving no hint of the heat of her soul. Her sharp cheekbones and the uncompromising line of her jaw accentuated the resolute mouth. No, she would never be pretty or beautiful; but she was a compelling woman that men desired.

Night had fallen swiftly as it does in the desert. Little Bird sat with her back against one of the intricately laid stone walls of the room that Cody Bent Knife had chosen. He had covered the floor with fresh sage, and the sweet wild scent filled the room. Little Bird closed her eyes and breathed deeply. She loved the smell of sage and smoky mesquite.

"Here's tea, Little Bird," Cody said politely, setting a rough earthenware cup down by her side, then moving to the other side of the fire. The primeval light made grotesque shapes on the walls of the small room and lit Cody's face with a primitive hunter's light. His dusky skin and eyes were dark mirrors of the flames, and Little Bird studied his face with narrowed eyes. He sat down, not next to her as most men would have done, but squatting on his heels across the fire. As he sipped his tea, his eyes over the rim of his cup showed amusement at her perusal.

"Don't you like girls, Cody?" Little Bird asked caustically.

"That's like asking a man if he likes food," he answered wryly.

"What is *that* supposed to mean?"

"I mean I like some kinds of food but not other kinds. I like venison but I don't care for snakes."

"You're saying that you like some women but not others."

"Isn't that the way it is with you? If I asked you do you like men, you wouldn't answer yes or no. You'd say I like this one or I don't like that one."

The sophistry of his reply irritated Little Bird, even though it had been close to her own private reflections of just a few moments before. "I think there's something wrong with you. You're not normal."

"Plenty would agree with that," he remarked calmly. "Why do you ask? Do you need a man?"

His bluntness irritated Little Bird. "No, I don't need any man, but if I did, I wouldn't ask you."

"But you just did."

"No I didn't, I was just talking about you and women in general. That's all."

He shrugged carelessly, his expression still tainted with laughter.

The conversation displeased Little Bird. She was not accustomed to having to draw men on like this. "Don't you get lonely?" she finally asked. "Don't you need anybody?"

"Everyone gets lonely. Everyone needs human contact," he answered remotely.

"You don't ever show it. You're the most isolated human being I've ever seen—except for that retard Zoan. You cut yourself off from everyone."

Cody did not answer for a time. "I've always been outside somehow, Little Bird. I can't explain it, but it's as though everyone else forms some sort of group and I can't join it."

"Well, what about all of us who have come to follow you? Don't you feel a part of us? Of our search, of our dreams, our hopes and visions?"

"It's just—different for me," Cody said rather lamely. The actual truth was that since they had met Zoan, and had come to Chaco Canyon, Cody had felt less secure in his mission, and more cut off from his followers, than he ever had before. He had tried to analyze these unwelcome changes in his spirit, but he felt as if he'd been disconnected from his anchors of visions and beliefs. Somehow Zoan had jarred him loose from his internal moorings. He simply wasn't communing with anyone, not with himself, not with the spirits he'd come to believe in, not with his followers—not even with his spirit-father, Benewah Two Color.

But sometimes these thoughts and responsibilities were just too burdensome and murky for Cody Bent Knife. Yes, he was a visionary, and yes, he was the last warrior of his people . . . but he was also a flesh-and-blood young man of only nineteen years. His thoughts and longings became more simple and tangible as he considered Little Bird and her awkward invitations.

The hungers that come to all men stirred within him. Little Bird was wearing a pair of faded jeans and a tight-fitting white shirt that outlined her figure, rich and sensuous. He knew suddenly that she was aware that he was looking at her as a man looks at a woman—and waiting to see what he would say.

Dropping his eyes, he murmured thickly, "I can't explain it to you, Little Bird. I'm not like other men. I have different wishes and longings and hopes, I guess, and women haven't been a part of my life."

"I thought," she said, breathing a little unevenly, "that you wanted me."

He looked back at her then, with no pretension on his face or coloring in his voice. "I do."

"But you've got other things on your mind." She leaned back defeated, feeling the roughness of the stone. "This place . . . I don't like it at night." She shivered slightly.

"Why? I find it very comforting."

"It's full of ghosts or—or evil spirits."

She thought he would laugh at her, but instead he nodded thoughtfully. "The Old Ones, they used to call this the place of the 'evil ancestors.' They never knew, of course, that the Anasazi, for all of their intelligence and shrewdness and scientific advancement, were actually savage cannibals. That's why they died out, you know. But our great-great-grandfathers knew nothing of that." He smiled a little at her. "They just felt that the place was full of ghosts or evil spirits."

She smiled back. Picking up a stick, she put the tip of it in the fire, and waited until it caught. She held it up like a candle before her face, studying the yellow flame, saying nothing for a while. Outside the stillness was complete except for the howling of a coyote far away. It was a lonesome sound and echoed the mood that had come to her recently. Still, she watched the flame until it burned down, then restlessly tossed it back into the dying fire. "I don't know *what* I believe. My grandfather believed in those things. He couldn't have been wrong. He was too wise for that. But I don't know about God."

"Neither do I."

"I thought God led you out here. At least that's what everybody says."

"They didn't hear it from me," Cody said wearily. "Your grandfather was a Christian, wasn't he?"

"Yes. Just about the only one I ever saw that I respected. Except for a couple, some friends, old friends . . . but they left. They're gone." She looked into his shadowed eyes and said, childlike, "Everyone leaves. We all wander, aimlessly, and we're all really alone. I'm afraid, Cody."

Cody Bent Knife met her gaze steadily. "I think most people are afraid."

"Are you?"

"No."

It was this strength and the simplicity of it that stirred Little Bird. She lifted her arms. "Hold me."

It was a simple but eloquent plea and one that Cody Bent Knife had never expected to hear from this woman. With silent grace, he moved to her and pulled her to her feet. He held her in his arms and she clung to him like a frightened child. "Don't be afraid. We've been brought to this place for a purpose, Little Bird, and we will find out what it is."

Little Bird felt that the shelter of his strong arms was a citadel. She clung to him tightly, savoring the strength of his lean body, the sureness of his voice. She felt the stirrings of his heart and her own responded, so she lifted her head and when his lips came down to touch hers at first it was gentle, but then she drew him closer, her fingers and lips fierce. Finally, when she drew back, she whispered huskily, "I'm tired of being afraid, Cody, and I'm not as long as I'm with you."

The smells of the desert wafted gently to Zoan where he stood on a high ledge overlooking the stark expanse. He always loved the raw smell of the wilderness and it came to him now in a way that, perhaps, no human being had ever known. The makeup that had emerged from his strange birth had sharpened his senses so that now he smelled the pinon trees and the hot breath of the thin grasses that grew under his feet. From the distance he caught the odor of burning wood and over all of this he smelled the strong odor of the jaguar who lay prone at his feet licking her fur.

As he savored the night beauty of the stark desert, his pupils grew extraordinarily large, gathering in each bit of light. Men had invented clever devices to give them night vision but Zoan had no need for such tricks. He never analyzed this gift that had come to him. All he knew was that at night he could see things others could not see. Now he looked up and saw the stars splashed across the sky, myriad pinpoints of light, some pale and almost invisible and others blazing as if a hidden fire had broken out in the heavens. The moon was only a pale scimitar overhead, but Zoan could see as well by its ghostly light as other men could see in the morning sun.

He rarely formulated his thoughts, but now he was pleased as he stood there, for he was thinking, *I'm not alone.* Looking back over his life, he realized that he had always been alone, a different being, and a solitary one. Although he had drawn as close as he could to Niklas Kesteven—and in Zoan's simplistic way, he did love Niklas—he had become aware of the lack of solace in a one-sided friendship.

Since Cody Bent Knife and his followers had come, however, Zoan's life had been different. Most of them were a simple people and willing enough to share their lives with Zoan. He had been accepted by most of the Indians in a way that he had never been accepted by the scientists and technicians in the laboratory. Part of this relationship between Zoan and the Indians had been of necessity, for they had been forced to survive by joining together in that most primitive of drives—the gathering of food. Hunting had become an important and valuable facet of their friendship. Zoan, who loved all animal life, had nevertheless realized that they must survive by finding game. To the surprise of all the Indians, Zoan was invaluable in the hunt. He himself never killed anything, but he (and Cat) unerringly led them to where the plentiful deer were running. He could lead them to the herds of antelope and the dens of prairie chickens. In fact, he had kept the pot filled for the small group, and for this skill they honored him.

His thoughts turned to Cody Bent Knife and in his visceral way he considered his favorite friend. Like the odd turn his life had taken after he had left the lab, so he had found that his friendships were not at all what he would have thought. So far, none of the people that had come to Zoan were Christians, and Zoan had been certain that God had sent him to the desert to prepare a place for His children. Still, as Zoan was the simplest and most faithful of men, he believed that all men were God's children, whether they knew it or not; and maybe somehow, sometime, the Indians would forget their spirit ancestors and spirit animals and come to know the True One.

"Especially Cody, he's tired and he doesn't know what to do now or why he's here . . . He needs You, God, to help him and to tell him." Zoan barely knew that he had spoken aloud, and certainly didn't realize he was praying. He was just talking to his Father God.

There was something in the tall, young Indian that Zoan felt very strongly tied them together. Zoan had tried and tried to figure out what it was that had immediately bonded the two. Finally he had given up but still was aware that the two were closer than most men ever get. "We are both different," he said, nodding with certainty. *I've always been different, and so has Cody.*

Thoughtfully he lifted his head to study the satin-and-diamond night sky again. Then, directly over his head, a streak of light suddenly ignited. It shot low on the horizon and he knew instantly it could not be a star or even a meteor, which he had seen often enough in the thin air of the high crust of the earth.

He stood very still, watching the garish light streak to the earth, concentrating very hard. The yellow trail disappeared, then his sensitive ears gathered in a faraway *whump*. A lurid red ball of light suddenly swelled in the darkness far to the south.

Zoan knew what had happened, though how he knew was infathomable. A plane had crashed.

Quickly he whistled and the sibilant sound brought his old friend the stallion to him. He was temperamental, stamping and snorting, but he allowed Zoan to mount him. "Thanks, Horse," he murmured. As the stallion broke into a dead run, Zoan trusted him to find his way down the rock-strewn gully. In fact, the horse's night vision was not as good as Zoan's, but he was strong and smart and agile. Zoan occasionally guided him by simply exerting pressure with one knee or the other. Quickly they reached the floor of the southern desert, and the stallion began running in earnest, stretching out his neck and heading confidently toward the light.

The fire from the explosion grew larger as they approached and he could soon hear the roaring of the flames. *Nobody could live in that,* he thought.

The stallion abruptly pulled up, snorting and skittering nervously, frightened by the heat and the flames. Zoan slapped his lathered neck. "It's all right, Horse, I'll go by myself," he said, then slipped to the ground. Approaching the wreckage, he tried to shield his face, but found that the brilliance of the flames blinded him, in effect taking away his greatest advantage. Turning his back, he circled the raging wreck.

Zoan wasn't consciously aware of how he found the man in the impenetrable darkness outside the blinding ragged circle of flame. He might have heard him scrabbling in the sand and moaning above the fiery roar, or his sharp night-eyes might have caught his helpless movements. He was lying on his stomach, crawling, groaning and bloody.

Zoan walked right up to him. "Hello," Zoan said, kneeling by him. "I think you better stop moving." The man lay still, breathing laboriously through his mouth. Gently Zoan rolled him over, then pulled a cloth out of his pocket and began to cleanse his face. The injured man reached out blindly and Zoan caught his hand. "You're hurt, but I'll take care of you," he said.

The sound of Zoan's voice seemed to reach the injured man although he was only semiconscious. Zoan asked, "Can you stand up—if I help you?"

The eyes opened then, at least partially. The lips moved as if they were numbed. "Don't know . . . I'll try."

Clumsily Zoan tried to help him to a standing position, but immediately the man's legs shakily collapsed. His head lolled, and he moaned softly.

"It's okay, I know what to do," Zoan assured him as he lowered him into a sitting position. Lifting his head, he whistled sharply, and the man stirred. The stallion appeared out of the shadows beyond the fire, stamping and neighing in protest, but he did come. Zoan went to him, and he allowed the small man to stroke his neck. "We need your help, Horse. Okay? Don't be scared. I'm not. But you'll have to be easy."

Still skittering, but obedient, the horse allowed Zoan to lead him to the pilot who was still sitting on the ground. Zoan put both arms around the flier and, groaning with exertion, managed to get him on his feet. The man tried to help, but he was weak and passing in and out of consciousness. Finally, somehow, Zoan got him on the horse, facedown, head on one side, legs dangling on the other.

"That was good, Horse. Now let's go home. But he can't fall off, you know." The stallion moved carefully along. Zoan kept one hand on the man's shoulder, steadying him, but the horse seemed to be deliberately trying not to jog with him.

The journey back to the village was slow, and occasionally the injured man groaned, but he did not speak again.

It was late, and the Indians, as was their wont, were scattered all through the great sheltered canyon and had evidently not seen or heard the plane go down. No one greeted Zoan and Horse and the injured man. No light streamed from any of the window squares of the crude stone huts.

In front of his hut Zoan stopped the horse with a low word. He touched the man's shoulder and said, "We're home." But there was no reply, and Zoan wondered if the man was dead. Sighing, he pulled the flier from the mare's back. The body was completely limp, and Zoan struggled, for he was a large man. It never occurred to him to wake anyone and ask for help. It took him a long time to carry the man into his hut.

Moving through the low doorway, he placed the injured man on his pile of Indian blankets and sleeping bag, and then stood staring down at him. "You're not dead," he said dully. "You're breathing."

Sensing rather than hearing, he turned; Little Bird stood in his doorway. "Hello, Little Bird," he said, lighting two of his precious candles.

She took a tentative step into the small room, her eyes big and dark. "Who is he?"

"I don't know his name. His plane crashed. He got hurt."

"Yes . . . he . . . that cut on his head is bad . . ." She was tentative, unsure.

"Will you help me take care of him?" Zoan asked simply.

Little Bird's head snapped up, and her eyes grew sharp. "I—I don't know."

Zoan blinked. "Why not?"

Little Bird stared at him irritably; conversations with Zoan were always jarring in their simplicity. Zoan was looking at her, with mild and innocent curiosity, but with no reproof at all. Such judgments simply were not in him. A smile as arid as their world touched Little Bird's mouth. "Okay, Zoan, I'll help you. But I'm no doctor." She shrugged carelessly. "He may be hurt so bad that we can't fix him."

"Maybe, but we have to try. You know that."

"Yes. I know that. All right, you build up the fire, get me some clean cloths, and heat some water."

The coals of Zoan's little fire were still glowing and he quickly put on an iron pot of water to boil. He watched as Little Bird carefully felt along the man's arms and legs, abdomen and sides.

"Zoan, we're going to have to get this jumpsuit off. I think his side's injured."

The two of them managed to get the pilot's uniform off and they did discover a long, ugly cut on his right side. They couldn't really tell how deep it was, but the bleeding was minimal. He was covered with scrapes, some deep, and both his shins were bruised and beginning to swell. But Little Bird didn't think any bones were broken. She couldn't know if he had internal injuries, however, until the man was awake and could tell them if and where he was in pain. Unless he had brain damage from the head wound, and never woke up . . .

Sighing, she said, "Bring the water over. At least we can clean him up." She had taken over naturally. As she sponged the filth and the blood away from the man's face, she studied his features carefully. He was, she saw, a rather handsome man although the rough wound on the left side of his head was deep and ugly. He had crisp brown hair with a slight curl in it and rather sensitive features. Little Bird reflected that, somehow, he looked like a nice man, a kind man.

Suddenly his eyes opened, though they were unfocused. *"Vas haben zie gesacht . . . ?"*

"That's not English," Zoan observed, rather unnecessarily.

The man's dark eyes slid questioningly over Little Bird, then he focused on Zoan with some recognition. "I—I can speak English . . ."

He tried to lift himself, but his face crumpled, he cried out involuntarily and then slumped back.

"He's unconscious again," Little Bird murmured. "I don't know . . . but I guess we should at least sew up this head wound while he's unconscious. Do—do you know how to do that, Zoan?" In her whole life, Little Bird had only had two stitches in a skinned knee when she was a child. She hadn't looked while the doctor was sewing, and she'd never seen anyone do stitches since.

"I've sewed up animals before," Zoan answered.

"Well, it's about the same thing, I guess." Laying her hand on the man's forehead, she then touched his neck and chest. "He's feverish."

At her touch, he moaned, shifting restlessly, then began speaking in English, though his eyes didn't open. Leaning forward, Little Bird heard the words, "Must not have sprayed enough . . . Lost all electronics . . . It's going! The coating . . . didn't work!"

"He's out of his head," she said in a low voice. Little Bird wondered just how badly the man was hurt. It looked to her like he was in trouble, and Little Bird was surprised to find that she cared. *Not about him,* she thought critically as she stared at the pilot. *He's no one to me, a stranger . . . but I hate for Zoan to be hurt . . .* This was quite a change from the way she'd always dismissed Zoan as the weird retard.

With an almost guilty glance at the still and silent man beside her, Little Bird said softly, "Let's sew him up. I'll help you."

"Thank you," Zoan said quietly.

"You—you're welcome, Zoan."

The men, the unelected but understood leaders of the Indians, came to look at the wounded German pilot.

Ritto Yerington grunted, "German pilot. Be better if he dies.

We've had a hard enough time staying away from the commissars. Don't need to get the military on us." Ritto was mean and savage at times although his strength and his hunting ability had been of great value to the group. Ritto's dark eyes lit fiercely. "Think about it, Cody. They're probably going to come looking for him. It'd be better if we go dump him back into the wreckage of the plane."

"No," Zoan said evenly. "No killing."

"I'm not talking to you, little man," Ritto said, gritting his teeth. "I'm talking to Cody Bent Knife. I follow him, not you." Ritto and his little sister, Layna, had lost their parents in the plague, and they had led a rough life indeed. It had turned Ritto into an angry brute, and it had turned Layna into a painfully shy and doelike girl.

The pilot, still lying on Zoan's pallet, looked up at Ritto and Zoan with an peculiarly clinical interest. He said nothing.

Cody Bent Knife, as was his habit sometimes, crossed his arms and watched Ritto and particularly Zoan, refusing to speak. He always was fascinated at how Zoan dealt with the Indians—on his own unearthly terms. Somehow Zoan always managed to hold his own, and keep the respect of these rough desert wanderers. Cody knew he couldn't give that to Zoan. Zoan could only earn it.

Zoan, who dealt only with one problem at a time and one person at a time, was staring at Ritto Yerington. He knew that he would not be able to stop Ritto, for the strength of the Navajo was tremendous, and Zoan was much smaller than him. But with certainty Zoan shook his head. "No. We're not going to kill him. He has been sent to us."

Ritto, who sensed Cody's distance, stubbornly held his ground. "We don't need him here, and we don't want him here. I think we need to get rid of him. He's nothing but trouble."

Layna Yerington, a small shadow behind her brother's bulk, reached out suddenly and took her brother's hand. "I don't think so, Ritto," she said in a timid half-whisper. "Zoan is right. Kill him? In cold blood? You can't do that. You *wouldn't* do that."

Bluestone Yacolt spoke up in his usual cynical and bored tone. His bright blue eyes flashed oddly in his flat bronze face. "I don't trust him—why should we? Not good, not good at all, Cody, for a German soldier to know we're camped out here. He's the only outsider that's ever found us."

"I found you," Zoan said. "I'm an outsider. So is Cody. But we're friends now. This man is an outsider, yes. But he could be a friend."

This discomfited Bluestone Yacolt and even derailed Ritto Yerington's barely concealed savagery. Cody Bent Knife looked slightly amused, and pleased. He winked at Zoan, though Zoan never responded to such signals. He just didn't understand such things as winking or body language or the meaning of facial expression.

Now Benewah Two Color spoke. Everyone knew that the old man had wisdom beyond the natural, and even Bluestone and Ritto respected him. "If you met him on the field of battle, it would be different," Two Color said calmly. "But now he is injured and no danger to us. What do you think would be the fair and honorable thing for them to do if you had been captured by his people?"

The question fell quietly into the room and Ritto shook his head and turned. "All right, Two Color," he grunted. "I'll leave him alone. But I'm not going to baby him or nurse him or help with him. And neither is Layna." He left, pulling his sister with him, and the others followed.

Cody lingered in the doorway, staring assessingly at the pilot, at Zoan, and then gave Little Bird a small smile. "You took good care of him, you two. If I'm ever injured in battle, I want you to take care of me. Will you?"

Little Bird swallowed hard, then said gutturally, "If there's a battle, I'm going to be fighting, not holding someone's hand."

"I'd take care of you, Cody," Zoan said.

Cody nodded and left.

Through all of this the pilot had said not a word. Now he reached up and touched the rough bandage that covered his head.

Zoan sat cross-legged on one side of him, and after a moment's hesitation, Little Bird sat down on the other side.

His eyes moved to Zoan whom he studied carefully, and with some guarded gratefulness. Then he looked at the young woman beside him in a guarded way; she was much more of a cipher than Zoan's open kindness. With some stiffness he said, "I am *Oberleutnant* Reinhart Angriff."

"I'm Zoan. That's Little Bird."

"I—must thank you for your protection, and your care."

"Who are you?" Little Bird asked, more sharply than she had intended.

"I am in the Luftwaffe." He saw that the words meant nothing to the two and he amended it. "I'm a flyer for the German air force, the 77th Air Wing, based at Holloman Air Force Base in New Mexico." Tentatively he touched his head again, and moved restlessly, but it caused him pain, and he grimaced. "My side, too . . . Did you two do these stitches?"

"Zoan did," Little Bird said with a careless air. "You would have died, I think, if he hadn't gone out and gotten you and brought you back."

Angriff nodded, and a lurking amusement lightened his pain-clouded brown eyes. "Yes, so I've heard. To some of your people it would seem that it would have been preferable if Herr Zoan had not saved me."

"He is not as wicked as he sounds," Zoan said seriously. "Or looks."

Reinhart Angriff lay flat on his back studying the two. Ever since his plane had gone down he had been wandering in a fog of feverish pain and confusion, but now he was beginning to gather his senses. Captain Reinhart Angriff was a reserved man of twenty-eight, an outstanding and dedicated flier for the Luftwaffe. When he was not bruised and bandaged, he was the handsomest of men, the true Nordic male beauty that has always shone best in the men of his race. In contrast to the stereotypical Nordic traits, he was a reserved man, and was indeed as kind and gentle as his looks had suggested to Little Bird the night before.

"Still, it seems that I owe you for my life, Herr Zoan, not once, but twice. How did you get me away from the wreck? And where am I?"

Zoan stared at him, his eyes dark and fixed in his odd way, then he nodded to himself. "I will tell you everything, Mr. Pilot, but first you need to eat. You're getting well, but you're weak. You need food."

"I suppose I do," Angriff said wearily, for he did feel treacherously weak. "And once again, I must say thank you."

"No need for that," Zoan said. "The time will come when you can repay me."

Reinhart lay quietly in his bed. The pain was lessening to some extent. He had, of course, ejected from his dead plane that had been heading nose-down to earth as fast as a bullet. Ejection from a sinking jet generally saved the pilot from serious injury—as it had Angriff—but always there were cuts and bruises and scrapes. Angriff felt as if he'd fallen to earth instead of parachuting down. But then, he had ejected at a dangerously low altitude, and he'd landed really hard. It was a miracle he hadn't broken something. It did seem that Zoan and the girl had attended to his wounds effectively, even with their obviously primitive conditions.

The late afternoon sun was feeble and pale and now he turned his head to look at the man who sat patiently beside him. Reinhart had thought—as all people did when first encountering Zoan—that the simple young man was little better than a half-wit. Yet now, after listening to him and watching him, Reinhart could see that Zoan was not a half-wit, he was not even really "simple."

There was more, much more to him—something, perhaps, that might be superior to most men. Reinhart licked his lips and asked, "Can I have a drink of water?"

Zoan, without speaking, moved over to his ola, filled a cup, and brought it back. "Do you want to sit up?" he asked.

"Yes, I think it would be better if I tried to move some." Reinhart, with Zoan's help, struggled to a sitting position. Insisting on holding the cup himself, he gratefully drained it dry. "*Danke,*" he said.

Zoan did not reply. He simply took the cup, filled it again without being asked, and Reinhart again drank thirstily. The pilot really didn't know what to say to Zoan, or how to talk to him. He was so different, and didn't seem to follow the rules of normal conversation. Reinhart studied Zoan's eyes that seemed to be all pupils. That was another thing; Zoan met people's eyes directly, openly, and endured scrutiny patiently. He looked back at Reinhart Angriff, and suddenly the pilot knew he must try and help this man. Not the rest of them—even the girl was hostile to him—but he was obligated to Zoan for his life, forever.

Licking his dry and burned lips, he said, "Zoan, do you understand that your country is in trouble? Do you know what's happened?"

Zoan was still staring at him in that patient way. "I know that the darkness has come."

Reinhart's eyes narrowed. "Have you been to a city?"

"No."

"I mean—in the last two or three days."

"No. I've never been to a city."

Reinhart frowned. This was more difficult than he had anticipated. "I see that you don't have—lights and Cyclops and electricity out here. What I'm trying to tell you, Zoan, is that the cities are dark now."

Zoan simply watched him, and the German could not ascertain how much he understood. "We're just trying to help," he added, rather lamely. For some reason he could not meet Zoan's gaze, and so he dropped his eyes. "I—I was on a reconnaissance patrol, you see. That's all . . . just to observe. I flew over Albuquerque and Santa Fe. They're cities just—uh—southeast of here, I think. They went dark. They—they don't have power." *Projekt Schlußenheit . . . We all knew it had to do with the power grid, they at least told us that—but they couldn't prepare us for what a—shock, a terrible shock it was to see the world go dark! And I wonder . . . how many of us went down? How many planes weren't adequately protected?*

WE did this, we must have! Otherwise, how could we have had the spray, the sealant to keep out . . . what? Some kind of virus? It's a live thing? We've unleashed some doomsday bug on America? Or—or—perhaps it just came, and we found a weapon, a defensive weapon?

Will I ever know?

Interrupting Reinhart's dark reveries, Zoan asked quietly, "You won't tell about me and my friends being here?"

Bleakly Reinhart replied, "It's against the law for you to be here, isn't it?"

"I guess so."

"No. I won't tell. And besides, I don't think your commissars will be worrying about you and your friends, Zoan. They have other things to worry about."

"Maybe," Zoan said cautiously. "But I think they'll be looking for us soon. So you won't tell?"

"No, I won't," Angriff said with a touch of impatience.

Zoan suddenly smiled, which was a rare thing for him; and this time Reinhart could swear that there was pity in Zoan's steady gaze. Suddenly a feeling of guilt swept over Angriff. "I swear I won't tell anyone," he added vehemently. "I swear to God."

"It's not a good idea to swear to God. It has a way of coming back on you."

"I don't know why I said that, I don't even believe in God."

"That doesn't mean it won't come back on you. Anyway, I believe you." For some reason this simple assurance made Reinhart feel better. With Zoan's help he lay back down and immediately began to drop off into a sleep. He had not quite drifted into unconsciousness when Zoan, in an almost inaudible whisper, said, "He's not here yet, is he?"

Startled, Reinhart opened his eyes with an effort. "Who's not here?"

"Him—your countryman. The—the wolf. The wolf of the evening."

Now Angriff was sure that Zoan was slightly retarded at least, and delusionary at worst. "The evening wolf? I don't know what you mean."

"He loves the dark. He can see at night. He's the one who made this darkness. You know that."

Suddenly Reinhart Angriff stiffened. "You mean Commandant Tor von Eisenhalt?"

"Yes . . . yes . . . that's his name . . . at least this time, for now . . ."

Reinhart was baffled, but there was one small part of his mind that understood to some extent what Zoan spoke of. There was something mysterious—perhaps even inhuman—about Tor von Eisenhalt. *Oberleutnant* Reinhart Angriff had an overwhelming respect for Tor von Eisenhalt, for the man was a military genius, and understood the mind and heart of the German people—particularly the soldiers—far more than any man had for centuries. Of course, Angriff had never met von Eisenhalt, but he had seen him and heard him, and he was drawn to him. Still, Angriff had seen that Tor von Eisenhalt was a man greatly to be feared.

And his insignia was, after all, a wolf.

This, of course, must be purely coincidental to Zoan's dark musings.

Still, Angriff answered Zoan respectfully. "No, Zoan. My commandant is not here in America."

A heavy, thick silence filled the room and Reinhart thought at first that Zoan had not heard him, and then the words came. "He's coming, though. I can see in the dark too . . . And I can see him coming." Zoan fell silent, then added in a small voice, "I hope he can't see me."

Reinhart lay silently, and he knew fear then; he wasn't sure if he was just responding to Zoan's fear or if somewhere, deep down inside him, he was feeling the first dark and cold fingers of dread himself. He had not been half so frightened when he knew that his plane was going down, when it simply stopped functioning. He recalled, then, that he had thought that not only was his plane going down but the whole world was going down. The sight of the lights of the cities going out had gone deep into his spirit and it was as if his spirit, too, were flickering out. Now he stared at Zoan, and he whispered, "I—I hope he can't see you, either, Zoan. I truly do. And I swear, he'll never learn of you from me."

EIGHTEEN

———•———

FORT CARSON WAS DARK, silent, and dead.

The 502d Infantry Regiment of the 101st Airborne (Air Assault) Division called the southwest quadrant of the fort home. The area was the closest to the main landing strip, control tower, and communications center. It was no mistake that the most crack unit in the whole 101st had been assigned to this particular quadrant.

For a full five seconds after the blackout, the men of the 502d who were on duty outside could only stare at one another and send questioning, stony looks of disbelief at the giant grid to their north. The sudden consummate silence and obsidian blackness on a two-thousand-man fort was unthinkable; indeed, a few had a natural feeling of vertigo as their normal world of harsh sound and intricate lighting deadened to the effect, for them, of being inside a tightly closed crypt.

The silence disappeared when, seemingly as one, they all began scrambling, cursing, and shouting orders to one another. The infantrymen—"grunts"—dashed for their barracks, where they'd find their trusty weapons and shelter. Those who were assigned to Humvee V's hopped into their vehicles, struggling to see the normally well-lit numerical keypad located on the console to enter the four-digit starting sequence. A few entered the wrong sequence because of the darkness, but the ones who managed to enter it correctly got the same result as the ones who didn't: nothing. No vehicle snarled to life.

The artillerymen, known as "cannon cockers" since time out of mind, scrambled around and over their British-made M151 radar-guided "boomers," the great guns, which now looked to them like dark hulks of junk metal without the glowing green lights of the Laser Imagery Display (LID) on the sightings panels. Many of the men cast wary, wide-eyed looks toward the starry sky, searching for the very intruders they were assigned to take down before reaching the base. To a man, they knew that if they made a visual sighting, it was way too late to do anything about it. They were trained on the boomers to eliminate any threat from up to twenty miles away with V-12 rockets, and any visual sightings were left up to the "duck hunters" with shoulder-launched surface-to-air weapons called "Scorpions."

The duck hunters themselves were staring at their dead cylindrical weapons as if they'd never seen them before. One of them actually banged his Scorpion against the side of a boomer, as if that would somehow bring back his small-range display screen. The only result he got from this action was a flurry of curses from the boomer crew.

Division support maintenance teams ran for the FK-120s, CJ-33 supply choppers, and Apaches to check on their conditions and discovered the same ominous results. The teams responsible for the ultra-sleek, high-tech FK-120 stealth fighters were especially horrified. This was the Army's best offensive plane. Now it was about as useless as a wet firecracker.

In Colonel J. P. Nix's aviation squadron, Fire Team Eclipse was scattered all around the quadrant, very much as puzzled and uneasy as the rest of the 101st. Except for two of them—Vashti Nicanor and Ric Darmstedt. From inside Surplus Warehouse C-6, they stood in a freight elevator halfway to the ground from their little excursion to the third floor. The elevator was caged, fifteen by fifteen, and from their vantage point they could see only a slightly lighter sliver of gray from the outside door they'd left partly open.

Vashti couldn't see Ric, but she could sense his presence close to her and heard his quickened breathing when the huge phosphorescent lights overhead blinked out. "What happened?" she asked, noticing for the first time how eerily their voices echoed in the cavernous warehouse.

Ric answered in his lazy drawl, "Guess some clown fell asleep at the power grid."

"And this happens often in America?" Vashti muttered.

"I was only joking, Colonel. All power stations and lines are tied in to Cyclops. I don't even know if they man the grids at the plants anymore." Vashti heard his clothes rustle, then he said in a slightly uneven tone, "The GL's out. That's new."

The GL was the Grid Locator, a handheld device that was programmed to recall the exact position of every member of Fire Team Eclipse who was carrying one. Hating to admit it to herself, Vashti felt a current of dread run through her; never had she heard Ric Darmstedt sound unsure of himself. Trying to make light of the situation, she said tentatively, "At least my feet aren't hurting."

A distracted grunt was his only reply.

Earlier that evening, the fire team had been eating supper with the grunts, a habit the whole fire team had fallen into, except for Captain Con Slaughter. Suddenly Ric had turned to Vashti and asked about her feet.

"My feet? What about them?"

"Which one hurts?"

"How do you know one of my feet hurts?"

Hiding a smile while spooning an alarmingly yellow pudding into his mouth, Ric had replied, "It's called simple observation, Colonel. You're limping like a three-legged mule. If you'll pardon the comparison."

Vashti had been having trouble with her right foot ever since she and Colonel Ben-ammi had been issued the boots worn by the fire team members. Their daily runs of five miles—and then their punishment runs of an additional two miles—had turned into tests of Vashti's ability to hide excruciating pain, as well as exhibit endurance. For some reason she just couldn't make the boot settle into the contour of her foot. Two weeks before, Vashti would have undergone torture on a rack to keep from revealing a weakness or a sign of pain to another soldier. Now, after working closely with Lieutenant Darmstedt and learning—a little reluctantly—to respect and even admire him, she admitted the problem to him.

Ric had thrown a Proto-Syn green bean at a tech-head (it bounced) across the table and asked where the surplus boots were stashed. After getting his answer, Ric asked if there was anything else interesting in there.

The tech-head rolled his eyes. "You know the army. They've changed the official snaplight color to blue again. For real, for good. Uh-huh. 'Til for real, for good next time."

Ric had taken her to the warehouse and, of course, had found her a perfect fit. Again she'd marveled at his ability to help a female soldier—even one that outranked him—without showing any signs of condescension or inappropriate intimacy.

Now, in the frozen elevator, she was becoming more disturbed the longer his silence lasted. "Lieutenant? What's wrong?" He didn't answer for a long time, and she used his Christian name for the first time since they'd met: "Ric?" The name felt alien on her tongue, yet comforting at the same time. Something was wrong. She wasn't frightened, exactly, but she was glad, just now, in this situation, to be with Ric Darmstedt.

Slowly Ric said, "I was just thinking about the time in airborne training when I graduated from maggot to worm."

"What? What?" Vashti asked, bewildered.

"We were training, I was on Defense Team Blue, I remember. There were two other offensive teams, Red and Green . . . anyway, they blacked out our command center. I was training on satellite solo imagery, and when the room went dark as the inside of a tomb, no one even breathed. We were completely defenseless against the commando teams. I got this weird panicky feeling even though it wasn't for real. Everyone started hollering and running around and pushing dead buttons that they couldn't even see—just general chaos really. Then the backup power generators booted up and everything came back on like nothing had happened, and it hit me—that was the first time I'd ever experienced a real and total blackout, even for just a few seconds."

Vashti heard a ripping sound, then saw his face suddenly illuminated by a green light, and she gasped before she realized that it was only the sound of Velcro cover separating and the glow from his watch as he checked the time. He looked alien in the green glow. She asked, "But are you saying this is a total blackout? I mean—I thought that maybe it was just the warehouse, a—a—what do you call them? Breaks?"

The green light disappeared and Ric answered with uncharacteristic shortness, "Breakers. But it's been almost five minutes. Why hasn't the backup generator kicked in? Every building the army owns is on a separate generator."

Vashti frowned. "I don't know. And what does this have to do with maggots and worms?"

"Huh? Oh. Yeah. Well, I was the only one in the command room that night who thought about putting extra guards on the backup generators in case the commandos took them out," he explained with a touch of his normal Texas cowboy bravado. "So the captain graduated me from maggot to worm." Abruptly he turned back to their odd situation. "Since the generators haven't kicked in, what's really happened here?"

Vashti still didn't understand either their predicament, or his worry.

"Colonel," Ric went on softly, and Vashti was never more aware of the complete silence than at that moment when his voice seemed to segment and rebound from everywhere at once. "What if there's been some sort of attack?"

A chill traveled up Vashti's spine to tingle at the back of her neck. "Impossible. We would be hearing sounds of combat—explosions, the artillery—"

"Maybe, maybe not. Anyway, we gotta get out of here, Colonel, but I can't see a blasted thing . . ." He trailed off until Vashti heard the slap of skin on skin, and realized that he'd slapped his forehead. "How could I be so *stupid*!"

"What is it?" Vashti asked anxiously. Then she heard thumps at her feet. "What are you doing?"

"Trying to get into this case of snaplights."

Now Vashti, too, felt foolish. She was the ranking officer, for goodness' sake, and here was this American lieutenant out-thinking her! Snaplights were small tubes of thick liquid that, if flexed slightly, would give off a flameless colored light that lasted for twenty-four hours. True to the tech-head's word, there'd been case after case of blue snaplights that were now the "official" color, replacing the green ones. Vashti had remarked that she liked the blue much better than the serpentine green, which was what the Israelis used. Promptly, and with solemn gallantry, Ric had "liberated" one of the cases and presented it to her. Her strong sense of military protocol had reared its head and signaled disapproval, but she'd said nothing, only smiled. He'd looked so boyishly pleased at his "gift."

The sounds at her feet became more violent, ending in a screech of wood giving way. "Ow! Man!"

"What happened?"

"Broke a nail."

In other circumstances, Vashti would have thought this funny, but all emotions except relief left her as she saw a snaplight come alive in Ric's hands.

"Here, Colonel, toss this down to see how far we are from the floor."

Vashti did so, peered through the grated walls of the elevator, then told him, "Twenty feet or so."

After bringing more lights to life, Ric threw three toward the wide door of the second floor, which consisted of collapsible bars spaced six inches apart. It was directly above their cage about five feet, and at a steep angle. "Can't jump that," he commented absently. "Here . . . help me." He began tugging on one side of the elevator door, while Vashti took the other. Once opened, Ric plopped onto his belly and waved a handful of lights around beneath the elevator.

"What do we do?" Vashti asked.

"Take off your shirt, Colonel."

"What?"

"Don't worry. I'll be taking mine off, too."

"That's not much consola—"

"Have a look, Colonel, ma'am."

Vashti lay down beside him and studied the gloom beneath them.

Ric pointed the snaplights to their right. "See that metal pole? That's one of the ones that the elevator slides up and down on. It's probably covered with little metal slivers that'll slice up your hands really good, so you'll need to use your shirt to slide down."

"Slide . . . down?"

In the dim blue light, Vashti could see Ric's boyish grin. "It'll be a breeze for you, Colonel. Easier'n rappelling out of a helicopter."

"It is?" Vashti said, gulping. It didn't look easier. It looked harder. And much more dangerous.

Unceremoniously, he threw some lit snaplights to the floor around the pole. It didn't provide nearly as much illumination in the vast warehouse as Vashti would have liked, but there was nothing to do about that. Ric hopped to his feet and began unbuttoning his shirt. "That pole's just a little too far from the door, so we'll have to make a jump for it."

Vashti stood and began working at the fastenings on her own shirt, telling herself over and over that they were just fellow soldiers with a job to do, instead of man and woman. It didn't help when he pulled his shirt off to reveal a sleeveless T-shirt and arms that were well-toned and undeniably powerful. Vashti shook off the thought and concentrated on the slide down.

Ric didn't so much as glance her way as she removed her uniform blouse. Underneath she, too, wore a sand-brown T-shirt, but hers was sleeved. Ric went to the box of snaplights and promptly slid them over the side to crash to the floor below. Finally he turned to her and said intently, "I'll go first. I know you can do this."

"Of course I can," Vashti answered, with more confidence than she felt.

The careless grin flashed again. "If you can't, I can always go down, then throw you up a rope and pull you down."

"Very funny. Go, Lieutenant."

Ric folded his shirt lengthwise three times, and she did the same. Then he sat down in the doorway and without hesitation sort of torqued himself down and around. Now he was swinging in midair, awkwardly holding on to the lip of the floor through his folded shirt. Ric eyed the pole, which was about five feet away, and began to swing his legs back and forth to gain momentum. Suddenly he let go with a grunt and flew toward the pole, first wrapping his legs around it, then his protected hands. Like an expert fireman he neatly slid to the floor.

"Nicely done," Vashti called down to him as she tried to ignore the knot in her stomach. What if she missed the pole?

Ric's face was a blue orb in the neon light as he gazed upward. "Piece-a-cake, Colonel."

"What does that mean?"

"Uh— never mind. You aren't scared, are you, sir?" he teased her.

"Of course I'm not scared!" Vashti sat down and immediately swung her legs over the side and did the same trapeze torque Ric had done. Keeping a hold on the lip of the floor through the shirt proved to be more difficult than she'd thought. One hand came loose, and with a gasp she nearly lost hold altogether.

"Hold on there, Colonel," Ric coaxed from below. "You're tough! You're Fire Team Eclipse! Huu-ahh!"

"That is easy for you to say, Lieutenant," Vashti returned through gritted teeth. "You're on the ground." Desperately she gained a better hold, and began swinging her legs toward the pole. It looked like it was fifty feet away instead of five. "Only five feet," she whispered to herself. "Five feet." She reflected that she wouldn't have been able to perform this feat before training in the personal program of weights and exercise that Ric had developed for her. She could feel strength humming through muscles she'd never known, and suddenly her confidence soared. Grunting "Huu-ahh!" she let go.

Vashti hit the pole so hard it knocked the breath out of her. Then she was sliding down too fast gripping the pole with her legs and hands as hard as she could to slow down. *Too fast . . . too fast!*

Strong hands stopped her just as she realized she was going to crash into the ground like a rock. Disentangling herself from the pole, pushing Ric's helping hands away, she muttered, "Just a slice of cake." She considered putting on the splinter- and oil-covered shirt, then threw it aside in distaste. Ric pressed a handful of snap-lights into her hand, and they took off running for the door, their heavy jump boots echoing loudly in the silent warehouse.

When they burst full speed from the doorway, Vashti was bowled over by another running figure. Together they went down on the ground in a tangle of arms and legs. Ric jumped on the man and jerked him up by his shirt.

"Watch where you're going! Mitchell? What the devil are you doin', boy?"

David Mitchell reached down to help Vashti to her feet with a plain look of horror on his honest face. "Golly, am I sorry, Colonel! But you just popped out right in front of me! No, I mean, I just popped out right in front of you—"

Vashti brushed grass from her T-shirt. "Never mind, it's all right, Sergeant."

"Mitchell, what's going on?" Ric asked as he looked around the completely dark facility. "Why aren't the backup generators—"

"It's worse than that, sir," David replied, waving a hand to the northeast. "Didn't you notice that the lights from Colorado Springs are out, too?"

Fort Carson was only five miles from the city, and one could normally see the lights as a hazy glow at night. Now, the stars could be seen clearly all the way down to the horizon.

"Yeah," Ric muttered. "And I guess your GL's out, too?"

David nodded.

Vashti was really worried now. "What does this mean?"

"I don't know, but I'd sure like permission to go to the airstrip, ma'am," David said, then turned to Ric. "There are two Stealths up there somewhere, they're almost out of fuel, and the world has disappeared, and I guess gone silent, right out from under them. Uh, sir, Joey Dane is one of the pilots. You remember him?"

Ric nodded. "Sure I do. Your funny redheaded friend from high school. You've got permission to go, Mitchell. We're headed to the command center. They must be going crazy in there."

David pointed to the snaplights. "Mind if I take a couple of those, sir?"

Ric handed him two of the lights. "Take care of yourself, Mitchell. And keep your eye out for other team members. We need to gather somewhere later. At the Apache, right?"

David was already running off, and called over his shoulder, "That's affirmative, sir!"

David Mitchell, unlike every other member of his specialized team, was trained to do *all* of their jobs. He was an adequate helo pilot, kept himself up as best he could on all new advances in electronics and weaponry, and had the most field training of any except Captain Slaughter. When he went with the team on training or, if the need ever arrived, a mission, his job was to fill the position of any man who was wounded or killed. He didn't like the idea of his job—sometimes he felt like a ghoul—but he and all his team members knew that it was essential.

Since David couldn't concentrate on only one specialty, his skill as a pilot couldn't equal Deac Fong, and there was no way he could outshoot Rio Valdosta. He wasn't an unfailing leader like Con Slaughter, and he wasn't a techno-genius like Ric Darmstedt. But David had worked hard to at least be *adequate* at every position. There was no way he would let laziness be a reason to let the team down should he ever be called upon. And he looked at his team as if they were all fingers on one hand—and he viewed himself as the thumb. The thumb could hardly function alone, like the other fingers could; but the whole hand couldn't work unless it had a thumb. It was a childish analogy, he thought, but it worked for him.

But even though David's loyalties, and yes, friendships, were strongest toward his fire team, he still had one especially good friend from his childhood, Joey Dane. A cheerful, energetic man, Joey had planned to be a Stealth pilot ever since he was five years old. He'd worked his whole life to that end. It had just worked out that David and Joey had been assigned to Fort Carson together, and their friendship had grown. When David had heard from a tech-head about the two planes in the air, he'd known that Joey was on a night patrol, so one of the pilots must be him. They never sent more than two of the outrageously expensive Stealths out. Immediately David had grabbed his NVG's—Night Vision Goggles—and set out for the airstrip.

The closer he got to the strip, the more he had to dodge other men running around. He wondered where they were all going in such a hurry, since there was no job that could be done without power. None. When the power had gone out, David had, of course, been confused, but only for a moment. Somehow he'd sensed the complete *finality* of the blackout, and he knew that flipping a switch wasn't going to set things right. It had disturbed him to think this, but it had also set him into action much more quickly than anyone else.

He rushed through all the confusion, by the cannon cockers and duck hunters who were still furiously trying to make their weapons work, and came to the N4 runway where the fighters would be landing. Quickly he donned the NVG's to scan the sky, and with the aid of the stars it seemed that it was full daylight through the lenses. He spotted the Stealths at once. They were coming in from the south, already descending in landing forma-tion, one right after the other. David looked down at the runway and his heart stopped.

There was a dead Humvee V sitting right in the center of the strip where the planes would be landing. It didn't matter that Humvees were strictly forbidden on the runways; the only thing that mattered was that it was there. At a hundred yards away, there was no way David could grab a couple of men and explain to them and then reach it and move it before the planes touched down. And it was far enough down the runway—almost at the very end of it, where planes didn't touch down anyway. That was probably why some dumb grunt had taken a chance on crossing there.

"Their landing lights will pick it up," he whispered to himself. "Sure they will . . ." Remembering those bright lights that illumi-nated the way for the planes, he removed his NVG's. If he'd been looking at the plane as they came on, he'd have been blinded.

The first Stealth hit the lights only a moment later, and David could clearly see the pilot make a last-minute correction to avoid the Humvee. Maybe these ultrafast jets *did* need that part of the runway for landing. The Stealth landed with a scream of reversing engines and taxied by, still at fully two hundred miles an hour.

"One down," David said, but was horrified to see that the other plane hadn't turned on his lights. "Turn them on!" he shouted hoarsely, but he could barely hear himself over the engines of the landed plane. He remembered the snaplights in his hand, and knowing it was a futile gesture, he sprinted for the Humvee, waving the puny lights over his head. "Turn on your lights!"

With a sinking feeling, David realized that the Stealth's landing lights must have malfunctioned. He had just enough time to wonder if that was somehow connected to this eerie power outage—and why the other pilot hadn't voice-warned the second pilot about the Humvee—then the underside of the Stealth barely touched the vehicle.

It was like a terrible nightmare. David saw the landing gear separate from the aircraft in small pieces and go flying. The Stealth itself listed to the starboard side, hit the runway, and wheeled horribly twice. The metal din was deafening. One wing shattered and tore from the fuselage, and the plane slid on its side directly toward David. He took a few steps backward on legs that were numb and yet shaky, his mind frozen in horror as the Stealth plowed into the earth beside the runway.

The aircraft came to a stop on its belly only a hundred feet from David, who stood with his mouth open, still not believing what he'd just seen. In the ensuing thunderous silence, David felt the hot air from the plane's momentum wash over him, carrying the acrid scent of jet fuel. This dangerous smell spurred him into action.

David sprinted to the aircraft, his mind ricocheting between praying that the copilot wasn't Joey Dane and praying that he was still alive. On the side where the wing had been stripped away, he saw shorted wires sparking along the torn part of the fuselage, and the fuel smell was now close to gagging level. One of the cockpit latches was still intact, and with quick, sure movements he disengaged the lock. The titanium enforced canopy was lighter than he'd thought, but it still took all of his strength to use leverage to break the other lock. When it snapped, David threw back the canopy and looked inside.

The pilot was dead. In all his training and travels, war games and rescue missions, David had never seen a dead human being before. This was no Ultimate Reality game on Cyclops where you blew raiders out of the sky, or gleefully mowed down enemies with assault rifles. This had been a living and breathing man, with family, friends, and dreams, who was now staring up at David with blank eyes from a head that was twisted almost completely around on his neck.

David felt his gorge rise, but he made himself look at the copilot. It wasn't Joey Dane, and he was still alive. His head was resting against the instrument panel, and when David gently pulled him back against the seat he heard a moan escape the man's lips. David could see no wounds except for the blood coming from the man's nose and trickling from his mouth.

David heard another snap from the shorting wires below, and knew they didn't have much time left before the jet fuel caught. David had had the minimum field medical training, and he was aware you weren't supposed to move an injured man until you knew the exact nature of the injury. But it was obvious he had to either get him out of there or let him go up in a flaming ball. David released the shoulder harness and easily lifted the man out, inwardly cringing at the protesting howl of pain that escaped the injured man, but determinedly dragging him clear.

David wasn't a big man, but he had an innate strength and vigor, and he had no trouble carrying the man a safe distance from the plane. He could tell, from the slight movements of the man's body, that he was broken, probably irreparably so. David would have kept going all the way to find some medical help, but somehow he knew that the flier didn't have that much time. It would be better to let him rest.

He laid the man down in cool grass and removed his helmet. The navigator was no more than a boy, and David held his snap-light close enough to make out the name stitched on his flight suit—Fleming. His eyes fluttered and he tried to say something, but he choked and began coughing.

"Don't try to talk, Fleming," David said calmly. "Help will be here soon." He looked up and saw figures running toward them in the distance, and could only hope that one of them was a real medic. At that moment, David would have gladly traded any of his million-dollar training to have taken more courses in Med-Aid. He was ignorant and he was helpless. For all he knew the kid could take his last breath at any time. He checked for broken bones in Fleming's arms and legs. When David touched his left arm, Fleming cried out.

"Fleming—" David began, then the plane exploded behind him. He covered the flier's body with his. Flaming debris fell all around them, but they went untouched. In the sullen glow, David could see the raw fear in the boy's dark blue eyes. "Fleming, listen to me—"

"God . . . God help . . . me!" Fleming whispered, and David could hear the liquid in his lungs through his gurgling voice.

David's heart wrenched, but he made his voice sound calm. "Fleming, listen to me. I really don't know how bad you're hurt. But I have to ask you this right now. Are you a Christian? Do you know Jesus Christ?"

He swallowed hard, but the result was only more blood seeping from his nose.

David watched him, trying to decipher the dying man's last breaths.

"No." The single gasped word was desolate.

"Okay, I can help you. I'm going to pray now, and if you want Jesus to come into your heart and save you, you have to pray it yourself, do you understand? He'll understand that you can't talk right now, but He knows your heart, Fleming, do you get it?" David took his right hand in both of his. "If you understand, squeeze my hand."

"I . . . under—" Fleming broke off into another coughing fit, but managed to squeeze David's hand. "Help me . . . I'm . . . scared . . ."

David closed his eyes and prayed, "Lord Jesus, have mercy on this boy and ease his pain. God, hear his cry as he confesses that he's a sinner, and has no hope except from You. Come into his heart as he asks You to do, and fill him with Your holy joy and ever-lasting peace. Heal him, or take him home, Lord. Thy will be done."

David paused and opened his eyes. He was surprised to find Deac Fong and Colonel Ben-ammi standing over him quietly, along with a few other men. Then he looked back down at Fleming. The boy was dead.

No longer was his mouth wrenched in pain, but it seemed that there was a ghost of a smile visible through the smeared blood. A figure moved to the other side of Fleming, and David saw a strong, meaty hand reach out and put two fingers to the side of the boy's neck.

"He's gone," Colonel Darkon Ben-ammi told David sadly.

To Ben-ammi's surprise, David smiled a little. "Yeah, and I know where."

Ben-ammi eyed him curiously, but merely said, "They're on the way with a stretcher, Sergeant. Guess there's no hurry now, though."

"It's all right," David said, gently wiping the boy's mouth and arranging his broken hands. "It doesn't matter to him now, for sure."

If Darkon hadn't seen what he'd just witnessed with his own eyes, he would have scoffed at anyone trying to tell him about it. He'd watched the young pilot while David had prayed over him. He'd *seen* the peace come into the shattered face, he'd *seen* the awful pain and terrible fear disappear as if they'd never been . . . he'd seen this boy die in real peace, without pain.

Darkon Ben-ammi had seen badly injured men die before. He'd never seen them die happy.

Though he'd never mention it to anyone, not even a fellow New Zionist like Vashti, Darkon had always been a little wary—almost afraid—of Christians. They had no *ceremony*, no *formalities*. Here they were in the middle of a massive power blackout of unknown proportions, an attack could come at any second, a $2 billion plane had crashed, and David could call on his Jesus to come into the heart of a boy he didn't even know. How crazy was that?

It's too connected with supernatural levels, with spiritual things, for an old earth-loving, life-loving soldier like me, Darkon thought. *There is only here, and now, and life, and this breath—*

And death, of course. This boy's death.

Where is he now? Exactly where is David Mitchell so sure, so confident, so happy, that this boy is now?

The evidence of David's faith was as plain as the peace on Fleming's face. And the evidence of Darkon Ben-ammi's confusion was, too, plain on his. As he always did, however, he denied it. This was not the place, and now was not the time. It never was.

"Colonel?"

With an effort, Darkon looked up from young Fleming to Deac Fong's anxiety-filled face.

"The Apache? I mean, we can't do anything else for him."

"All right, Lieutenant." Darkon turned to David and said, "Lieutenant Fong is, how do you say, busting to check on his beloved Apache. Are you coming?"

David slowly shook his head. "I'll stay with him until the medics get here with a stretcher. Then I'll be along."

Darkon patted his shoulder, and then joined Fong in a dead run for the helo yard. Being twenty years older than the hotshot lieutenant, he steadily lost ground in the race, but Darkon knew that the young pilot was as worried about his Apache as he would be about a sick puppy. He checked his watch and was astonished to find that only twenty minutes had passed since the power outage. It seemed as if it had been hours.

The thought of his beloved homeland crossed Darkon's mind. Was Israel, too, under this smothering carpet of darkness? What about his wife, Shira, and their four children? Were they frightened, were they hurt? The hunger to know threatened to consume him, but of course there was nothing he could do about it. A blackout this severe meant complete communication shutoff from the rest of the world, and there was no telling when power could be restored. Until then . . . well, until then Darkon would send prayers to the God of Abraham for his family, a God in whom he had never pretended to believe. Still, just in case . . .

Just keep them safe for me, God. If You will do this for me, I promise to learn more about You from David. Darkon shook his head in chagrin as he puffed and jogged along. That sounded weak even to him, and he doubted that Yahweh made deals like that. *So be it . . . that is my plea.*

Signs that the base was taking on some form of order were evidenced by the beefy MP who stopped him at the gate of the helo yard. He looked at Darkon's bronzed mideastern features suspiciously, then raised a wicked-looking double-edged bayonet. "What's your business, sir?"

Darkon raised his hands to signify innocence, saying, "I have papers right here in my pocket—"

"Corporal!" Deac Fong shouted, already halfway to his Apache. "He's on my team, let him through!"

With another uncertain glance at Darkon, the MP stepped aside. Deac waited for Darkon, and together they raced to their bird. Deac automatically hit the power switch to activate the door, and when it didn't open he slammed it angrily with his fist.

"Lieutenant . . . ," Darkon began, but he was interrupted by a dapper captain who was passing by, his face sorrowful.

"Forget about it, Lieutenant. They're all dead," the captain said sadly.

Deac looked at the man, but acted as if he didn't hear. He knelt down under the door and felt around for the manual override catch.

"Did you hear me, Lieutenant?" the captain asked in irritation. He was a slender man, with a thin mustache.

"H-U-A, Captain," Deac confirmed, and his face lit up when he found the catch and activated it.

"Then what are you doing? I just told you—"

Deac stood and put his hand on the door latch. "You don't mind if I check her myself, do you, Captain?" Though Deac was short and wiry, his demeanor had somehow turned dangerous.

The captain stiffened and took a step toward Deac. "Now, listen here, Lieutenant," he began, but then he stopped. The anger slowly melted from his face, and he sighed. "Never mind. Carry on, son. I know just how you feel." He turned sharply on his heel and marched away.

Deac wasted no time in lifting the door and stepping inside. Ben-ammi watched, fascinated, as Deac reached up and flicked some switches, then put his hand over the dark ignition keypad. "Come on, princess," Deac crooned. "C'mon, baby girl. You've never let me down, never . . ."

Darkon was amazed that Deacon Fong could even think there was hope in starting the Apache. Hadn't he seen what was going on?

Deac closed his eyes, sucked in his lower lip, and lovingly punched in the ignition code numbers. He hesitated with his finger over the Power Up button, and Darkon could clearly see the hope and anticipation in his normally impassive Oriental features. He pressed the button. When nothing happened, he quickly entered the code and pressed the button again. Then once more. And again.

Watching Deac's face became painful even for a hardened soldier like Colonel Ben-ammi of the Israeli air force. Besides that, he was a member of Fire Team Eclipse, and this was one of his men. Deac's smooth forehead accordioned, his eyes squeezed shut even tighter, and the corners of his mouth sagged. "Lieutenant," Darkon said softly. Deac's fingers were still racing over the keypad, performing the ignition start-up over and over again. Darkon lightly laid his rough hand over Deac's fine, sensitive one. "Lieutenant, she's not going to start."

Deac snatched his arm out from under Darkon's hand and slowly leaned forward until his forehead rested against the dead instrument panel. Shocked, Darkon thought he was actually going to cry. "It's not right," Deac whispered. "My poor princess, my sweet baby, it's not right."

Now Darkon became a little uncomfortable. The pilot was grieving as if he'd lost a comrade or a loved one—he was actually *talking* to the helo. With a start, Darkon realized that Fong *was* talking to a loved one. He'd seen the way the Apache performed in Deac's capable and, yes, loving hands over the months. He'd seen the pure joy on the helo pilot's face when he got the waspish and agile helicopter to perform a particularly dashing maneuver. Right or wrong, Lieutenant Deacon Fong was in love with the Apache.

Darkon suddenly remembered when he was Deac's age and considered himself the hottest pilot to graduate from the Israeli ranks. He could still remember his first fixed wing, a British P-12 Centaur. Aircraft were indeed like people, in that they all possessed little quirks here and there. The Centaur had been unusually touchy on banking right, and much more sluggish on the left. There was absolutely no logical or mechanical reason for the plane's peculiarities, and Darkon doubted that any other pilot would notice it, but it did have those personality traits. And it was, after all, *his* plane, and Darkon had come to understand her as he had his own wife.

A wife, yes, he reflected as he watched Deac lightly slide his fingers over the dark instrument panel. *That is how much this Apache means to Deac. Strange, but true.*

Darkon's meditations were again interrupted, because that's when the shooting started.

Sergeant Rio Valdosta had been on his forty-seventh push-up when the lights went out. He jumped to his feet at once and reached for his TechStar MK-20 laser rifle he'd left leaning against his bed after cleaning it. The barracks room he shared with David Mitchell had no windows, but even in the pitch blackness he found the door and opened it.

The barracks complex that Fire Team Eclipse occupied housed seventy-five men, most of whom were tech-heads. Rio didn't think they were a bad bunch. They were just wimps. He supposed that in some way their jobs were important, but they and their little chores didn't concern him. The only entity that mattered was his own fire team. Some of the tech-heads came out of their rooms and naturally drifted toward him in the hallway, where dim starlight came from a few skylights spaced at intervals along the ceiling.

"What's going on, Rio?" a sergeant named Masters asked.

"Hey, you're the tech-head, you tell me."

"I'm a tactical systems engineer," Masters responded in an offended tone.

"Whatever. With a fancy title like that, seems like you ought to be telling *me* how to turn the lights back on." Rio heard some shouting outside and ran to the door, with the others following in a bunch like bewildered sheep.

When they'd stepped outside, they all stared in wonder.

"Whoa!" Masters said. "I thought it was just our barracks. It looks like the whole complex is out."

"That's not possible, is it?" another man asked.

Masters answered smartly, "No. Guess it's a figment of our imaginations."

Rio's thoughts turned to his fire team, scattered who-knew-where around the quadrant. *If the whole base is down, then . . .* "We're nekkid, ladies," he told the others.

"Huh? What do you mean?" Masters blustered.

"I mean no radar, no satellite protection, no weapons . . ." Rio stopped, and with a sinking feeling looked down at his TechStar rifle. Flipping off the safety, he raised the rifle into the air and pulled the trigger. No laser bolt, no recoil. He engaged the laser sight, but no thin red line shot up into the sky.

A group of grunts trotted past them and noticed what Rio had done. They stopped as one, and everyone looked at the TechStar in Rio's hands with awe.

"It doesn't *work?*" one of the grunts asked in disbelief.

"'Pears not," Rio answered grimly. "Where did you guys come from?"

"The airstrip. *Nothing* works—no tracking grids on the artillery, no Scorpions, even the Vees won't fire up. Now the TechStars don't work?"

"Were there any officers where you were?" Rio asked.

They looked at one another. One said tentatively, "I think I saw a colonel standing around and scratching his head."

Masters looked warily around the base and said, "We could be attacked at any time. What do we do, throw rocks?"

Rio was thinking. Everything they had was useless because it all depended on electricity and power cells. What didn't? Suddenly he snapped his fingers. "PSA's. Any of you guys got PSA's?"

The grunts and techies looked blank. "What's a PSA?"

"Personal Side Arm, dummies. You know, guns? The little ones? The ones they give you when you get out of basic?"

"Oh, I forgot about that," the apparent leader of grunts finally answered. "Nah, I didn't take one. Why take a clunky old 9 mm when we had a TechStar?"

Rio was stupefied. "You mean they were going to give you a gun—for free!—and you turned it down?"

Upon completion of basic training, recruits were offered the old 9 mm laser-sighted pistol as a backup in case the TechStar malfunctioned. Captain Slaughter had insisted that every member of his fire team receive full training on the weapon. "You just never know," had been his simple explanation. He even had his grandfather's old Remington 12-gauge pump shotgun he'd let Rio fire a few times. Rio Valdosta, a true modern-day Paladin, had loved it.

Rio stuttered in disbelief, "You mean to tell me not one of you dummies has a nine-mil?"

"I think I do," one of the grunts finally said, and eventually one or two more thought they might have kept the old guns, if they could just remember where they'd put them.

"Okay, you girls that are armed, go fetch your guns and bring 'em out here to me. I know you don't know how to shoot 'em, so I'll shoot one or two of them to show you. At least the nine-mils should still work." With that, he dashed off to his own room and rummaged around in his foot locker, donning his NVG's and finding the nine in the bottom, gleaming dully. Pulling back the slide and injecting a round in the chamber, Rio whispered, "I sure hope you work, old man."

Outside, the tech-heads stared at him and the weapon with trepidation. "I've never fired one of those antiques," Masters sniffed. "They're just for parade dress, you know."

"Too bad for you, you don't know what you're missing," Rio said, grinning. To the pistol, he whispered, "Come on, baby," and raised it in the air. The explosion caused all of the tech-heads to jump in fear. "It works!" Rio cried, then fired off another round out of pure joy. More grunts emerged from their barracks and began testing their nines. A bullet whizzed by Rio's head, way too close. "Hey, stupid, watch where you're aiming!"

One of the grunts, a youngster with a shaved head and a goofy grin, said, "Sorry, Sarge. I'm used to having the laser sight. How are we supposed to aim these things?"

"Just point and shoot but not at human targets, you idiots! The bullet goes in the direction the barrel's pointed, you know! If you can't even hit the sky with it, give it up!"

"Hey, Rio," Masters called, "you got any more of those things?"

Rio remembered the other weapons his team had, but said, "What's the matter, Masters? Your fancy TechStar not good enough for you now?"

After a little more satisfactory shooting, and taunting the tech-heads who didn't have weapons, Rio slipped away from the group and returned to his room. Rummaging through David's footlocker, he found his nine and pushed both pistols into his belt. Each team member had been issued three boxes of shells, so Rio grabbed his field pack and stuffed the boxes inside.

In Captain Slaughter's room, he found his nine, pocketed it, and gingerly lifted the shotgun out of the footlocker. "Gotta be careful with this thing," he told himself, "I *know* what kind of damage you can do, Mr. Remington." He also found three bandoliers of shotgun shells, each loop filled with a brass-based load. "Oh, yeah!" he breathed, stringing the bandoliers over his neck and shoulder and placing the 9 mm shells in the backpack.

Rio found Ric Darmstedt's and Deac Fong's pistols and stuck them in his belt, too. After gathering the boxes of shells, he immediately began thinking of where to find more ammunition. After all, in a weird situation like this you could never have too many bullets. "Quartermasters, quartermasters, o' course," he muttered, and, weighted down with his distinct burdens, he went back outside.

"Rio?" Captain Slaughter called from his right just as he burst through the door.

"Captain, sir!" Rio did stop in his headlong run long enough to salute snappily.

Con Slaughter raked his gaze up and down his sergeant, taking in the beltline crowded with the handles of nine millimeters, the three bandoliers of shotgun shells, the bulging backpack, and the Remington itself. "Planning on starting your own little war, Rio?"

"Oh, here, Cap'n," Rio said, handing over the shotgun. "I wasn't liberating it, I hope you know. Seems like these old manual weapons are the only things that work around here. That's a kick in the pants, huh? Well . . . gotta go, sir."

"Uh—Hold up there, Rio. Just exactly where do you think you're going? Nowhere flammable, I hope."

Rio cracked a smile. "No, sir. Thought I'd go down to the quartermasters and see about some more ammo, sir."

"More? You've got enough right there to take down a Tornado! Change of orders—you're coming with me."

Of course Rio immediately fell in with his captain. "Sir, yes, sir. Where are we going?"

"To the Command Center first, then to the Apache. The GL's aren't working, did you know? No, you've been kinda occupied with the weapons. Anyway, I figure the team's probably reconnoitered there."

"That's affirmative, sir. Deac'll be there, at least."

Slaughter and Valdosta found Ric Darmstedt and Vashti Nicanor just exiting the command center as they reached it. Con hailed them, and when they met he asked, "What's the situation in there, Darmstedt?"

Ric shook his head. "Don't even bother, Captain, sir. That is unless you want to see a bunch of generals and colonels screaming at one another and everyone else. The whole thing's down, and nobody knows what to do about it except yell at everybody else."

"What about the rest of the team?"

"We haven't seen anyone but Sergeant Mitchell, Captain. We told him to meet us at the Apache. Figure the team will go there eventually." Ric looked at Rio's gear and asked, "Was that you doing all that shooting, Valdosta?"

"No, sir. Well . . . not *all* of it. The grunts were just happy to have something to use if the whole Chinese army showed up or something."

"Don't laugh, Rio. We don't know that's not going to happen."

Con Slaughter grunted. "We don't know if it hasn't already happened." This was a sobering thought to everyone, and he went on, "Okay, let's head to the helo yard. I want my team in order ASAP."

Vashti hurried over to Con Slaughter's side. "What do you think happened here, Captain?"

He gave her an odd look. "What do *you* think happened, Colonel? Has the Mossad ever run across something like this?"

Everyone knew that Darkon Ben-ammi and Vashti Nicanor reported to the Israeli intelligence agency, the Mossad. All Israelis did. It's just that it wasn't acknowledged in polite company. But Vashti Nicanor felt that they—she, her partner, and their fire team—were beyond such political considerations, so she answered Captain Slaughter honestly. "No, Captain, we've never encountered such a thing. Lieutenant Darmstedt said it may be solar flares. That would not be—an intentional strike, you see."

"Sure," Slaughter grunted. "And it could be little green men from Mars, or cave worms from the center of the earth. But our systems should have warned us of any of those things. Especially solar flares, Colonel. We should have had warnings for months— maybe even years—in advance. Besides, if it was solar flares suddenly interfering with the electromagnetic fields, all of the planes should have gone down, too."

Vashti tucked a thick strand of black hair behind her ear, then nodded resignedly. "I know, you're right, Captain, and Lieutenant

Darmstedt did say the same things. It would be a neat and comfortable explanation—if it fit. Anyway, what bothers me the most is that we don't know how extensive this is."

"If it took us out *and* Colorado Springs, I'd be willing to bet we're not alone, Colonel Nicanor."

They were silent the rest of the way, each dealing with his or her own thoughts and night-frights. When they reached the Apache, they found David, Deac, and Darkon sitting with their backs to the huge tires, talking quietly. They got to their feet when they saw Con, who asked, "I don't suppose I need a status report on the helo, Deac?"

"She's grounded, sir." Deac refused to use the word *dead*.

Vashti went to Darkon and asked, "Are you all right?"

"Of course, Vashti."

She leaned close and, like the father figure he was to her, he gave her a rare comforting pat on the back. She whispered, "Home. Have you thought about it?"

"I haven't stopped thinking about it, Vashti. But what can we do?"

Now this exquisite tool, this highly tuned weapon, Fire Team Eclipse, was together, healthy, at its peak and ready to fight—and they could do nothing. The team members looked at one another silently. For the first time, Vashti began to face the true impact of the blackout.

The truth was, they were helpless.

And they were alone.

NINETEEN

———◆———

To President Aristide Luca Therion, Project Final Unity was so pure and so perfect that he felt as if each moment of the past three and one-half days was like walking in his highest dream. Gazing around, an idyllic half-smile touching his woman-soft lips, he reflected that this room, these people, the images before his eyes and filling his mind and thoughts, were flawless, and the next moment would be equally whole and complete, and the next, and the next . . .

"Play the speech again, Commissar Mays," he ordered.

"Yes, sir," she answered, with professional neutrality. This was the third time the president had wanted to review his speech.

The room was a curious contrast of the old paths and the new. A formal sitting room, part of a bedroom suite on the third floor of the White House, Luca had never liked the coldness of the nineteenth-century furnishings, so he had set it aside for a secret Project Final Unity Situation Room. Two enormous Cyclops II screens had been added to the one, and now all of them were glowing, the images bright and sharp and compelling.

The first screen was a map of the United States. The state lines were faint gray, with co-op cities and the Man and Biosphere Project facilities vivid color-coded flashes. Overlaid across state boundaries, in bright green, were designated boundaries of the fourteen biomes.

The second screen was another map of the U.S., with major power grids depicted as spiky lines criss-crossing the continent. All co-op cities and other authorized directorate facilities were yellow dots, while areas blacked out by the ohm-bug were outlined in red, with major populated areas represented by red dots. For the last few days, since the execution of Project Final Unity, the cities, populated areas, and military bases that Luca and Minden had chosen to be blacked out had been without any power whatsoever. The German science team had achieved Project Final Unity with a 99.8 percent accuracy rate.

The third screen, now, showed the president of the United States making his declaration of a national emergency. It was short and forceful, reassuring to his allies, a warning to his enemies, Luca thought with satisfaction.

". . . early this morning. The Sixth Directorate has assured me that their emergency management personnel and transports will reach every affected area by this afternoon. Wherever you are, soon our dedicated commissars will be arriving, bringing water and food and medical supplies and attendants, and arranging for your evacuation to the nearest available facility.

"I must stress again: *Do not leave your homes!* And especially, do not evacuate to, or attempt to get assistance from, any military installation. At this time, I feel that I must tell you that I have placed our military forces on Priority Two Alert status, and our forces are therefore not available at this time for disaster assistance for our citizenry. But this alert, I assure you, is not because of outside threats. Though it grieves me greatly to confirm this, I feel that you, our peace-loving citizens of Earth's America, must know:

"We have determined that this massive blackout is the result of sabotage by disruptive forces within our own citizenry. The Secret Intelligence Division of the Sixth Directorate has found direct evidence of a conspiracy by an organization of religious fundamentalists—or perhaps I should say religious fanatics. As we have long known, these militant groups believe they have a commission from God. These men and women and—though it bruises me to know it—even children, see as their goal on this earth to punish, and ultimately rule over, those of us who are more tolerant and less blinded by notions of ruling men's minds. These religious conspirators have long been known to us as anarchists, but now we have evidence that they have committed this act of terrorism against the peace-loving people of Earth's America. This, then, is our enemy, and I give you my word that they will be detected, found, and brought to justice.

"In the meantime, my friends, remain calm and remain in your homes. Our dedicated Sixth Directorate commissars will soon be coming to your aid."

Minden Lauer, sitting close by him on the old Chesterfield sofa, smiled dreamily. "Your people love you, Luca, as they never did that hard and harsh Bishop Beckwith . . . already they have forgotten him as if he never existed. And after that passionate assurance from you, none of our people will fear."

That might have been true, at least for all of those who were not "religious fanatics." The president and all of the Project Final Unity team (the American team, anyway) thought that their reassuring broadcasts of salvation were going to all Cyclops users in the blacked-out areas, as all Cyclops had internal batteries that could last for up to four weeks. Upon losing the main power source, Cyclops automatically switched to full battery power for the first half hour, allowing a user to interface with any of its capabilities. After that, it switched over to a receiver-only mode to conserve the battery.

But of course, the ohm-bug had other uses for a 12-volt nickel cadmium battery. Cyclops' red eye had been dead in the blacked-out areas of the United States for over three days now. President Luca Therion had been talking to people who could not hear, and could not see. Neither could they go anywhere, unless they walked.

But President Luca Therion and his American Project Final Unity team were blissfully ignorant of this, too. It was the Germans' greatest triumph of deception: The ohm-bug was airborne. It was, in fact, almost omnipresent.

Luca and Minden resumed watching the tape of the broadcast, but soon Luca grew distracted by his chief commissar. Alia Silverthorne, a dark frown upon her tight face, paced back and forth behind the three commissars who were seated at the drones that were interfaced with the three Cyclops II screens. Her eyes darted back and forth, now between the first two screens only, as she ignored this third rendition of Luca's passionate speech.

Minden caught Luca's displeasure, and called out lightly, "Alia, you're like a cat in a cage. Come sit by me, and have some champagne, and stop making such grim faces!"

Obediently Alia came to stand by the sofa, but she asked courteously, "If you don't mind, I'll stand, My Lady. This operation is very complex, and I think I'd better go access another Cyclops II to start monitoring my commissar squads' status reports."

Minden laughed like a giddy young girl. "Did you hear that, Luca darling? Alia is being very grown up here, and she needs your Cyclops. Of course, she couldn't dare ask for it . . . but I dare. I dare anything." She dropped her eyes, then slid such a lascivious look up at Luca from under her thick lashes that it made his palms sweat.

"Go ahead, My Commissar," he muttered hoarsely. "I'll attend to Minden . . ." He reached for her, and with a slight grimace Alia hurried to stand behind Kev Jamison, her former bodyguard who was now her second in command of the commissars Alia had chosen to staff the monitoring of Project Final Unity. Along with his partner Schor Evans, these two bodyguards had pleased Alia with their meticulous attention and instant obedience to her command. Alia had also chosen Commissar Bennie Mays for the team, as the tall, gangly woman had made an impression on her at the lab on the day that Bennie had tried to shield Alia from the ire of the military men. Or perhaps it was the fact that Bennie was not attractive, and was no threat to Alia. She would never have admitted such a weakness and insecurity to herself, of course, but she did have a tendency to surround herself with women who could not compete with her.

Kev was seated at the third drone, and Alia murmured, "Incoming live comms?"

"Yes, My Commissar, five: from Lansing in the Fifth Directorate, and Little Rock, Jackson, Montgomery, and Atlanta in the Fourth."

"Give me Lansing first. No—strike that. Put them all in conference, split-screen, and notify."

"Yes, My Commissar." Kev's fingers moved lightly over the drone's keyboard; his small screen showed the commands he gave, while the large Cyclops II screens showed four men and one woman in separate boxes. "All stations, you are on tie-lines with Chief Commissar Alia Silverthorne," he said.

"Report, Lansing," Alia said curtly.

"All Unity teams are go, My Commissar," he said tightly.

"Any problems with the civilian population?"

"No, ma'am."

"Then Unity Teams Lansing are go. Little Rock?"

"All my Unity teams are go, My Commissar," she said in a soft southern drawl. "But I've received no communication from Hot Springs."

"None?" Alia said sharply. "No Cyclops comms at all?"

"No, My Commissar. And no refugees. There's been no—nothing."

Alia grimaced. "What about your civvies?"

The hard-faced, soft-spoken woman shrugged. "They're calm, My Commissar. A number of comm requests and questions have been directed to the commissary. But there has been no panic."

"Then Unity Teams Little Rock are go. Make Hot Springs first-line priority, Commissar. It will take how long for the team to reach Hot Springs?"

"About two hours, My Commissar."

"Report back to me personally in two hours."

"Yes, My Commissar."

"Commissar Jamison, who are those incoming?" In-line lights on Kev's drone keyboard were lighting up.

"Albany, Jackson, Mississippi, Orlando, Seattle—"

"All right, everyone's reporting in. Schor, you take the First Directorate; Bennie, you take the Second and Third Directorates; Kev, you take the Fifth Directorate, and I'll take the Fourth. Unless there's a trouble spot, you three handle the routine reports just as I have. Got it?"

"Yes, My Commissar," they solemnly answered, then started speaking softly into their transceivers. Kev Jamison managed to talk to his stations and put through Alia's Fourth Directorate commissars at the same time.

This went on for some time, as Alia watched the maps obsessively and Luca and Minden drank champagne and talked and laughed in low voices. This irritated Alia, as the president and his consort seemed to have no concept of the enormity of the project they were undertaking. They seemed to regard it as lightly as an Ultimate Reality game. Alia thought dryly that perhaps that's exactly what it was to them. To her, however, it was much more grimly real than any Cyclops-generated game.

Alia was pacing, her arms tightly crossed, behind her three assistants' chairs, her eyes continually scanning the wild colors and flashes of the map grids. Suddenly she stopped and stiffened. "Bennie? You have Albuquerque on-line?"

"No, My Commissar, they have already reported in and are go."

Alia's eyes narrowed to suspicious hazel slits. Bennie cleared her throat uncomfortably and said, "My Commissar? What is it?"

"Look at the Second Directorate map. Northern Arizona. There's a MAB Directorate facility . . . it's a lab, a classified underground facility that just went red. Lab XJ2197."

Bennie's fingers jabbed in the code. "XJ2197 is off-line, Commissar Silverthorne."

Alia stepped closer to Bennie, her eyes on the single flashing red dot. She made herself concentrate, though one little part of her mind was nagging, *Niklas . . . not trapped in that horrible buried coffin . . . Niklas . . .*

Finally she snapped, "Double-check Power Grid 36-SW1 through 41-SW8."

While Bennie was keying in the commands, a single green power grid line on the second screen suddenly turned red. Then another spiky line started flashing red, then another . . .

"Get me DFW right now!" Alia ordered harshly.

Bennie cleared her drone screen, hastily pushed buttons, and a smooth-faced young man popped up on the third Cyclops screen. "Y-yes, My Commissar?"

"Who are you?" Alia demanded.

"I—I'm Eric Lees, Third Scientific Minister, Konza—"

"Get me a high commissar. Now."

"Y-yes, yes—" He whirled and shouted in a high voice to someone out of range of the Cyclops eye. Helplessly he turned back to face the screen, swallowing hard. "One moment, My Commissar—"

More power lines in the Southwest were going out. Alia said with desperate calm, "Listen to me, Minister Lees. Do you have any Vindicators in the air?"

"Why—why, yes, of course, My Commissar. That's why—oh—thank the goddess—here's—uh—Commissar—uh—"

A stocky older woman appeared, and Alia commanded, "Get me a flyover of Albuquerque and Santa Fe right now, Commissar! I'm on-line until your Vindicators report!"

"Yes, My Commissar," the woman said, and instantly bent over a drone keyboard; Bennie put her image in one-fourth of the screen.

"Get me San Diego, Los Angeles, Denver on-line," Alia said tightly. "No—delay that. Get me NORAD. Now."

"Yes—" Bennie began.

One by one, beginning at the southernmost tip of California, the enormous co-op cities started flashing red, mocking winks from a vengeful Cyclops.

The commissar in Dallas, bending over her drone, her face dark, disappeared.

Minden and Luca stood up slowly, their faces blank.

Alia raised her voice for the first time. "Hurry! Get me NORAD now! Anybody!"

"Alia . . . ," Minden said tentatively.

"What—what's going on?" Luca blustered. "Commissar Silverthorne, I demand to know what's going on! Report to me right now!"

Alia ignored him. Grabbing Kev Jamison's shoulder, she said urgently, "What military bases are still on-line? Get me one of them now! Any of them!"

"Alia!" Minden's voice was a hysterical shriek. "Alia, call Tor! Call him now!"

Then the lights went out.

The Ranch House at *Shortgrass Steppe Biome,* *Lab XJ2197*

Niklas woke with a start, panting a little. The fading remnants of a nightmare came to him, one in which he'd been enclosed in a shiny steel box and unable to get out. It hadn't been a coffin, but that didn't matter; the claustrophobic feel had been scary enough.

He reached across the bed for Gildan, but found only empty sheets. That's right, *he thought groggily,* she's gone out to the barn to check on her—what was it? Cow? Vulture? Gopher? Whatever. Waste of time and sleep. *Then he noticed that he couldn't see her spot across the bed. He always left a muted light on in the bathroom, which normally lit the bedroom in a pale, bland light during the night. It was off now. The bulb must have burned out.* Blasted filaments, only last a few days . . . and my precious *chaco*—rotten little insects! You'd think they had organized a rebellion! *Niklas's lack of success with formulating the organism as his dreamed-of superconductors was actually what had set him off on this downhill slide of drink and mindless and careless intimacies with such women as Gildan Ives. It made his head ache to think about it.*

Groaning, stiff, the nightmare almost forgotten now, he groped his way to the kitchen of the ranch house, barking his shin on the edge of an end table on the way. "Man, this is some for-real dark," *he said aloud. He felt along the wall and pushed the light button near the sofa. Nothing. Niklas cursed and rounded the sofa, this time stubbing his bare toe, causing more, and more passionate, swearing. He found the remote to the Cyclops and by touch and memory pushed "on."*

The Cyclops screen remained blank.

For the first time he realized that the red eye of standby mode wasn't even glowing.

"What—what's happening?" Niklas muttered. If the Cyclops was

out—something that would never, ever be allowed to happen, food for the masses and all that—then that meant that there was no power. But how could there be no power? The lab had not one but two redundant power generators . . . And besides, what about the Cyclops internal battery?

The pain from his headache, barked shin, and stubbed toe faded away as he struggled to grasp the situation. "It's not possible!" he said aloud to the blank Cyclops screen. "If there's no power, even for a few hours . . ."

Suddenly he broke out in a sour sweat beneath his cotton pajamas. He groped his way into the elevator bedroom, his breath hitching in and out almost in hiccups. His eyes had grown adjusted somewhat to the inky blackness, and with a shaking hand he reached out and pushed the button to withdraw the phony wooden wall to reveal the elevator. It didn't budge. He pushed it again, more insistently, and then he was slamming the palm of his hand against it to no avail.

"This can't be happening. This is not happening!"

But of course it was.

He thought of the personnel trapped underground in the huge five-story facility. What must they be thinking at this moment? All two hundred of them? He had a good idea of what was going on beneath his feet, hundreds of feet down, and it was a lot worse panic than he felt at this moment.

Niklas stepped forward and pressed his ear to the wall. Suddenly he stiffened. The dream came back to him, his screaming and flailing at the lid of the box, trying to dig his fingernails into the smooth steel.

Niklas Kesteven, brilliant scientist, champion of the power of logic, thought he heard screams coming from the elevator shaft behind the wall. He knew, in the deep recesses of his mind, that this was a physical impossibility. The elevator and all levels below were hermetically sealed from the surface of the earth. Completely airtight. No human ear could possibly pick up any sound waves from that buried titanium-enforced steel canister.

But still he thought he heard faint, muted screams from two hundred doomed people.

Niklas raced through the great room, out into the yard to the woodpile, and snatched up an ax. His heart was pounding so fast and hard that it occurred to him that he might have a heart attack. But the horror of the screaming—it was getting louder, wasn't it?—pushed aside any thought of himself.

Back in the bedroom, he began swinging the ax into the wall with clumsy but powerful strokes. Sweat stung his eyes, but he didn't care. He couldn't hear the screaming over his own desperate gasps and the sound of the blade biting into the wood, but he knew the awful sounds were still there. The wall began to come apart, and he attacked with even more vigor. Once the ax head exploded through to strike the elevator door itself with a fearsome shower of sparks.

Finally Niklas dropped the ax and began tearing at the splintered paneling until he'd created an opening large enough for him to step through. He placed his ear against the cold, dense door and listened through his ragged breathing.

Still there. Faint, very faint, but still he heard desperate screams. Cries for help from his fellow scientists and coworkers. Some of them he called friends. Some of them he had even loved.

Niklas sat down heavily amid the litter of splintered wood on the cold floor and stared into the unforgiving darkness.

TWENTY

———◆———

Considering that there were almost five thousand commercial airplanes in the sky, and that all of America went dark in less than two hours, there were very few accidents. Those that were in the process of landing when they lost runway lights and communication were actually in the most danger, for by now the ohm-bug was fully airborne and started hungrily attacking the great electrical monsters as soon as they touched down. Most of the jets were starting to lose their systems by the time they were parked. Others never got to their designated terminals, and it didn't take long before the pilots started just heading off the runways anywhere they saw a hole as soon as they landed and slowed.

The air traffic controllers, in their tense and dark rooms, were always walking the thin edge of nervous breakdown anyway. When their screens went dark and their lights went out and their telephones went dead, most of the male controllers started sweating and shouting, while many of the women went into wailing hysterics. The ones in between were sort of catatonic, walking around with blank looks on their faces, pushing buttons and picking up dead Cyclops transceivers and humming little tunes.

The only thing that saved the thousands of people on the planes were the pilots and, of all things, the baggage handlers. The pilots, whose planes were functioning perfectly even if the ground was going nuts, went into automatic emergency mode, and stayed cool.

The baggage handlers, better than anyone, understood immediately how important it was going to be to keep all runways clear, all the side runs clear, and even the fields surrounding the airports clear. By the thousands, they formed into crews to get the planes that were still landing bunched up as close to the terminals as possible while they were still running. They were the ones who figured out that the cheap little flashlights worked when the big lanterns didn't. They were the ones who knew where the luminous signal lanterns were stashed in the cavernous storage spaces—now dark—under the miles of terminals. They were the ones who quickly formed into teams to get people away from the runways as they deplaned from the emergency chutes.

Still, there were terrible tragedies. At Chicago's O'Hare, a jumbo 810 landed and the pilot, who was nervous, jogged just a bit to the left. His wing barely tapped another 810 that had landed and only had time to pull off the runway onto the bordering field before it died. The moving 810 ricocheted like a wild bullet, spun around, then wheeled into the tightly packed row of stranded planes at the side of the long strip. The explosions that followed killed everyone on board the 810, eighty-nine others who were still evacuating a 787, and sixty-three people—mostly baggage handlers and airline crews—who were working around the planes. Fourteen other people who were standing almost half a mile away on another runway received second-degree heat burns from the fireball.

Twyla Lee Halston was piloting a GlobeNet 787 into John F. Kennedy Airport—or trying to. She had been in a holding pattern at 42,000 feet for six hours. The pilots of all the jumbos had immediately logged on to the emergency band as soon as they'd lost ground communication, so they were talking to one another. Soon an authoritative-sounding pilot for GlobeNet by the name of John Smithson had taken over the air traffic control, and so far he'd done pretty well. The smaller planes had all diverted to the private airfields so the seventy-nine jumbos circling the dark airport had managed to stay out of one another's way without getting swatted by, or barreling into, the little guys. Smithson had managed to get thirty-two of the jumbos landed so far.

But now three of them were in trouble, because they had been international flights and were low on fuel. Twyla Lee's bird was one of these, as she had just completed what was to be her last Paris run. Smithson hadn't tried to change everyone's altitude; he'd barely been able to compute who was where and get the bottom-most ones down first. Trying to land the jets according to any other priorities was just impossible.

"GlobeNet 555, this is Smithson. How you holding out?"

"Captain Smithson, I'm holding my breath so as not to use so much fuel. Is it our turn yet? I mean, I'm not too worried, but my copilot's in the john losing her dinner. For the fourth time." Twyla Lee tried to speak lightly, but she was still afraid that she sounded whiny. In the eerie green glow of her instruments, her plain features drew down into a deep frown.

John Smithson's even tones grew deeper. "555, you out of a copilot?"

Twyla Lee sighed, then cleared her throat before answering in a bloodless tone, "Yes, sir. My copilot is—unable to assist at this time." The silly girl had gone off the deep end in about thirty minutes. Twyla Lee had decided that her screeching and crying had been worse than facing this all by herself, and had sent the panic-stricken woman back to the cabin.

A long silence ensued, and it took all the self-control Twyla Lee had not to key in the mike and beg Smithson to talk to her.

Finally he came back and calmly said, "Twyla Lee, we've still got four heavies under you that we've got to get down and out of the way. That's about another hour. What do you think?"

Bleakly she answered, "I have about twenty minutes left, Captain."

Another long silence. Twyla bit her lip so hard that she tasted salty blood on her tongue.

"Okay, here's what we've got, Twyla Lee," Smithson said in a businesslike voice. "You could try Cannery Airfield in east Jersey. It's the only old military field that's got a runway long enough. But that's one of the old ones that some of the smaller planes were going to divert to—twelve that I know of. And you know we haven't had any communication from any of them after touch-down."

"Yes, sir, I know. Is that my only option?"

"That's the only airfield that might be possible. Your only other options are the interstates."

Twyla Lee swallowed hard, but when she answered her voice was as composed as John Smithson's. "Sir, do we have any idea at all about the auto traffic? Are the roads cleared, are they congested—can anyone even see anything on them?"

"Sorry, 555. No word on them, except that a couple of the landed flights have reported that even the interstates are blacked out."

"But—what about car lights?" Twyla shot back.

"They—it would seem that either there aren't any cars on the interstates, or . . ."

"Or they're stacked up there, dead," Twyla Lee finished in a dry voice.

No answer.

Finally Twyla Lee keyed in her mike, and said quietly, "Captain Smithson, it's been a pleasure doing business with you. You've been a real hero."

"No. You're the hero, Twyla Lee," he said quietly. "God go with you."

So quietly she could scarcely be heard, John Smithson heard her say, "Pray for us. 555 signing off."

Twelve minutes later GlobeNet Flight 555 crashed into a line of cars on 278 on Staten Island. All 273 souls aboard perished, and 18 stranded motorists were killed.

At 28,000 feet above John F. Kennedy Airport, John saw the fireball rise into the sky and whispered, "Hail Mary, full of grace, the Lord is with thee, blessed art thou among women and blessed is the fruit of thy womb, Jesus. Holy Mary, Mother of God, pray for us sinners, now and at the hour of our death . . ."

———•———

In the United States of America in the year 2050, a total of 743,989 elevators rode their vertical cables every day. However, only about half of them were ever in use at one time, mostly because of the massive migration to the huge co-op cities. Had the ohm-bug struck during peak business hours, the results would have been much worse, but that was little consolation to the 232,620 souls who became trapped in these elevators, some as high as seventy stories.

Quite a few industrious and athletic individuals climbed out and brought back help for their stranded colleagues. Some of the elevators stopped exactly even with a floor, and the occupants were able to jam open the doors through brute strength and escape. Others were saved by relatives or friends who figured out where they were over the next two days.

Others weren't so lucky.

Those who had no loved ones and weren't able to get out numbered 1,236. Eventually they succumbed to exhaustion and thirst. One hundred and twelve people plunged to their deaths trying to climb the grease-slick cables. Sixty-four perished from medical conditions ranging from heart attacks to lack of maintenance drugs for certain illnesses. Not all rescue attempts were successful: 144 people died from panicked attempts at getting them out, some falling down the shafts, some slipping from inadequately secured lines, some simply losing their grips on the last human touch—a rescuer's grip. Claustrophobic suicides, some ill-disguised as escape attempts, numbered twenty-three. Murders numbered eighteen.

The tragedies did not discriminate between young and old, rich and poor; all races and religions and political persuasions were included. Forever after, elevators were simply referred to as "death boxes."

Senator Donald Black of Wyoming had decided to treat some of his aides and good friends to a ski trip as reward for their hard work in getting him reelected to his fourth term. No partners or wives were present, but the senator—ever the accommodating host—had arranged for companions for everyone according to their particular tastes. All were in a fine mood as they rode the ski lifts to the top of the mountain for one last dash down the slope. When the lifts came to a dead halt halfway up, they laughed it off, joked about how the Jackson Hole ski lift system was about as reliable as Congress, and enjoyed the view from their fifteen-hundred-foot height.

Night fell, and with it came the biting wind and a few flakes of snow from an oncoming blizzard they had been warned of, but had not cared about on that bright and silvery morning. Their screams to the operators and people on the ground could be heard, at first, anyway. Of course, there was nothing anyone could do. A healthy, fit Wall Street executive named Banyon fell to his death as he tried to climb back down the cable. In the cruel cold, his strength left him after only a few hundred feet. A few others tried, with the same result. Their screams as they fell echoed magnificently.

Senator Black had never comprehended just how cold his home state could get in the heights of the Rocky Mountains. That night he finally understood. He and his companion, a wispy-faced boy of only twenty, huddled together through the night, trying to keep themselves warm through the blizzard. It worked for about two hours, and then they went to sleep and never woke up.

Ski lift deaths across the icy West totaled 578.

———

Besides being an island, Manhattan had been a world unto itself for over a century, and in the previous four decades that had changed the face of America forever, Manhattan had remained largely untouched. The only major difference the dictates of the Man and Biosphere Project had made to the island was the fire that had devastated Central Park in '22. The park had been mandated for "re-wilding" in 2010, which meant that the awful, dirty, polluting people had been forbidden to enter the park, except for the wide walks around the perimeter. The interior was soon ruled by brambles and thickets, rats and noisome insects. No one ever knew how the fire started, but after twelve years of human neglect, the wilderness was impenetrable to fire teams and the hydrants were long lost and gone. The park burned for four days, and within a year new spiky MAB high-rise apartments covered the lost paradise.

Apart from that, Manhattan was much the same as it had always been. The population was about four million, and most of them had never been off the island. Many of them had never been to either side of it. Why should they? Seventy-eight percent of them lived in Man and Biosphere housing, working via Cyclops, with everything they needed either under their roof or delivered to their doors. The Upper West Side was a gated Structured Dependence Facility, and certainly they never left their drug-saturated community. So the island was still a world unto itself.

In that world, and even in the real world, the New York Stock Exchange was still a center of interest, and it was one of the few places where most of the employees still physically went to work. In fact, with the seamless and instantaneous Cyclops-linked networking of brokers, dealers, and exchanges around the world, the New York Stock Exchange never closed, and many of the employees almost lived there. Angstrom Klerk was one of these.

He was young, only twenty-eight, and he'd been designing computer models at the NYSE since he was eighteen. He'd quit an MS fellowship at MIT because it was boring him. Thin, with unruly black hair, premature eye wrinkles from squinting at a computer screen, and a kid's grin, his mathematical genius was almost immeasurable. He began by designing models for financial derivative contracts, and then—as an amusing sideline—he began structuring the contracts themselves. Financial derivatives, highly leveraged, speculative mazes of investments, were incomprehensible to all but a few computer wizards, mathematical prodigies, and financial geniuses. Angstrom Klerk was all of these; he was also incredibly wealthy, and still he was bored.

But he hadn't been bored for the last three days, because the markets, of course, had been performing bizarre permutations since the blackout had hit the United States. Of course anything that affected America's market affected the entire world, and Ang had amused himself for almost an entire day constructing a model predicting what each market in the ten spheres of economic influence would do next. His modeling had proved to be, so far, 82 percent correct, and he'd made another million or so adjusted dollars for himself and had almost single-handedly managed to stabilize the tantrum-prone globally based financial derivatives market.

But now, on the third day of the blackout, he was getting bored again. The floor of the exchange was still lively—in comfortable times it was quiet, with muted and dignified voices talking into SATphones and the drone of Cyclops-generated audio—but for the last three days there had been lots of shouting and hysterics.

Too much for little blackouts in the hinterlands, Ang thought with irritation. *Everything's smoothing out again—the Euromark hardly even flinched, after all! Don't these imbeciles realize that nothing really important has been affected . . . just some squatters in Texas, I guess, and some yahoos in the South . . . and some apple farmers in the Northeast. None of the co-ops have been affected, the imports are still*

*coming in, the exports are still going out, and Cyclops is still hum-
ming . . . what's the uproar all about?*

Of course, Angstrom Klerk, being much smarter than most
human beings, didn't have all of his wealth tied up in the never-
never cyberland of the stock market. For years he had been stash-
ing gold and silver coins and precious jewels, and they weren't
stashed in any inaccessible bank vault, either. He'd designed a
home safe and security system, and then had actually built and
installed it himself, with his own hands, and all without Cyclops's
red eye ever seeing a thing. Ang certainly wasn't one of those weird
end-of-the-world militants; it was just that it had given him great
satisfaction to completely insure himself against any force or man
or woman or organization or entity.

After lunch, the buzz was decreasing somewhat as the numbers
flashing across the hundreds of Cyclops screens continued to stabilize. Ang leaned back in his creaky but comfortable chair and
grinned, running his hands through his hair. Two more benchmark
securities that were touchstones of his model had just done exactly
what he'd predicted they'd do. Life was good.

The lights went out. Ang could have sworn that his beloved
Cyclops sighed, and then went dark.

The silence was heavy, assaulting the ears with its oppressive-
ness. It seemed to last for a long time . . .

But then the screaming began.

After two minutes, eight people were already dead from
being trampled in the inky blackness, forty-six others had broken
bones, and eighty-two others had gotten bruised and scraped and
bashed.

Still in his private cubicle, still sitting in his personally modeled
ergonomic chair, Angstrom Klerk began to laugh wildly, though
tears were rolling down his face.

His vault, his lovely safe he'd created and formed with his own
hands to hold his treasures, was behind two inches of titanium-
reinforced steel.

There were no manual controls to open it.

Angstrom Klerk began to think that maybe he wasn't so smart after all.

⸻

On Directorate Highway 94 just west of Denver, the traffic flowed heavily but smoothly down the four-lane mountainside, which happened to be particularly steep at a 12 percent grade. Most of the vehicles were commuters from the big city, the lucky and rare few who still owned property in the foothills. Mostly through bribes they were able to hold off the Sixth Directorate's increased pressure to assign them to the Man and Biosphere co-op cities. Some of them were relatives of high-ranking officials in the organization, and thereby retained favor. No matter who they were or who they knew or what they'd done, every passenger of every car lost their breath with fright when their cars quit.

When the batteries in the cars went out, so did the brakes, thanks to an engineer named Sevvy Quint who'd invented a braking system powered by the battery rather than the ancient fossil-fuel method that was polluting our beloved Lady Earth. Very quickly, a few of the drivers on Directorate Highway 94 began to wish mightily that Sevvy Quint had never been born.

The cars heading down the dangerous incline began picking up speed, and then bouncing off of one another, too crowded to leave the road and nowhere to go if they could. Drivers going up the mountain were faced with the impossible prospect of steering straight while their vehicles lost power and began backing down the slope. These turned out to be the fortunate ones, however— much more fortunate than their fellow drivers moving down at increasing speed. All of the backward moving cars eventually spun sideways into the side of the mountain from which the highway had been cut, or into the median wall. Most of them came to a stop, and those that somehow managed to turn all the way around had their progress stopped by the immobile ones. All of them were left with the horrifying sight of the cars in the lanes thundering downhill at terrifying speeds. A little more than halfway down, at a very sharp right curve, these juggernauts jumped the median retaining wall and crashed headlong into the immobile drivers. This area soon became a death pit.

Those that managed to fly past the curve were faced with a left hand curve every bit as vicious at the one they'd just successfully navigated. The guardwall didn't last past the second vehicle that hit it, and it collapsed to allow car after car to plunge off into the canyon. It was a 2,200-foot drop to a shallow, icy creek below.

Gazing at the bottom, when it was finally over, one old-timer said that it looked like the old tin-can garbage dumps of the earlier century, where he used to go and shoot rats with his .22 pistol.

———————

Even the most militant Greens of the Man and Biosphere Project cared little for North Dakota. Plans for an Arctic biome were still far in the future—because the snow would live. Even humans couldn't conquer and kill the snow wilderness.

Darlie Lundvaal, now sixty-two years old, reveled in the fact that she still lived alone, self-sufficient and triumphant, in her grandfather's house by the shores of Lake Sakakawea. She was a stark and bony woman, her limbs strong, her skin like blistered leather from the decades of savage winters. Her hair, now as white as the eternal snow surrounding her, was still thick and luxuriant, and reached below her waist. She brushed it twice a day, and shampooed it every other day, drying it by the fierce heat of her fires. The only thing that Darlie resented about getting older was that she couldn't get warm as easily as she could when she was young and vigorous. That, and the fact that she had outlived her husband by three years now. They'd been lonely years, but still Darlie had no wish to go live in her designated retirement co-op city of Helena, Montana. She'd been to that sprawling Gotham once. Once was enough.

Grunting a little, she heaved a fat oak log onto the fire.

"Last one, Lord," she said, pursing her lips and narrowing her eyes. "Those good aged oak logs burn fine and long. But then . . . but then . . . the cold."

She pulled her ancient rocker up as close to the stone hearth as she dared. Darlie already had on several layers of clothing, with the oldest but warmest pure wool on top. She also had a sassy orange wool cap that she'd knitted herself and wool gloves that her husband had given her for the last Christmas they'd celebrated together. Staring down at them, she smiled to herself and reflected dryly, "Shows you how foolish all my squirreling stuff away is . . . I never wore these gloves, they were so fine I was 'saving' them. Well, for certain I won't be wearing them out now . . ."

Rocking steadily, she ate and drank her last cup of tea with the last dollop of sugar and the last homemade bran muffin. All to go with the last oak log. She ate and drank slowly, with relish, thinking how very good everything had tasted for the last three days.

"All together, I tell You, Lord, it's been a good life," she murmured calmly, laying her head back and closing her eyes. "And it looks like I'll be just going to sleep. And, Lord, I say that it'll be a good death."

After a little while she whispered, "Even so, come Lord Jesus."

The western desert in the heat of the day

Reinhart looked down at the old city of Albuquerque, New Mexico. Part of the city was burning, and part of it looked as though it had been bombed. A squadron of his beloved F16 Tornadoes flew off in an arrow-straight formation toward the south. Reinhart backed his horse, and motioned Zoan to pull back farther into the shelter of the overhanging cliff behind them.

The horse beneath him was flecked with frothy white sweat and blew her lips together with a slobbering sound. Leaning over, Reinhart patted the horse and thought for a moment about the four days he had spent with Zoan in the Indian camp, and the two days and two nights they had spent crossing the empty desert. Those had been strange days for him. He would not easily forget Zoan and his friends.

"A long ride, my friend," he said rather awkwardly. When Zoan merely nodded, Reinhart slipped off his horse and handed the lines of the simple rope bridle to him. Uncomfortably, Reinhart tried to think of some way to adequately express his gratitude. Finally he said, "I'm forever in your debt, Zoan. I would have died if it hadn't been for you. I hope that I may have the opportunity to repay you someday."

Zoan smiled and it lightened his whole face; he looked like an innocent young choirboy. "I'm glad we met, Reinhart. And I think we will meet again."

At those words Reinhart felt that Zoan, perhaps, still thought that Reinhart might betray him. The German felt the need to, once again, impress on his friend that he would never reveal the secret. "I won't tell anyone." He smiled then. "I won't swear because I know you don't like it, Zoan. But I will not tell anyone about you and your friends and the canyon."

Zoan did not answer. His unusual eyes grew darker as the pupils *dilated, and he seemed to look through, and beyond, the German for a moment. "If he finds out," he said quietly, "you'll die."*

Oberleutnant *Reinhart Angriff, a loyal German of the Luftwaffe, a professional soldier and warrior by heart and blood and history, felt a terrible fear at Zoan's calm words. Rigidly controlling the bile in his throat, and deepening his voice to a growl, he said evenly, "On my honor as a soldier, Zoan. I will never speak of you to anyone. Now— I must say good-bye. Thank you once again, my friend." He bowed slightly and clicked his heels together, a long-forgotten gesture of respect from men of his race.*

Zoan said, "God go with you, Reinhart Angriff. I'll pray for you. And I'm glad to call you friend." Then he turned the stallion back to the north and disappeared into the heat-shimmers of the cruel desert.

TWENTY-ONE

THE CITY OF HOT SPRINGS was old, its homes aged, its commercial buildings antiquated. The soul of the town—and most of its square mileage—was actually a two-centuries-old national park, with fine old hardwoods carefully tended through the years. Hot Springs burned like a dead dry thornbush.

The fire was started by an old couple who, in their fear of the anarchy that resulted from the blackout, shakily lit candles in every room in their old house. The parlor's green velvet drapes that dated from the antebellum era burned in less than thirty seconds. Ena Drennan, at seventy-four years old, was overcome by smoke in less than five minutes. Her husband, Mackey, died a few minutes later, trying to drag her out. The house burned down to the ground in about twenty minutes, and the brisk, rising fall breeze carried the sparks from street to street.

The Commissary Headquarters for Hot Springs was located in the old Arlington Hotel. Commissar Xanthe St. Dymion had a third-floor room with a single dingy window that had ages ago been painted shut, so the fires, and the confused shouts of the people outside, didn't awaken her.

But the screaming did.

She had come starkly awake, then jumped out of bed and yanked the dusty velvet curtain back from her window. The raging fire lit up the night sky. At the great intersection of Grand and

Central, she could see people running, yelling, pointing, panicked. The screaming woman was somewhere in the building, maybe on the first floor. Along with all this Xanthe's quick mind registered another odd and frightening thing: *All the power is off. No lights.* She glanced back at the ever-present Cyclops screen inset into the wall. *Even the red-eyed monster, as Brother Mitchell called it, is dead. That's why I haven't been called out . . . no one knows how to communicate without Cyclops anymore. No high commissar would ever think of having to knock on doors to call out the troops by voice command . . .*

"A complete breakdown," she murmured. Quickly she dressed and left her room. The elevator was dead, so she groped her way carefully down the stairs. The screaming had stopped, but she could hear more muffled shouts from the street.

Outside she saw a stygian scene of confused and frightened people running, shouting, sometimes pushing others and fighting. Some of the shouts, as she moved along, turned into screams of fear. She moved toward the center of the intersection, where the big decorative fountain formed the center of a little-used traffic circle. Many people, mostly men, were milling around aimlessly, although some did seem to be trying to organize a bucket brigade. The ancient Grand Hot Springs Hotel, on one corner, was ablaze and somehow that gave her a wrench. The old twelve-story building was beautiful in a way. Xanthe had loved the hotel's faded grandeur, but now yellow tongues of flame licked from every window. Even as she watched, a woman in a pale pink nightgown threw herself out of a window on the top floor uttering a shriek that was cut off as she struck the pavement.

Xanthe was thunderstruck; until now she hadn't actually comprehended the dangerous scenes around her. She stood still, trying to decide what to do. A man pushed her, his face distorted with fear and rage, and Xanthe pushed him back. He ran off, cursing.

She was confused, disoriented, and growing more afraid. Frowning, she took a step toward the men who had managed to form a shaky line and were passing buckets back and forth from the fountain to the Grand Hotel. It was a hopeless exercise, she realized, and stopped again. Even as she watched, three men ran by, chasing a young girl who looked behind her as she ran fleetly, her face white and terrified. With sudden decision, Xanthe ran back to the Arlington. Commissars were running around outside, as confused and frightened as the mobs. And now Xanthe could see that two of the windows on the top floor—the fifth—were smoking ominously.

Running hard, she flew in and up the stairs to her room. Already she could smell the harsh, acrid smoke, though she couldn't see any yet. With quick and sure movements, she gathered up her weapons and snapped them onto her belt and side holster: an Israeli-made Uzi, stubby but deadly; her personal side arm, a Glock 9 mm; her baton-Tazer; and a long, slender dagger that fit into a sheath in her right paratrooper's boot. Quickly she loaded her munitions belt, cramming her breeches pockets full of the half-empty boxes of cartridges. Without hesitation, leaving her few personal possessions, she turned to run out of the room. But at the doorway she stopped, then hurried back to the scarred wooden dresser and opened the top drawer. Her gray eyes thoughtful and faraway, she took out the brooch that Noemi Mitchell had given her. Xanthe started to put it in her pocket, but then she snatched off her black beret and pinned it over the jaguar insignia on the front of the band.

"I need to . . . feel close to you, Sister Mitchell," she whispered. Then she added hesitantly, "And You, too, God. You, too. Help me, please. Just—help me to do the job You've given me to do. I'll do whatever You tell me."

Even die?

Xanthe didn't know if God had asked this hard question, or if she was testing herself.

But she knew the answer, because she'd heard it from the wisest old man she'd ever met: *Though He slay me, yet shall I trust in Him!*

The sound of a high-pitched scream penetrated the deep sleep of Allegra Saylor. She was a light sleeper and the harsh sound brought her back to the world with a start. She sat up and searched for the alarm clock, but total darkness met her eyes. She groped for the lamp, threw the switch. Nothing.

"Blasted power's out . . . ," she muttered. Rising, she fumbled a little in the cluttered drawer of the nightstand until she found the tiny flashlight. She flicked it on, the small one-inch beam an instant comfort.

Hurrying across the hall, she found that her four-year-old son, Kyle, was still asleep. Unlike her, he was a heavy sleeper. Allegra watched him for a long moment, part of her reveling in the simple joy of watching her child sleep, part of her filled with confusion.

Leaving Kyle's room, she went into the living room, stubbing her toe painfully against the couch. Moving to the window, she drew the heavy drapes back—then gasped with fear. The entire street across from her little cottage was blazing! Instantly she knew that her little old wooden house was doomed. Dashing back into her room, she dressed, mumbling furiously to herself at the difficulty in finding suitable clothing for the cold night. *And we'll have to leave—! I've got to get some clothes—Okay, calm down, take one minute to save a lot of heartache later . . .*

At the age of twenty-two, Allegra Saylor was a lovely, waifish-looking woman, slender, willowy, and delicate. But at the same time she had enough strength of mind and willpower, said her husband, Neville, "to stock a store." Neville Saylor, a Marine pilot, was based at Twenty-Nine Palms in California. Allegra and Kyle had come to Hot Springs for a two-week visit with her parents, Merrill and Genevieve Stanton. They lived in a big Victorian house just down the street, but Allegra had stubbornly insisted on renting this little cottage. She knew that her son could be a handful, and her parents deserved all the peace and quiet they could get after raising five kids. No need in them starting all over again at their age . . . she was suddenly very worried about them. Quickly she took another look out the living room window and saw some dark shadows breaking into houses across the street that hadn't caught fire yet.

"What in the world is happening?" she whispered. Where were the commissars in their big, rumbling Humvees? Where were the fire trucks? "We've got to get out of here. Get it together, Allegra!" she scolded herself. The clothes she stuffed into a canvas shoulder bag would have to do. She went in and woke Kyle up. He reached up for her, chubby and stubborn, a big boy four years old with sandy brown hair and big sparkling brown eyes. "Whass all that noise, Mum?" he asked sleepily.

"There's a fire. We've got to go to Grandpa and Grandma's."

Instantly, Kyle's eyes widened and he asked questions steadily as she dressed him. Quickly, Allegra added some of his clothes to her own, and then she took his hand. Together they went outside. The fire was roaring, and now Allegra could see that houses behind hers were burning, too. This was one of the oldest neighborhoods in Hot Springs, and all of the houses were wooden. They weren't going to last long.

People were aimlessly milling around the street, crying for help, shouting in anger. Almost running, Allegra towed Kyle down the street to an old Victorian house painted sky-blue and decorated with white gingerbread trim. Mounting the stairs to the wrap-around porch, she banged the brass knocker. Instantly the door was yanked open by Merrill Stanton. He was fully dressed, and his face was tense. "I was just coming over to get you. Are you two all right?"

"We're fine. Is Mother okay?"

"Yes, we're both all right. She's still getting dressed. The whole town's on fire and the power's out. Phones won't work, either. And another thing—even the cars won't work. Never saw anything like it!"

Allegra said, "My cottage is probably burning by now. And, Father, I think the fire's going to spread. Some houses over on the street behind you are already going up. And . . ." With a cautious look down at Kyle, she whispered, "I saw some looters. Everyone's panicking. Panicky crowds turn into mobs."

Merrill's gentle features were grave. He murmured, "This is going to be hard. Especially on your mother."

Allegra nodded; her parents had lived in this house for thirty-five years. "I brought everything I could put in my backpack."

"Then, little girl, you can help me load the garden cart. I'm going to gather all the medicine and medical supplies we've got. Why don't you go into the pantry and grab all the food that won't spoil. Take your time, and think; get stuff that's solid, like rice and dried beans, but easy to carry. No jars. I've got a feeling food's going to be hard to come by."

Allegra's mother, Genevieve, joined her in the roomy pantry. "How are you doing, Mother?" Allegra asked softly.

Genevieve Stanton, a gentle and quiet woman of fifty-seven, sighed but answered gamely, "As well as can be expected, Allegra, considering I can't find two socks of your father's that match, he's lost his favorite wool jacket, and you're turning my pantry upside down. Other than that, I'm doing very well, thank you."

Perhaps Allegra had, after all, gotten some of her heart from her mother.

The loading of the garden cart did not take long and finally the four of them went outside. They stood hesitantly on the front walk, looking around blankly. With a shock, they saw that one of the ancient oak trees in the Stantons' backyard was burning; at that moment, an enormous limb fell on the roof. Part of the roof caved in, and the house started burning with loud crackles and roars. "We've got to get away," Merrill muttered, "but to where?"

Suddenly Kyle began to cry. "I forgot Benny."

"Oh, no," Merrill moaned. Benny was his grandson's stuffed bear.

Allegra said, "We can't go back in there now, Kyle."

"But I can't leave Benny! He'll burn up!" the child wailed.

"I'll go get Benny," Merrill said decisively. "Where is he, Kyle?"

"In the bafroom, I think."

Merrill made a quick dash into the house and was out almost at once, coughing. He held a stuffed bear, which only had one eye. Kyle took it eagerly, saying politely, "Thank you, Grandfather."

"You're welcome, Kyle," Merrill said, managing a thin smile. He looked around briefly at the inferno that had been his home for so long. "Let's go. Now."

"Where will we go?" Genevieve asked. Her voice was even, but tears were rolling down her cheeks.

Merrill Stanton lifted his head and said in a stronger voice than he'd been able to muster that whole terrible night: "Where we always go when we need help, Genevieve. To the Lord. We'll go to His house. When we're there, He'll give us a sign. I know it."

Allegra sighed, "A sign? Father, what are you talking about?"

"A sign, Allegra. I don't know what it will be, but we must look for it, for it will give us hope. It will be a beacon of hope in the darkness."

Jesse Mitchell started with such violence that the entire bed shook. Confused and disoriented, he pulled himself up and sat staring across the dark room. His wife's voice was fully aware and alarmed. "What's wrong, Jess?"

"Something's happened, Noe. Something bad."

Throwing the cover back, Noemi lit a coal oil lamp beside the bed and turned to face Jesse. Pushing her braids back, she reached out and anxiously grabbed his thin shoulder. "Are you sick?"

"No, no, nothing like that." Jesse got out of the old bed and stood uncertainly in the middle of the small bedroom. Uncertainty swept across his face and he began to pray silently while Noe waited. Finally he pulled on his favorite overalls and moccasins. "I'm going to go out, Noe. "

"You don't know what it is or where you're going?"

"No. Not yet."

Noe watched as Jesse rose to his feet. "I'm feeling something, too. And you're right, Jess . . . it's something bad. Let's pray before you go."

The two knelt beside the bed and for ten minutes they prayed, sometimes silently, sometimes aloud. It had become a way of life for the old couple. Prayer was their element as water is a fish's element. Finally Jesse said, "Amen and amen!" then got to his feet. As he helped Noe up, he urged, "Go back to bed, Noe."

"No. I'll stay up. You may want something to eat when you get back. And I'll keep praying."

Jesse grinned then pulled her to him, and kissed her resoundingly on the cheek. "It's not bigger than God, whatever it is."

Turning, he left the cabin and walked up a well-worn western path. Overhead the stars were crisp and cheerily uncaring of little men and their little problems and fears. A sliver of a moon slunk behind a cloud. Jesse quickened his pace, threading his way easily through the trail he'd so often walked. Finally he arrived at Sky Rock, a big, flat promontory that crested one of the high hills overlooking a vast bowl of a valley. He stopped dead-still and caught his breath in shock.

Hot Springs is burning . . . !

The sight of the cherry red glow could be nothing else. Ordinarily the lights of Hot Springs could be seen, but now there were no lights—just a dull red flickering glow that could only be a massive fire.

He continued to pray unconsciously and when no word came, he muttered, "Lord, why are You hiding Yourself from me? If I ever needed You, I need You now."

Still no wisdom came to him, so he watched the ominous glow in the west grow brighter. As always, when he reached a point in his life when he was confused or had no guidance, he simply waited. As he watched the city burn, and he thought of his and Noe's isolation, he felt a tremor of fear. *What if . . . the whole world is burning? Something bad is happening, some meanness of the evil one . . . Both Noe and I have sensed it . . . and here we are, two old fools out here all alone, with no help . . .*

And he can see us.

This errant thought brought Jesse Mitchell up short. "Who? Who can see me?" he cried into the night.

Still nothing, and no one answered him.

But now Jesse had that old, too-familiar and close skin-crawling feeling he'd had ever since they'd left New Mexico. He felt as if someone (*some thing?*) was looking for him—like a searchlight, kind of. It probed here, and then swiveled over there—it might just hone right in on him, standing on this big rock in the wide open—

Jesse actually wheeled and started to run back to the house.

Behind him he saw two red eyes.

Jesse stopped, his old heart hammering like a young wild buck's against his thin chest.

"Oh, God, my God!" Jess managed to cry.

The red eyes disappeared. The searchlight swung by, not even touching a hair of his head.

Jesse turned and threw back his shaggy white head to stare at the uncaring stars. The last few minutes—the fear, the panic, the confusion—was it all an illusion? Was he, perhaps, losing his grip on sanity?

Again he felt a little twinge of fear, but this time he faced it with his whole mind and his strong spirit. "Well, for goodness's sake, my Lord, how I'm puttering on! And here You are, of course! Right here, right now, and who am I to demand that You talk to me or You show me something or do a trick for me, like You're my

trained pet? Where was I when You laid the foundations of the earth? Who laid the cornerstone and the foundations, and for You all the morning stars sang together, and all the sons of God shouted for joy? Forgive me, dear Lord, I am but a beast before Thee!"

In spite of his harsh self-recrimination, Jesse Mitchell was suddenly filled with joy and even laughed. He turned, dancing a little jig, and called out, "Hey, you, old red-eye! I know what you are, and I know who you answer to! Get thee hence, get thee behind me, Satan, I command you in the name of all power, Jesus Christ!" Dusting his hands together in a businesslike manner, he said, "So that takes care of that. Now, Lord, what do You want this old fool to do about all these shenanigans?"

Growing somber now, he studied the conflagration in the west. "There's going to be people who need help. People who are scared, and lost. It looks like the whole city's burning up."

As soon as he had muttered these words, the Scripture came into his mind. *A city that is set on a hill cannot be hid.*

The thin frame of Jesse Mitchell suddenly grew rigid. "That's it! A city set on a hill! Of course, now I know what to do. Thank You, Lord."

Quickly he began gathering dead wood. Old fallen branches were easy to find in these thick piney hills. When he had gathered a large stack, he fumbled in his pocket and brought out a box of small wooden matches. Kneeling, he struck one, cupping the tiny blaze in his hand, savoring the dry, sulfury smell that brought to mind thousands of comforting home fires Jesse Mitchell had lit. Soon it caught and a brisk night breeze fed it quickly to the dead wood. Soon a great bonfire, blazing six feet into the sky, its sparks flying up as high as the stars, was a strong beacon in the gentle old hills.

Jesse Mitchell stood, pulled off his old Stetson hat, lifted his lined face to the heavens, and spoke in a loud voice:

"But ye, brethren, are not in darkness, that that day should overtake you as a thief. Ye are all the children of light, and the children of the day: we are not of the night, nor of darkness. Therefore let us not sleep, as do others; but let us watch and be sober!"

His voice dropping to a whisper, he finished, "And the grace of our Lord Jesus Christ be with you, amen."

PART IV

———✦———

FALL, DYING

The righteous perisheth, and no man layeth it to heart: and merciful men are taken away, none considering that the righteous is taken away from the evil to come.

—Isaiah 57:1

O the mind, mind has mountains; cliffs of fall
Frightful, sheer, no-man-fathomed.
—Gerard Manley Hopkins, No Worst, There is None

Death, be not proud, though some have called thee
Mighty and dreadful, for thou art not so. . .
—John Donne, Holy Sonnets

TWENTY-TWO

——◆——

THOUGH HE MAINTAINED A strict parade-ground stance at attention, and he was supposed to focus straight ahead, Captain Con Slaughter's sharp brown eyes slid around to take in the changes in his CO's office.

"That's right," Lieutenant Colonel J. P. Nix asserted. "SATphones and drone went out the window. Covered up that useless Cyclops screen with a map." Chewing on his ever-present cigar stub, he mouthed dourly, "Map still works."

"Yes, sir!" Con agreed smartly.

"At ease; sit down, Captain. So what's your bug today?"

"Uh—yes, sir. My bug. It's my team, sir. They're restless, I guess you'd say."

"Yeah?" Nix responded acidly. "Well, Captain, we're all kind of antsy, sitting here and waiting to get nuked or gassed or anthraxed or for the sky to fall in or the ground to open and swallow us. Suck it up."

Con swallowed hard but pressed on. "Yes, sir, we know everyone's optempo stinks right now. But we have an idea for a mission, sir."

"Con, everybody wants to go kill something, including me," Nix sighed. "But you know the drill. With no communication, no command, and no intelligence—and I don't mind admitting that I feel like the least intelligent of anybody—we maintain a defensive posture. That's our only option. That means sitting here and waiting, playing with our little toy guns."

"Yes, sir, but our mission isn't offensive in nature. As a matter of fact, it might help you feel less—er—I mean more—intelligent." Colonel Nix's bulldog frown was so forbidding that Con went on hastily, "I mean, sir, that's what this operation is designed for, actually. To gather intelligence, to research reestablishing communication—and also, maybe to—uh—gather some useful supplies and equipment."

Nix's eyes narrowed. "Okay, you got my attention."

Con still wasn't too confident. Colonel Nix was a fair man, but sometimes when he looked at you it made you feel as if you were donating bone marrow without anesthesia. "Thank you, sir. If I may use your map? Here's Fort Carson. Fire Team Eclipse has gathered extremely detailed information about the areas to the southwest, sir. We know that here"—he pointed confidently—"a large herd of wild burros wander about a seven-square-mile area, but they always come to this small canyon to drink. There's a stream that must be spring-fed instead of rainwater-fed, because it never dries up."

"Burros, huh?" Nix said slowly, but his dark brown eyes flickered with interest. In these medieval days, pack animals could be very useful.

"Yes, sir," Con said, his confidence growing. "But even better— over here are horses. Hundreds of them."

"Horses? What do you mean? Wild mustangs?"

"Yes, sir. You see, there is a ranch right here, right out in the middle of nowhere. But we've observed Vindicators and Humvees there several times, and the ranch is quite large and well-equipped. And then there are the horses. You know no private individual could possibly have gotten licensed to own so many horses. So it must be—"

"A Green-head ranch," Nix growled. "Maybe some kind of experimental biome station for wildlife management."

"Has to be, sir."

Colonel Nix, being the kind of man he was, had scrounged around until he found an old scarred metal desk from the previous century and an old wooden chair with a hard uncushioned seat and slatted back. He wore, and had always worn for his thirty-six years of service, an old Colt M1911 .45 caliber automatic that had been issued to his grandfather back in the 1970s when Jacob Paul Nix joined up with the 101st and was sent to an obscure little Far Eastern country called Vietnam. Now J. P. Nix, his namesake, swung his chair around, and the wheels creaked and the swivel squeaked, and he felt like an old, old man. He stared out the window behind his desk, and the bright wash of sunshine made Con squint to see him clearly.

"Captain Slaughter, I guess you know about General Wallace taking his tank-heads and marching to NORAD the day after the blackout?" the colonel asked in an unusually subdued voice.

"Yes, sir."

"You know he got back last night? With not one whit of information—except that Cheyenne Mountain is still standing. Anyway, out of that tanker company of one hundred and fifty-three men he started off with, he only got back with sixty-two of them."

Con merely nodded, and though Nix wasn't looking at him, he seemed to receive his acknowledgment. "We've had over two hundred desertions in just this week, Con," he continued in a voice deepened with anger. "And I can't tell you how proud I am that not a single one of them has been from the 502d. So far, anyway."

Con stiffened and his tawny eyes flashed angrily. "Colonel Nix, I assure you that I and my men have no intention of deserting. If you order us to, we'll stay here 'til doomsday."

"Calm down, Con, I wasn't accusing you of making this elaborate scheme just so you and your team can desert. Blast it, you and I both know you could just walk off if you wanted to," Nix rasped, now turning to face him. "Besides, boy, you're a really bad liar. You couldn't fool a six-year-old kid if you weren't telling the straight truth. Now sit down, you're blocking my view of the map."

Con sat.

Nix studied the map through a dreamy-looking but foul-smelling gray-blue haze of cigar smoke. "So you're telling me that your team has maps better than Cyclops II recon records? Maps so good that you know where all the little bunnies are, and the yellow flowers as opposed to the red ones, and every anthill?"

"Well, sir, Sergeant David Mitchell—he's our Everyman—has done some manual observations during our helo exercises," Con explained enthusiastically. "Sergeant Mitchell's a very conscientious soldier, sir, and he takes the Cy II recon maps and makes meticulous notes on them. Says he figured it would sharpen his navigational skills, and they also would be good references just in case. Would you like to see?"

"Sure would."

Con unfolded a detailed topographical map that was actually a perfectly clear satellite photo that Cyclops II had interpolated and labeled. On it, in a tiny and neat block handwriting, were such notes as "Old Graybeard Rock," and "Eagle's Dare," and "The Grove."

Colonel Nix burst out laughing, something he had not done for many days now. "Lemme guess. This is where the burros are?"

Con grinned tightly. "You got it, sir. Donkey's End."

"Remind me to give that boy a commendation. Smart and a sense of humor, too." Nix leaned back, his chair squealing in protest, his eyes roving over the map. He grew somber. "So, Con, are you talking about going on to the ranch? In one operation?"

Con answered uncertainly, "Sir, the team and I have made alternate mission plans, and I decided to present them both. Plan One is to just go as far as—er—Donkey's End, capture some of the animals, and bring them back to the base. Also, of course, we'll be on an alert for any intelligence and/or communication possibilities with civvies or whoever's out there. Plan Two is to pick up the burros, and then proceed on to the ranch. We think they might still have some kind of communication capabilities with the Man and Biosphere Directorate. At least that'd be a start. And I do think we could bring back at least a hundred horses. Maybe twice that, if we're lucky."

"The mean Greenies aren't going to give 'em to you, you know," Nix grumbled. "Blasted tarantula-kissers."

Con shrugged carelessly. "Sir, of course I'm well aware that civilian goods may not be confiscated by the military without adequate compensation. But these horses, sir, are not civilian goods. The MAB has ensured that. They're America's resources. That makes them available for conscript in a national emergency, for the good of the common defense."

"Sounds right to me, but you better get ready for some cryin' and sobbin'," Nix asserted. "Assuming you can confiscate them. Horses are kinda hard to draft, you know, Captain. You can't just walk up to a herd of mustangs and order them to surrender themselves for the good of the common defense."

Con's mouth twitched. "No, sir, I know that. But I was raised on a cattle farm in Alabama, and we always used that as an excuse to keep horses. In fact, my parents and grandparents are still licensed, and between their two farms they still have about twenty horses. I can bring you back some horses, sir. Now the burros—" He made a wry face and shook his head. "I don't know anything about them. But Sergeant Mitchell says he and his grandfather used to wake up every morning and start the fight with their mule. Says the two of them won by early afternoon. Most of the time. He's pretty sure he can handle the burros."

Nix was amused. "Okay, if you got a cowhand and a mule driver, you might be able to come through. But there's just one more thing we gotta talk about, Con. You're telling me you can go over the Sangre de Cristos—and the San Juan range, in winter?"

"Over the Sangre de Cristos, yes, sir," Con answered sturdily. "But through the San Juans. Sergeant—"

"Mitchell found a passage," Nix completed for him.

"Uh—sir. It'll mean an extra travel day or two, but it'll keep us from having to go over Wolf Creek Pass."

"You don't wanna try that on foot in wintertime, son, not even Fire Team Eclipse," Nix said in a low voice. He stared at the map a while longer, then sighed deeply. "Two weeks there, two weeks back, at the very best. A month, maybe a month and a half . . ."

"Yes, sir. Unless the lights come back on. Then we'll commandeer the nearest car or truck or bicycle or whatever we can get our hands on and double-time it right back here, sir."

Nix swiveled again to stare out the window. "They ain't comin' back on, Con. Not for a while, anyway. So permission is granted for you and Fire Team Eclipse to undertake this mission. Go ahead and go the distance, Captain Slaughter. Plan Two. I'll have you some written orders in an hour."

"Thank you, sir," Con said sincerely.

Nix was silent for a long time, his back to Slaughter. "Wish I could go with you, Con. I surely do. But my duty is to sit here and wait . . . for whatever comes. And something's coming, you know. This is no natural phenomenon and this is not an accident. Something's coming along behind it, oh, yes sir, and it ain't good . . ."

Con didn't know what to say, so he stood at attention until finally Colonel Nix said quietly, "You remember the Airborne Creed, Con?"

"Of course, sir."

"Good. You'll need to remember that creed, Con. Especially this: *In battle, I fear no foe's ability, nor underestimate his prowess, power, and guile. I fight him with all my might and skill—ever alert to evade capture or escape a trap. I never surrender, though I be the last.* Remember that, Con. You stand by it. Even if you're the last."

Fire Team Eclipse was once again a team on the move. But this time they weren't soaring, powerful and indestructible, high above the ground. They were making a journey in a way that men had done since the beginning of time: each man by his own strength, carrying his own sustenance, using his own eyes and ears and cunning to find the way. It was a little bit exhilarating to all but Lieutenant Deacon Fong, who still mourned for his beloved Apache. He hated walking. He hated marching. In fact, he hated everything about being bound to the earth. But it was unthinkable to him to either complain to his team, or to contemplate not going. They were a team, with or without a helicopter. He was just like an arm, or an eye. They wouldn't be Fire Team Eclipse without him, just as they wouldn't be whole without any other member of the team.

And now, incredibly, that included two lost Jews. It never occurred to either Colonel Darkon Ben-ammi or Colonel Vashti Nicanor not to go on this mission with the team. They simply did the military courtesy, following correct protocol, and alerted Colonel Nix that they would be going with the team, and that was that.

After all, Fire Team Eclipse was the only home they had now.

They were traveling in a steep southeasterly line, crossing the barren plains that led up to the Wet Mountains, which they were going to barely skirt around the southern end. The morning was crisp and fine, the sky clean, the sun pale but cheerful. The tip of Vashti's nose was cold, but otherwise she was fairly comfortable. American military clothing was expertly designed for all kinds of climate. The cold-weather Syn-tex underwear was light but very warm. They wore solid black "battle dress uniforms" of rip-stop Ty-canvas, which was sturdy and of a slightly heavier grade than summer BDU's. Over this they all had long, roomy desert camouflage waterproof ponchos. Vashti secretly thought that the mottled light tans and beiges of the desert camos were the least flattering to her complexion, but there was nothing to be done about that.

Lieutenant Ric Darmstedt slowed down his long-legged step to fall in with her. "You going to make it okay with those boots, Colonel Nicanor?" he asked. He wasn't just making light conversation; long hikes with less than perfect boots could cause very serious problems. And on a mission of this type, it could mean problems for the whole team, not just Vashti's discomfort.

"I assure you, I'm fine, Lieutenant Darmstedt," Vashti replied a little stiffly. "I would have thought I had proved by now that I won't hold the team back."

"Huh? Hold us—but I was just worried about you, Colonel," Ric assured her. She snapped her head back to look up at him, and could see he was telling the truth.

He always told the plain truth. He was like that. It unsettled Vashti sometimes. "Oh. Thank you, Lieutenant. I'm fine," she said awkwardly.

"Good. 'Cause I'm not. I'm staggerin' already, and we've come, what—fifty feet? Who knew we were gonna have to march over half of America with packs like this?" Ric declared. "One hundred and seventy pounds for combat drops isn't really too bad, all you gotta do is waddle onto the plane. But this—"

"Weighs about thirty pounds and you know it, Lieutenant," Vashti said with amusement. He was indulging her, she knew, because she'd insisted on carrying the same as everyone else, and it was harder on her than anyone. That was just a fact. Darmstedt was just trying to make her feel better ahead of time, because it was almost certain that she'd have to have some help near the end of their planned ten-hour marches. She dreaded it, but she knew it was inevitable. But she was going to carry this pack until she couldn't take another step. Then, she knew, Ric Darmstedt would carry it for her, and probably try to do it so the rest of the team wouldn't notice. "Don't worry about me, Lieutenant Darmstedt. Not yet, anyway. Ask me again after lunch."

He nodded, understanding perfectly.

They walked steadily, not pushing it. This hike was going to take careful pacing, and Con Slaughter wasn't having anyone overexert themselves and then have to hold up the entire team to wait for someone to rest up. He'd planned frequent stops during the day for rest and long halts at night for sleep. In this climate, at this altitude, carrying these loads, even he and Ric Darmstedt were going to have a tough time.

Colonel Ben-ammi dropped into step at Vashti's other side. He looked as if he were enjoying himself. Ben-ammi was such a big man, with such a natural strength, that his paunch and his lack of enthusiasm for an exercise regimen weren't really disadvantages to him. He was like an ox plodding along, never flagging. "This is a beautiful American morning," he pronounced grandly. "Not too hot, not too cold. Just right. Like the Three Great Bears."

"Uh—" Ric began, then shrugged. "The Three Great Bears, yeah. So you must be Goldilocks, huh, Colonel Nicanor?"

Vashti looked utterly bewildered. "Who are the Goldilocks?"

"Didn't your parents ever tell you fairy tales?" Ric demanded.

"Yes. They told me that all of the evil trolls and goblins and monsters are tall blonde Germans," Vashti replied innocently, looking up at Ric Darmstedt's Aryan features and hair.

"Now that is a fairy tale," Ric said gravely. "I'm a good guy."

The sun climbed, and Vashti's nose warmed up. The Wet Mountains materialized to their right, ghost-hills of gray shimmering in the distance. The ground they traveled was flat and hard, covered with short, rough brown grass, small dull rocks, and an occasional spiky succulent hugging the ground. The team, instead of walking in a straight formal line, meandered back and forth with one another, talking in quiet voices. Except for Con Slaughter, who took point and didn't talk to anyone. Sergeant Mitchell stayed close behind him, because he had the compass and was checking their course. Sergeant Valdosta stayed close behind him because that's what he'd always done, stuck close to his captain and watched his back.

Vashti was watching Mitchell thoughtfully. "The compass, I understand, has proved that the blackout is not due to solar flares? That a solar flare of the magnitude it would take to cause this widespread blackout would certainly affect the electromagnetic field of the earth?"

"That's correct, ma'am," Ric Darmstedt answered. He walked with her a lot.

"But—suppose the compass is affected, and we don't know it?"

"Because we've got three, and we check 'em all against one another. If they didn't read the same, then we'd know something's whacked."

"Whacked," Vashti repeated thoughtfully, cataloging the word. She liked learning American idioms.

"Whacked," Ric repeated solemnly.

"So—so what is it?" Vashti murmured, returning to the same question that almost every person all over America was asking over and over. "Is it some sort of other natural phenomenon? Is it sabotage? Is it an attack? By whom? And why?"

"Colonel, if I had the answers to those questions I would inform you immediately," Ric intoned.

"You would? Really? Even though—" Vashti stopped, shocked. She had actually been about to say, *Even though I'm Mossad.* The first rule in covert operations was that you *never admitted being a covert operative,* not to friends, not to family, not under any circumstances. Even when you knew they knew, you just never, never discussed it. What was the matter with her? Was she losing her mind? Some sort of trauma reaction? She stumbled a little, and Ric quickly grabbed her arm to steady her. Still bemused, she yanked it away. A tightness came over his features, but quickly he smoothed it out.

He shifted his backpack, making a great show of it, then sighed theatrically. "I think maybe my pack's heavier than everyone else's," he groused. "Just because I'm bigger and in better shape than everyone doesn't mean I'm gonna carry—"

"Hold up!" Con called harshly, stopping quickly mid-stride.

"What's up, Captain?" Ric called.

"Can it, Darmstedt! Don't you hear something?"

"Yeah, I hear my lungs bursting—"

"I hear it," Vashti said, her dark eyes searching the sky. "Planes."

Deacon Fong, who was slogging along rather dejectedly with Colonel Ben-ammi, suddenly became animated. "Choppers, maybe?"

"Maybe . . . ," Darkon muttered, his eyes searching due south.

"There, Captain!" David Mitchell pointed.

Sure enough, coming out of the south, headed northwest, was a formation of planes. Deac, who had the sharpest vision of the team, said in wonder, "It's the Luftwaffe. Must be from Kirtland. They're Tornadoes."

Valdosta had already dumped his pack and was rifling through it. "Flares—I got flares—"

"No!" Con shouted. The noise of the Tornadoes' engines was becoming very loud, and their signature high-pitched scream was indeed deafening.

"No is right!" David shouted, eyeing the planes with growing trepidation. "They're sure flying low, Captain, almost like they're—"

"In attack formation," Con finished. "Everybody down! Now! Hit the deck!"

They had done this drill about a hundred times since they'd formulated this mission. But none of them had truly thought they'd have to hide from air surveillance, and all of them were a little stunned. Still, they followed orders without question, and moved fast.

They threw their packs down, shed their ponchos, then lay down flat in the sand with the packs at their heads. Quickly they threw the heavy ponchos over themselves, pack and all, and scrabbled some sand up over the edges. Now they were invisible to a quick surveillance with the naked eye at least.

Deacon Fong, pilot in blood and bone, reveled in the sound of aircraft actually in the air again. *Maybe it's over!* he thought exultantly. *Maybe I'll get my baby back!*

Both Vashti and Darkon had the same images burned into their minds, and they brooded on it: the ancient Iron Cross glittering on the black fuselages of planes.

David Mitchell still felt a flicker of hope at the sight of something electrical actually working, but within moments his sense of foreboding had drowned it out. *Wait a minute—Tornadoes? Of course, dimbulb! The spray! They sprayed everything . . . that has to be an antidote, or preventive, or something . . .*

Prevent . . . then they knew?

The Germans are behind this?

Dear Lord, is it war?

The hard, cold ground beneath them shuddered. A few seconds later, the sound waves reached them.

They're bombing the base! Ric Darmstedt started, jerked so hard that he almost dislodged his poncho. *They can't do that!* he absurdly thought.

But by the force of the shaking ground and the continual bass reverberations of explosions, he knew the truth, and it almost made him ill. They *were* doing it, and probably with the same stern, methodical German precision with which they (and he, though he didn't realize it) performed all other tasks. Ric was only two generations removed from having been born in Germany. It suddenly hit him that if he had been, *he* probably would have been up there, bombing defenseless American soldiers. The thought sickened him.

Rio Valdosta was a simple man, and a good soldier. His last order from his commanding officer had been to conceal himself, so he was doing that, and he wouldn't move so much as a little pinky until he was ordered to. Otherwise, considering that Rio Valdosta was also a warrior, a man whose blood ran hot, a man who did not have a lust for killing but certainly did have the skills for it, he would have jumped up, grabbed Slaughter's 12-gauge, and taken the head off one of those fine flyboys as they whizzed by only a couple of hundred feet above. He probably could have done it, too. He wanted to, real bad. But Rio just bowed his head and made a vow. *Every German I meet from now on is crow feed. 'Til I'm dead and cold, they're gonna pay!*

Captain Con Slaughter was becoming more furious with every thud heard and felt. It took every ounce of his will not to leap to his feet and start running back to the base. So terrible was the struggle within him that he literally trembled. *We can't do anything, we can't stop it, we can't protect anyone. If we tried, we'd die—or be captured. Never surrender, that's what he said. Never surrender . . .*

The carnage was complete.

Fire Team Eclipse, as one, stopped walking when they saw the first dead body. He wore a cannon-cocker's patch, and he still had a 9 mm Beretta clenched in his hand. He had run far before they'd strafed him; he lay just at the edge of the base perimeter. They gathered around him in a ragged circle. Captain Slaughter and Sergeant Valdosta looked enraged. Lieutenant Deacon Fong's face was expressionless, but his nostrils were white with tension and his jaw was like flint. Lieutenant Ric Darmstedt's smooth and hand-some face was so chalky he looked ill. Sergeant David Mitchell looked grief-stricken.

Colonel Darkon Ben-ammi, in spite of the fact that he cared for these men, was still a New Zionist, and still was Mossad. He was sorry for the deaths, and appalled by the viciousness of an unannounced act of war against defenseless men, but he could not stop himself from observing these elite American warriors in their first combat situation. *So far,* he reflected, *they are stricken, but controlled. That is good . . . for me and for my country.* The real fear didn't strike him until he realized that his country's strongest and most feared ally in the whole world had been brought to its knees, just as these men had been.

Colonel Vashti Nicanor had been in combat before—from the comfortable height of thousands of feet above the ground. That was the best thing about being a fighter pilot. You didn't have to deal with the dirtiness of death, the shock, the uselessness, the tragedy. She stared at the dead soldier, a man she had never seen before, and felt a soldier's pity for a comrade, but her revulsion was even stronger. She was the first to turn away.

But it did no good to turn away, for wherever one turned, death waited. All of the buildings had been bombed by the precise and deadly Skoll-10 missiles, and all of them were blasted piles of rubble. Some incendiaries had been used—particularly around the armory—so there had been tremendous fiery explosions when the armaments went up, and much of the nearby piles of debris were still burning.

They saw hundreds of bodies—and hundreds of body parts around the armory. Vashti walked up on an arm, severed at the shoulder, but the uniform sleeve was curiously clean and unmarked, with a lieutenant's stripes. The hand was still holding a box of 9 mm cartridges, unexploded. She turned around and with her head held high and her eyes dry, she marched to the edge of the camp and sat down on the ground, alone. No one stopped her or commented. They barely noticed.

"I heard helos," Fong said numbly to Colonel Ben-ammi. "This precision shooting wasn't done by fighters. I wanted to look so badly, because I thought they must have been the new Messerschmitt-Daimler Daggers. The precision of this strafing . . ."

"This is no strafing," Ben-ammi sighed heavily. "This is meticulous execution. One shot, one death. They must have a new targeting system for small arms. Based on something like your Baby BAD, maybe."

Fong nodded blankly, then wandered off.

David Mitchell's worst fear was realized; he found his friend Joey Dane, the Stealth warrior. He'd been running for his plane—perhaps for a last good-bye. He was sprawled in the grass of Runway N4, shot through the back with a single 50-caliber shell. David simply couldn't face turning him over, and not just because his chest would be gone. It was his face—bright, laughing, freckled, always so *alive*—that David didn't want to see. Like a man in a deep trance, David knelt by him and picked up his hand. It was already stiffening, and so cold. David stayed so long that his legs went to sleep.

All of them found scenes of horror. Rio Valdosta found a woman, just a girl, really, who wore a nurse-corpsmen's uniform. She was lying on top of a young boy who was lying facedown in the street, obviously trying to shield him. They were both dead.

Lieutenant Deacon Fong saw, with longing, that none of the base's planes or helicopters had been touched. *Goth rats are coming back to get 'em, huh? Not my baby! I'm gonna go burn her myself!* He actually took a step toward the helo yard, then stopped. This was no time to think of his helicopter. This was a time to mourn and honor the dead. Lieutenant Fong turned himself smartly around and made himself go to every single body he could find, and stop, and look at them. He committed them to memory, each of them. That was his way.

Lieutenant Ric Darmstedt ran straight to the command center. His closest friends outside the team were the electronic intelligence men, the tech-heads who operated all the complex equipment and interpreted the results. Ric liked doing that kind of thing for fun, and he'd made friends with several of the earnest droneheads. But the command center, which had been a three-story brick building with a basement, was now level with the ground. It had been so pulverized by numerous Skolls that not even a brick was left whole. The men inside, too, must already be little more than ashes and bone. *Ashes to ashes and dust to dust . . . no more than dust . . . none of us are any more than a little smear on this earth anyway . . . God's little worker ants . . . Wonder if He's noticed this atrocity yet?* Ric thought with galling bitterness.

Ric was joined by Con Slaughter, who was moving as slowly and painfully as a seventy-year-old man. His weathered face was riven with sorrow and horror. Together they found their commanding officer, Lieutenant Colonel J. P. Nix.

He was lying right outside where the door of the command center had been, in a curiously defiant position; one knee was still jointed, so that from a long way off it might look as if he were lying down, relaxing at a picnic. His arms were spread-eagled perfectly, and Con thought numbly that he must have still been firing two-handed even as he lay on his back, his left leg almost blown off. His old Colt .45 was in his right fist, and a cold dead cigar was still clenched between his teeth. Numbly Con tried to push his leg down, and lay his hands across his chest, but rigor mortis was already setting in, and the limbs wouldn't budge. Con kept trying. Ric was staring blankly down into Colonel Nix's face, which still grimaced with defiance. Even in death he had not admitted defeat.

"Captain Slaughter," a deep, kindly voice said behind Con's right shoulder. "You can't move him, you know. Leave him."

"Wha—what?" Con jumped up and whirled around, furious, to face Darkon Ben-ammi. "Leave him! Over my cold dead body! We have to—to—bury all of them, with full honors, and—and—or burn them, at least! A funeral pyre!"

He was up in Ben-ammi's face, shouting, the furious spittle flying from his lips actually touching the older man. Still, Darkon Ben-ammi merely looked sad. He laid his meaty hands on Con's shoulders. "Son, you're not thinking straight, and you're not thinking smart. You're the last officer here, Captain Slaughter."

Con reeled backward a step as if Ben-ammi had struck him hard across the face. He staggered, then recovered, but his head was down and the hand he dragged across his face was shaking. "I'm—the last?" he mumbled.

Ric stared at him, and Colonel Ben-ammi's horsey face was filled with pity. Neither of them spoke.

Captain Con Slaughter, as the colonel and the lieutenant knew he would, recovered quickly. His back straightened, his face set in grim lines, and his voice hardened. "You outrank me, Colonel Ben-ammi, and so does Colonel Nicanor, and I won't ever forget that. But you're right. I'm the ranking American officer here, and more important, I'm the leader of this fire team." He looked around at the devastation, and his voice grew hoarse. "They'll come back, won't they? The Goths. Bound to. If nothing else, they'll want to pick up all those expensive toys out there."

Colonel Ben-ammi nodded, though Slaughter wasn't looking at him. "They were pretty thorough here, Captain Slaughter," he said quietly. "They killed everyone. Do you understand? *Everyone.*"

Slaughter said grimly, "Not everyone. But they don't know that, do they?"

"Not now," Colonel Ben-ammi said as calmly as he could. "But they would if we honored these men and women—"

"And children!" Rio Valdosta growled from behind him. Ben-ammi hadn't even known he was there.

"And children," Ben-ammi added, his voice catching slightly. "They would know if we honored them in death, Captain Slaughter. They would know, and they would hunt until they found us. And then we would die, just as uselessly as these men have."

Con Slaughter swallowed, and he looked around again, almost in bewilderment. "My—friends," he said gutturally. "My friends, my comrades . . . I never thought I'd leave them for the vultures."

No one said anything.

He saw Lieutenant Deacon Fong's small figure in the distance, kneeling down by a small lump on the ground. He saw the sun in the west, glowing a cruel orange, riding low. He saw smoke, and smelled burning metal and running blood and the foul stench of death.

"Let's go," he said, his voice dropping to a half-whisper. "We can't stay here tonight. I'm getting you—my team—as far away from here as possible."

Turning, he knelt again by his commanding officer's body. With gentle hands, he reached out and unpinned the silver eagle from his chest. "I don't think you'd mind if I keep this, sir," he murmured, "to help me remember. I swear to you, old man, that I'll die as good as you did. I'll never surrender!"

TWENTY-THREE

A HARD HUNTER'S MOON GLARED down on the Gulf, making spiky sparkles on the barely lapping waves. Victorine stared up at it, unblinking, the monochrome planes of her face set and unyielding. Her mother, a slight, fragrant rustle behind her, murmured, "It's going to get cold. I can feel it."

Victorine said nothing. She merely stared at the moon.

Tessa Kai, with a small sigh, went on, "Dancy's asleep. I guess I'll go to bed, too."

"Would you stay here tonight, please?" Tessa Kai, independent as always, insisted on sleeping in her own condo.

Victorine still wasn't looking at her. Tessa Kai stepped closer and stared up into her daughter's too-still face. "Why?"

"I'm going—out."

Incredulous, Tessa Kai scoffed, "Oh? To the opera, or the symphony?"

Victorine didn't smile as she finally turned. "I'm going to go down to White Dunes to see if Gerald's there."

"Victorine, it's dangerous. What if those filthy Pikes or those awful Spikes are out pillaging?" Tessa Kai spat out Dancy's given names for the gangs that were roaming the beach. The Pikes, the first gang they'd seen, had been bad enough. About twenty men and a dozen or so women, they'd been drunk, drugged, and so dirty that Dancy had sworn she could smell them coming. They roamed up and down the key, breaking into cottages and condos.

Three more times they'd seen the Pikes. Victorine had seen their torches in the distance, and had heard them shooting, and after they'd left she'd gone to investigate. They seemed to like breaking into the condominiums—at least the ground-floor units, they were evidently too lazy to go up stairs. They also seemed to prefer staying in the cottages across the street from the beach. There were many more of them than there were condominiums, and some of them were big and elegant. The gangs would pick a place, stay for a night or two, and then destroy it, slashing the furniture and carpets and scrawling obscenities on the walls and shooting out the windows.

But even worse was the women's gang—the Spikes. They had come staggering down the beach one night, carrying torches and long, sharpened sticks like spears and baseball bats. Victorine and Tessa Kai and Dancy had heard them screaming and shrieking like madwomen long before they could see them clearly. When they finally grew close to the condo, Victorine had seen that they were dragging two men with ropes around their necks. The men had been barely dressed in tattered rags, and they were barefoot and bloody. Victorine had never even heard of some of the obscenities the women had been screeching. She'd shut Dancy and Tessa Kai up in the front bedroom, and had huddled by the balcony door with her father's old .38. When the banshees and their two captives had kept marching down the beach without a second look at the dark and apparently deserted Summer Sea, Victorine had felt nothing except a furtive disappointment that she hadn't had an opportunity to shoot one of the women. The Spikes didn't have guns. Somehow, on some level, that made them seem much worse.

"I know it's dangerous," Victorine answered coldly. "But it's dangerous to be here, too, Mother."

"Yes, it is. But it's courting danger to go five miles down the beach on a night with a full moon, Vic."

"I don't think so. I can see my way without having to use a

flashlight. I'd be able to hear and see any gangs coming for miles, and I'd have plenty of time to hide."

Tessa Kai considered this, and finally nodded. "True. Of course I'll stay, Vic. But I do want to ask you—why are you doing this? We have plenty of food and water. I know you like Gerald, and he's been good to come help you out, but why should you take such a risk to go see him?"

In a brittle voice, Victorine answered, "It's been two weeks since the blackout, Mother. I want to know what's going on. It's only logical: Gerald is the nearest person we can contact. It's seven miles to the Commissary Supply, and it's only five miles down to White Dunes."

Tessa Kai nodded, but her voice was sad. "Just logic, I see. Victorine . . . you know that Dancy and I are not afraid, don't you? I mean, we're doing very well under the circumstances. And you— you're not responsible for what's happened to us. Neither are you responsible for—for our lives."

"What an idiotic thing to say, Mother," Victorine said tightly. "Of course I'm responsible for you. Dancy is my daughter, and you are my mother. I'm perfectly capable of taking care of you and protecting you."

"I know," Tessa Kai said, with awkward gentleness. "It's just that I wish you weren't so greatly troubled. It's not your burden to bear."

"Of course it is," Victorine retorted, with a touch of anger.

Stubbornly Tessa Kai shook her head. "No, it's not, Victorine."

"Really? Then whose is it?"

Tessa Kai's luminous brown eyes met Victorine's glittering gaze. "It's the Lord's."

The harsh moonlight made the stark black and white planes of Victorine's face shift jarringly, but in the next moment she was as coldly composed as ever. "Until the Lord sends us sea gulls with berries in their mouths, and bottomless jars of Proto-Syn soybean oil and baskets of wheat meal, I think I'd better start scavenging around for normal humans and some information. God helps those who help themselves."

"That's not in the Bible and you know it," Tessa Kai muttered. "And it's terrible theology besides."

Shrugging, Victorine said, "I'm leaving now. You have your guns?"

"Of course." Tessa Kai had two small .22 magnum Derringers, little twin ladies' guns that her husband had given her more than forty years ago. She'd never used them, never even fired them—until two weeks ago, when they'd first seen the Pikes. "Cleaned, polished, loaded, and ready," she said with relish, pointing to her ever-present floppy handbag.

Victorine nodded, and quickly dressed in the warmest clothes she had. That meant piling on several light layers, for in this subtropical climate, they'd never owned very much heavy clothing. Victorine, in fact, had only one coat, a bright red skier's canvas jacket that her ex-husband had bought her when they'd had the good fortune to draw a Diversionary Retreat in Denver, Colorado, once. It had a removable Syn-Fleece lining that provided warmth, but Victorine had lost the lining long ago, as it had never seemed cold enough to use it. Now she wondered whether this autumn was colder, or if it just seemed so since they had no pleasant Cyclops Enviro-Control to keep every room at a constant 75 degrees. She always seemed to be chilled, and she was sure Tessa Kai and Dancy were, too. It worried her, but she hadn't had a chance to go scouting for some warmer clothing for them.

Finally she left, going down the cavernous stairwell. She'd hated this ever since the night of the autumn equinox. Victorine flatly refused to admit to herself that she found the blackness and eerie echoes in the stairwell frightening. That made no sense. Therefore, it had no place in her considerations. Still, she ran down the stairs.

Rolling the bicycle to the entrance of the parking lot, she carefully scanned up and down the road and strained to hear any sounds of Pikes or Spikes out "pillaging," as Tessa Kai had called it.

The silence was complete. As she rode down the deserted beach road, she reflected that this, perhaps, was one of the hardest things to bear: the oppressive silence. Especially on the rare nights like this, when no wind stirred and the tide was sullenly low. Sometimes, on quiet nights like this, they heard far-off cries of coyotes and even wolves' howls. Perdido Key, being a tiny barrier island, had not been repopulated with native wildlife, although there were an uncommonly large number of foxes. But just six miles to the north was a wide belt of thick southern wetlands and woods, and for the last twenty years since the migration to the co-ops, the deer, wolves, coyotes, bears, cougars, rabbits, raccoons, snakes, alligators, millions of birds, and billions of insects thrived. For the last three years Victorine hadn't allowed Dancy to ride her bicycle over the bridge to the mainland. Just on the other side of the man-made inland waterway that cut through to the ocean on the Key's west end was the wilderness.

She rode fast, not enjoying anything about the ride. The night was chilly and damp, and her hands and feet felt like clammy lumps. The exotic landscape that she had known all her life now appeared forbidding, too sharp-edged and flat. The piercing moon and prickly stars felt hostile.

Finally she reached White Dunes, a condominium complex completely unlike the glossy high-rise Summer Sea. White Dunes was very old, a wooden structure with the two-story units built up on stilts. It had weathered to a gentle sand gray, and had a nostalgic aura of old and slightly tacky beach kitsch.

Victorine stared up at the sharp roofline of Number 5, Gerald's home.

He was hanging from the roof.

Gerald was tall, with sandy blonde hair, and she could see the slender wand of his body, gently swaying, and the moon gleaming in his light hair. She couldn't see any other details, and for this she was very grateful. Her breath caught in her chest, and in the stillness she could hear a slight creak as his body swung back and forth lightly.

Victorine stood motionless, her face as still and unmoved as if it were sanded in cold marble. She swallowed. There was no need to blink back tears, for she had none. Only a sickly burning sensation in her throat and a heaviness in her chest.

Gerald Ainsley had been an artist who painted indifferent seascapes, but had the passion of a genius. He'd been a gentle and kind man, timid and a little effeminate. He'd never given her what Victorine called the Look—the automatic assessment men made of women who'd caught their attention. Victorine had sometimes wondered about his personal life, but either he was chaste or very discreet, for he'd been the hospitality manager of White Dunes for thirteen years, and she'd never known him to have a consort or even a relationship. He'd always been good to help her out when she'd needed it. Suddenly, oddly, it occurred to her that Gerald had never asked her for help at White Dunes, and she was sure there must have been times in summer when he could have used some help with the crowds of middle-class vacationers that always overran him. This realization struck her like a thrown rock, and she swallowed again, gritting her teeth.

It's too late, he's dead, and there's nothing to do about it now.

"I'd better bury him," she said.

But she made no move to do that.

After all, the Pikes or Spikes or whatever hellish creatures had done this would probably come back and relished their great victory. Great warriors they were, with their triumph over gentle and lonely Gerald Ainsley. If she cut down and buried the display of their prowess, they would know that someone else was on the Key.

After long moments, she remounted her bicycle and turned her back on her dead friend.

It was only logical.

"Please, Mom? Please?"

"No."

"Please, Vic? Please?" Tessa Kai echoed Dancy's childish plea, her eyes twinkling.

"No."

"Mama Vic," Dancy sighed, "you're just no fun anymore."

Victorine started to snap at her. But seeing her pretty heart-shaped face upturned, her sparkling blue eyes, her face alight, she thought, *Isn't this what I'm trying to do? Make her and Mother happy? So why should I insist that they be clench-jawed and strung piano-wire tight like I am? Isn't that why I didn't tell them about Gerald, why I've tried to minimize . . . everything?*

Still . . .

"Dancy, I know it's hard. But I just don't think it's a good idea for you and Mother to go outside yet," Victorine replied as casually as she could.

"But it's such a beautiful day, and so warm! And it's clear, so clear we can see to the Yucatan peninsula, practically! We'd hear those nasty Pikes or Spikes coming hours away." Dancy's pert nose wrinkled. "And I swear I could smell the Pikes as soon as they came over the bridge."

Victorine frowned.

Dancy drooped. "All right, Mother, I understand. But do you suppose we could eat out on the balcony? It'd be almost like a picnic."

"You know the sea gulls would swarm. We might as well hang a sign out on the balcony."

Defeated, Dancy nodded and turned away.

Tessa Kai stepped in front of her daughter, glaring up at her, bristling. "Victorine Flynn Thayer, you are a good mother to

Dancy and a good daughter to me. But I am still your mother, and I'm pulling rank this time. We've been imprisoned in this apartment for almost three weeks now. We need to get out."

Victorine was a strong-willed woman, but she was not in the habit of disobeying her mother. She had always honored her parents, and besides that, she did respect her mother's judgment. Rarely did Tessa Kai disagree with Victorine's decisions, but when she did, Victorine had always obeyed her.

Now, though she felt thoughtless rebellion, she did consider the circumstances. Dancy had been looking—not panicky, or frightened out of her wits—but just pinched and pale. Her wide eyes seemed too big for her face. Dancy had always been an affectionate child, but since the blackout she had been positively clingy to her mother and grandmother. Today, when Tessa Kai had suggested that they go down to the beach for a picnic, Dancy had been more animated than at any time in the last three weeks. Some semblance of a pale pink blush had colored her cheeks, and her eyes had sparkled.

Victorine reluctantly admitted to herself that maybe such signs of life in her daughter were worth the risk. "All right, you two tyrants," she finally muttered.

Dancy grabbed Tessa Kai's hands and they whirled around, laughing. Victorine grumbled on, "But listen to me, little girls. There are some conditions."

"All right, grumpy old bear," Tessa Kai teased. "Anything to get out of this place and in the sun and sand and sea!"

"No swimming!" Victorine ordered. "It's warm today, but the water will be cold, and we certainly don't need to get sick!"

"But Mom, these birdbaths we're taking—" Dancy begged.

"No swimming," Victorine said flatly. "You'll dress warmly, and you'll wear two pairs of thick socks and your Wellies. No wading, either."

"She's right about that, Dancy-doodle," Tessa Kai said lightly.

"The sun's warm, but the water, and that light north wind coming in, is cold. No swimming and no wet feet."

"All right," Dancy grumbled.

"And both of you do me the courtesy of not tramping all over the beach," Victorine said, with mock sternness. "We can take short walks, but only below the tide line."

"But why, Mom?" Dancy asked.

Victorine's face fell. Now that she'd decided to take this risk, she was determined to make it as much lighthearted fun for Dancy as she could.

Tessa Kai, with a quick glance at the deep worry on her daughter's face, spared her. "Because, Miss Fit, if those stinking Pikes see your tiny little footprints all around the condo, they might decide there's a fairy around here dancing in the light of the full moon, and come looking for her."

Dancy's eyes grew wide and stark again, but only for a moment. "Oh, I see," she said quietly, then smiled again. "It's all right, Mother. Don't worry. I'm not scared."

Victorine smiled weakly back at her, but Tessa Kai thought, *I wish you weren't so scared, Vic . . . Of the three of us, you are both the strongest and the weakest. I've never understood this in you . . . until now.*

"I'm hungry," Dancy announced, pulling the sleeve of Tessa Kai's sweater. "And I'm thirsty, and I want to go outside and play!"

"Dress first, like I told you," Victorine said. "Then we'll eat, drink, and be merry!"

Dancy dashed off to her bedroom, and Tessa Kai smiled as she watched her. "Victorine, you are a wonderful daughter, and I love you with all my heart. But that child has been my delight. She's filled my life with joy, and the only sadness she's brought me is that your father didn't live to see her and know her."

Victorine was unaccustomed to such outward expression of emotions from her mother. Both of her parents were warm and loving in their demeanor, but neither of them was very physically affectionate. Rarely did they express emotions in words, though Victorine had always known a security in their love and support. Because her ex-husband had been a touchy-feely sort of man, Victorine had taught herself to be more physically affectionate both with him and Dancy. But still, she had never felt comfortable talking about her emotions, either good ones or bad ones, and she felt awkward now. "I'll go on down and build the fire and take the food," she murmured, dropping her eyes. "Do you think you and Dancy can manage the basket and blanket?"

Tessa Kai nodded, smiling up at her daughter with understanding and a hint of regret. "Of course. I'm old, not crippled."

"You're not old, you're seasoned," Vic retorted automatically, an old joke between them. "And make sure Dancy dresses warmly."

"Yes, Drill Sergeant," Tessa Kai responded.

Victorine dressed, marveling again at the oddities that her mother had stashed over the years. Tessa Kai had come up with a box of old cable-knit fishermen's sweaters, not old enough to be made of natural fabrics like cotton or wool, but still bulky and floppy and warm. With an undershirt, they were usually more than enough for the mild winters on the coast. Almost smiling, Victorine put on two pairs of thick socks and pulled on her "Wellies." Her father, while traveling in England, had bought several pairs of the sturdy rubber boots, which had been long absent from America's cyber-stores. Even though her father had died seventeen years ago, Victorine still missed him. Her mother's words about him—he had died in a helicopter accident—had wrenched Victorine, though she hadn't shown it. She'd been pregnant with Dancy when Victor Thayer died, though she didn't find out she was expecting until three weeks after the accident. It had been a terrible time for her and her mother, so Dancy's arrival had indeed been like the only light in their lives. Sometimes it still seemed that way, especially to Victorine. It had never occurred to her, and did not even now, that she, her mother, and Dancy had formed a tight circle that had excluded her husband, Indie Galloway. By the time he deserted Victorine, he was barely a part of her life or thoughts.

Her thoughts now, however, were centered on the logistics of having a picnic on the beach when murderous gangs might be lurking around. The sheer insanity of the situation didn't escape Victorine's notice, but with a tight control she dealt with the problem as if it were what to serve at a dinner party for six third ministers, or how to decorate a condo for a high commissar and his consort's month-long Diversionary Retreat.

Grabbing the two heavy iron Dutch ovens that Tessa Kai had always used to cook, her backpack bulging, Victorine headed down to the beach. Before she did anything, she took a pair of fine binoculars she'd stolen from the deserted commissary and checked out the beach. The binoculars were hardly needed. The day was so clear and fine she could see for miles both east and west. Cautiously she went out on the road and checked up and down. There was not a sign of a living human being. As had so often happened in the last days, the reality of their isolation made Victorine feel a frisson of dread, but she smothered it quickly. Businesslike, she went to the maintenance room and got her supplies.

Returning to the beach, she smoothed out a nice level place with a shovel to put the blanket and build a fire. Then she built a shallow pit and ringed it with old bricks. With mathematical precision, she laid out a fire of odd pieces of driftwood, old dune fencing, pieces of wooden pallets that she'd scrounged. Frowning with disgust, she laid what looked like ugly pockmarked pieces of red mortar on top of the wood.

"Stupid Proto-Syn lava rocks, my eye," she grumbled to herself. "No telling what they really are. Melt and smolder more than glow." Still, they did retain more heat than small pieces of old dried wood that burned fast and hot and then were gone. The fire lit easily. She placed a piece of a lacy wrought-iron fire screen over it, then set the two pots and an old tin coffeepot on top with satisfaction.

Tessa Kai and Dancy came running up, Tessa Kai breathlessly protesting and Dancy teasing her. "I'm so hungry, hurry up, T. K.!"

"It's not time to eat yet, little bird, so you just go amuse yourself for a bit," Tessa Kai retorted. "Shoo! You wanted to come outside, now here you are! Run and play!"

Dancy turned in a circle, twice, her arms held out and her face lifted up. Then she ran along the beach, waving her arms at the precocious sea gulls that were already gathering. "I'm here, I'm here, and I've got a treat for you, you rascals . . ."

Victorine frowned. She didn't want Dancy going too far.

"Relax, Vic, you'll be able to see her even if she runs five miles," Tessa Kai declared. "What a perfectly glorious day! Let the child breathe, for heaven's sake."

Victorine sank down on the blanket, sighing. "I know, I'll try."

Tessa Kai lifted the top of one of the pots, sniffed suspiciously, and asked Victorine, "You didn't do anything to this, did you?"

"No, Mother, I didn't even open it up to see what it was," Victorine answered, with amusement. Victorine was an indifferent cook at best, while Tessa Kai was a throwback to the days when women cooked from scratch, never knowing exactly how much of anything they used, and everything they cooked was wonderful. Victorine's cooking was the only thing Tessa Kai ever reproved her about, for Dancy's sake, which was unnecessary because Tessa Kai cooked for the three of them. She always had.

"Good," Tessa Kai grunted, unaware of Victorine's dry amusement at the not-so-subtle criticism. "This—this—dog food is going to be bad enough as it is."

"It'll be wonderful, as your cooking always is, Mother. It surely does smell good."

"Hmph."

Victorine shaded her eyes to watch Dancy. She did look wonderful, like an art montage on Cyclops. Dancy was wearing Victorine's bright red jacket with her red Wellingtons, and she was surrounded by hundreds of sea gulls, that wheeled and cried as she threw them old bread crumbs and pieces of stale crackers. As far as the eye could see, an empty white beach stretched behind her, with a cheerful blue sky and the luscious azure-and-jade sea framing her. The sight filled Victorine with such fierce longing to protect her, and sorrow for the hardships and dangers they were facing, that she almost choked.

For perhaps the thousandth time since the blackout, fear and panic rose in Victorine. *What in the world am I going to do? How do I handle this? What's the best thing for us?* Her eyes fell on the piece of fire screen that she was using for a grill. She'd taken it from a condominium complex down the beach, between Summer Sea and Gerald's White Dunes. It was named Perdido Quay—Lost Key—and it was an elegant high-rise with twelve floors. Lost Key was closed except for the three months of summer, when the first ministers and congressmen and foreign heads of state sometimes vacationed there. It had never been as popular as Summer Sea, however, mainly because there had never been a concierge as dedicated to maintaining the facility and providing the quality of service as Victorine did at Summer Sea.

But the twelfth-floor penthouses are marvelous . . . and they have fireplaces, Victorine reasoned. *Cooking . . . it's such a terrible hardship.* They'd been building small cooking fires in one of the vacant units between Victorine's condo and Tessa Kai's. It had Mexican tile, and Victorine had simply outlined a circle on the floor with bricks. They opened the balcony doors to let the smoke out. When it was visible, Victorine had to stand and fan vigorously to dissipate it so the telltale smudges couldn't be seen against the clear skies.

Fireplace . . . you could still see the smoke . . . unless . . . I wonder about some kind of turbine on top of the chimney, that would turn with the heat?

Victorine frowned darkly. *But Tessa Kai . . . how in the world would she cope with twelve flights of stairs? Seven is bad enough!* Anger grew in her then, an aimless but savage fury for what had happened to them. Their lives had been turned upside down, they'd been deprived of everything: a sense of security that had always seemed to be their birthright, the essentials of life, freedom from personal danger, even the freedom to go outside on their own property. It was outrageous, and Victorine could hardly contain the bitterness she felt.

Glancing at her daughter's dark face, Tessa Kai said quietly, "You know, Victorine, there's something that I've been meaning to talk to you about for the last few weeks."

With difficulty, Victorine pulled herself out of the blackness of her thoughts. "Oh? What's that, Mother?" she asked politely.

"It's about the Lord," Tessa Kai said, not without discomfort. "You know that your father was a much stronger Christian than I. And after he died, well, I just sort of . . ." She shrugged, then spread her hands. They were old hands, but still lithe and pretty. "But now, since these terrible days have come, I've come back to Him. It was hard. I felt"—she smiled with irony—"sort of like the soldier in the foxhole. You know what I mean. Like: 'I know I've been ignoring You for years now, Lord, but now I'm in trouble, so I want to come back so You can take care of me.'"

Victorine dropped her eyes. "I see."

Tessa Kai took a deep breath. "Do you?" She waited.

Shifting restlessly, Victorine muttered, "I don't know. What's your point, Mother?"

"The point is, *do* you see? Do you know what the Lord's answer to my shamefaced little confession was?"

Finally Victorine answered, "No, I don't suppose I do."

Tessa Kai smiled. "It was just two words: 'Welcome home.'"

Victorine said nothing, and still didn't meet her mother's steady gaze. She was making meaningless little tick marks in the soft white sand.

"That's all He's ever said to me. I mean, that's all the words I've heard clearly in my head, I guess you'd say. But I know He's real, Victorine, and I know the Holy Spirit is in my heart, and in my soul, and in my very breath. So when I tell you that I'm not frightened, that's what I mean. I'm not. I—I—worry, I suppose you'd say, and I'm concerned, and I try to—figure out how to—fix things. But I'm not afraid, not at all."

Victorine was quiet for a long time. Then, in a voice so low and strained that Tessa Kai could barely hear her, she asked, "And Dancy? Is she afraid, or is she—like you?"

Softly Tessa Kai answered, "Victorine, I think you don't understand Dancy, much as I've never completely understood you. There's nothing wrong with that, you know. It doesn't mean that I love you, or you love Dancy, any less. In fact, sometimes I think that means that the love you have for someone you can't always comprehend is deeper, more dedicated, than the love you have for someone with whom you have a perfect rapport. Anyway, to answer your question, Dancy is at peace. Yes, she's afraid, in a way, because she's just a child and doesn't have the mental stamina and stability that the simple process of living gives an adult. But still, Victorine, she has a very close relationship with Christ. There's something even I can't quite . . ."

Now Victorine looked up sharply. "What do you mean?"

Tessa Kai frowned, then dismissed her words. "Oh, nothing, Vic, you know I think she hung the moon and stars. Anyway, what I wanted to say to you is that I'm worried about you."

"About me? Why? I'm doing just fine."

"Are you?" Tessa Kai said mildly. "Well, anyway, there's just one other thing I wanted to say to you. It's sort of a message, I guess you'd say, from the Lord."

"Oh, Mother, please—" Victorine was now embarrassed.

"No, let me finish. It's just this: *Come unto Me, all ye that labour and are heavy laden, and I will give you rest. Take My yoke upon you, and learn of Me; for I am meek and lowly in heart: and ye shall find rest unto your souls. For My yoke is easy, and My burden is light.*" She finished awkwardly, "I wrote it down for you. Here."

Victorine took the plain white sheet of paper and stuck it in her pants pocket. "Thank you, Mother."

"You're welcome, Victorine. And I love you very much."

Victorine finally looked her mother in the eye. "I love you, too. Very much. Now, how about some food?"

The night before, as Tessa Kai had secretly been planning a special day for Dancy, she'd taken all the rest of their dried beef strips and soaked them overnight in cooking sherry. Early that morning she'd wrapped the softened meat strips around pieces of Asian pears, which kept forever. Tessa Kai had always said it was because they were actually wooden fruit: Their consistency was like soft wood, and they certainly tasted like it. Still, when cooked with spicy meats, they made a good, mild-flavored base.

Then she'd started a long and slow-cooking sauce made of satsumas—that rare citrus fruit still grown in a few places in the South that looked like old dried-up oranges and tasted sweeter than sugared tangerines—and butter. She'd also made a dish of julienne potatoes and onions diced into tiny bits, with a sauce made of powdered cream and butter. She hoped it would be something like lyonnaise, though it was unlikely, with the tasteless Proto-Syn cream.

It was delicious, perhaps the best meal they'd had since the blackout, even though Tessa Kai insisted that it was like dog food. Every morsel was carefully wrapped for snacks later. Victorine allowed Dancy to have two cups of heavily sweetened and creamed coffee, while she drank the heavy, bitter brew—it was boiled—black. She liked it. Actually, it was a little like the espresso her father used to buy and share with Victorine. Suddenly Victorine longed for an espresso, in a tiny, delicate china cup with a twinge of lemon peel waved over it . . . *Odd the things that occur to you, that you miss and want . . .* For the first time since the blackout, Victorine let her mind and thoughts wander a little. She relaxed.

The sun was deliciously warm, and even burned a little on Victorine's face and hands. Tessa Kai and Dancy started picking up shells and making little drawings in the sand that the waves promptly erased. It was an idyllic day, and Victorine thought that she could almost forget—not completely, but almost—the terrible days that they had been through, and the ones that were surely to come. Lying back on the blanket, she closed her eyes, though she didn't drowse. She just concentrated on relaxing her aching leg muscles, the tightness in her shoulders and neck and jaws. She thought of her father, and she thought of Tessa Kai's words about her heavenly Father, too.

Something was wrong. Victorine shot up and looked around wildly.

Dancy and Tessa Kai were standing in the little surf. They had grown quiet, and their sudden stillness and silence were, perhaps, what had startled Victorine. Dancy was gripping Tessa Kai's arm, hard, and her face was strained and white. "What is it?" Victorine called, running to them.

"I—I—don't know," Dancy said. She sounded confused.

Tessa Kai said in an urgent tone, "She told me to be quiet. She said she heard something."

"Heard something? Like—like what?" Victorine demanded.

She and Tessa Kai looked at Dancy. Dancy was pale, the color draining from her cheeks. Her eyes were unfocused, staring into the far distance to the east. Then she tightened her mouth into a small, straight line and said, "Someone's coming, Mother. They're coming."

Victorine froze, then whirled and searched frantically up the beach. It was empty, deserted.

Dancy looked chagrined. "Maybe—maybe on the road—"

Victorine said quickly, "It doesn't matter. You two go upstairs. Now." She turned and ran back to the fire, frantically kicking sand over the flames. Then she grabbed the shovel and started covering it good. It would have to be better than good—it would have to be out and covered with clean white sand. Dancy and Tessa Kai ignored Victorine's command to run upstairs. They both now sensed that Victorine wouldn't have time to erase all traces before they got close.

Dancy muttered to her grandmother, "They are on the road, Grandmother. And I think—I think it's the Pikes."

"Filth," Tessa Kai sniffed. "I'll get the food and things, Dancy. You start sweeping up our footprints, okay? Hurry, child, hurry!"

The three worked so fast and hard that Victorine didn't even have an opportunity to order them upstairs again. Within minutes, the fire was out and covered, the few footprints on virgin sand had been swept, and the litter from the picnic had been whisked up. They hurried to the condo, with Victorine coming behind, quickly sweeping up the marks of their steps.

If Victorine had thought quickly enough, they could have gone up the west stairwell and then, perhaps, the gang walking from the east would never have seen them. But then, Victorine thought of many, many things, for a long time, that she might have done, or should have done differently. As with all regrets, they did no good whatsoever.

Without speaking, making as little noise as possible while carrying so much, they hurried up the stairs. They reached the landing between the third and fourth floors, and to their horror, the gang had reached the condos. Framed in the open portholes in the east-facing wall, Victorine, Dancy and Tessa Kai were exactly in the line of vision of the men and women only fifty feet away on the street.

Victorine froze. "Don't move," she whispered furiously. "Can see movement in peripheral vision better . . ."

The three of them stood perfectly still.

The men, laughing and talking loudly, were swaggering along, some brandishing baseball bats, some holding guns. One even had a horsewhip he was cracking on the road and making hooting cattle calls. They could see three women, walking tiredly. One of them stopped, pulled a bottle out of the pocket of her leather jacket, and swigged enormously, then wiped her mouth. Her hair was tangled and matted, and when she swiped at her face it left a dirty streak across her mouth. It was very hard for the three not to move while she stood there, idly looking around. Once it seemed that she looked straight at them. But then, carelessly, she tipped the bottle again and took a long hard drink, then capped it and slouched on. Victorine started breathing again, and Dancy made a small, high noise in her throat.

The last of the group—there were about thirty of them now, Victorine thought—were straggling on, and she was thinking, *We made it, we did it, they didn't see, they can't see . . .*

Unbelievably, beside them, was a horrible clang and then a shriek, quickly cut off. Tessa Kai had dropped the iron pot she was holding, and was clawing at her face.

Before she had time for a conscious thought, Victorine pulled Dancy down to the gritty, cold floor, beneath the sill of the opening.

Tessa Kai grimly pulled a spider out of her hair, then, with great deliberation, threw it down and stepped on it. As if she were in a dream, Victorine watched, her eyes on her mother's cheerfully bright yellow Wellie as she ground it back and forth. "Well, that's done it for sure," Tessa Kai breathed.

They were shouting. A man's rough voice called, "Hey, Brucie Goose! You hear that! Somebody's up there—look! On the stairs!"

Though she tried to move quickly, Victorine couldn't seem to control her body. She felt as if she were underwater, far underwater, with weights all over her, weighing her down, burdening her, so she could only move in slow motion . . . she raised her eyes to her mother's kind brown ones.

Men's voices were shouting, while some of the women were calling shrilly. They heard footsteps, hard and loud, in the parking lot. Men were running toward the stairs.

"I love you both so much," Tessa Kai said sweetly. "And it won't be long before we're together again. But right now"—incredibly, she smiled at Victorine—"I'm going home."

Clutching her funny big pocketbook close, Tessa Kai turned and walked down the stairs.

Victorine and Dancy both felt as if they were indeed in a horrible, uneasy dream, unreal, stifling, where you can neither move nor speak.

Tessa Kai disappeared.

A man's greasy voice echoed in the stairwell: "It's an old woman! C'mere, Bruce, look! Hey, Grandma, how you dealing with it, huh? You can't be by yourself . . . who else is up there, taking care of you?"

Dancy, in Victorine's arms, stiffened. Victorine felt her deep intake of breath as she opened her mouth to shout.

And then Victorine did something that forever after both horrified her, but also gave her great gladness. She clapped her hand over Dancy's mouth, and held her arms in a vise so she couldn't move. Dancy whimpered, but the tiny sound was lost.

"You filthy pig—no, that's an insult to pigs," Tessa Kai was saying calmly. "Well, whatever you are, I can take care of myself. See?"

"Lookit that! Grandma's got—two! Two little popguns! Hey, look—"

A gunshot. It sounded very loud, and echoed deafeningly, in the tunnel of the stairs. Dancy flinched, her whole body jerking spasmodically.

He bleated, "Shot me! You—" Scuffling noises. Another shot, then two more.

His voice was black with rage. "Shot me! Old woman *shot me!* C'mere, you idiot, help me! Get me back to the doc, now!"

Their footsteps receded. Crouching on the floor, Victorine still holding Dancy in a stranglehold, they heard the gang shouting, then laughing. The man's rumbling growls faded.

It was quiet again.

Victorine and Dancy got up so slowly; they looked as if they were old, old women. Victorine put her arm around Dancy's waist, and together they walked down the stairs. A soft twilight was enveloping the world. They didn't see Tessa Kai until they were standing right over her.

She was sprawled in an awkward position on the second and last steps. Her handbag was still threaded on her left arm. Both of her ladylike silver .22's were gone.

It took Victorine and Dancy a long time to carry her up to her home. They washed her and did her hair, and dressed her in an old white dress that she had always liked, and had worn every New Year's Eve. They laid her in bed and perfumed her. Victorine took a long time arranging her hands outside the perfectly smooth coverlet. Dancy took Tessa Kai's old Bible and read Psalm 103. Tears streamed down her face, but her high, childlike voice was steady and calm. Victorine didn't cry.

When they left, Victorine locked the door. She never saw her mother's house again.

The White House
Washington, D.C.

"Wha—"

The president's voice cracked. He cleared his throat, a dry, choking sound, and began again. "What are they shouting?"

"They want in." Alia Silverthorne spoke in terse sentences these days.

"But why?"

Stiffly and slowly, Alia moved to stand in front of the roaring fire in Luca and Minden's formal sitting room. There was no nonsense about "Project Final Unity Situation Room" now. Cyclops, and the White House, and Washington, and perhaps the whole world, had been dark for more than three weeks now. "They're cold, hungry, angry, and scared. Just as we are. Sir," Alia added as an afterthought.

Luca remained motionless at the window. It was bleak outside. Even the light of day seemed halfhearted and weary.

"Sir, you really must move away from the window," Alia said—for at least the hundredth time. President Therion just didn't get it. The hundreds of people besieging the White House were angry and determined to make someone pay for what had happened to them. And President Luca Therion's defenses were very weak, indeed. But he just couldn't seem to comprehend that, either.

"I don't understand," he murmured, an eerie echo of Alia's private thoughts. "Why are they threatening me and Minden? I told them . . . I told them that it was a conspiracy, a dangerous fundamentalist religious faction . . ."

"Yes, sir, they understand that."

Finally he turned away from the window to face her. "How do you know, Commissar Silverthorne?"

"Because last night they hanged four people from the gates," she answered neutrally. "They have signs hung around their necks that say 'religious fanatic' and 'traitor.' One of them was a priest."

Luca's sensitive face was unreadable, especially in the uncertain firelight. Alia studied him carefully, and he seemed unaware of her scrutiny. He really is perfectly self-deceived . . . he has truly convinced himself that somehow this disaster has nothing to do with him or Minden or the ohm-bug or the Germans—

Or me, *one part of her disciplined mind tidily supplied.*

She was much too fatigued to go into that mental minefield again.

"Where is Minden?" she asked, choking back a yawn by sheer willpower.

"Meditating," he answered, nodding toward the adjoining bedroom.

"Sir, I really must stress again that neither of you should ever be alone for any length of time," Alia said as severely as she could manage. "Will you go get her, or do you want me to?"

"Neither," he said gruffly. "Leave her alone. And I will ask you to keep silent, please, Commissar Silverthorne. I'm trying to meditate myself."

Alia considered this, and decided to let it go. There was no outside entrance into the bedroom. Minden and Luca were probably as safe as they could be with Alia guarding them, for she was fairly certain that in the end—which could come any day now—she was going to be the only one left standing with them. She leaned against the mantel, savoring the warmth of the fire, trying to regain some strength from it. Blinking heavily, she let her eyelids shut only for a moment . . .

All this . . . because of that silly little germ, *she daydreamed.* And Niklas . . . Niklas . . . I wonder . . . if he's dead . . . horrible, unthinkable way to die! Smothering, dying, sick, thirsty, starved, shut up with hundreds of dead and dying people in the dark . . . Entombed, alive, entombed, alive, entombed, alive . . .

With a smothered half-scream, Alia woke up.

She'd fallen asleep, standing on her feet, leaning against the mantelpiece.

Guiltily she glanced at Luca Therion. He didn't turn around.

"Alia, go to bed."

"I can't, sir, I—"

"I order you. I'm still president of the United States of America. Go to bed."

Alia straightened to her full height of five feet, four inches tall. "I'll obey your order, sir. But I ask permission to sleep on the sofa."

"Permission granted," he said dully. "It doesn't matter anyway, does it, Alia? Aren't we all going to die?"

"Not on my watch, sir," she said evenly.

She settled down on the hard sofa, and Luca returned to the window. "Sir . . ." she said in a soft, pleading voice.

"Aren't the snipers on the roof?" he asked carelessly.

"Yes, sir, but they can't shoot a bullet heading for your head."

"Isn't this window bulletproof?"

Alia sighed. "Yes, sir, it's supposed to stop up to a .50 caliber."

"So?"

"So there are always M-60's, sir."

"Ah, yes," he said gravely. "There's always a bigger gun out there, in the dark, where you can't see it . . ."

Minden came floating in. It really did seem as if she were floating, for she wore a filmy white dress trimmed in a long airy fur, like the finest ermine. She was radiant. "Oh, wonderful, Alia, you're here! No, no, sit down, here, right by me. Luca, come here, my darling. I have such good news, such wonderful news!"

Alia immediately became concerned for Minden's sanity: there was no such thing as news any more. There was no Cyclops. There were no newspapers, or SATphones, or even radio waves or electromagnetic impulses. The ohm-bug had eaten them all . . . Alia was fuguing out a little, and made herself concentrate on Minden's raptures.

" . . . ritual cleansing is the first step. I insist, Luca, that you do it tonight. Now."

Luca wearily took her hand and stroked it. "Minden, dear, there's no water. Remember?"

She jerked back her hand and said irritably, "Don't talk to me as if I'm a troubled child, Luca. There will be water. Trust me. We will have water. Then—then—you must do the invocations. It's taken me so long—I've been so blind! But the invocations and incantations, Luca, open the door . . . and then comes the empowerment."

Luca looked uncertain. "The—empowerment?"

"Oh, yes," Minden said in a low voice. "You have no conception, Luca, no possible comprehension of what I have learned, what I have finally seen . . . It's a miracle."

"What—how—"

"Tor," she said in an almost inaudible whisper. "Tor showed me."

"Tor—von Eisenhalt?" Luca was losing ground.

Impatiently Minden jumped up. "It took me three weeks to—to—find it, Luca. It'll take you a little while, I know. But look—"

She rushed to the window, flinging the heavy draperies aside impatiently.

Luca and Alia gazed after her, mystified. Alia, her mind slow and stupid, finally got up. "Minden—My Lady—" she said helplessly.

Minden turned around, and for a moment Alia thought she saw—something. Something Else. Not Minden, not a woman, not even a human. Something pale, forbidden, of the wraiths, the ghouls, the gray and tattered spirits of ancient tales told in darkness . . .

I must be hallucinating from fatigue, Alia said, shutting her eyes tight.

When she opened them, Luca was standing by Minden, touching her face. "You're bleeding," he said. He sounded afraid.

She touched one long pale finger to the corner of her eye. "It doesn't hurt," she whispered. Pointing with her blood-tipped nail, she said, "Look. It's snowing."

The three stood, unmoving, watching clean fat flakes swirling down.

Alia turned and ran from the room.

She had to get containers onto the roof fast.

At least they wouldn't die thirsty.

TWENTY-FOUR

COLONEL DARKON BEN-AMMI, who was the steadiest hiker of them all, stumbled and fell to his knees. Vashti Nicanor wondered at it, but only for a moment. She knew her Mossad comrade very well, and knew that he had done it on purpose. He was walking by Captain Con Slaughter's side.

Slaughter roused from his daze and hurried to help the older man to his feet. "You all right, Colonel?"

"Sure, sure," he grunted. "Just a misstep."

He rose, dusted himself off, then the two started walking in step again. At least Con had come out of his semi-catatonic state. His eyes were focused, and he began to look around at the landscape in an assessing way.

Lightly Colonel Ben-ammi said, "I was wondering how long we would march today. How far is it to Donkey's End?"

"Uh—I'm not sure," Con hesitantly replied. He seemed a bit surprised that he didn't know.

But Darkon Ben-ammi wasn't surprised at all. In the aftermath of the massacre at Fort Carson, the team had just walked off the base. All of them, except Darkon, had seemed stunned, as if they had concussions. It was just a sort of autopilot, Darkon was certain, that had made Con walk out in the same direction they had started on that long-ago morning—southwest, toward the small box canyon where the burros roamed.

Darkon had given it almost the entire day, judging whether Con Slaughter was going to recover and take command again. As evening crept up on them, Darkon could see that Con was still unable to come out of his darkness, so Darkon had decided to try to help him along a bit. As it turned out, it didn't take much. Con Slaughter was a natural leader of men, and this deep instinct was bound to come alive in him. Darkon—the entire fire team—just really needed it to be sooner rather than later.

"Hold up, people," Con suddenly ordered. The straggling team's footsteps eventually lagged to a stop. "Sergeant Valdosta and Lieutenant Fong, scout around over there in that stand of rocks and see if there's a good place to camp. Darmstedt, Colonel Nicanor, you check over to the east. Looks like a loss, but there may be a sheltering ravine or gully."

Valdosta and Fong took off immediately, but Ric Darmstedt blinked a few times. Vashti touched his arm. "Come, Lieutenant, I'll take point."

"Sure, ma'am," he said blankly, following her obediently.

"Mitchell, where are we?" Con demanded.

David looked bemused. "I—I'm not sure, sir. I haven't been— uh—"

"Neither have I, and neither has anyone else, except the colonel here," Con said brusquely. "So get on it. I want a spot on the map. How much time do you need?"

David straightened, and like the others, his eyes seemed to come alive. Searching around, he answered, "I need some height, I need the 40K night binocs. Give me half an hour, sir."

"Fine. Go climb a tree or run up a hill or something. Be back in thirty."

"Yes, sir." David hurried off to the east after Valdosta and Fong.

Con Slaughter turned to Colonel Darkon, his face careworn and old-looking. "Sir, I'm the captain of this team, and I appreciate you and Colonel Nicanor putting yourself under my authority since you've joined up with us. But right now, I'd sure like the advice of a superior officer—and a more experienced soldier and wiser man than I am."

Politely Colonel Darkon replied, "I don't know how qualified I am, Captain, but I'm at your service."

Con looked off into the distance, after his team. "What the devil do I do now?" he muttered.

Colonel Ben-ammi eased the pack from his shoulders and rubbed his right shoulder contemplatively. Con Slaughter waited, his tawny brown eyes troubled and murky. Finally Ben-ammi said rather coolly, "I may outrank you, Captain Slaughter, but I have no training in commanding a small combat unit. That is why I am here, to learn—from you. You are the leader of this so-elite and highly trained team."

"That doesn't help me much, sir," Con observed darkly.

"No? The only other information I can give you, Captain Slaughter, is what I would do if this were a flight team downed in hostile territory."

Wearily Con asked, "And what would you do, sir?"

Heavily intent, Darkon replied, "I would order them to hide, and wait. Wait for some real soldiers—someone like Fire Team Eclipse—to come rescue them."

Con's careworn face blanched, and he seemed momentarily stunned. After long moments his lips set in a tight line, but all he said was, "Thank you, Colonel, for the advice."

They camped underneath a brooding pinnacle of red sandstone, huddling close together in their sleeping bags. It was bitterly cold, and the air was so dry that their lips were already beginning to crack. When David Mitchell realized this, he sternly made everyone apply lip balm. That was the sum total of the activity, and the conversation, of the night.

None of them thought they would sleep, but the first indication that they were real soldiers was that they fell asleep instantly.

Men of war did that. Sleep was a healer, and sleep was precious. Time for sleep was never squandered.

In the first bare gray of dawn, Con Slaughter was surprised to awaken refreshed, alert, and with a clear mind. He woke up first, and he kindled the dead fire and started the coffee and even boiled a separate pot of water for tea for the Israelis. No one else stirred.

The high plains mornings were so crisp, so stringent, that it stirred a man's soul and strengthened his will. *These men are my responsibility, and that is the saving of me . . . ,* he reflected with uncharacteristic self-analysis. *Otherwise, I'd be lost, tearing at my hair and howling at the moon. But I have a duty, I have responsibilities, I have obligations, and no one—not even Colonel Ben-ammi—can or should take them from me.*

So that's my mission . . . to lead them.

So what's my crisis? he thought with sudden invigoration. *I have a mission, I have a plan, I have the best team in the army . . .*

"Wake up, people!" he stood up and roared. "It's a great morning to be alive!"

He was impatient, and while they were still grumbling and moaning, he began his work.

"They're dead," he said flatly. "Never forget, but never let it devour you. No team of mine is going to grow weaker because of the deaths of honorable comrades in arms. This will—it has to—make us stronger.

"We're Fire Team Eclipse. We are soldiers, we are professionals. No more stumbling around like brainless civvies. We're lying low here for the day, then we resume night marches. We've got a mission, and a plan, and it's time to get back to work.

"We're going to hunt for food to save our MRE's. We're going to conserve our water because it's been a dry summer and it looks like the winter's gonna be the same. We're gonna grab some pack animals and use 'em, but we're not gonna bleat if they're needed to carry water or wood while we're still haulin' our packs. We're going on to that ranch for horses. Along the way we're going to help out any civvies we can, any way we can. And sooner or later, we'll fight, and we'll never surrender. We fight—even if we're the last!"

———

David Mitchell, by some skill, some deep instinct, and some mystical gift, led them directly to the ranch. They'd found a gully about four miles from the ranch, and they'd parked there until dawn. Con had decided to reconnoiter the ranch in daytime, and not go crashing in like some SWAT team in the middle of the night, just in case there were only scared civvies there.

From two miles out, David could see clearly across the flat waste of sand the big house and the outbuildings with the ART III power scope that was originally made for snipers' rifles. Laser Imaging Targeting, however, had made all visible imagery technology obsolete, until the blackout, of course. David had had the foresight to scrounge around in the base supply warehouses and find all kinds of things that the army had no use for anymore but would never throw away.

"No horses," he reported to Con. The entire team was lying flat on their bellies on the last small rise before the startling green line of the ranch house grounds. Two miles back in the gully, their four burros chewed contentedly on some tumbleweeds that Ric Darmstedt had managed—rather comically—to capture. The burros were surprisingly amiable, David had said, and they ate anything and everything with relish. The worst trouble the sturdy little animals had given them was when one that David had named Cookie had almost eaten Captain Slaughter's right boot. The four burros even seemed to be growing attached to David and Ric.

"One Vindicator, two Hummers," David continued, peering intently through the contraption. "No sign of people outside, but there's smoke coming from the chimney."

"Smell any Germans?" Con asked cautiously. They had seen no sign of Germans anywhere on the ground, only flyovers by a squadron of Tornadoes and the occasional helo or two. In fact, they'd only seen other humans once, in a ghost town named Canto. The people had run into the thick forest that hovered over the dusty little town when Con and Rio tried to approach them. Con, sighing, had let them go. No sense in running after them and really terrorizing them.

"Not really, sir. I just don't think it's feasible," David was finally answering thoughtfully. "Surely they're sticking close to their bases. And this facility sure isn't like a pleasure resort or something. I doubt if they'd take any notice of it."

Con took a few moments to consider, then he turned to his right-hand man. "Rio, you got a nose. What do you think?"

Con had become skillful at honing in on each person's unique capabilities and using them at every opportunity. This was one of the things that had saved the team in the last weeks. Rio Valdosta relished being called on by his captain, as did each member of the team. "Gimme that spyglass, Mitchell, let me take a look-see. You're a pretty smart little puppy for liberating this jewel."

"Can the wise sage routine, Rio, you're the same age as I am," David scoffed.

"Puppy bites," Rio teased. He studied the ranch for a while. "The helo and Hummers have sand piled up on the north side. Must not be any commissars there . . . they wouldn't stand for that, even if the blasted things don't run. Corral's broken down in two places."

He peered through the scope for a few more minutes, then said confidently, "Captain, I think we got some scared Green techies in that house. No way of knowing how many, but it wouldn't matter if it was a hundred. They ain't gonna give us no trouble. They'll probably cry with joy all over their little green coveralls to see some people who have a clue."

Yeah, we do have a clue, Con thought with satisfaction. Standing up, he shouldered his pack. "Then let's ride to the rescue. C'mon, slugs, daylight's trekkin'."

A covert approach to the ranch, which was smack in the middle of a vast barren plain, was not impossible but probably would've taken the team a day and a night, crawling on their bellies. Con's instincts told him that the risk wasn't worth the effort, so they simply walked up to the front door. Con knocked politely. "Hello, the house! Anybody home?"

The door was almost yanked off its hinges. In the doorway stood a man with thick unkempt hair and beard who looked as if he'd been wandering in the wasteland for years.

"Soldiers?" he clamored. "People? Live, breathing, real people?" His crazed brown eyes suddenly grew wary. "You're— you're alive, aren't you? You're real . . . really . . ." His great meaty hand shook as he reached out and poked Con Slaughter's chest.

In his rough half-whisper, Con told him, "Mister, if you ever do that again I'm gonna put some more spaces in your teeth."

Niklas Kesteven's muddied brown eyes widened. Then he threw back his shaggy head and roared with laughter. "He's real! Never knew a Screaming Eagle that could stand being poked at! Glory be!" In the next moment, he threw his great gorilla arms around Con Slaughter, bulky pack and all.

Though it was difficult for him, and Rio Valdosta never let him forget it, Con did manage to keep from making good his threat.

━━◆━━

They met Gildan Ives, who was like a thin wraith, only with cherry-colored hair. She cooked for them, and though it was pretty good food under the circumstances—salt-cured slabs of beef in a creamy sauce, Proto-Syn spaghetti and meatballs, a big stew of vegetables—

the team was rather surprised that it all tasted offensively plasticine to them. Rio Valdosta had turned out to be an expert hunter, and they'd been eating well. They just hadn't realized it until now.

Dr. Niklas Kesteven talked incessantly, pacing the floor, fiddling with the food, ordering Gildan around. "Sure, this is a Shortgrass Steppe Biome facility. Who else would be stuck out in the back end of nowhere like this?" He was nervous, ducking his head and refusing to look them in the eye.

Con had a feeling, an itch, that something was wrong; not something dangerous, not something deadly, just that there was something else he needed to know about this place. Something that Niklas Kesteven really didn't want him to know. He just couldn't figure out how to find out what "it" was.

"You two have had a hard time of it, all by yourselves?" Colonel Darkon Ben-ammi asked kindly.

"Uh—we—that is, yeah, it's been hard," Niklas stuttered. They were in the enormous kitchen, seated at a rough oak table that must have weighed four hundred pounds. The fireplace was right by the table, and Gildan was kneeling close, tending to the pots that hung on clever swing-out hooks. She made an odd little gulping sound, then clamped her mouth shut.

"We—that is, we're short on water," Niklas blathered on. "That's why we've got to move on now, Captain Slaughter. No use staying here. No water."

"No water?" Colonel Ben-ammi repeated with great surprise. "But surely you have a well? Surely the commissary didn't haul water to this facility!"

"No. I mean yes. It's dried up, though," Niklas answered vaguely. "Gildan, you have any more of that beef stroganoff? The colonel here needs some more."

"No, no thank you, I'm quite full," Vashti said hastily. "It's very good, but I've had more than enough. In fact, if you will all excuse me, I believe I'll take a short walk. I've overeaten, and I'll grow sleepy if I don't walk some of it off." Without waiting, she hurried out.

Niklas looked after her, chagrined. But there was nothing he could do, short of tackling her or shooting her. "Uh—so. We need some help, Captain Slaughter. We can't stay here. Not another night, not one more night!"

Slaughter and his team exchanged wary glances. Something was definitely wrong with this man. And the woman—she looked as though if anyone touched her she'd shoot straight into the stratosphere.

Slaughter nodded, but he managed to signal Ben-ammi to keep the man talking. Colonel Ben-ammi knew how to make people tell things. Con Slaughter knew some ways to get people to talk, but such methods weren't quite appropriate to use on this poor half-demented big-brain. *Being that smart always makes you nutty*, Con reflected, not without some pity. *And being scared makes it worse.*

Colonel Ben-ammi turned on his buttery teddy-bear act full blast. He began telling Niklas all about how he looked too fatigued to embark on a difficult march to anywhere, he must be exhausted, such a strain for such a keen and highly intelligent man, blah, blah, blah . . .

And he was oh-so-solicitous of Gildan, who practically dissolved in front of their eyes. After being slathered with this warm oil for a few minutes, both Niklas and Gildan were lulled into an almost hypnotic state.

Finally Vashti came back in. She stood by the table, hands on her hips, and addressed Con Slaughter in a slow, methodical voice. "Captain Slaughter, there are two Humvees here, and a Vindicator. Where is the pilot? And please—a Humvee apiece for these two? Even the MAB directors don't get personal Humvees. Also, there are three corrals, two barns—one that has two enormous tractors stored, and much other machinery—and there are four other outbuildings. I looked in one, and it appears to be some sort of medical facility, only a little cruder than normal. Probably a veterinary clinic. A big one. What I am saying, Captain, is that this facility is much too well-equipped and complex for just two people."

Gildan, who had sat down in a chair close to Darkon Benammi, was staring vacantly into space. When she spoke, it was as if she were reading off a Cy-prompter. "I told you I'm a veterinarian. That's what we do here. Care for the wildlife in the biome. I let them all go, you see . . . all the animals. Except the horses."

Con turned to Niklas Kesteven, who had finally sat down and buried his face in his hands. "Sir, where is the pilot of the helo? And I know that all MAB facilities are equipped with commissar security details. Where are they?"

"There—were two . . . men. They started fighting over Gildan. I couldn't let them—hurt her . . . I took their guns. But I didn't kill them. I just threatened to. They—they ran out. I didn't even think about the horses. They took two of them, and let the rest of them go." Niklas's normally booming voice was hollow and weak.

Con listened and decided he was telling the truth—just not all of it. "Tell me everything, Dr. Kesteven, or I'm not going to help you."

"It's—it's got to be a lab, sir," David said suddenly. "A secret lab. Biochem weapons research. The ground, the layout—it's like it was laid down over—"

Ric Darmstedt, who said very little these days, suddenly jumped up. "Not underground. No, man, don't tell me that—"

Niklas looked up and his face had deep crevices and lines, his eyes were as dull as if he were unconscious. "You can't help them. No one can. I couldn't. I tried, I really did . . . It's too late. I was too late . . ."

"Spread out, find the elevator," Con ordered. The team jumped and ran. Rio Valdosta called out, "Here, sir!"

The team saw the splintered pile of paneling shards, the broken ax . . . the thick daubs of blood from Niklas's fingernails scratching on six inches of titanium-fortified steel.

"They died," he whispered raggedly. "They've been dead for weeks. I know that. But I still hear them . . . at night . . . every night . . ."

Con Slaughter looked at the door, looked around at the horrified faces of his team. "Stay frosty, people," he said in a clipped tone. "We got work to do. Get these two people packed and loaded up. Liberate anything we need. We're moving out."

Vashti Nicanor, whose rich, olive-colored skin was now a sickly jaundiced yellow, pleaded, "When, Captain?"

Con answered, "The man's right. We can't stay here, not even one night. No man should have to." He turned to Niklas and Gildan, who were sagging against each other outside the doorway. "Tonight you'll sleep. Tonight we'll watch, and you can sleep."

Niklas bowed his head and wept.

Chaco Wash, an indifferent stream fed by summer thunderstorms and starved by arid winters, meanders down northwest New Mexico from the San Juan River and peters out completely somewhere close to the Continental Divide. Ten or twelve miles of its wanderings came to be called Chaco Canyon, although it is really only a broad depression, from one-half to three-quarters of a mile wide with its deepest cut between mesas measuring about eight hundred feet. It is a desolate valley. Dull ocher and sienna sandstone rocks are the sole color palette. Pinon trees and tortured mesquites and stubborn desert grasses are the only textures. Haunting remains of long-dead peoples are the only evidence of a desiccated husk of life.

A biting wind numbed Gildan Ives's face as she forced herself to trudge wearily along the narrow trail. She had always heard that the night was darkest just before dawn, and now she could well believe it. No stars dotted the ebony canopy that draped itself over the desert, and she felt like a blind woman groping toward some sort of terrible disaster.

Gildan had only thought that she felt old on her thirty-second birthday. Now she felt aged, weak, infirm. She had never been in any sort of condition to undertake such a journey. Niklas was a little better off; he appeared to have a measure of natural stamina. But Gildan had no reserve, no natural strength of body or will or mind. She was, perversely, a little peeved at Fire Team Eclipse. They were all so tightly conditioned, so confident, so controlled, so resolute.

They even laugh sometimes, she thought irritably. *How can they laugh and make jokes? They must not have been through the awful, horrid things I've been through . . . but it does seem that they would at least have the courtesy to—to give me a little more care and compassion!*

Actually, the team did care for her. They made sure that she didn't harm herself, and they had allowed her to pack her belongings onto one of the heavily laden burros. They had given her and Niklas more water than their own allotments. But no, they had not babied Gildan, which was what she really wanted.

That slayer Ric Darmstedt has tried to be nice once or twice, Gildan reflected bitterly, *but it seems like that snooty Israeli woman just won't leave him alone . . . He'd do better to forget her—she's like a Ultimate Reality Cy-warrior—and concentrate on a real flesh-and-blood lady in distress . . .*

And Niklas, after two nights away from that horrid crypt, had reverted to his usual thoughtless self. He walked with Gildan and sometimes seemed to be trying to help her, but mostly he was moody and uncommunicative.

Gildan sighed deeply, and it came out as a soft moan. Every joint and muscle in her body ached, and the bleakness of the night quenched her spirit. She longed to simply lie down and sleep. "I don't think I can go on much longer, Niklas."

"You don't have any choice." He spoke with absentminded

curtness. Niklas was reflecting that he had managed to withstand this journey because he'd done some hiking and rock-climbing on some of his diversionary retreats.

Like that trip to the nameless Caucasus mountain, where I found the greatest treasure that man has ever known . . . , he thought bitterly. *Or so I thought. I know this whole scourge is my ohm-bug . . . What did you do, Alia?*

What did I *do?*

They had traveled at a torrid pace, always by night, and now they were ascending the last line of jagged sandstone hills just to the west of the Anasazi ruins and the mesas where herds of wild mustangs roamed. Or at least David Mitchell had so assured them. He had also stoutly maintained that if there were horses, there was water. The team seemed to accept this from the young sergeant as if it were a known fact, though Niklas had recovered enough of his natural rebellion to grumble about it. Still, here they were, and they had nowhere else to go. Especially Gildan and him.

Gildan Ives stumbled and would have fallen if Niklas had not grabbed her arm and held her. Ordinarily Niklas had little sympathy for anyone except himself, but unexpectedly he felt a stab of pity for Gildan. Any virtue from the sentiment was marred, however, as he also felt a superior sense of pleasure to know that somewhere hidden under his strata of selfishness a little pity for someone else still survived. "You can make it, Gildan," he said stoutly. "Don't give up."

All the members of the small party were filthy, and their water had run low so that thirst had become a torment. The soldiers had endured this stoically, and as Gildan had so bitterly reflected, even made acidic jokes about it sometimes. But Gildan's tongue felt swollen in her mouth and her lips were cracked. She had drunk the last of her water and was too ashamed to ask for some of Niklas's share, which he probably wouldn't give her anyway. The ground was sandy and the sand poured into her low quarter shoes.

Grabbing onto Niklas's arm, she had to stop, balance herself as best she could on one leg like a wild stork, and shake the rock out.

"I'd give anything for a bath," she mourned. "I've never been so dirty in my life! I didn't know there was so much dirt in the world!"

"A bath!" Niklas laughed harshly. "I think that's the least of our worries. If I had a bath, I'd drink it dry."

"Ma'am? Are you all right?" Vashti Nicanor's polite voice sounded behind them. Tonight she was the "pickup man," which meant walking last, leading the burros. Gildan thought it was an oddly apt name for Colonel Vashti Nicanor.

"I had a rock in my shoe," Gildan answered stiffly.

"Are you all right now?"

"No, I'm not. I'm tired to death and thirsty and filthy and my foot is killing me." Gildan hated herself for sounding so petulant, but something about this calm and competent woman made her want to screech long and loud.

"I am sorry, Miss Ives. But we must move on. I've lost sight of Lieutenant Darmstedt." Ric was walking just ahead of Niklas and Gildan.

"I doubt that very seriously," Gildan snapped, then walked ahead with such a flounce that Vashti reflected dryly that of all Gildan's ills at least her foot must feel better.

Finally Con Slaughter called a halt to confer with David Mitchell. "It's almost daylight, Sergeant Mitchell. We're going to have to make a hole here pretty quick. What do you think?"

The rest of the team gathered around, while Gildan curtly agreed to hold the burros while Vashti conferred with the team. Niklas sank to the ground. Actually, she liked the little burros, as she did all animals. She petted Cookie's soft nose and whispered baby talk to him.

"All I can tell you, sir," David was saying as he closely perused his map by a pencil-fine red flashlight, "is that I've noted that what seems to be the largest herd runs most often in the northeast quadrant of the canyon."

"Okay, switch off the light," Con said cautiously. He turned and considered the relatively low and gentle slope they faced. With quick decision, he said, "No time for a recon and report, so let's double-time it up to the top of this hill. Maybe there'll be a shelter close enough in a northeast line so we can head that way and find water before we have to dig in."

"Sounds good, Captain," Rio Valdosta said. He took a deep breath and eased the straps of his heavy pack for a moment. When Slaughter effortlessly trotted off, he was right at his side. The others hurried to keep up. In the rear, the raw hacking of Gildan Ives's rough breathing sounded as loud as a blaring horn to the fire team.

They had almost reached the top when David Mitchell half whispered, "Captain Slaughter."

"What?"

"Can't you smell that, sir?"

Slaughter sniffed the air carefully. "I don't smell anything except myself, Sergeant. What is it?"

"Smoke, sir. Wood smoke."

Instantly Slaughter ordered, "Everyone down!" He threw himself down flat, and the rest of the team was belly-down in an instant. Vashti, as pickup man and mule driver, was still near the bottom of the slope. Quickly she led the burros back down to the bottom and lined them up in single file across the shallow gorge of the hill's base. It wasn't much cover, but it was the best she could do in a hurry. Then she flattened herself in the sand, too. Niklas was slower than the soldiers, but grunting, he did kneel, then lay down. Gildan knelt but fidgeted, protesting, "I just hate it when we have to do this! It's so *dirty!*"

Just ahead of them, Ric Darmstedt whispered furiously, "Please be quiet, ma'am! A little dirt won't hurt you."

"A *little*," Gildan retorted sarcastically, but she did lie down and cover herself with an extra poncho.

"Okay, Sergeant, you get to play with the big gun again," Slaughter growled, handing over his precious 12-gauge. "We'll crawl to the top. The rest of you break out your nines and wait for my signal." The fire team still had their short-range walkie-talkies, which, luckily, were powered by 1.5 volt batteries. But unluckily, carrying extra batteries was too much weight, so they had to stingily conserve all battery-powered equipment.

"Yes, sir," Rio breathed happily, caressing the deadly-looking gun.

Shaking his head slightly at Rio's love affair with his shotgun, Con said, "Eyes wide, Rio. Shoot if you see anything that needs killing."

Carefully Slaughter moved upward, using his elbows to propel himself along. The desert quiet was so absolute that all sounds seemed to be magnified. He could plainly hear his own breathing and that of Sergeant Valdosta, the tumbling of small pebbles and the soft swish of the sand as they scrambled up. At the pinnacle, a five-foot shelf of rock angled slightly upward. Carefully Con pulled himself up, and at the same time put the binoculars to his eyes.

What he saw, at first, made no sense. He thought the binoculars were faulty, and shook them slightly, but it didn't change the meaningless image.

Then his brain clicked, and he recognized what was framed in the binocular's lenses. It was—*a giant boot*!

"Hello."

Whatever Slaughter was expecting in that tense moment, it was not the calm greeting that he heard. Con almost dropped the binoculars, then snapped his head up at an impossible angle to see the shadow of a man looming over them.

At the same time he heard the dangerous sound of a 12-gauge round being chambered: *CHUK-CHOCK!*

"Hold up, Sergeant," he commanded sharply.

Rio Valdosta could not decide whether to shoot Zoan first—or the jaguar that had come to stand beside him. His finger tightened on the trigger, he was that much on edge. But Slaughter said calmly, "He's unarmed, Rio."

"That tiger isn't," Valdosta said acidly.

"She's Cat. I'm Zoan."

Con Slaughter scrambled to stand up, with Rio crowding so protectively close to him they almost both fell down. He gave his sergeant a step-back signal, and reluctantly Rio gave him about two inches. Con said to Zoan, "I'm Captain Concord Slaughter of the 101st Airborne, Fire Team Eclipse. This is Sergeant Rio Valdosta."

"I'm Zoan. You're soldiers, aren't you?"

"Yes, we're soldiers," Slaughter said, glancing at Rio. Their looks said, *Desert-fried brains . . .*

Zoan was peering around them. "Why don't the rest of your friends come up?"

Con Slaughter swiveled his head around quickly to see if his team had shown itself, but he could see no sign of the team, even the civvies. "How do you know about them?" he demanded sharply.

"Why, I see them—right there. And anyone could hear those four burros down there. What are they chewing on?" Zoan asked with mild interest.

Valdosta also turned and squinted against the darkness. *With NVG's you might be able to see some kinda suspicious-looking lumps, but with the naked eye . . . can't see a thing. If that guy can see the rest of the team, he must have eyes like—like that tiger's, there.*

"Who are you?" Slaughter demanded.

"My name is Zoan. This is Cat. Are you thirsty?"

"Wha—uh—" As happened to many people, Con Slaughter felt as if he were having some sort of synaptic lapse as he conversed with Zoan.

"We can go get some water." Zoan peered up at Slaughter, his eyes wide and dark, and then he nodded with finality. "Let's go get some water for you and them and the burros and then I'll take you to meet my other friends."

An alarm went off in Slaughter's head. "Wait just a minute. How many of you people are there? Who are they?"

"There are thirty-three of us. We're all friends."

Slaughter's eyes narrowed speculatively, while Rio caught his attention and gave his head a slight shake. "I'm not so sure we're all going to be such good friends, Zoan," Con said cautiously. "I need to know who's here, where they are, what they're doing, and I need to know why you're all here."

The sky overhead was beginning to clear now and the first faint gleams from the east lit Zoan's curiously placid face. "We're all friends," he repeated softly, then added, "God sent you here, didn't He?"

Valdosta snorted and Con frowned. "I'm afraid not. We've got other business."

Zoan nodded. "I know. You're tired, and thirsty, and scared. But God did send you here, Mr. Slaughter. All of you."

In the clear air of the desert, the rays of the sun penetrate quickly. Now, almost as if pulled upward by an invisible cable, the burning globe was being lifted over the jagged tops of the saw-toothed mountains far in the distance.

Con Slaughter sighed and said resignedly, "Well, right now we need water and we need cover. If you can give us that, we'd appreciate it."

"You mean you want to hide?"

Rio muttered threateningly, but Con just answered dryly, "Uh, yeah, that's about the size of it. My sergeant, here, just doesn't like to call it that."

Zoan, of course, had no notion of such dry humor. He said earnestly, "I can show you where to hide. The German soldiers won't find you here, though."

Instantly Con Slaughter stiffened and the dark mahogany eyes of Rio Valdosta bored into the strange man in front of them. "How do you know?"

Zoan's voice was the calmest thing on the plateau. "Because this place is the cleft of the rock, where God's hiding His people. You can all rest here and be safe. For a while, anyway."

Slaughter hesitated only a moment, as he studied Zoan's face. The he ordered calmly, "Sergeant, go down and bring the team up."

To Rio's credit, he hesitated only a fraction of a second, in spite of his grave misgivings. But Rio Valdosta had never questioned an order in his life, and he trusted Con Slaughter more than he'd ever thought he would trust an officer. "Yes, sir!" he said snappily, then turned and agilely slid down the slope.

When he reached the group, who were still obediently huddling face-downward in the sand, he said, "Captain Slaughter says we're going up."

"Who's up there? Did you find anything?" Lieutenant Darmstedt asked as everyone struggled to their feet.

"A half-wit and a lion," Rio intoned.

"What?"

"You'll see, sir." Rio turned and hurried back up to be close to Captain Slaughter. He still was holding the 12-gauge at half-mast and watched Zoan and Cat with equal suspicion.

Zoan walked ahead, with Cat padding along beside him. At a safe distance Con and Rio followed. The team was close behind, though Niklas and Gildan and Vashti, with the burros, straggled a little.

Without looking behind, or to the right or left, Zoan led them to a deep crevice between two of the peaks, then took a sharp left into a deep ravine. The floor of it climbed upward at a steady angle, though it zigzagged raggedly back and forth. The ground, however, was hard and easier to negotiate than the sandstone crust of the hills.

David Mitchell sidled up to Con Slaughter to ask, "Who is he, sir?"

"His name is Zoan. That's Cat," Slaughter replied wryly.

David Mitchell stared at Zoan's back and murmured under his breath.

"What's on your mind, Mitchell?" Con asked curiously.

"Did you see his eyes, sir?"

"Yeah. Weird-looking. Pupils dilated. I think he's on some kind of drugs."

"I don't think so, sir," David Mitchell said softly.

"Why not?"

"Well, sir—I think he's the Lizard Man."

"He's the *what?*"

"The Lizard Man, sir. You remember? The Lizard Man, with X-ray vision."

"Mitchell, it's been a long night. What are you talking about?"

"You remember on her trial run, Baby BAD found him. Riding with that wild herd of mustangs, sir. I just remembered it."

The memory of that first recon with the Israelis swept over Slaughter. "Yeah, sure! I'd forgotten about that. What was it Baby BAD found?"

"Minute traces of reptilian DNA. Highly acute vision, both regular and night. Ultrasensitive hearing."

Slaughter pondered what his sergeant had said, then muttered, "He's different all right. I want you to talk to him, Mitchell. He's some kind of dunkhead nut." With a quick sidelong glance, he added, "No offense."

"None taken, sir," David said cheerfully. "Us dunkheads understand one another pretty well."

Just behind Zoan, they heard the welcome sound before they saw it. A slight musical whisper of water, as delicate as wind chimes tripping over flat stones, sounded as they entered the grotto of Zoan's hidden pool. Zoan and Cat watched curiously as the soldiers filed in, then the two civilians, and finally Vashti Nicanor. She'd left the burros tied up in the ravine, but she brought a bucket to take them some water first. Con watched with approval. You had to treat your work animals well. Niklas and Gildan threw themselves down and drank and splashed loudly. The soldiers were more cautious, Con noted with great satisfaction. They looked around, then paired off into their normal two-man buddy teams. One drank while the other watched. Darkon Ben-ammi helped Vashti water the burros, then they came and settled on a big, flat rock overhanging the stream to drink.

When Dr. Kesteven finally stopped drinking and splashing, he looked at Cat, and then at Zoan, curiously. The water drops sparkling brilliantly in his wild beard, he shook his head impatiently, then his eyes flew open. "Zoan! It's you!" he boomed. Standing up, he almost ran to the slight young man, but pulled up short of giving him a bear hug. "It's me, Dr. Kesteven! Don't you recognize me?"

"Yes, sir; I know you. Hello, Dr. Kesteven."

"But—I can't believe we met up! Though I knew you must be out here wandering around somewhere," Niklas said with enthusiasm. He was a little amazed, himself, at how glad he was to see Zoan. "How've you been, Zoan? You've been all right, have you?"

"I've been fine," Zoan answered. He had looked at Dr. Kesteven, and addressed him as politely as he ever did, but he seemed distracted.

Suddenly Niklas was extremely embarrassed. It seemed that he was much more glad to see Zoan than the young man was to see him. Curtly he said, "Good to see you again," then went back to sit by Gildan.

David Mitchell moved over to stand beside Zoan. "Hello. I'm Sergeant David Mitchell."

Zoan's X-ray eyes zeroed in on him as he said, "I'm Zoan," and then turned away.

"Sure glad we happened upon you, Zoan," David said warmly. "Thanks for helping us out."

Zoan didn't answer. David Mitchell sensed that he wasn't being rude—he didn't seem to know how to be, or to be extremely courteous—but that Zoan was merely concentrating hard on something else. Following his glance, David saw that he was looking at Colonel Darkon Ben-ammi and Colonel Vashti Nicanor very closely. Just as David was going to offer to introduce them, Zoan suddenly turned and walked over to the two Israelis.

He stopped and said simply, as he always did, "I'm Zoan."

Amused, they introduced themselves.

At first, Vashti thought maybe the young man was smitten; she affected some men that way, sometimes. But he was so still, so intent, and had such haunting eyes, that finally she grew nervous.

"Haven't you ever seen a woman before?" she asked tersely.

"Yes, ma'am."

"Then what are you staring at?"

"Are you some kind of Indians?"

Ben-ammi chuckled. "You've never seen anyone from the Mideast?"

"I don't know. You're—different."

"And?" Vashti retorted rudely.

"Well, you're pretty, ma'am, but that's not why I'm looking at you. It just seems that you're different."

Vashti seemed taken aback, so Darkon said patiently, "We're from the Middle East. We're New Zionists."

"Zion?" Zoan showed the first traces of emotion they'd seen on his face: He looked eager. "You mean you're Israelites?"

Now Vashti was amused. She and Darkon exchanged quick smiles, and Darkon said in a kindly tone, "Well, I suppose you could call us that. We're from Israel."

"You're Jews?" Zoan asked, stepping closer.

Ben-ammi shifted a little uneasily. "We're, both of us, of the Israeli race, but we don't practice the Jewish religion."

This distinction meant nothing to Zoan. His eyes gleamed like black pearls. "You're real Israelites—God's chosen people. You're so lucky. It must be just the best thing to be God's favorites! And I'm so glad you're here. That means that God will really bless us, and watch over us. For you."

TWENTY-FIVE

B Y THE GRACE OF ALMIGHTY GOD, Jesse Mitchell had only
been sick enough to be bedridden maybe four times in his
entire long life.

"It's hard to understand God's purposes sometimes, Noe," he
said unhappily, picking at the heavy Syn-tex blanket, one from the
case that Xanthe St. Dymion had provided for them. His voice
sounded as if he were speaking from the bottom of a barrel, and his
n's and m's were flat.

"Now settle down, Jess." Noe Mitchell laid her hand on his
forehead, then dipped a cloth in cool water, scented with some
fresh sprigs of peppermint that still grew heartily by the cabin
steps. The scent was as refreshing as the spring's first warm breath.

"Got to go out and tend the fire," he muttered, impatiently
pushing her hand aside.

"I can take care of that," Noe said in a no-nonsense tone that
she very rarely used with her husband. Jesse had started off with a
cold, then it had gone down into bronchitis. Noe was afraid that if
he kept galloping around outside in the wet, cold night air he'd
come down with pneumonia. Jesse, who knew well when to listen
to his wife, lay back down and closed his eyes. She leaned forward
and sponged his forehead again and prayed for a few moments.
Then she saw that he had dropped off into an uneasy sleep.

Moving slowly and trying to ignore the pain in her arthritic
joints, she put on an extra pair of socks and a pair of boots. She

pulled on a heavy black coat that had also been in one of the boxes Xanthe had given them. Again Noe was grateful for Xanthe St. Dymion's gifts. She and Jess owned very few clothes as it was, and had never collected much heavy clothing. Even though the temperatures were lower in the desert, the cold here seemed to creep into your bones as if you'd been shot with a hypodermic full of ice shards. That's the way it seemed to Noe, especially in her hands. The coat came down almost to her ankles, and was a distinct military cut. She pulled on some of the finest real black leather gloves she'd ever seen, and then, with only the slightest hesitation, pulled one of the commissary berets over her gray head. "Don't guess anybody'll give me any trouble," she observed to herself. "I know I must look just like one of those big, mean commissar women." The thought tickled her, even in her worry and pain.

It was a long, cold walk, it seemed, to Sky Rock. Jesse had piled up enough wood to last, she estimated, for two days. As she started the hard work that it takes to build a fire, she wondered, *And what am I going to do after all this wood's gone, Lord? Break out an ax and chop down one of these trees? That's about as likely as me wandering around and dragging up all this wood like Jess does . . .*

But Noemi Mitchell was a practical and solid woman, and had learned to deal with the problem at hand. With a measure of satisfaction she reminded herself, *Sufficient unto the day is the evil thereof . . . and these days are evil enough, yes, Sir, Lord, without me shopping for trouble. I'll build this fire, and I'll tend it, and then tomorrow we'll see about that fire, and then the next night You can just tell me what to do, and that'll be the end of it.*

It took a long time, but she started from the beginning with small twigs and got a blaze going, then began to add bigger chunks. Soon the fire was roaring and she stayed so close that her clothes began to smoke. Finally the blaze reached up over her head. She walked back down to the cabin, a forlorn figure, so tiny that it seemed she was a child dressed in her father's overcoat.

The night passed agonizingly slowly for Noe. She kept watch over Jesse and she kept watch over the fire.

Sometime around midnight something happened to Noe. She was trudging back up to Sky Rock, exhausted and depressed, when suddenly she felt something . . . it was not a physical sensation like a wind or frigid air or wetness or rain, but it was like something surrounding her, pressing upon her, just the same. She stopped walking, but didn't look around. Though it might have been the most difficult thing she'd ever done, for her heart quailed with fear, she bowed her head and closed her eyes. It was there, everywhere, a dark presence, a malevolent sense that someone—or worse, some *thing*—filled with hatred and darkness was hovering over her. It was as if she were a tiny little frantic fish, and it was looming huge over her, with a net, an inescapable net, and she would struggle and cry out but in a minute, in a second, it would see her, the poor little helpless fish . . .

"Oh, Lord," she muttered, her eyes tightly shut. "When the enemy will come in like a flood You've promised to raise up a standard against him. The devil is here, Lord, but You've overcome the devil . . . in Your blessed Son Jesus' name, and by His blood . . ."

She didn't exactly know how long she stood there, crying out to God, her eyes and heart closed to the evil that pressed in on her. But when she started walking again, each step was so difficult, and her entire body was so heavy and pained and cold, that she almost wept. She stoked the fire one last time, for she sensed, rather than saw, that dawn was not far off. By the time she made it back to the cabin, it seemed that the darkness had turned into a soft twinkling gray.

Jesse was worse the next night. Noe was so sore from the previous night's work, and her hands hurt so badly, that sometimes she caught herself jerking and staring down at them to see if they were on fire. She tended the signal fire, though Jesse had gotten so bad that he seemed lost in a fog of fever. He wasn't delirious, but he was dull-minded and slept heavily.

The sense of evil, and the battle, was worse that night, too.

The next dawn, Noe was sitting in the rocking chair by the fire, staring down at the black leather gloves she'd kept on all night. She had a terrible delusion—just for a moment, but it was wrenching just the same—that if she took off the gloves, raw sinews and throbbing, swollen joints and cartilage would be there instead of skin. Shaking her head to clear it of the gory vision, she bowed her head, and finally the tears came. "Lord, that's all the wood, and Jess is worse. Please tell me what to do."

The answer came, though it took a while, and the pain in Noe Mitchell's hands did not lessen.

A wise woman buildeth her house . . .

That was all, and it was enough.

Noe raised her faded, tearstained blue eyes and smiled wearily. *God is good,* she thought gratefully. *Here is my place, and here is my ministry, right here in my house, taking care of my husband. That signal fire, those people, are Jesse and God's business. This is mine.*

And so, for five nights, while Jesse Mitchell wandered in the grip of fever and illness, and Noe Mitchell stayed by his side, the desperate people wandering in the forests far below them saw no beckoning fire in the hills.

———————

They had all been drawn to it, and by it they had been united, by their belief in it and their dependence upon it. The night of the blackout, twelve people had hurried to Tybalt Colfax's church, frightened, confused, looking for their shepherd. Tybalt and Galatia Colfax, in spite of great misgivings, had led them out of the burning city toward the beacon in the hills that all had seen as a sign of hope and deliverance.

Along the way, more stragglers had fallen in with them, so that there were twenty-one of them now, two weeks later. It had been a difficult time for them all, and some of them were wavering, weakened from the great physical demands of living under such primitive conditions, the terrible food, the long marches in the cold. They were like newborn kittens. None of them had any skills in woodcraft, hunting, constructing shelters, building fires. Of all of them, Allegra Saylor had been the one who had just worked and experimented and thought until she figured out how to do things. Surprisingly, her meek and gentle father, Merrill Stanton, was usually the one who decided *what* to do.

"What's Perry's story, Mother?" Allegra Saylor asked, her eyes fixed on a young man wearing a dirty yellow macintosh over a violently green sweater and sagging Ty-jeans. He was slogging along determinedly behind Allegra and Kyle and her mother as they toiled up one of the countless hills.

Genevieve Stanton had to work to gather enough breath before she could answer, stifling an unreasoning surge of envy at Allegra, who was not even breathing hard. Genevieve had been lithe and energetic like that when she was younger. *But then again, I'm not fifty anymore,* she reflected with grim humor. She eased the straps on her backpack for a few moments. Though her burden wasn't very heavy—neither Merrill nor Allegra would allow her to carry much—the straps had been cutting grooves into her shoulders. But Genevieve Stanton had not complained. That just wasn't her way, and she disapproved of people with those kinds of ways. Arching her back to ease the strain, she answered quietly, "He comes to church every time the doors are open. But I've never seen him with anyone else, no parents or friends. He must be a child of one of those 'non-nuclear' families," she pronounced with disgust. "Hmph! Nonexistent is what I call them. Merrill and I always speak to him, but we've never asked him home for dinner or anything . . ." Her voice, suddenly pained, trailed off.

Sturdily Allegra said, "Well, you've adopted him now, Mother. At first I thought he had a crush on me. Then I decided that, really, he was more taken with Kyle; he probably would love to have a little brother. But now I think he's really hoping you and Dad will be his surrogate parents."

Genevieve said quietly, "I think all those things are true. The Lord has said He will set the fatherless into families, and I think He's set Perry into our family. And I thank the Lord for him."

Allegra said nothing, though she thought her mother was a little strange for thanking God for Perry Hammett. Perry was caught in the awkward half-child, half-man stage at seventeen years old. His worn frayed Ty-jeans sagged in all the wrong places on his chubby body. Poor Perry, with the painful blush and desperate shyness and embarrassing clumsiness and teenage acne, had been their constant companion for the last two weeks. *What am I so grumpy about?* Allegra scoffed at herself. *At least he's quiet.* At that moment they heard a deep thump behind them, and dry sticks breaking and pebbles rolling and Perry crashing to the ground, for the second time that day.

Winking at her mother, Allegra hurried back to the boy. "Are you all right, Perry?" she asked, offering him her hand. He kept his head down, but Allegra could see the scarlet tops of his ears.

"I'm fine, thank you," he said faintly. "I'm getting good at it, as a matter of fact."

Allegra was stunned; she hadn't been aware that Perry had a sense of humor. But maybe that was because he was always red-faced and tongue-tied around her. "Okay, glad to see you have it under control," Allegra said, trying hard not to laugh. She returned to her mother and Kyle, who was toddling along gamely, holding on to his grandmother's hand.

"Is Perry okay?" Kyle asked anxiously. He liked Perry very much.

"He's fine. How are you doing, little bear?"

"I'm going to go see Perry," Kyle announced, wrenching his hand loose. Allegra let him go to Perry, watching him indulgently.

He was wearing about five layers of clothing, and he looked like a stuffed sausage. Over it all he wore his favorite, a bright red sweatshirt with a picture of Benny the Blue Bear on it. He loved Benny the Blue Bear's adventures on Cyclops, and had named his teddy bear after him, though the stuffed bear was not blue and only had one eye. He'd been Neville's bear when he was a boy . . . the thought pained Allegra. She missed her husband terribly, and wondered constantly about him. But a hint of a smile touched her lips when she saw Perry offer to hold one of Benny's hands. He and Kyle walked along, holding the small bear between them.

When they finally crested the hill, they found Merrill Stanton waiting for them. He was always in the advance group that went ahead and chose a campsite and gathered firewood. Now, when he saw his wife's pale face, he hurried over to her. He had his father's .45 magnum stuck inside his belt, and as his black-and-red mackinaw swung open he brushed it with his fingertips, as if reassuring himself. It was the only weapon they had for the entire party. He felt ludicrous, carrying the enormous revolver, and worse, he knew he looked ridiculous. Merrill Stanton was the mildest of men, with kind eyes, a gentle manner, and a balding head. But somehow, he felt as if it were a part of his responsibilities, and he wouldn't contemplate offering it to anyone else to carry. Besides that, it had been his father's, and he'd managed to keep it even though the licensing had cost him dearly. He would never have been able to get a license to own a private firearm, except for the fact that he had been a pharmacist in the federalized health care system, and knew enough bureaucrats to shuffle the eternal coil of papers for him.

"Here, let me help you, dear." Stanton lifted the heavy knapsack from Genevieve's shoulders, and she gratefully allowed him to. "Go thaw out by the fire. Hot soup, Kyle! Better hurry!"

"Okay, Grandpa. C'mon, Perry, hot soup," he coaxed.

"Got your mug?" Perry asked him. "Oh, look! Here's a Benny the Blue Bear mug in my backpack! What do you mean, it's yours?

I thought it was mine . . ." Perry took Kyle in hand, while Genevieve and Allegra gratefully stretched and rested for a bit before going to get their ration of soup.

It took nearly an hour for all the stragglers to arrive. One older couple, the Hartleys, in their sixties, were barely able to walk. Quick compassion came to Allegra as the pair simply slumped down under a tree, unable to go another step. *They're too old for this sort of thing,* Allegra thought, and a sense of raw rage came to her, aimless, helpless fury at whoever or whatever had created this misery.

And what in the world are they doing out here, anyway? she thought rebelliously. *My parents, luckily, are young enough and strong enough for this . . . but the Hartleys are so frail . . . and what about that poor Wheatley woman and the little girl? What in the world happened to them? They're both almost catatonic!*

Allegra had wildly mixed feelings about this quest. Although she was a Christian, and on the night of the blackout, she had devoutly believed that the gleaming fire in the hills was a signal straight from God, well, things had changed since then. A moral and upright woman, strong in her beliefs in right and wrong and good and evil, she still was doubtful about Christianity being a deeply spiritual minute-to-minute force in a person's life. To Allegra Saylor, it was much more like a creed, an oath taken, a promise made to God to live a moral life, raise your children in church, and follow the Ten Commandments. Allegra had always been faintly amused at her parents' stout devotion—at least until now. Now this blind faith in something as unknowable as what was probably a squatter's hunting fire in the hills was far from amusing. It was frightening.

But Allegra Stanton Saylor, who had her mother's solid determination and her father's compassion, still kept going, following that light. She really didn't know if it was something deep inside her spirit pressing her on, or if it really was just devotion and loyalty to her parents. It didn't matter. It was her decision, and once made, Allegra followed through and toughed it out, always. She never gave up.

Now, as she sipped at her mug of hot soup that her father had already prepared for them, she sighed deeply. *I just can't stand it anymore . . . we've got to figure out some better way of helping the weaker ones. Poor Dad, he's already forged ahead, hiking farther and faster than he really should, and scouted for this place, and gathered firewood for three fires for the night and then built the fires . . . but the Hartleys are simply too exhausted to even cook for themselves. And they can't have much food in that pitiful little suitcase Mr. Hartley's lugging . . . And poor Olivia Wheatley, does she even know how to cook? So far all I've seen her do is huddle by the fire and eat pieces of that dried Proto-Syn fruit. And she practically has to spoon-feed that little girl, when she can gather her scattered wits enough to remember to eat herself . . .*

"Mom . . ." Allegra nodded toward the fire across from them, built in the shelter of two soaring pines. Mr. and Mrs. Hartley were clinging to each other, Mrs. Hartley's head on his shoulder, her eyes closed with exhaustion. On the other side, Olivia Wheatley was sipping from a cup of coffee that her father had given her. She took a sip, her eyes wide and unseeing, and then offered it to her seven-year-old little girl, Dana. Dana automatically took a sip, then offered it back to her mother. The two did this over and over again, without speaking or looking at each other. Their listlessness was pathetic, and somehow frightening to watch.

"I know," Genevieve sighed. "I've been thinking about them, of course. We'll just have to help them, Allegra. I can't bear it another minute."

She nodded numbly. It wasn't just a question of having a charitable heart. Out here, in the wilderness, taking responsibility for other human beings was becoming a life-and-death decision. For one thing, food was critically short. Allegra had, as her father had told her to, "packed smart" when she was loading up foodstuffs from their pantry. She'd brought rice, bouillon cubes, dried meats and vegetables, crackers, dried beans, all things that were relatively light to carry. Her mother had thought to bring the lightest and most efficient utensils. Her father, naturally, had packed badly needed medicines and medical supplies. Altogether, their family was fairly well-equipped for such an arduous journey.

But they were not well-equipped to care for more than four people for very long.

Merrill, who was still moving around the laggers—who had in some nebulous way become "his group"—hauled a fallen pine branch to the Hartleys' fire and began breaking it up and tossing the smaller branches on to stoke it. It blazed up, crackling and spitting ominously, and he said something to the four of them. None of them replied, though Mr. Hartley gave him a grateful glance.

Merrill came back to his family, his face troubled. "I can't stand it anymore," he declared. His kind face was lined with worry.

Allegra gave him a desert-dry smile. "I was just thinking that, and Mom just said it. Great minds think alike, huh." Standing up, she dusted off her posterior in a businesslike manner. "Okay, we've got soup. Do they have any cups or bowls, do you think?"

Merrill gravely told her, "You know, Allegra, I haven't been certain about taking them on. You and Kyle and your mother must be my first concern. And I'm just not sure that we have food enough for them."

Perry Hammett, who was sitting by Kyle and telling him a Benny the Blue Bear story, looked up. "Mr. Stanton, I've got lots of food. More than enough for one person. If we all threw in together, maybe?"

Merrill smiled warmly at him. He knew that Perry, in spite of his ample size, wasn't really very strong, and also he was really still a child. He'd packed like a child. He had chocolate and candy and cookies and potato chips and sweet powders for drinks, and even sugar lumps. The solid food that he'd had was what Merrill cooked for them and they shared with him.

But he shared with them, too, eagerly, and Merrill thought that maybe it was harder for this chubby boy with the sweet tooth to give Kyle his cookies than it was for them to give him their soup.

"You know, Perry," he said with an air of thoughtfulness, "I think that's a really good idea. And the Lord will bless you for it."

Perry blushed and ducked his head, and his words were almost inaudible. "I know that, Mr. Stanton. He's already blessed me with—with you and Mrs. Stanton and Miss Allegra and Kyle. I'm—I want to help."

Allegra said sternly, "Dad, I can take care of the Hartleys and Olivia and Dana right now. Why don't you just sit down for a minute, and rest? And talk to Mom, please. She misses you. We all do."

Efficiently, Allegra marched over to their fire and said in a no-nonsense tone, "Mr. Hartley, we've got soup and crackers, but we don't have many dishes. Do you and your wife happen to have bowls, or—of course, those coffee mugs will do. Give them to me. What about you, Olivia? Olivia . . . yes, Olivia, I'm talking to you . . ."

Looking after her, Merrill, who had sunk gratefully down by his wife's side, shook his head, smiling a little. "She looks as frail and wispy as a light summer breeze. But she's more like a stout headwind, when she gets going." He pinched his wife's arm lightly. "Like you."

Genevieve retorted smartly, "And you look like an accountant, but you act like Marcus Iago in *Southern Terrors.*"

"Too bad it's not the other way around."

"Not for these people," Genevieve said, suddenly somber. "I think it's a shame that we've splintered up like this. The group that Pastor Colfax is baby-sitting doesn't seem to need much of anything, while somehow you've gotten stuck with shepherding all the poor, lost little lambs." Though the group traveled together, along the same paths and stopping and starting at the same times, they had loosely split into two groups. Tybalt Colfax led a group of eight people, while the weaker ones had tended to become Merrill's "group." Ty Colfax was the leader, effectively. But because finding good campsites for twenty-one people was so difficult, Merrill had eventually started scouting for the group after lunch, moving ahead, finding a site, gathering firewood. Ty, his wife Galatia, and their "group" always seemed to move faster than the others, reaching the campsite first, choosing the best places, starting their cooking and setting up their shelters before the rest had even arrived. The six people who traveled with them were a couple in their thirties with two children, and another athletic young couple in their twenties.

Merrill's "group" had become the weakest, like the Hartleys; the misfits, like Perry; and the lost, like the Wheatleys. Two other couples, all of them in their early forties, sort of scrambled along between; they stayed with Ty Colfax and his group as long and as much as they could, but often they couldn't keep up and ended up rather shame-facedly camping with Merrill's group and depending on his fires.

Now Merrill, gazing sadly around at the fourteen people huddled around his three fires, said in a low voice to his wife, "I just don't understand it, Genevieve. I'm not cut out for this. I'm not the kind of man to lead these people. It doesn't make sense."

She looked up at him and smiled a little. "But it does to the Lord, Merrill. It must. He's set you in this place, with these people, and though you don't seem to know it, you've done miracles, every day. So I guess you are *exactly* the kind of man to lead these people."

He was a little taken aback—and also exhausted. "Let's go ahead and get the blankets out and settle down right over there, by that stand of big rocks. I've figured that's going to give us a good view of the fire." Every night, Merrill chose a place that would allow them to drink good, sweet coffee, eat some of Perry's choco-late, and gaze at the signal fire. It was a good time for them. It gave them hope, and peace.

But that night there was no fire.

For the next four days the group wandered, lost and hopeless, in the old and hostile hills.

"I tried to talk to your father before he went ahead," Ty Colfax said in a tone that begged Genevieve and Allegra to see reason. "But he simply wouldn't listen. I must say, Mrs. Stanton, that I believe Merrill may be suffering from some form of exhaustion. He doesn't know where we are, and he certainly doesn't know which direction that signal fire is. Or was. If it was ever there at all."

Genevieve sighed wearily, while Allegra's blue eyes sparked dangerously. She didn't think much of Tybalt Colfax, but especially she didn't like his wife, Galatia. Though Ty Colfax had never said much to Allegra, Galatia was extremely cool to her. Allegra didn't know what she'd done to offend the woman, and she didn't care. She'd never said anything, for Ty was her parents' pastor, and they seemed to respect him. But Merrill and Genevieve were saddened when Allegra refused to go to church with them. Now, however, she couldn't escape them, as they'd dropped back to present their pleadings to Genevieve and her, for some reason.

"I don't understand exactly what you want from me, Pastor," Genevieve finally said stiffly.

"Well, Galatia and I think that it would be much better to turn back, and return to Hot Springs," Ty explained. "We were hoping you would persuade Mr. Stanton to turn around."

"What difference would it make?" Allegra said acidly. "You obviously don't have a clue where we are, and you think my father's lost. So why do you think he can lead you back to Hot Springs?"

"Allegra," Genevieve said quietly. Allegra's delicate features looked mutinous, but she kept silent as Genevieve went on calmly, "Pastor Colfax, I'm afraid I can't help you. My husband makes his own decisions, and so far they have been very good ones. I support him. Right now, he's finding us a campsite. My plans are to follow him, and then camp when and where he tells us to. If you wish him to do something different, then you really must speak with him about it."

Tybalt and Galatia, who was looking pretty rough without all her cosmetics and creams and collagen plasters, exchanged glances. Tybalt looked uncertain, while Galatia looked positively furious. Quickly Ty said, fumbling a bit, "I—understand, Mrs. Stanton, if—you'll just excuse us—come along, Galatia, we're falling behind . . ."

He led her ahead, but her hissing whisper could be heard clearly by Genevieve and Allegra, "Ty, you're the leader of this group! This is ridiculous! You don't need to ask anyone's permission, much less grovel to that—that little nobody and his wife . . ."

He said something in a low voice that they couldn't hear, and then they were out of earshot.

With a warning glance at her daughter's savage face, Genevieve said, "Allegra, such behavior is beneath your notice. You're better than that."

"Oh no it's not, and oh no I'm not," Allegra muttered.

Ignoring her dire mutterings, Genevieve went on calmly, "Galatia appears to be one of those people who doesn't do well under stress."

"Stress! Mother, you call this—this—disaster just a *stress*?"

"Calm down, Allegra. You're shrieking." Genevieve searched Allegra's face, which was working as she tried to get her emotions under control. "You're all right, aren't you, Allegra?" her mother asked, now with anxiety. "I mean, of course this is a terrible hardship. But—you don't agree with the Colfaxes, do you?"

When Allegra tried to answer, but couldn't, Genevieve's placid features suddenly filled with understanding. Shouldering her pack more securely, she nodded. "I understand. I'm sure most everyone here really feels the same way, Allegra. It's confusing, and it's frightening, especially since the signal fire has disappeared. But your father and I have prayed without ceasing in the last two days, and both of us know in our spirits that God has prepared a place for us. We've determined to go on until we find it, knowing that He will somehow guide our path."

Even though she felt ashamed, she murmured, "Even without food?"

Confidently Genevieve said, "The Lord will provide. He has promised that His children will never have to beg for bread, and I believe in that promise."

They rested after lunch. Their rests were getting longer, their meals scantier, their marches shorter. It was cold, though nowhere near freezing, because a damp mist, so light it was invisible, fell all during the dull, smoke-colored day. The hills were wreathed in a sullen smoke about their summits, and leaden curls of mist rose from the ground.

"But just up about a mile, Pastor, is a fine campsite very close to a fast-moving stream," Merrill said. It was almost three o'clock, and with the low clouds and mists, evening would be coming soon—too soon. "We need to get everyone moving now. We can't possibly let the older people and the children go stumbling around in the dark. Someone's bound to get hurt."

"Merrill, I'm afraid you just don't understand," Colfax said, shaking his head sorrowfully. "My people don't want to go on. They want to go back. And I'm afraid most of your people feel the same way."

Merrill Stanton's rounded shoulders sagged even more heavily. "But, Pastor, surely you can't think of camping here. This just won't do. It's not close to water. The trees are sparser and stunted here, on the west side of the mountain, it'll be hard—if not impossible—to get enough wood for everyone."

Tybalt Colfax, who had chosen this site for a cold lunch and a rest, bristled slightly. "But this rock shelf provides some excellent protection, Merrill, and it looks as if it's going to drizzle all night. There's even a small cave. We could—fit a couple, perhaps, and all four of the children in there."

Merrill Stanton's kind, rather weak blue eyes widened with alarm. "A cave? Have you lost—I mean, Pastor Colfax, surely you don't propose to go into a cave! With all the wild animals in these hills? You can't do that!"

Colfax pulled himself up to his full height, which was considerable, and spoke with ringing authority. "I beg your pardon, Mr. Stanton, but I think you should show a little more respect. I'm not a fool, you know. I looked in the cave, and there's nothing there, nothing at all. Now, if you don't wish Kyle to have warmth and shelter for the night, then so be it. That will allow some others who might appreciate my efforts a little more room. If you'll excuse me—"

His face drawn into a mask of disbelief, Merrill sat back down with Allegra and Genevieve. Behind them, Kyle and Perry sat. Perry was showing Kyle some of the old, dark Renaissance pictures in his enormous Bible. But his full-moon face was troubled as he listened to Colfax and Merrill, and he watched Genevieve and Allegra with sympathy.

"I just can't believe it," Merrill murmured, taking his wife's hand as if to draw strength from it. "I can't believe anyone could be that foolish."

Olivia Wheatley suddenly appeared in front of them. She looked ghastly, with a pinched face and wild eyes and pale hair sticking out in wet strings under a Ty-wool cap. "Did he say there's a cave? C'mon, Dana, let's go see . . ." It was the most animation she'd shown in the entire two and a half weeks.

Merrill started to get up, calling, "No, Mrs. Wheatley—" but Genevieve's hand clutching his arm froze him.

"You can't stop them, or anyone, Merrill," she said quietly. "They do have the right to make their own decisions."

He sat back down, then buried his face in his hands.

They had stopped on a small west-facing shelf of one of the highest mountains they could see. Pines were the only trees hardy enough to grow here, and they were as twisted and distorted as if a bonsai master had been tending them. Above them, the mountain's heights loomed to about five thousand feet. There were some stands of tall firs and pines and a few cedars farther up, but the ascent was steep, and hauling any deadwood back down would be treacherous. And, of course, as Merrill had said, there was no water here.

They were debating whether to go on to the campsite that Merrill had seen. About a mile ahead, the shelf widened out to a level plateau, and the mountainside was not nearly so precipitous above them. A small stream trickled out of some rocks and flowed merrily by a glade that was three feet deep in still-fragrant brown pine needles. But Allegra said unhappily, "It's too late, Dad, for the Hartleys, at least. Look at them. It'd take them hours to stagger a mile."

"But—" Merrill never completed the sentence, for out of the great thick of boulders they were facing, a man stepped out.

A man they had never seen before.

He was of medium height, and as thickly built as a wrestler. He was dressed in a dull green poncho and had a shapeless hat jammed on his head. Cradled carefully in one arm was a deadly-looking rifle with a big bore and a long barrel.

Allegra—and everyone else—froze, rather comically, in mid-gesture and mid-word.

With exaggerated slow and large movements, the man held up his rifle, barrel pointed upward, and then lowered it to the ground and leaned it against the rocks. His hands still up in the air, he said in a deep, resonant voice, "Hello, the camp. Nobody has to be scared, all right? I'm harmless."

Coming to his senses, Merrill scrambled to his feet, shoving back his mackinaw to expose the butt of the .45. But he felt like a pure fool, and looked worse, of that he was certain, so he didn't touch it. "Kind of foolish, isn't it? Sneaking up on a man's camp like that?"

The man's face was shadowed by the slouchy hat, but they could clearly hear the exasperation in his voice. "Mister, I made enough noise to disturb a deaf man's sleep. I thought about just hidin' and yellin'. How do you think that would've gone over?"

Merrill Stanton seemed half angry, but then he was overcome by amusement. "I probably would've shot at you, but then again you probably wouldn't have been in much danger. I'm Merrill Stanton."

"Riley Case." As if aware he presented a rather mysterious and dangerous sight, he slowly removed his cap, then nodded at the ladies. His hair and eyes were as dark as a starless night, and his face was pugnacious, with a strong, full jaw outlined with a heavy beard-shadow and a high forehead. "I'd like to talk to you people," he said in his slow way, "but I think, Mr. Stanton, that you and me better go get those imbeciles out of that cave first."

Stanton's mouth worked. "Is it—bears?"

"No, sir," Riley said, and his dark eyes dusted over Allegra once, quickly, as if they shared a secret joke. "Worse, in my opinion. Skunks."

"Oh, Lord, let's hurry," Stanton said, striding off toward the maze of rocks, his coat flapping.

"Ladies," Riley Case said. Making a small, mocking bow, he replaced his floppy hat, picked up his big rifle, and followed Merrill Stanton.

It didn't take long to roust the people out of the cave, for it hadn't turned out to be such a great shelter, after all. At least they hadn't wakened the skunks yet, though Merrill could smell their musk—which was simply part of their normal scent—so strongly that he wondered that any of them could bear it. Later he found out that, of course, they had smelled it; it was just that Galatia Colfax had told them it was probably some kind of fungus growing in the cave, like mold. None of them had ever smelled a skunk, and neither had Merrill Stanton, but he finally and secretly admitted to himself that Riley Case had called it right. It took an imbecile not to recognize that odor for what it was: a sign of danger.

Aside from that, they'd tried to build a fire—far back from the cave entrance. The cave, of course, had immediately filled with smoke. Also, there were mice and spiders and other things that crawled. The only reason the people stayed there was that Ty and Galatia had insisted that it was still better than being outside in the dampness. But even they seemed relieved to leave the place.

Though it grew dark quickly, and the path they were on was extremely treacherous, Riley Case had brought four torches he'd made from hollow copper pipes he'd had, with a gummy mixture of pine resin and needles and small sticks wrapped around the end. They burned surprisingly long, though they smoked and stank. But none of them had batteries left in the few flashlights they'd brought. That was one reason they didn't try to travel at night.

Finally they reached Merrill's campsite, which was, indeed, perfect. Quickly, Merrill, Ty, and Riley made fires, the women started cooking, and everyone started nesting, as humans invariably do when in strange and bewildering places. They searched around, looking for just the right place to pitch a tent or set up a bedroll, and arranged their personal belongings, no matter how scarce, just so.

Merrill—for once not letting anyone else overrun him—staked out the sheltered glade by the stream for his family, and though he helped the others in his group get settled and helped build their fires, he stayed close to Genevieve and Allegra and Kyle and, of course, Perry, who was just one of them now. Riley Case looked around, seeing that everyone was settling in, and said to Merrill, "I killed a deer today—"

Kyle, who was standing by his grandfather and staring up at the mysterious stranger with wide-eyed fascination, breathed, "You *did?*"

Case looked down at him and answered gravely, "I sure did. A big ten-point buck. Man can't eat a deer that big all by himself. You hungry, boy?"

"Boy, am I!" Kyle said enthusiastically. "But what you gonna do wif that deer you killed?"

Kyle, of course, couldn't be expected to comprehend. Killing wild animals had been outlawed since long before he was born; in fact, back in the MAB-dominated world, the penalty for killing a deer was as stiff as a manslaughter sentence. It never occurred to Kyle—or indeed to most people—that these animals had once been killed for meat, because people were hungry. Such things had never been a part of even their darkest dreams.

Case's dark eyes flashed with amusement. "Well, I think I'll let your mom explain all about that. Now I'm going to leave for a while—"

"Can I come? And Perry?" Kyle asked eagerly.

"Not this time," Case answered. "But I'll be back soon, and then we'll have something really good to eat."

True to his word, Case returned quickly with big slabs of raw meat. Allegra, who had very confused feelings about killing wild animals, suddenly found that her confusion was greatly cleared when she ate the delicious steaks fried over an open fire. They didn't even eat any vegetables. Case also produced a sort of heavy, doughy bread, and they greedily sopped up the juices from the cooking pan with it.

"I got a Dutch oven, with a lid," Case said to Genevieve. "She's a real backbreaker to carry, but it's worth it. You can cook anything in it, even bread."

Allegra stared at him, then wiped her mouth with her hand. It was slightly greasy, but she didn't care. Licking her lips with enjoyment, she finally asked, "Who *are* you? Some kind of guardian angel?"

He shook his head vehemently. "No, ma'am, I'm sure not."

Merrill said slowly, "How long have you been out here, in these hills?"

Riley Case took a sip of coffee from his tin cup, then threw the grounds into the fire. It hissed as if in anger. "I left Hot Springs the night of the blackout."

"So—you've been following us?" Merrill asked evenly.

It might have been called a smile on another, less grim man, but on Riley Case it was more like a twisting of his mouth. "Mr. Stanton, when you march you straggle out anywhere from a mile to three. You sound like a herd of buffaloes tramping around. You leave a trail half a mile wide. It's not that I've been following you. It's that I can't get away from you."

"You could," Stanton remarked casually, "if you weren't following the same path as we are."

Case nodded curtly. "The signal fire. That's where I'm going. Where you people are going is your own crisis, and I don't believe in poking my nose in other folks' business."

"Then why did you help us today?" Allegra challenged him.

"Because, Mrs. Saylor, you people are going downhill fast. I'm no one's keeper, but I don't want these hills littered with bodies, either. So, if you decide to go on, then I don't see why we can't travel together, and maybe I can help out some. At least keep some of you from dropping dead on the road from starvation. Or getting killed by some bear or mountain lion."

Genevieve reached over, took Case's empty cup, and refilled it from the enormous old blue tin coffeepot that she used to use for a flower vase. "Mr. Case, may I ask you something?" she politely inquired.

As Case was a rough-edged man, with little use for niceties, he considered the question before answering with brutal honesty. "You can ask, ma'am."

A ghost of a smile lit Genevieve's smooth, sweet features. "If you left Hot Springs on the same night we did, and if you are going to the signal fire—may I ask what's taken you so long? Surely a man such as you would have reached that mountain long ago, if you'd simply gone straight to it."

As will happen in men unaccustomed to even polite deception, his eyes gave him away. They slid to Allegra—for the briefest of moments—and then he looked down and deliberately took a long sip of coffee. "Mrs. Stanton, I don't believe I'm going to answer that question. Let's just say that I'm enjoying the journey, so I'm not in any big hurry."

Merrill Stanton, like most men, hadn't noted the significance of the exchange, or Riley Case's unspoken meaning. Both Allegra and her mother had, though they gave no sign. Merrill said quietly, "Do you still know where the path lies, Mr. Case? Since the fire's gone out?"

He answered quickly, "I do. And so do you, Mr. Stanton. You're leading these people in the right direction."

"Am I?" Merrill sighed.

Case's impenetrable gaze raked over him. "Let's get something straight, Mr. Stanton. I'm no dunkhead. I'm no mystical Moses leading people around in the wilderness. Looks to me like that's your department. If you people are going on, I'll help. If not, I'll see you in the next life."

Merrill Stanton nodded, then straightened his shoulders and set his face. "We're going on, Mr. Case. By the grace of God, we're going on."

EPILOGUE

COMING AWAKE WAS FOR ZOAN very simple. In the depths of his mind, which no man, only God, would ever plumb, would come a knowledge, a silent signal, and he would pass through a doorway from the place of shadows and whispers and wanderings to the place of light and sounds and visions.

He lay quietly under the rough blanket, immediately aware that though it was still night, the dawn was near. With his curious synchronization, all of Zoan's senses were resurrected at one time. The alkali odor of dust and ancient stones was mingled with the aromatic and pungent smell of pinon trees. Miles away, a coyote called, a lonely and poignant song. A whispering sound as of old dead voices came to him, but it was only the wind caressing the worn stones of the houses. Darkness was heavy in the small room. Most men, with their puny earthbound vision, could have seen nothing. But Zoan could see everything, every one of his few precious possessions, every wrinkle in his blanket, the clever mortaring between each stone.

He could even see the painting, though it was done in dull earth tones of ocher and brick and sand and had faded in the centuries. But because it pleased him, he kept his gaze on it for some time. The scene was of a stick-man lifting a spear to throw at a stick-deer, no more than this. But for long stretches of time Zoan had sat, thinking about the artist, even seeing him, a short man with a flat face and sparkling, lively eyes and stubby, agile fingers. Though Zoan didn't understand exactly what he saw, or how he saw it, he did comprehend that the man was now no more than bones in a shallow grave. The few lines captured the vivid action of the hunt in a mysterious fashion, and Zoan knew that the artist had been greatly gifted. He never would have said so to anyone. Zoan never, unbidden, offered his opinions about anything. It never occurred to him that anyone would ever be interested.

With quick movements, Zoan threw back his blanket and stood. Moving to the door, he stepped outside and lifted his eyes. He watched as a small sailing cloud raced across the sky, and then it hit the moon. The cloud seem to nibble at the moon, for piece by piece the silver disk was lost, and only the light of the stars reached the earth.

Chaco Canyon brooded around him, majestic, mysterious, timeless. Aeons of living had worn the stones, smoothing them with wind and the action of fine sand. Zoan's eyes were filled with the vision, his ears full of the music; he even sucked in its breath, loving this land and aware that others before him had stood and loved even as he did.

An impulse came, touching his mind even as the most fragile strand of a spider's web will brush against the face. He had learned to obey these silent commands. With quick, efficient movements he pulled on his boots and wrapped his treasured Navaho blanket—a gift from Cody—around his boyish shoulders. Hurrying out into the path, Cat appeared mystically at his side and walked with him. Her sleek body moved as if propelled by steel springs, her satiny, silvery fur gleaming in the moonlight.

Overhead, Bird was circling, waiting for dawn. Glancing upward, Zoan was pleased, as always, by the smooth patterns that the creature made. Now the huge raptor doubled up into a stream-lined missile and dropped from the sky. Zoan could not see the impact, nor did he especially trouble himself to envision it. But he knew that death had fallen out of heaven on some living thing. He accepted this facet of existence as he accepted the sunshine and the rain and the slow turning of the earth itself.

Zoan stopped before one of the huts that stood alone, high on one of the smallest mesas in the canyon, in splendid solitude. He did not enter but called out softly, "Cody . . ."

Bent Knife came awake instantly. His awakening was somewhat similar to that of Zoan's for he never had the moment-by-moment processes of awakening that other men seemed obliged to pass through. At the first sound of the soft call, his eyes flew open and his body stiffened. Automatically his hand reached for a weapon, closing around the shaft of the razor-sharp knife that he always kept on the table beside him.

Coming off the bed smoothly, he did not pass at once through the door. Deep, almost buried and forgotten instincts, slowly coming alive in him, made him cautious, and he stood to one side waiting. The voice came again and Cody recognized Zoan's voice. This astonished him; he could not recall the strange young man ever initiating a conversation.

Stepping outside, he greeted Zoan, then, as was his curious custom, said, "Hello, Cat," in a tone of respect. The form of the jaguar, shadowy and silvery and fearsome in the moonlight, as always, imprinted Cody with the cold touch of a primeval fear. The animal was under control, it seemed, but he recalled without volition the lines of a poem that he had read long ago:

Tyger! Tyger! burning bright
In the forests of the night,
What immortal hand or eye
Could frame thy fearful symmetry?

The simple, deadly elegance of the lines—and the jaguar—bemused him. Cody Bent Knife was sensitive to such moments of revelations of beauty, and he allowed himself to enjoy it for a brief time. He knew that Zoan would wait.

Finally, his eyes still on Cat, who was watching him as if she could discern his fear and reverence, asked, "What is it, Zoan?"

Zoan did not speak, which was not unusual. Language for him was a different thing from what it was for other people. He had long known that. What they could put into words and phrases and sentences came to him almost like visions, with intricate words like deep colors, and lovely phrases like the canyon at sunset and leaping sentences like Cat as she ran . . . he could see the words, drink them in, even love them, but could never quite use them right. People laughed at him so often when he tried. It didn't really hurt his feelings—the concept was foreign to Zoan—but it frustrated him. He simply stood there, mute, frowning a little.

Cody sighed and slipped the knife into his belt. "Well, Zoan, you've got your little band of lost souls here now and I've got my followers." He bit his lip for a moment, considering Zoan, whom he loved but had no idea how to tell him this or anything else. He began again, awkwardly, with a topic that was close to Zoan's heart, he knew, and hoped maybe this was what he really wanted to talk about, and so sadly, could not. "This is a perfect hiding place. I'm even starting to wonder myself if your God hasn't had something to do with it."

The silence ran on for some time and finally Zoan spoke haltingly and with some difficulty. "That's why I woke you up, Cody." This seemed to exhaust his stock of words for a moment but then he managed to add, "That's why I needed to talk to you."

Cody smiled, thinking that Zoan could not see . . . but of course, he could. "I understand. Go ahead."

After an inner struggle that was apparent from the way his features twisted, Zoan whispered, "We're not hidden."

Cody was startled, wary. "We're not hidden? What do you mean?"

"He doesn't know yet—exactly—where we are."

"Who is *he*, Zoan?"

Again Zoan did not seem to hear. "He'll try—to—he's trying to find us. He'll come looking for us."

Cody Bent Knife was a man of great physical courage, even though he was young. Long ago Cody had envisioned, and come to grips with, his own death, and once a man conquers that fear, all others seem to pale beside it. But this conversation, Zoan's words, Zoan himself, was strange and unsettling and even beyond the ken of contemplating death.

Cody Bent Knife, though he shunned it, was afraid. But his courage, like his will, rose to combat, as it had done his whole life. He spoke with surety, showing nothing of his deep foreboding. "Zoan, try to explain. Try to tell me who is searching for us, who is coming to look for us."

Zoan's voice dropped to a hoarse whisper of such an unearthly timbre that Cat half growled deep in her throat in an uncanny response. She moved forward, lifting her enormous head, seemingly to search Zoan's face and to listen.

"The wolf . . . the wolf of the evenings." Zoan swallowed and touched his lips as if he were shocked at what they had uttered. "He can see in the dark, you know . . . like me."

Cody Bent Knife could not move; he felt as if bands, tighter and tighter, bound not only his legs and arms but also his mouth.

Zoan went on in the cadences of a poet and a prophet: *"Their horses also are swifter than the leopards, and are more fierce than the evening wolves: and their horsemen shall spread themselves, and their horsemen shall come from far; they shall fly as the eagle that hasteth to eat."*

Zoan fell silent. He looked up.

Zoan's eyes caught the reflection of the moon so that they themselves seemed to be pure silver for a moment. Cody flinched, physically, visibly, as suddenly he was loosed, but he felt so weak he thought he might fall. The dread that was trying to overcome him was like a terrible specter, floating, touching and tapping with dead fingers at the window on a dark night when the wind is howling . . .

"The horsemen are loosed, Cody," Zoan whispered, and now he sounded merely tired, and sad. "The horsemen are loosed."

Cody blinked, still unsure if this was some uneasy dream. "What—what can we do?"

Suddenly Zoan moved forward. Oddly—he had never initiated a touch of another human being, as far as Cody knew—Zoan grabbed his hand, then placed it on his own chest. He then placed his hand over Cody's heart. For a moment, Cody imagined that their blood became intermixed, interwoven, and flowed from their hands to their hearts in a symbiotic, never-ending circle.

Then Zoan whispered, "We are the last of our people, Cody. You and I are the last. And we must overcome!"

For two nights the heavens had displayed a celestial fireworks that dazzled, and delighted, the eyes. The moon itself seemed to be twice its normal diameter—whether from some trick of the atmosphere or whether the size lay in the eyes of the beholders was not entirely certain to Noemi Mitchell as she stood quietly beside her husband. The two of them had come out to Sky Rock. Together they stood, silent, looking up at the myriad of pinpoints of light flung by a mighty hand with awesome power to spangle the sable curtain of the skies. Stars were falling, dying. Six shot across the horizon as they watched, leaving dusky streaks of light as their trail.

The wind made a keening sound; it was fitful on this full moon's night. A hunter's moon, Jesse had always called it, when the moon was larger than it was supposed to be, thrice a year, a special gift to the hungry ones so they could find and kill their food more easily. It was an oddly predatory fairy tale. But Noe reflected, bathed in its eerie light, that the story made sense for this, the earth that was the Lord's, and all the beasts therein. It wouldn't fit in Eden, but here, now, in this time, it was the way He had ordered it.

"It's giving the wolves a good hunt tonight," Noemi said quietly.

"The wolves and the foxes and all of the fiercest beasts, the Lord has provided for them, too," Jesse replied. "But some of these wolves, now . . ."

With clear reluctance he dropped his eyes from the heavens to the troubled earth below. "They'll be here tomorrow, maybe the next day," he said in a low voice. "If they can stand fast, and make it through."

"We'll pray them through, Jess," Noemi said confidently. "God is on His throne, and His paths for us are set. All those poor wanderers have to do is stay on His path. They'll make it through devil-wolves or no."

"I know you are right, Noe, 'course I do, but sometimes it's hard to live with miracles," Jesse said dryly. "Kinda hard to get used to, isn't it? We're just dust, just little bits of dust, and it'd kill us dead if we saw more than the tiniest glimpse of God's back as He passes. It's almost beyond our ken that we're here safe, and those poor people are coming on through the darkness, even though we haven't been able to light the signal for them." Jesse was still too weak to gather firewood, but God had shown him that the refugees—some of them anyway—were coming on. Jess knew, too, that one of them had died, though he hadn't mentioned this to Noemi. Sometimes God told him things he had to keep to himself.

Another star flamed, burned brightly in its death throes, and then was lost forever. Noe asked calmly, "Jesse, do you think this is the end of the world?"

No immediate answer was forthcoming. The old man stood there and Noemi knew that he was listening more to the whisperings deep inside his spirit than to the moanings of the wind that lay heavy on Blue Mountain.

After what seemed a long time, Jess spoke. His words did not seem to have anything to do with the question. Nevertheless Noe listened closely.

"I remember my grandpa telling me about World War II. People now—kind of arrogantly, I've always thought—call it the Last Great War. He was at Normandy, you know. The big D-Day invasion."

Noe said nothing but, of course, she knew the history of Jesse's great-great-grandfather very well, for his exploits were one reason her beloved grandson David had joined the army, and fought to get accepted into his elite division. Kaleb Mitchell had been in the 101st Airborne assault on Utah Beach. He had been one of the few who survived that bloody day, and one of even fewer who outlived the war.

Jesse's voice went on, not strong as it had been in his youth but still clear and commanding. "When Hitler conquered Europe it looked like he was going to conquer the whole world. Those must have been terrible days, dark days of fear. Grandpa Kaleb said Christians then were sure they must have been living in the last days. Preachers were preaching about it from every pulpit. Prophets were jumping up all over the place proclaiming that the last and greatest evil had come, and soon Jesus must return. I guess it did seem like the end of the world to Christians at that time."

Noemi nodded thoughtfully.

"I don't read much poetry but there was one poet—forget his name—who said something like, 'Why do we talk about bad times coming as if there were ever anything *but* bad times?' Don't guess that fellow knew the Bible, but the Scripture says: *Man that is born of a woman is of few days, and full of trouble.* I guess that the people who died in concentration camps thought the end times had come. And it had. For them."

"But this—now—is something different, isn't it?" Noe asked hesitantly.

Jesse sighed. "I don't know, Noe, I really don't. And we can't know. Not even the Son knows that hour. One thing I have learned in my long life is that we're so self-centered, we always think we're the very center of the universe. If the end of our world comes, then we think it's the end of everything."

Noemi considered this carefully, as she did everything her husband said. But she was tired, and it seemed as if the future was too huge, too dangerously complicated, to look ahead and try to plan. She was suddenly aware of how cold her hands and feet and face were. The pain in her hands was dull now, but she knew that with the chill would come a price to be paid.

Suddenly, Jesse turned to her and took her hands in his. Immediately, tangibly, Noe felt warmth flowing into her, and with warmth comes strength. Noe had seen the sick healed instantly when Jesse touched them. But the source of the strength, Noemi Mitchell knew, did not come from the physical body of the small man who stood beside her. She saw that Jesse was staring blindly, his eyes wide but unseeing, over the dim depths of the valley stretched out below them. "What do you see, Jesse?"

"I can't see much of anything in this darkness that's come upon us." His grip tightened. His grip hurt her, but Noemi gave no sign. "But sometimes you don't need to see to recognize someone . . . I don't know if these are the last times or not. I do know that there's an evil loosed . . . He's out there, he's—close, and he's coming on . . ."

Noemi swallowed hard. " Jess. . . who? Who is—"

Abruptly, Jesse relaxed, and shrugged. "You know who. He's always the same old devil, but he takes different tacks and names and faces and ways, but he's always the same. That's why I don't have to see him. I recognize him, for I've seen him too many times before. But I know there are two things that we can do. The two things that God's people can always do."

"Yes. . . with the Lord. . ."

"We can fight—and we can win!" Now he smiled, already in triumph.

But Noemi Mitchell, though she was a woman of strong faith and will, had fears and weaknesses and doubts that it seemed her husband did not share. Her eyes fell, and she gently rubbed her knuckles. "Fight . . . maybe a war?"

Jesse replied with a touch of sadness. "I know, Noe. David. But it's his path, you know that. And there'll be others who have to follow that hard way."

He fell again into that stillness that sometimes came to him and turned his head as if listening. Finally he said in a voice strong and sure, "Here's what I see, Noe, because I choose to look at Him instead of the enemy: *They overcame him by the blood of the Lamb, and by the word of their testimony*—" He broke off suddenly and watched her, waiting.

Noe finished the quotation, for she knew it well ". . . and they loved not their lives unto the death."

"Even so," Jesse Mitchell cried exultantly, "come Lord Jesus!"

And as He sat upon the mount of Olives, the disciples came unto him privately, saying, Tell us, when shall these things be? and what shall be the sign of thy coming, and of the end of the world?

And Jesus answered and said unto them, Take heed that no man deceive you. For many shall come in my name, saying, I am Christ; and shall deceive many.

And ye shall hear of wars and rumours of wars: see that ye be not troubled: for all these things must come to pass, but the end is not yet.

For nation shall rise against nation, and kingdom against kingdom: and there shall be famines, and pestilences, and earthquakes, in divers places.

All these are the beginning of sorrows.

About the Authors

Dr. Gilbert Morris is a retired English professor from a Baptist college in Arkansas. His first novel was published in 1984. Since then, he has become one of the most popular fiction writers in Christian publishing. He is the author of over 80 novels, many of them best-sellers. Some of his most popular series include: The House of Winslow, Appomattox Saga, and The Wakefield Dynasty. His daughter Lynn and son Alan have co-authored many books with him.

Lynn Morris has a background in accounting. She worked as a private accountant for twenty years before she began collaborating with her father on the series, Cheney Duvall, M.D. This series has sold nearly half a million copies in five years.

After a working in the armed forces and the U.S. Postal services, Alan Morris began co-authoring books with his father. Their historical series, The Katy Steele Adventures, launched Alan's highly successful writing career. He is the author of The Guardians of the North Series, and is currently collaborating with best-selling author Robert Wise on a new series.